His car was an old Anglia, in only slightly better condition than her father's van. The engine groaned in complaint when he switched it on and gave an anguished sigh when it was turned off outside the Brennans' cottage. They'd hardly spoken to each other in the time between.

'Thank you for the lift,' Marie said. 'Are you going back to the wedding now? Marguerite will be wondering where you are.'

'Then Marguerite can go on wondering. I managed to escape once, I'm not going back to be captured again.' He folded his arms, grinning. 'I was hoping you'd ask me in for a cup of tea.'

'Would you like to come in for a cup of tea, Mickey?'

He jumped out of the car with alacrity. 'I would indeed, Marie. By the way, what's happened to your freckles?'

Marie was rooting in her bag for the key. 'They're covered with make-up.'

Mickey put a finger under her chin and tipped her face towards his. 'I prefer you with them,' he said softly, kissing her cheek.

Maureen Lee was born in Bootle and now lives in Colchester, Essex. She has had numerous short stories published and a play staged. *The Old House on the Corner* is her twelfth novel. *Stepping Stones, Liverpool Annie, Dancing in the Dark, The Girl from Barefoot House, Laceys of Liverpool, The House by Princes Park, Lime Street Blues, Queen of the Mersey, The Old House on the Corner, The September Girls, Kitty and Her Sisters, The Leaving of Liverpoool* and the three novels in the Pearl Street series, *Lights Out Liverpool, Put Out the Fires* and *Through the Storm* are all available in Orion paperback. Her novel *Dancing in the Dark* won the 2000 Parker Romantic Novel of the Year Award. Visit her website at www.maureenlee.co.uk.

By Maureen Lee

THE PEARL STREET SERIES
Lights Out Liverpool
Put Out the Fires
Through the Storm

OTHER NOVELS
Stepping Stones
Liverpool Annie
Dancing in the Dark
The Girl from Barefoot House
Laceys of Liverpool
The House by Princes Park
Lime Street Blues
Queen of the Mersey
The Old House on the Corner
The September Girls
Kitty and Her Sisters
The Leaving of Liverpool
Mother of Pearl

The Old House on the Corner

Maureen Lee

An Orion paperback

First published in Great Britain in 2004
by Orion
This paperback edition published in 2005
by Orion Books Ltd,
Orion House, 5 Upper St Martin's Lane,
London WC2H 9EA

An Hachette Livre UK company

Copyright © Maureen Lee 2004

The right of Maureen Lee to be identified as the
author of this work has been asserted by her in accordance
with the Copyright, Designs and Patents Act 1988.

A CIP catalogue record for this book is
available from the British Library.

Typeset by Deltatype Ltd, Birkenhead, Merseyside

Printed and bound in Great Britain by
Clays Ltd, St Ives plc

The Orion Publishing Group's policy is to use papers that
are natural, renewable and recyclable products and
made from wood grown in sustainable forests. The logging
and manufacturing processes are expected to conform to
the environmental regulations of the country of origin.

www.orionbooks.co.uk

For my friend, Margaret Sarsfield

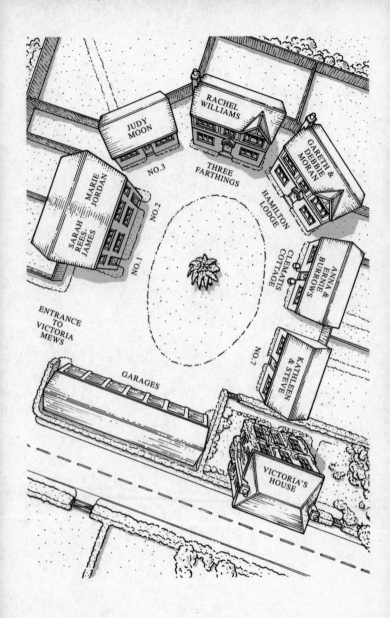

Saturday

7 JULY 2001

Chapter 1

Victoria looked out of her bedroom window at the new estate where Macara Removals & Storage used to be. It was only a tiny estate, surrounded by a shiplap fence, and comprising just seven houses; two mock black-beamed Tudor detached with four bedrooms each, a pair of redbrick semis, and three small, double-fronted bungalows, neatly rendered and painted white, set around a communal, oval-shaped lawn with a freshly planted willow tree in the centre.

To her left, out of sight, there was a row of garages, one for each house. Victoria's own house, more than a century older than its neighbours, was in a corner facing the road. The pretty garden was packed with sweet-smelling lavender, broom, and dazzling pink peonies, hidden behind a thick privet hedge. Golden ivy covered the walls and had curled itself around the chimneys.

At only half past six on a beautiful July morning – a Saturday – all the curtains were closed and there was no sign of life until two sparrows landed on the willow tree, madly fluttering their wings and making the lacy tendrils shiver delicately.

She had wondered how the builders would persuade people to buy properties crammed so closely together: no front gardens unless you counted the narrow strip of grass barely two feet wide, and not much behind either, but the new development had been christened Victoria

3

Square, giving it a posh, exclusive sort of air, and all had been sold long before the building work was finished. Six were occupied – one bungalow was empty and waiting for the new owners to move in. Three even had names; the detached ones were called Hamilton Lodge and Three Farthings, and one of the bungalows was Clematis Cottage – the tiny green shoots in tubs each side of the front door might well be baby clematis, Victoria couldn't tell from this distance. The remaining four properties were, so far, unnamed and making do with numbers.

There were some faded photographs in the loft, a century old, showing the land when it had been like a miniature park, full of trees and shrubs and winding paths and even a statue or two. This was before her great-granddad, Fraser Macara, had started a removal business and covered it with tons of concrete, leaving his wife only a fraction of her lovely garden.

First, there'd been just four horses and two carts, but the firm had quickly expanded until the horses and carts had trebled and the animals were accommodated in a row of ramshackle stables. Not long after the First World War, the company had been equipped with lorries – there were photos in the loft of these too; boxy, top-heavy vehicles parked at an angle in a neat row of eight about a metre apart, the drivers wearing coat overalls and bowler hats and standing to attention beside their cabs. It was Macara Removals' boast that they were the first company of its kind in Liverpool to convert to mech-anized transport. The stalls had been removed from the stables, furniture instead of horses had been kept in the run-down building, and the words '& Storage' added to the company name.

'What would you say if you could see the place now,

4

Gran?' Victoria mused aloud. 'We should have done this ages ago. Think of all the money we would have had!'

Things had been tough since Granddad had died leaving behind loads of debts that Gran had been determined to settle. Granddad hadn't had his father's flair for business. The company had been a burden he'd found too heavy to bear and had been going steadily downhill for years.

Something was happening in the square. Three Farthings' front door had opened and a woman emerged, clutching what looked like several envelopes. Victoria had become friends with the developer and knew most people's names. The woman was Mrs Williams, her husband was a motorcar salesman, and they'd just moved from a place called Lydiate on the outskirts of Liverpool. They had two children, a boy about twenty and a girl a bit younger.

Mrs Williams went next door to Hamilton Lodge and put an envelope through the letterbox. She did the same to the other five houses. 'I wonder if the Williams are throwing a party or something, Gran.' Victoria still talked to her grandmother, even though she'd been dead for more than two years. 'Oh! If it's a party, she must be inviting me?' Instead of returning home, Mrs Williams had left the square and, a few minutes later, the letterbox at the front gave its rather rusty clatter.

Victoria shot downstairs, still in her nightie, and opened the door just as Mrs Williams was walking away, having deposited a postcard on the tatty doormat. 'Hi!' Victoria beamed.

The woman nearly jumped out of her skin. 'Good morning, Miss Macara. I hope I didn't disturb you.'

'No. I've been awake for ages. Me Gran was an early riser and I don't think I'll ever get used to sleeping in.'

She picked up the postcard. 'A barbecue! Thanks, I'd love to come. Would you like a coffee? I was just about to make some. Or tea, if you'd prefer.'

Mrs Williams's face creased into a worried frown, as if she'd been asked to solve a major world crisis. 'I really should be getting home.' Then her expression cleared. 'Oh, it'll be ages before the others wake up. Coffee would be nice, thank you. I'm glad you can come to the barbecue – bring a friend if you want. You're my first acceptance. I thought it was about time we all got to know each other.' She sniffed, rather pathetically. 'Kirsty, she's my daughter, is all for it, but my husband thinks I'm a terrible busybody and my son, James, is inclined to agree.'

'You're nothing of the sort.' Victoria led her visitor into the kitchen, flooded with sunlight. 'I think it's a brilliant idea, except I won't have much time to get to know people. I'm off to America a week tomorrow. Sit down and I'll put the kettle on.'

'Oh, I say! What a lovely big room. It's like being in a time warp.' She immediately looked flustered. 'I hope you didn't mind my saying that. Some people might regard it as offensive. What I meant was . . .' She ran her hand through her short, untidy hair. 'What I meant was . . .' She paused again, unable to find the words.

'I know exactly what you meant,' Victoria said soothingly. 'It *is* in a time warp. Gran didn't approve of change unless she saw a reason for it. She liked the kitchen the way it is, with a nice deep sink and wooden draining boards. The gas cooker's ancient, but she wouldn't be parted from it, although she bought a fridge, and there's an automatic washing machine and a spin dryer in the outhouse and a great big telly in the parlour – the parlour's even more old-fashioned than the kitchen. Me, I don't care what the place looks like as long as it's cheerful. Mind you, once Gran died, I bought meself an electric kettle and a microwave.' She filled the kettle and switched it on. 'Sit down, Mrs Williams,' she said, nudging a chair when she became aware the woman was still standing in the middle of the room, looking lost.

'Call me Rachel.' She sat on a creaky pine chair and leaned her elbows on the creaky pine table. 'It's got loads of character,' she whispered, glancing admiringly at the yellow and white gingham curtains that Gran had made, the grey slate floor, the pine dresser that took up half the wall and was filled with crockery that didn't match, most of which had been there since before Victoria was born. The window sill was full of pot plants.

'I'm Victoria or Vicky, I don't mind which.'

'I'll call you Victoria. It's such a pretty name. Is the square called after you?'

'Yes.' There wasn't much that could make Victoria blush, but she blushed now. She was a tough young woman, unfashionably sturdy, with beautiful skin, thick black curly hair and fearless brown eyes that regarded the world with an unflinching stare. 'The developer didn't tell me until everything had been settled, the name approved by the council, that sort of thing. He thought I'd be flattered, but it makes me feel uncomfortable, like having a statue erected in my honour.'

'I'd be embarrassed too.' Rachel Williams seemed the sort of person who would be embarrassed easily. Her eyes were pale and nervous and looked as if they were used to tears. She gestured all the time with her hands, as if she hadn't enough confidence in the words themselves, or her voice, to convey what she meant. A sad cotton dress, badly in need of ironing, strained against her stout figure and there were spaces between the buttons down the front. Her large feet were encased in mannish leather sandals. 'Have you got a job in America?'

'In New York, yes. I'm really looking forward to it.'

'I bet you are. I've only been abroad a few times, mainly to Cyprus where my brother lived. It must be nice to be young, have the world at your feet sort of thing.' She looked at Victoria enviously. 'I've never done anything exciting with my life.'

Victoria snorted. 'You got married and had two children, didn't you? That's more than I've ever done. And I'm not all that young. I'm twenty-seven.'

'You don't look it.'

'Well, I am.' The kettle boiled. Victoria got to her feet and made the coffee. 'Do you take milk and sugar?'

'Just milk, please.' Rachel's head drooped. 'My husband and children don't think much of me.'

Rachel Williams was beginning to get on Victoria's nerves, but she had a kind, generous heart and felt more sorry for her than irritated. The woman was badly in need of a kick up the behind. Having no idea how to respond to this rather gloomy assertion, she said the first thing that came into her head. 'Your children are very lucky to have a mum. Mine died when I was only two. I only know what she looked like from photos. Then me dad left because he couldn't cope and I came to live with me gran and granddad.'

Rachel looked as if she was about to cry. 'I'm so sorry. What did your mother die of?'

'Cancer. She was only twenty.'

'That's awful. You must have been very unhappy.'

'Not a bit of it,' Victoria said cheerfully. 'I suppose I was sad at the time, I can't remember, but I've been happy ever since living here.'

'Gosh! I do admire you for not giving into things. I give in at the drop of a hat.'

'Well, you shouldn't.' Victoria hoped she didn't sound too brusque. She thought it was time to change the subject. 'Have you spoken to any of the neighbours yet? I haven't had the opportunity. I only left work yesterday – for good, that is. Next week, I'll be getting ready for America.'

'The people in Hamilton Lodge seem very nice.' Rachel perked up a bit. 'Gareth and Debbie Moran, though I can't help but wonder how such a young couple managed to afford such an expensive house. He's something to do with computers: a database developer, whatever that is. Frank, that's my husband, said he wouldn't earn all *that* much.'

Victoria grinned, showing a mouthful of strong, white teeth. 'I'm in the same field meself, except I design websites. *I* didn't earn all that much either, although I will in America. Maybe the Morans have got a big mortgage.' She felt slightly guilty for receiving such a whacking great sum for the land, thus adding thousands of pounds to the cost of each property.

Rachel Williams said sadly that she couldn't understand computers. Her children had one, Frank used one at work, but she was hopeless. Before she could list all her other inadequacies, Victoria forestalled her by asking if she'd met the people in Clematis Cottage on the other side of Hamilton Lodge.

'Mr Burrows? He seems very nice, but I didn't meet his wife, she's an invalid. I've spoken to the pretty girl in one of the semis, Sarah. She has two young children and a baby. I got the impression she'd just separated from her husband and the poor girl doesn't seem able to cope. I offered to babysit if she ever wanted to go out. The Irish

9

family in the semi next door keep very much to themselves, and so do the couple in the other bungalow, number seven. Have you seen them? The woman looks about forty and she's absolutely beautiful.'

'I haven't seen her, no. I saw the girl called Sarah. She looked terribly harassed. She has a hyphenated surname, Rees-James. The Irish family are the Jordans and they have two teenage boys. I don't know who's in the other bungalow.' A speculator had bought number seven with the intention of renting it out and the empty bungalow had been the last to be purchased: she had no idea by whom. 'If you're wondering how I know so much, it's because I'm nosy. I inherited it from me gran. She was the nosiest person in the world. I was dead miffed, being at work and missing everyone moving in.'

'You're just interested in people, that's not being nosy.' For the first time, Rachel allowed herself a brief smile, though it quickly vanished. 'Anyway, I hope they all come to the barbecue. If it's a wash-out, Frank will only say, "I told you so." '

Tell Frank to go screw himself, Victoria wanted to say, but it didn't seem exactly tactful. 'I'm sure it will be fun, even if not everyone comes.'

'I thought we could have it on the communal lawn. We could put up a big tree there at Christmas, have firework parties, and that sort of thing.' Her voice trailed away. 'I suppose people will think I'm just being a nuisance.'

'I think you're marvellous. And if Gran were here, she'd think the same. It's really nice, getting everyone together, making friends. I almost wish I wasn't going to America and could become part of it.'

Rachel's cheeks flushed and her watery eyes brightened. Victoria wanted to throttle Frank Williams for not offering his wife more encouragement. Gran had always taught her she could do anything she wanted and Victoria had grown up believing this to be true.

In Three Farthings, Rachel found Frank in his pyjamas in the kitchen reading a magazine. 'The kids are still asleep. Where have you been all this time?' he enquired in his booming voice. He was a big man, six feet tall, and heavily overweight. He was fifty-two and his sandy hair was rapidly receding, exposing more and more of his red, shiny scalp. Despite these signs of ageing, women continued to find him attractive, mainly due to his brash, outgoing personality and the fact that he flattered them mercilessly.

'I've just delivered the invitations to the barbecue,' Rachel said meekly, knowing he would disapprove.

'And woken everyone up in the process,' he sneered.

'I was very careful not to make a noise, Frank,' she stammered. 'I slid the cards through the letterboxes as quietly as I could.' He was only being awkward. Normally, he loved entertaining.

'It took you long enough. It was barely daylight when I heard you leave.' He grinned, but it wasn't a very nice grin. 'You woke *me* up.' Everything he said held an accusation or criticism of something she had, or hadn't, done, making her feel that she would never get anything right.

'I'm sorry, Frank. The reason I was so long is I've been talking to Victoria Macara in the old cottage. She's ever such a nice girl, old-fashioned. She works with computers, like Gareth next door; a web designer, I think she said.'

'An old-fashioned web designer?' Frank guffawed. 'Bit of a misnomer if you ask me.'

'Well, it's true,' Rachel said doggedly. 'Anyway, she thinks the barbecue is a brilliant idea.'

'I'm glad someone does.'

Rachel sighed and glanced around the dazzling white kitchen with its gleaming surfaces, matching cupboards and stainless-steel sink. It looked very clinical, like an operating theatre. 'Later, when we go to the supermarket,' she said, 'I'll get some plants for the window sill.' She wouldn't tell Frank she wanted her smart new kitchen to look a bit more like Victoria Macara's time warp, he'd only laugh.

The sound of the doorbell took them both by surprise. Rachel went to answer it and found a tiny girl outside wearing only a grubby vest and knickers. She carried a teddy bear close to her chest. It was Sarah Rees-James's eldest child, Tiffany, who was four, and as heartbreakingly pretty as her mother.

'Good morning,' Rachel said brightly.

'Mummy's dead,' Tiffany announced in a matter-of-fact voice. 'I can't wake her. I want a glass of milk and there's none in the fridge.'

'Oh, my God!' Rachel's hand went to her throat. 'Did you hear that, Frank? I'm going over there.'

'I'll be there in a minute,' Frank replied tersely, 'as soon as I'm dressed.'

'What about my milk?' Tiffany wailed when Rachel raced down the path and across the lawn to number one where the front door was wide open and the house looked as if a hurricane had swept through it, although it had been the same when Rachel had glimpsed inside the other day. There were dozens of cardboard boxes and plastic bags in the hall and living room waiting to be emptied. She ran upstairs, doing her best to avoid the clothes and toys left dangerously on each stair, into the front bedroom, where Sarah lay, face down in a froth of frilly bedclothes, wearing a dirty T-shirt, and apparently dead to the world.

Rachel shook the inert woman vigorously and after a while a groan emerged. 'You're alive!' she gasped, sinking thankfully onto the edge of the bed.

Sarah groaned again, turned over, and screamed when she saw Rachel, whom she hardly knew, sitting on her bed. 'What the hell are you doing here?' she demanded shakily.

'Tiffany said you were dead. She gave us a dreadful fright.'

'I was asleep,' Sarah said in a croaky voice, 'fast asleep, having a lovely dream. I didn't drop off until about three o'clock. Alastair's teething. I need some of that stuff you dab on gums, I can't remember what it's called, and baby Aspirin and Calpol and hundreds more nappies, but before I can buy anything, I have to get money from somewhere. Are there any cash machines around here?' She sat up, swung her legs out of bed, and looked around the untidy room, as if expecting to see one amidst the jumble of bottles and boxes on the dressing table.

'I'll find out,' Rachel said helpfully. 'There's bound to be some on Smithdown Road. If not, I'll lend you some money. And my husband and I are going shopping later. We'll get the stuff for you and anything else you need.'

'Thank you, you're very kind – I can't remember your name. I've no idea where Smithdown Road is. I don't know anything any more,' she wailed. 'And I need all sorts of other stuff: a kettle, for instance, and an iron, not that I know how to use one, and one of those big flat things you fry things in.'

'My name's Rachel, dear, and what you need is called a frying pan.' She patted Sarah's hand. 'Smithdown and

13

Allerton Roads are no distance away. They're full of shops and there's a lovely big park directly behind called the Mystery where the children can play when they get older. You'll find this a really convenient place to live. Liverpool city centre is only a bus ride away. It's hardly worth taking the car.'

'This time last week, I lived in a seven-bedroomed house and had a nanny for the children. I'm finding it hard to get used to this – but I *will*. I've promised myself that I will.' Sarah brushed back her thick, fair hair with a determined gesture. Her dishevelled appearance, and the fact that she smelled a bit, couldn't disguise how lovely she was, with perfect bone structure and huge blue eyes surrounded by thick dark lashes. Her legs were long and brown and as perfect as her face. She wore brief shorts to match the T-shirt. It was one of those modern sleeping outfits – Rachel's daughter, Kirsty, wore the same sort of thing.

Frank arrived. He came bounding up the stairs and into the bedroom, puffing slightly. 'It's bloody hot out there,' he panted. Rachel noticed the way his eyes narrowed calculatingly when he saw the long-legged Sarah. It was a look she'd seen before. Frank had always been a flirt, but it was only recently he'd started to have affairs. Sarah would be perfect for him: just separated from her husband and feeling very vulnerable – and living right under his nose.

'Well,' Frank drawled. 'You're clearly not dead. That's a relief.' Sarah smiled tremulously and fluttered her eyelashes.

'Where's Tiffany?' Rachel enquired.

'I woke up Kirsty, she's with her.' Frank didn't even look at his wife, having eyes only for Sarah's shapely breasts – the nipples were enticingly visible through the thin cotton top.

A little boy came wandering in, completely naked, sucking the corner of a scrap of blue blanket. It was Jack, who Rachel remembered was two and a half.

'Oh, hello, darling.' Sarah regarded him listlessly. 'Is Alastair still asleep?'

'Alastair not there,' Jack said through a mouthful of blanket.

'Perhaps he went walkies with Tiffany,' Frank suggested.

'He's only seven months old,' Sarah screamed. 'I've just remembered. I had him in bed with me. I might have smothered him.' She dragged back the duvet to reveal a plump baby lying with his face buried in the pillow. 'Alastair, darling.' She picked him up and clutched him to her chest. 'He's still breathing,' she announced tearfully.

'Thank goodness.' Rachel suddenly felt very tired and wanted to go home. Sarah Rees-James and her offspring were very wearing.

She therefore wasn't quite sure how it happened that, two hours later, Frank drove to the supermarket with a list of groceries, accompanied by Sarah Rees-James, while Rachel was left to look after the children. Why couldn't Sarah have written a list and looked after her own children? Come to that, how come the two women hadn't gone and left the children with Frank?

Why didn't I think of that before? Rachel wondered, too late.

Anna Burrows was sitting up in bed when her husband came in with breakfast on a tray. 'There's some children playing on the lawn, Ernie. They're awfully sweet.'

'I hope they're not making a noise,' Ernest growled. 'That's why we moved, to get away from the noise.'

'Only of never-ending traffic, darling. I love the sound of children playing,' she said wistfully. The Burrows hadn't been blessed with children. All they had was each other. She surveyed the contents of the tray. 'I'll never eat all this, Ernie. Just the toast will do fine. Oh, you've got gooseberry jam, my favourite,' she added gaily when she noticed his disappointed face. 'You have the fried stuff. I know you can find the room.' He had the appetite of a horse.

'If you're sure, luv.' He took the plate. It held only a single sausage, one slice of bacon and an egg, but Anna seemed to be eating less and less these days. 'Would you like to go for a walk later? It's a lovely day outside, going to be another scorcher.' They'd hardly been out since moving to Clematis Cottage a week ago – it had been Anna's idea to give it a name. He'd been too busy laying carpets, arranging furniture, putting up curtains, making the house perfect for his beloved wife. Ernest was eighty-one, but had the health and strength of a man half his age, as well as a full head of silver hair and all his own teeth. He only wore glasses for reading.

'I'd love to go for a walk. I'm longing to see where we're living now. Can you get the lid off this jam for me?'

'Sorry, luv. I should've done it before.' He unscrewed the lid. A small child could have easily done it, but Anna had hardly any strength left in her hands. She'd had multiple sclerosis for almost a quarter of a century. At first, it hadn't been too debilitating, but now she could hardly walk. There were days when her speech was slurred, she couldn't concentrate, felt giddy, though today she seemed as bright as a button. She had borne her illness with infinite patience, rarely complaining.

Ernie regarded her tenderly as she pecked at the toast like a bird. He was her willing slave, her cook, her nurse. When they'd first met, he'd risked his life on her behalf. Then, her hair had been pure gold and her cheeks as pink as roses. Now the hair was silver, like his own, and her face was lily-white and wrinkled. But Ernie still loved his darling Anna just as much, if not more.

'I forgot to say, a postcard came this morning. The woman in Three Farthings has invited us to a barbecue next Saturday.'

Her blue eyes glowed. 'We'll go, won't we? I won't find it too tiring, I promise. You know how much I love parties.'

'I know, luv. As long as you're up to it, we'll definitely go.'

An hour later, after Anna had washed and Ernie had helped her into a smart purple cotton dress and dangly red earrings – today, she had managed to put on lipstick and brush her lashes with mascara – they set off for a walk; Anna in her wheelchair, Ernest pushing.

The children were still playing on the lawn, a little boy chasing a butterfly while managing to carry a piece of blanket, and a girl slightly bigger doing cartwheels, watched over by Mrs Williams from Three Farthings who was sitting on the grass nursing a baby and not looking very happy about it. The girl came running over. 'Why are you in a pushchair?' she wanted to know.

'Because I'm ill, dear,' Anna told her. 'I can't walk, least not very far. What's your name?'

'Tiffany. That's Jack, he's my brother. Alastair's my other brother. He's got a pushchair, 'cos he can't walk either.'

'Yes, but one day he'll learn. Hello!' Anna waved at Mrs Williams who was struggling to get to her feet while holding the baby. 'Don't get up, we'll come to you. You've got a lovely family,' she said when Ernie had parked the wheelchair beside the heavily perspiring woman.

'They're not mine. I've got three children too, but they're much older. James's twenty, and Kirsty's nineteen. They've both gone into town.'

'And how old is the other one?' Anna enquired.

'Oh!' Mrs Williams's moist face went very red. 'I'm sorry, I meant two, two children. These belong to Sarah Rees-James from number one. I'm just looking after them while my husband takes her shopping.' She looked at her watch. 'It's time they were back,' she muttered.

'It must be you who's having the barbecue. Let's hope the weather's as good as it is today. Ernie and I would love to come, wouldn't we, dear?'

'Yes,' Ernest mumbled. He hated socializing and wouldn't have gone near the barbecue if it hadn't been for Anna.

A bright red car drove into the square and parked outside one of the garages, windows open, music blaring. The music was turned off and a young man got out. He wore heavy, horn-rimmed glasses that made him look rather owlish, jeans, and a T-shirt. His brown hair was tousled and he was badly in need of a shave. 'Hi, Rachel – we'd love to come to the barbecue, by the way. Hi, kids. Hi, folks.' He smiled cheerfully. 'I'm Gareth Moran. You must be Mr and Mrs Burrows. Pleased to meet you.' He shook hands with them both.

'Call us Anna and Ernie,' Anna trilled. This was what she loved, Ernest thought fondly, being surrounded by people.

It took quite a while to extricate her from the crowd – it was a crowd by then, as Frank Williams had returned with the children's mother, Sarah, who was a fine-looking girl, Ernest had to concede, though not a patch on Anna at the same age.

'I'm ever so glad we moved, Ernie,' she said breathily as they left the square, an elderly man out with his invalid wife. They probably looked very ordinary, very boring. Ernest chuckled to himself, and supposed they were, now. But they hadn't always been.

'Debbie,' Gareth shouted when he went into Hamilton Lodge – he loathed the name, considered it pretentious, but Debbie had insisted. He was relieved that she had decided Moran didn't sound as grand as Hamilton and had used her own name instead of his.

There was a note by the phone. 'Gone to town. Let's meet for coffee in Bluecoat Chambers at 3.30. Deb.'

He searched for his mobile, found it in his jeans pocket, and texted her a message. 'No can do. C u at home.' She would be cross, but he didn't care. He had work to do in his office upstairs.

In the kitchen, he wrinkled his nose when he saw the place was a tip. A fluffy tortoiseshell kitten jumped off the table and rubbed itself against his leg, purring loudly.

'Nice to see you too,' Gareth muttered, giving it a saucer of milk that looked slightly off. The kitten had already been christened Tabitha before they had discovered it was a tom, by which time it was too late to change the name and confuse it.

'Well, this is a fine old mess,' he sighed. That morning's breakfast dishes were piled on top of last night's dinner dishes. Gareth was perfectly willing to do his share of housework, but Debbie had taken the day off and it seemed unreasonable that she hadn't washed up while he was at work. He sniffed virtuously. The other way round, he'd have done the dishes like a shot.

Debbie wanted a cleaner. 'I can't be expected to clean a big house like this on my own,' she complained, although they'd barely been in the place a fortnight. She was irritated when he pointed out they hadn't had to buy such a big house in the first place. He'd been keen on moving to the square, giving up the flat in Woolton that cost an arm and a leg in rent, expecting to pay much less for a mortgage on one of the semis or a bungalow, but Debbie had insisted on this one, although they had no need for four bedrooms. Both were too busy with their careers to think of having children for years. Debbie was a beauty therapist and wanted to open her own salon one day.

I should have put my foot down, Gareth told himself. Easier said than done when faced with Debbie's appealing little face and appealing little voice. 'Oh, go on, Gareth, we can afford it.' She could wrap him around her little finger and Gareth, who loved her to bits, was only too willing to let her. It accounted for why the house was full of dead expensive furniture and Debbie wore dead expensive clothes, why they were going on holiday to Barbados in October, why, any minute now, he would get rid of the old Ford Escort that he was rather fond of and buy a ghastly four-wheeled drive thing called a Prairie Dog that he considered as pretentious as the name of the house. He sighed, picked up his mobile and texted another message. 'Changed mind. Meet u 3.30. OK. Luv u. G.'

Victoria was still badly missing her gran. There was something very unsatisfactory about having one-sided conversations with a woman who'd been dead for two years, no matter how dear to her she'd been. From her window, she had seen the Burrows speak to Rachel who was looking after Sarah Rees-James's children, seen Gareth Moran drive in and join them. Then Frank Williams and Sarah had arrived, and Victoria was about to go round and introduce herself, when the Burrows left and Rachel went indoors, Gareth Moran disappeared into Hamilton Lodge, Frank carried Sarah's shopping into number one, Sarah carried the baby, the other children followed, and there wasn't a soul left on the grass.

It frightened the usually fearless Victoria that things could so quickly change. One minute there was a crowd of people yet, in a flash, all had gone. The same thing had happened with her mum and dad, who'd vanished from her life within the space of weeks. Gran was old and apparently in the best of health, but had died quite unexpectedly in her sleep, leaving Victoria without a soul in the world to call her own. The boyfriend who had expressed his undying love only a few months ago had turned out to have a very pregnant wife, although Victoria tried hard not to think about that particular episode in her life. She would get over it one day soon.

She told Gran that Mrs Burrows looked very sweet and glamorous and her husband was remarkably handsome for his age; that Rachel had seemed rather fed up, though it was difficult to tell from so far away; Gareth was nice and she'd quite like to talk to him about his job; Frank Williams was terribly over-bearing, though she'd already guessed that from what Rachel had told her, and he was paying far more attention to the delicious Sarah than was decent, which was probably why Rachel was fed up.

'That's about it, Gran. If anything else happens, I'll tell you later.'

The morning had been spent sorting through her clothes, wondering what to throw away, what to give to a charity shop, what to take with her to New York, or whether to get rid of the lot and buy a whole new wardrobe. If so, should she buy it in Liverpool or wait until she was in America? It was great having money for the first time in her life, although she wished Gran was still around to enjoy it with her.

She decided to go round to Three Farthings and offer to give Rachel a hand with the barbecue. It was merely an excuse because Rachel had seemed so down and would almost certainly like someone to talk to.

There was no reply when she knocked on the Williams's front door. Rachel and the children must have gone out – Frank could be seen in the Rees-James's where he was putting up a mirror over the fireplace. She was on her way home, when two boys turned into the square. They were examining a computer game they must have just bought.

'Hi, what's that called?' she enquired, stopping in front of them. They were very alike, obviously brothers, with heavily freckled faces, green eyes, and dark ginger hair.

'Moon Rider,' the younger one replied. He looked about fourteen. The older one regarded her suspiciously. Perhaps he thought she was about to molest them.

'I've got Moon Rider Two,' she said. 'It's much better, more exciting.'

'Yeah, but our computer isn't powerful enough to take it.' He had an Irish accent. They must be the Jordan boys from number two.

'Mine is, it's sixty-four Ram. You can come round

and use it if you like. I've loads of games. I live in the old house over there.'

His green eyes lit up. 'Can we come now? Ours is only sixteen Ram.'

'If you like.'

The older boy spoke for the first time. 'We can't, Danny,' he said shortly. 'Ma will have the dinner ready for us.'

'I'd forgotten.' Danny bit his lip. 'I'm sorry, we can't come. But thanks for asking,' he added politely.

'That's all right,' Victoria said easily. 'Any time.'

The other boy virtually dragged his brother away. The door to their house opened a crack and a woman shouted, 'Patrick, Danny, your dinner's ready now.'

Victoria waved in the direction of the voice, but there was no sign of its owner. She shrugged, vaguely hurt. She'd only wanted to be friendly.

Marie Jordan stood in the hall, her hands on her hips. She was angry, and when Marie was angry, her green eyes blazed, her freckles glowed, and her red hair looked as if it was on fire. Her heart was leaping all over the place after spying her lads conversing with a stranger directly outside the house.

'What did that woman want?' she demanded hoarsely.

'She said we could play on her computer,' Danny explained.

'He'd have gone an' all,' Patrick said coldly, 'if I hadn't stopped him. He's an eejit, Ma.'

'Did she ask any questions like?' Marie put her hand on her breast in an effort to control the beating of her heart.

'Only what our new game was called.' Danny looked

23

defensively at his mother. 'She was a nice lady, Ma. She only lives in the ould house on the corner.'

'I've told you before, Danny, mind who you speak to. You can't be too careful, none of us can.'

'It's possible to be *too* careful, Marie.' A man was coming downstairs, slight and not very tall. He always reminded Marie of Jesus Christ himself, with his long brown hair, beard, and calm brown eyes. His voice was soft and gentle. 'We should mix with the neighbours, not draw attention to ourselves by being rude and unfriendly, making people wonder what we have to hide. Come on, lads,' he put an arm around each of the boys' shoulders, 'your ma's made us a fantastic salad, seeing as it's such a hot day, with trifle and cream for afters.' He led them into the kitchen diner and they sat at the table. 'No grace,' he warned when Marie clasped her hands ready to pray. 'No more grace, no more going to Mass, no more holy pictures on the walls. The Jordans are no longer a religious family, not after what happened in London.'

In London, they'd gone to Mass one Sunday and, a few aisles in front, Patrick had spied a boy who'd gone to the same school as he had in Belfast. He was with his family – Marie recognized the mother slightly. Perhaps aware she was being stared at, the woman had turned her head and Marie could have sworn she recognised *her*. The Jordans had left the church immediately and moved to Liverpool with all possible speed.

'I'd forgotten, Liam.' Marie would never get used to calling him that.

'It's hard to forget the habits of a lifetime. Shall we eat? And afterwards, I suggest Danny goes round and plays on the lady's computer. Just watch what you say, lad. If anyone asks, your daddy's a salesman and he travels a lot, you'll both be starting your new school in September, and you come from County Donegal, where your mammy was born. Is that all right with you, Marie?' His calm gaze rested on her anxious face.

'It is indeed, Liam. Whatever you say.' Her heart was beating normally again. It was the effect he had on her. She'd over-reacted earlier. 'I might go round with our Danny, say hello like. He's right. She looked a nice young woman. She waved, but I just ignored her. She'll think I'm desperately rude.'

'A card came this morning, inviting us to a barbecue. Can we go to that too?' Danny enquired eagerly. 'It's next Saturday, our Patrick's birthday.'

'We can,' Liam replied. 'We'll take a bottle of wine and Patrick his guitar and give everyone a song.' He smiled and Marie's erratic heart turned over. 'But none of that Irish protest stuff, lad. Stick to rock'n'roll or rap or whatever's in vogue these days.'

At this, the usually dour Patrick looked quite pleased. 'I'll do some Blur and Oasis numbers – I'll start practising after dinner.'

Anna returned from the walk quite animated, insisting she was drunk.

'You only had a single glass of wine, luv,' Ernie remarked. 'You can't possibly be drunk.'

'Ah, but I *feel* drunk,' she insisted. 'I feel completely sozzled, if you must know.'

'You'd better have a little nap when we get home.'

'I'll do no such thing, Ernie. I *like* feeling drunk. We must go to that pub again. Everyone was so friendly. I'm ever so glad we moved. Queen's Drive was very nice but, apart from being noisy, there were no shops around, no pubs. I really enjoyed going in Woollies.' She had an assortment of plastic bags on her lap, having bought a pair of ghastly hoop earrings, a box of chocolates, some blue eyeshadow, and a bottle of Irish whiskey for Ernest – he was partial to a dram before going to bed. 'I wonder who lives in the next-door bungalow?' she said when they turned into Victoria Square. 'Have you seen any sign of them, dear?'

'It's a couple, middle-aged. They were in the kitchen when I was hanging out the washing the other day.'

'Did they see you?'

'They weren't exactly looking out the window, luv. They were in the middle of what we used to call a good old necking session. Nowadays, I think it's called a snog.'

'You mean they were kissing?'

'Kissing with knobs on.' Ernie had felt a bit like a stalker.

'Isn't that nice.' She sighed. 'We used to do it all the time.'

'We'll do it again, as soon as we get in,' Ernest promised, and Anna shrieked with delight.

'People will think this house is empty,' Kathleen whispered after Steve kissed her again, very long and very hard. 'I don't think anyone's seen us yet.'

'Who cares about people?' Steve stroked her face, her neck, her breasts. His hands were rough and coarse against her delicate skin. She shivered ecstatically and he took her again. She'd lost count of the number of times they'd made love that day.

'It's nearly three o'clock,' she said. 'We've been in bed for fifteen hours.'

'Who's counting?'

'Me. I'm hungry and I'd love a cup of tea.' She sat up and he ran his fingers down her spine. She shuddered again. 'That tickles.'

'Stay there and I'll make some tea.' He got out of bed and stood beside her, naked, his broad, muscled body as hard and solid as a rock. She felt dizzy, already wanting him again.

'No,' she said determinedly. 'I'm getting up. We need groceries. At this rate, we'll never eat again. There's hardly any milk left and I'm out of cigarettes.'

'It's time you stopped smoking. I'll put the water on.'

'You'd better get dressed first. There are no curtains in the kitchen. If someone sees you, they'll think we've started our own nudist colony.'

He looked at her, one eyebrow raised quizzically. 'That's an idea – it might catch on.' He pulled on jeans, shrugged his massive arms into a check shirt, and threw a scarlet satin dressing gown in her direction. It was part of her 'trousseau'. 'Come on. You're right. It's time we came up for air. It's a nice day, we can go for a walk. Hey, there's something come through the letterbox. We've got mail.'

'What is it?'

'Three Farthings have invited us to a barby.'

'What's a barby?'

'A barbecue. By God, you're an ignorant woman, Kathleen Quinn. I suppose you don't know what a telly is, either. Or a chippy, or a cossy, or a butty. What's a nana?' he demanded.

'A banana, and I know all the other things apart from a cossy.'

'It's a swimming costume.'

He went into the kitchen. Kathleen got out of bed and languorously stretched her arms. In the wardrobe mirror, she watched herself put on the satin gown. Her cheeks were flushed, her hair was loose, her eyes like stars. She looked sexy, wanton, wholly satisfied. 'I've never looked like this before in my life,' she said, and the reflection smiled in agreement.

'Shall we give *our* house a name?' she asked when she followed Steve into the kitchen. 'Would the landlord let us?'

'*Our* house!' His deep, gravely voice was full of wonder. 'Our *house*.' He took her in his arms. 'Let's not ask. A number's good enough for me.'

'And me. Number seven sounds better than Three Farthings.'

'Any day. Would you kindly let go of me, Mrs Quinn? The water's just about to boil.'

They moved reluctantly out of each other's arms. Kathleen washed two mugs and put a teabag in each. 'We need a teapot,' she said fussily. 'And a cosy, and all sorts of other things, like pans, more towels and bedding, crockery . . .' Her voice trailed away. There were too many things to list.

'We'll get 'em today.' They sat down, one each side of the small table, and looked at each other for a long time. 'I love you, Kathleen.'

'I love you, Steve.'

The phone rang. She got up and went into the living room to answer it. Strange, she thought, no one knows our number. She didn't even know it herself, she realized when she picked up the receiver and said, 'Hello.'

'I'd like to speak to me dad,' a woman's voice said curtly.

Kathleen went cold. Steve came in. 'Who is it?' He refused to meet her eyes.

'I think it's Brenda. It's one of your daughters.' She shrugged, pushed the receiver at him, and returned to the kitchen. There was an ashtray on the draining board, full of butts. As yet, they hadn't got a wastebin to empty them in. She took a lighter from the pocket of the scarlet gown, chose the biggest butt and smoked it until it reached the tip, then the next-to-biggest.

He'd let Brenda have their number. He'd promised her – and she him – that they would start a new life together, just the two of them, leaving the past and all its various unpleasant attachments behind. This wouldn't have been necessary had his four daughters been even vaguely sympathetic to the fact he'd fallen in love with another woman. But they hated her. She was the harlot who had stolen their father away from their mother, his wife, the clinging, helpless, whining Jean, to whom he hadn't made love since the youngest girl had been born twenty-four years ago.

Steve was standing in the kitchen doorway. 'I'm sorry,' he said humbly. 'It was Brenda. I rang the other day, just to see how Jean was. She must have pressed 1471 and got our number.'

'Didn't it cross your mind that's exactly what she would do?'

'I didn't think of it.'

'I might ring Michael later, see how *he* is.'

'I'm sure Michael's fine.'

'And I'm sure Jean is too. She's probably watching television. According to you, that's all she ever did.'

He shoved his hands in his pockets, still refusing to meet her eyes. 'Brenda ses she's not stopped crying since I left. The girls are worried sick about her.'

'What do they expect you to do? Go home and kiss her better?'

His shoulders hunched. 'I don't know what to do.'

'I would have thought the obvious thing to do was nothing, but if you're actually thinking of going home, Steve, then don't bother to come back.'

'You don't mean that!' He looked deeply hurt.

'I do.' She was lying through her teeth, wanting to hurt him, yet knowing she would die if she never saw him again. 'I'm not sharing you with a wife who lives miles away, you rushing back every time someone rings to say she's cut her little finger. Would you mind if I went to see Michael at the same time? He's bound to be lonely on his own.'

He shook his head. 'I'd hate it.'

'Well, now you know how I feel.' She badly wanted to cry herself, feeling totally let down, betrayed. She'd given up everything for him: her husband, her home, her job, her friends, and had thought he'd done the same. It terrified her that he could so easily be persuaded back to Huddersfield, leaving her on tenterhooks that he might not return. 'What are you going to do?' she asked.

'Nothing, like you said.' He came and sat at the table. 'Tea's cold,' he said, taking a sip. 'Jean'll get over it. I've got you to think of now, haven't I?' He reached for her hand. 'I can live without Jean, but I can't live without you, Mrs Quinn.'

'It's just coming up to midnight, Gran. I'll be off to bed soon, after I've made meself some cocoa. It's been a funny old day, you'd have loved it – *I* did. A boy came this avvy, Danny Jordan, and we played Moon Rider Two on the computer. I beat him every time, but he looked so downhearted I let him win the last few games. His mum came first, just to say hello. Her name's Marie and she's as Irish as the pigs of Trocheady, as you would say. They live in one of the semis, number two.

'Right now, I'm in my bedroom, sitting by the window. It's a fantastic night, still warm, and the sky is an amazing dark blue and littered with stars. Victoria Square looks dead pretty in the dark. There's a lamp by the garages where you come in and another outside Hamilton Lodge. The houses look as if they've been there for ever, not just a few months. It'd make a great painting.'

Victoria rested her arms on the sill and put her chin in her hands. She sniffed loudly. 'Our garden smells like heaven, Gran, particularly the lavender.' She felt almost dizzy from the strong scents that wafted from below. 'Remember when I was little and used to dry the blossom in the airing cupboard and make little lavender bags for you and all me friends? There's still some around the house.'

'I can hear Sarah Rees-James's baby crying, poor little lamb, and there's music coming from Hamilton Lodge. What else happened today? Oh, Rachel Williams came at teatime to say nearly everyone's coming to the barbecue, so she's dead pleased. Her husband spent virtually the whole day in Sarah's, helping her unpack, putting up pictures and stuff – she wasn't too pleased about *that*. Then Mrs Burrows from Clematis Cottage came tottering over – she can only walk a bit. She said I'm to call her Anna and invited me for coffee on Monday morning.

'Anyroad, Gran, goodnight and God bless.' Victoria blew a kiss at the star-spangled sky. 'I'll speak to you again in the morning.'

Kathleen and Steve

Chapter 2

The clerk of the court's voice was deep and gravelly, carrying to all corners of the wood-panelled room. 'On the second of November, two thousand, it is alleged that the accused, Steven Alan Cartwright, threw stones at Colthorpe police station and assaulted a police officer, namely Constable George Parsons.' He turned to the magistrates, two men and a woman, seated behind him, and gave a little nod.

The woman looked at Steven severely over her gold-rimmed spectacles. 'Please state your date of birth, Mr Cartwright.' In contrast to the clerk, her tone was light and cool.

'The twelfth of September nineteen forty-nine, your ladyship,' Steven replied with a broad grin.

'And how do you plead?'

'Guilty on both counts, your ladyship. It were the tenth anniversary of the pit shutting down and I'm quite likely to do it again on the twentieth.'

'I trust that wasn't a threat, Mr Cartwright. And I am not your ladyship. If you want to call me anything, call me madam.'

'As you wish, madam,' Steve replied with an even broader grin. There were titters from the back of the court where the general public were sitting.

The magistrate opened her mouth to say something, but must have thought better of it. She bent her head towards the clerk who whispered something in her ear. Nodding impatiently, she conversed with her fellow magistrates, then turned towards the accused man, who still bore an amused expression on his tough, handsome face. He was a tall, dignified man, at least six foot, with massive shoulders and powerful arms. There was a suggestion of a curl in his short brown hair that was a slightly lighter shade than his smiling eyes.

'Steven Alan Cartwright, this court finds you guilty of the offences listed. This being your first offence, we do not feel a prison sentence is necessary at this time. I am therefore fining you the sum of two hundred and fifty pounds and would like to offer some advice.' She leaned forward, looked earnestly at the accused, and said in the manner of an adult addressing a child, 'Mr Cartwright, you are fifty-one years old, yet have behaved like a teenager. May I suggest you grow up?'

'Thank you for the advice, madam,' Steven said meekly, although his tone was mocking.

'May I suggest you grow up?' Bert Skinner mimicked in the pub about fifteen minutes later. 'Snooty bitch! She had eyes like icicles. Mind you, I wouldn't have minded giving her one. She were a corker.'

'Was she?' Steve could only remember the voice, not the face. She could have looked like Julia Roberts and he wouldn't have noticed.

'I bet she's a wild animal in bed,' Fudge said with wistful sigh. 'Those cold women usually are.'

Steve laughed. 'How would you know, mate? Have you ever slept with a cold woman?'

'Nah, but I've read about 'em in books. The colder they look, the hotter they are, least so the books say. Anyroad, Steve,' Fudge went on, 'you don't have to worry about finding the whole two hundred and fifty quid. We'll have a whip round in the club tonight. We were all involved, but you were the only one who were caught.'

'George Parsons knows me from the strike. He was getting his revenge, a bit late in the day, mind. Who'd like another drink?'

'Keep your hand in your pocket, Steve. This is on us.'

'I'll have another bitter, just a half, this time. I don't want to be done for drunk driving, I might find meself up before Lady Muck again.' He made a face. 'I'm already in Jean's bad books, not that that's unusual. "What'll people say when they read about you in the papers," is all I've had for bloody weeks. She'll have a fit when she finds she might have to pawn her engagement ring towards that bloody fine, not for the first time, either.'

It was February, snowing, had been for days. The roads out of Huddersfield were thick with it, the surfaces hard and slippery. Steve drove carefully, worried about the thin tyres on the Micra – twelve years old and unlikely to get through its next MOT. The heater didn't work and the car felt like a fridge. Snow piled in clumps on the windscreen, the wipers were useless. He shivered violently inside his anorak, wishing he hadn't worn his best – and only – suit for his appearance in court. It was some sort of man-made material without an ounce of warmth. But Jean had insisted he put it on in case his photo got in the paper.

'Local man sent to the tower to be beheaded,' Steve had quipped. 'I'm not exactly a murderer, luv. All I did was throw a few stones and give George Parsons a bit of a shove.'

He'd phoned Jean from the court, told her the verdict. By now, she'd have contacted the girls, and they'd all be there when he got home, giving him filthy looks, telling him he was a disgrace to the name of Cartwright. It was like having five bloody wives nagging at him all at once.

It had never used to be like that. Until ten years ago, he'd worked down the local pit, starting as a potboy when he left school. He was proud of himself, of his job, fond of his mates, enjoying the camaraderie that existed between them. Then bloody Heseltine had come along and shut the mines down – coal came cheaper when it was imported from abroad where the miners were paid a pittance. Steve had been out of work for two long and very tedious years.

Jean behaved as if the whole thing was his fault, as if he was personally responsible for closing the mine. His four daughters, who'd once idolized him, began to look upon him differently once he was unemployed, lounging listlessly around the house, getting under their mother's feet, hanging round Bert Skinner's allotment for something to do and spending his evenings in the Working Men's Club, letting a single pint of ale last till closing time. Jean and the girls scoured the papers, pointing out vacancies; van drivers, store men, labourers, bin men – nowadays called refuse disposal technicians or something equally daft. But the blood that ran through Steve's veins was mixed with coal dust, and it took a long while before he could imagine working anywhere but down the pit. Only another miner would have understood his feelings. Jean didn't even try.

He eventually started work as a hospital porter, earning less than half he'd done before. It was a useful job, but that's all it was, a job, whereas the pit had been part of his very existence. And now the bloody hospital was closing down. It was a decrepit place, an old mental home, built in eighteen something, bits added over the years. Departments were gradually being transferred to a brand, spanking new hospital on the other side of town. Come July, his services would no longer be required. He'd be made redundant for the second time. His daughters, all married by now – most of his redundancy money had gone to pay for their weddings – had already begun to look in the paper for suitable vacancies.

He reached the outskirts of Huddersfield. Colthorpe, the village where he'd been born and had lived his entire life, was another five miles away. By now, his teeth were chattering and the steering wheel felt as if it was made of ice. Soon, he was driving through fields of snow, the ground falling away to the left of him, rising smoothly on his right in a gently curved blanket of white, the surface broken only by the occasional bush or tree. The sky looked as though it might collapse under the weight of heavy, grey clouds.

There was very little traffic on the road and the isolation was affecting him, making him feel very much alone, wondering what the hell would happen to him when the hospital closed? Where would he end up next time?

He reached the top of Cooper's Hill, awed by the vast white world that lay before him, drove slowly down because the little-used surface was as hazardous as an ice rink, packed as it was with hardened snow. Further down, almost at the bottom, a car had stopped. When he got nearer, he saw the left back wheel had slid into the ditch at the side of the road. The exhaust emitted clouds of white smoke as the driver attempted to go forward, but the car, a black Mercedes, whirred angrily and refused to budge.

Steve eased the Micra to a halt. He jumped out, approached the Mercedes, and banged on the window. It opened a few inches. 'Need a shove?' he asked.

The driver was a woman, encased in a chunky sheepskin coat, a thick woollen hat pulled down as far as her eyebrows, and a matching scarf knotted under her chin. She turned off the ignition.

'Would that help?'

Steve shrugged. 'It might.'

'I tried to ring a garage, but my mobile isn't working. It must be the signal.'

'Start her up, and I'll give her a push.'

'Thank you very much.'

He went round to the back of the car, put one foot in the ditch, and pressed his shoulder against the gleaming metal. The car started with a jump, his heels skidded on the ice, and he fell back into the ditch, uttering a roar when the ice at the bottom broke and water, freezing cold, seeped through his clothes and down his neck. The top half of him was soaked. He heard the car door open and close and the woman appeared.

'What happened? One minute I could see you through the rear window, next minute you'd disappeared.'

'You bloody idiot!' he yelled. 'You took your foot off the clutch.'

'Did I? I'm so sorry,' she said abjectly. 'I wasn't thinking. Are you all right?'

'Course, I'm not all right. I'm about to freeze to death down here. Don't just stand there gawping, woman, give us a hand out.'

She extended her hand. Steve contemplated pulling her into the ditch with him, see how *she* liked it, but it seemed unnecessarily cruel. She helped him out and he stood there, shivering, his body chilled to the bone.

The woman regarded him with concern. 'You'd better get out of those wet clothes before you catch pneumonia,' she said, stating the obvious. 'Look, my car is still stuck. If you're up to driving yours, I live less than a mile away. You can get warm and I'll give you some of my husband's clothes. I can ring the garage from there.'

'Sod the bloody garage. Just get me into some dry clothes,' he snarled.

Neither spoke during the short journey to her house, until she said, 'Turn right here,' and Steve drove down a long path lined with trees, stopping in front of a large, bleak Victorian house. The woman leaped out and unlocked the door. Steve could hardly move in his frozen clothes. He managed to extricate himself from the car, which he'd always found too small, and stagger towards the open door.

The woman was running upstairs. 'Come on up,' she called. 'I'm going to run you a hot bath. That'll soon warm you up. I'll leave some clothes outside. Just throw your things on the floor and I'll have them cleaned. I'll get coffee on the go. It'll be ready by the time you've finished.'

'Ta,' Steve muttered ungraciously.

Five minutes later, soaking in a warm bath in a warm bathroom, encased in bubbles that the woman had been kind enough to add, he didn't feel so bad about things. At least it saved going home, being the object of derision by all and sundry. He wouldn't ring Jean. It wouldn't hurt to let her worry for a bit.

Another five minutes had passed when there was a knock on the door. 'Are you all right in there?'

'Fine, ta. I'll be down in a minute.'

41

The bubbles were getting cold. He pulled out the plug, wrapped himself in a snowy white bath towel, and gingerly opened the door. Clothes were folded in a heap outside: a maroon fleece tracksuit, two T-shirts, dinky underpants, socks and a pair of velvet mules. He put everything on, they just about fitted, apart from the mules that were much too small, and went downstairs.

Music was coming from a room at the end of a long, gloomy corridor that he deduced must be the kitchen. He peered through a half-open door as he went towards it, the mules flapping uncomfortably with each step. A living room, the furnishings and decoration fitting the period in which the house had been built: satiny wallpaper, velvet tasselled curtains, a richly patterned carpet, over-large furniture, everything too dark for his taste. It gave the impression of being little used.

'I thought I heard a noise.' The door to the kitchen opened, taking him by surprise. The woman had removed her bulky outer clothes to reveal an elegant black suit over a white polo-necked jumper. He'd thought he'd never recognize her again, but he did, even though she no longer wore glasses.

'You!' he gasped. Bert Skinner had said she was a corker and now that Steve had a proper look he reckoned Bert was right. Her voice was different and she looked smaller, thinner, not so haughty, now that he was looking down on her and not the other way around. Her brown hair was shoulder length, very thick and wavy, making a perfect frame for her beautiful, delicate face: fine nose, perfect lips, high, moulded cheekbones. Her grey eyes were very large and rather sad.

'I thought you recognized me earlier.' After fining him a small fortune, she had the temerity to smile.

'If I had, I'd driven right past.'

'I hope you don't expect me to apologize for what happened in court. You only got what you deserved.'

'I hope you don't expect me to be grateful for all this.' He indicated the clothes, the coffee pot and a plate of sandwiches on the table. 'Because I'm not. If you hadn't taken your foot off the clutch, there'd be no need for it. By the way,' he added childishly, 'I prefer tea.'

'Then tea you shall have,' she said with a gracious wave of her slender white hand. 'Sit down and I'll make it. Have you warmed up after the bath?'

'Yes,' he said grudgingly. The kitchen had its own little dining area in an alcove in the corner. He sat on a padded bench in front of a dark oak table and thought how much Jean would have loved it. The room was about twenty feet square, modern, but made to look Victorian, like the rest of the house: oak units, copper pans on the wall, cream lace curtains suspended from a brass rail, through which the snow could be seen, falling heavier now. Lights gleamed underneath the vast array of wall cupboards, making the room look faintly exotic, more like a nightclub than a kitchen. An Aga kept the place comfortably warm. The music came from a small radio on the stainless steel draining board.

'Do the clothes fit?' Lady Muck enquired.

'Where they touch.'

'I thought as much. My husband has smaller feet and is much slimmer than you, that's why I gave you the tracksuit, it stretches. I'll fetch your shoes down in a minute and put them on the Aga to dry and find you an anorak or something to go home in.'

'Ta.'

Her back was to him while she made the tea, and he was horrified to find himself admiring her slim ankles, her neat bottom, the way her hair flicked up at the ends and how the lights made it appear more red than brown. He'd always considered magistrates to be barely human, let alone sexual beings. *'I wouldn't mind giving her one,'* Bert had said.

She turned, caught Steve's gaze, and the world seemed to stop as something indefinable passed between them. Apart from the hum of the fridge, the silence was total. Then, 'Oh, dear,' she said shakily when the tea slopped into the saucer. Blushing, she changed it for another. He guessed she wasn't as sure of herself as she made out. His flattened ego raised its head a little. He'd been over-awed, first by the car, then the house, and the fact she'd turned out to be Justice of the Peace, but the blush had shown she was just an ordinary woman.

'What does your husband do?' he asked.

'He's a doctor.' She put the tea in front of him and slid into the bench opposite, rather reluctantly, he thought. 'Do you mind if I smoke?' She waved a pack of Dunhill's at him.

He shrugged. 'It's your house.'

'So it is.' She lit the cigarette, breathing in the smoke and letting it slowly out, as if it was the first ciggie she'd had in years. 'What about you? What do you do?'

'I *was* a miner, now I work in a hospital as a porter.'

'Of course, the pit closed, didn't it?'

'I'm surprised you noticed.'

She blushed again. He was enjoying her discomfort. She shouldn't have told him to grow up. 'I couldn't help but notice, could I? I'm a doctor too. I was suddenly inundated with miners' wives suffering from depression.'

One of them could have been his own. Jean had been taking tablets 'for her nerves' for years. 'What's your name?' he demanded rudely.

'Quinn. Kathleen Quinn.' She pushed the sandwiches in front of him. 'I made these for you.'

He took a bite of sandwich. It was ham. 'Got any mustard?'

She fetched a jar and put it in front of him. 'It's polite to say "please"?'

'Mebbe I will when I grow up.' The barb had hurt far more than the fine.

'Wasn't it rather childish to throw stones at a police station and assault the officer who tried to restrain you?' she said coldly.

Steve held up his hands in an attitude of surrender. 'As I said in court, it were ten years to the day that the pit closed. We were merely commemorating the fact. I suppose we could've laid flowers, wreaths, said prayers, sung a few hymns, but we weren't exactly in the mood. Throwing stones seemed more fitting, as it were, though if we'd had a few sticks of dynamite, we'd have blown the bloody place up. Coppers weren't exactly the miners' best friends during the strike.'

Her lips pursed. 'That was fourteen years ago.'

'Fifteen, actually, but it seems like only yesterday to me and me mates.'

'It's time you stopped living in the past and moved forward,' she said primly in the voice she'd used in court.

'Except I've nothing much to look forward to.' Steve lost his temper. 'Can't you ever forget you're a magistrate? Is that all you ever do, give advice to people when you know nothing whatever about them? Mebbe you'd like a bit of advice yourself – unless anyone asks, in future, keep your opinions to yourself.' He smeared mustard on a sandwich, shoved in his mouth, and nearly choked. He'd used far too much.

To his intense horror, two tears ran down Kathleen

45

Quinn's thin cheeks. 'I wish I'd just driven away and left you in that ditch,' she said. 'It's been a horrible day and you're the last straw. Once you've finished that sandwich, I'd be obliged if you would leave.'

'You couldn't have driven away,' he reminded her, rather more gently now. He was a sucker for tears. 'Your back wheel was in the ditch, you were stuck. I'll leave, don't worry. You'd better fetch me shoes first.' The black lace-ups would look daft with a tracksuit, but he wasn't planning on prancing up and down the catwalk, not today.

'They'll still be wet. You can't possibly leave in wet shoes.' She rubbed her cheeks with the back of her hand and gave him a tremulous smile. 'I'm sorry. It's just that I had some upsetting news this morning. You were awfully kind, stopping and helping me like that. Finish the food and there's more tea in the pot.'

She went upstairs for the shoes. Steve spread another sandwich with mustard, more sparsely this time. He felt very odd, almost drunk, as he sat there, waiting – no longing – for Kathleen Quinn to come back.

The telly was on when he got home. Jean was watching *Countdown*. 'Oh, Steve,' she cried tearfully, though didn't get up. 'I thought you'd had an accident.' She noticed his outfit. 'Where on earth did them clothes come from, luv?'

'I *did* have an accident. I skidded a bit, then got stuck in a ditch, and only fell into the bloody thing when I tried to get out the car.' He'd decided not to mention Kathleen Quinn or he'd be cross-examined about it for weeks. 'Some chap in a lorry hauled me out. He loaned me his tracksuit and some other stuff.'

'But where's your own clothes?' she wailed. As usual,

she was turning the situation into a tragedy of Shakespearean proportions.

'The chap said he'd leave them in the dry cleaner's for me.'

'Which dry cleaner's, Steve?'

'For Chrissakes, Jean! I can't remember. Anyroad, does it really matter right now? I'm bloody freezing, and I'd like a cup of tea, not the third degree.' He was pleased to note the girls weren't there. They must have gone home to get the kids their teas. The thought had barely entered his head when the phone in the parlour rang. Jean went to answer it.

'Yes, he's home Brenda, luv,' Steve heard her say. 'Had some sort of accident. Oh, he's all right, just chilled to the bone, that's all. Ok, luv. I'll see you later. I doubt if your dad'll be going out again tonight.'

A few minutes later, Maggie rang, shortly followed by Sheila, then Annie. Jean more or less repeated what she'd told Brenda and, from what he could gather, all four were set on coming round that night, in which case, Steve decided, he'd call in the club for a pint.

'Would you like more tea, luv?' Jean asked when she'd finished telling the world and his wife about his accident.

'Wouldn't mind,' he said in a surly voice. He shut his eyes, but couldn't shut out his surroundings. He'd been sitting in the same chair in the same room for nigh on thirty years. The curtains had changed with each decade, the wallpaper, there was carpet on the floor when there'd used to be lino, but the furniture was hardly different. It had been bought new when he and Jean got married: two armchairs, a dining-room suite, no sideboard, because it couldn't be squeezed into the tiny room. As

47

the girls grew bigger, they'd objected to sitting on hard chairs to watch telly. Jean had reluctantly given in and let them use her precious parlour, sit on her precious moquette three-piece, to watch the new colour telly.

Money hadn't been a problem in those days, not like now. Years ago, Steve had wanted to move out of the small, cramped terrace and buy a new house on the edge of the village, but Jean had refused. They'd had some flaming rows about it. She'd wanted to stay with her friends, her family, all living close by. Then, just to be awkward, once he'd lost his job, she'd suddenly decided she'd quite like a bigger house. By then the girls were in their teens, still sleeping in bunk beds for lack of space. There'd been more rows.

'No one'll give me a mortgage, not now,' he'd told her, but Jean only heard what she wanted to hear. There was no point giving her the facts once she'd shut her ears to reason.

There was a photo on the sideboard of Steve and Jean's wedding. He was twenty-one, she nineteen: a blonde, fairy-like girl, vivacious and full of fun. What had happened, Steve wondered, to turn her into the shapeless, pasty-faced, complaining woman she was now? Most miners' wives had stood by their men when they'd been given the boot, supported them, gone out and got jobs themselves. With a bit of help, he might have pulled himself together sooner, not hung around the house for two years feeling useless.

But it wasn't fair to put the blame on Jean for everything. 'It's time you stopped living in the past and moved forward,' Kathleen Quinn had said. All of a sudden, he visualized her in the kitchen, her back to him while he admired her slim figure. She'd turned around and something had passed between them. He remembered Bert's words again, '*I wouldn't mind giving her one . . .*'

In his mind, Steve carried Kathleen Quinn upstairs to one of the bedrooms in her big house. Tenderly, he laid her on the bed and undressed her, slowly, taking his time, anticipation growing, wanting to hurry, yet enjoying the wait. He exposed her small, white breasts, kissed them, unpeeled her tights – by now, his hands were shaking – removed her pants, then stared at her, laid out on the bed like a sacrifice, waiting for him to take her.

Which Steve did, no longer tender, but roughly, urgently, losing himself totally in her soft, warm body . . .

'Here's your tea, Steve. By the way, did they take your photo in the court? Steve, wake up.' His shoulder was given a hard poke. Now that she had got used to the fact he was alive and well, Jean was back on the attack. 'You don't realize what a terrible afternoon I've had,' she said querulously. 'I was worried sick, wondering where you'd got to. Why didn't you telephone? You're a very selfish man, Steve Cartwright, no thought for anyone but yourself.'

'That's not true, Jean.' He hardly listened while she railed at him, his mind preoccupied with Kathleen Quinn.

Steve worked regular shifts at the hospital, six in the morning until half past two. He arrived home from work a week later just as the telephone began to ring. He went into the parlour, picked up the receiver, and growled, 'Hello.'

Jean appeared in the doorway, hands on hips, looking annoyed. She preferred to answer the phone herself.

'Who is it?' she demanded before he'd had a chance of finding out.

'I've had your clothes cleaned, Mr Cartwright.' Kathleen Quinn spoke in her magistrate's voice, cool and detached. 'Would you like to collect them? I can have them delivered if that's what you'd prefer.'

'No, I'll collect them. Tomorrow afternoon, about three?'

'I'll see you then.' The line went dead.

Jean was standing over him, waiting for an explanation. 'That was the cleaners,' he said. 'My things are ready to be collected.'

'Will you have to pay?'

'Of course I'll have to pay,' he said impatiently. 'It's a cleaners, not a bloody charity.'

'Where is it, the cleaners?'

'Huddersfield,' he grunted.

'I'll come with you. I want to take that cardy our Maggie gave me for Christmas back to Marks & Spencer's. It's too small.'

Steve hunted wildly around in his mind for a reason to turn down this perfectly reasonable suggestion. 'I'm going straight from work,' he said. 'It'd hardly be worth your while if I came home first to collect you. Why don't you go to Huddersfield on the bus, make a day of it?'

She frowned, then her face cleared. It would seem she found the suggestion acceptable. 'I'll go tomorrow. I wouldn't mind a day out for a change. But if that's the case, I might as well pick up your cleaning.'

'You don't want to be carting that lot around, it'd be too heavy. Anyroad, I thought I might take the opportunity of calling in the Job Centre, see what's going.'

'We could meet up for a cup of tea and I could come home in the car.'

'Best not, luv,' he said easily. 'If there's anything decent, I might be a while, filling in forms and stuff. Best you make your own way home on the bus.'

The snow had almost gone, the temperature having risen a few degrees over the last few days. The soil in the fields was black against the stark patches of white that still remained and the roads were wet and slushy.

When Steve left the hospital, he drove like the wind, water spitting from the tyres. He was unfolding, becoming someone else, experiencing emotions never felt before, or at least not for a long time – when he was younger, perhaps, much younger.

He turned into her house, noticed it had a name on a board tacked to a tree: Threshers' End. He was wondering where the name had come from, half expecting to see a couple of dead threshers lying amongst the trees, when he arrived at the front door, got out of the car, and rang the bell.

It was quite a while before she answered, wearing a bathrobe and a towel tied around her hair. 'You're quarter of an hour early,' she said shortly. 'I thought we'd agreed you'd come at three.'

He hadn't thought that time mattered all that much. 'Sorry,' he said humbly. 'Me watch needs a battery and the clock in the car don't work.'

She stood aside to let him in. Their arms touched as he brushed past. She closed the door, stood with her back to it, looked at him. There was longing in her grey eyes and she was breathing heavily, as was Steve himself. He reached for her, rested his big hands on her waist, and pulled her towards him. She came willingly and didn't protest when he undid the belt of the robe and began to caress her damp, naked body. Nor did she protest, when he picked her up and carried her upstairs, as he had done so many times over the last few days in his imagination.

But making love to a flesh and blood Kathleen Quinn was immeasurably, indescribably better than it had been in his dreams. He touched, and kissed, every intimate part of her, while she did things to him that Jean wouldn't have countenanced in the days when they used to make love. Not that he gave much thought to Jean that afternoon in Threshers' End.

When it was over and they lay naked on the bed, side by side, utterly sated, she said shyly, 'That was wonderful, thank you.'

'It were bloody marvellous. Thank *you*.' He'd just shared something that could only be described as magnificent with a woman he hardly knew.

'I've been thinking about you,' she whispered, 'ever since last week, wanting us to do . . . what we've just done. When I phoned, I was dreading you'd tell me to have the cleaning delivered.'

'No way.' He turned on to his side and stroked her hair, dry now, and all mussed. Her lips were swollen from their lovemaking and there was a bruise on her shoulder. 'What would your husband say if he knew?'

'He'd be upset. What about your wife?'

'She'd bloody kill me and if she didn't manage it, me daughters would pitch in and finish me off.'

'How many daughters do you have?'

'Four.' He didn't mention his seven grandchildren. Right now, he felt too young to be a granddad. 'Have you got any kids?'

'A son, Conrad. He's twenty-one and lives in Denmark.'

'You don't look old enough to have a son of twenty-one.' He'd thought her in her mid-thirties.

'I'm forty-two,' she said surprisingly. 'The reason I was so upset last week was because Con had rung that morning to say he'd just got married. I felt gutted, not being there, the mother of the groom, that sort of thing. He's emailed since and it turns out that no one else was there, just him and Lydia. They did it on impulse. Mind you, it still hurts a bit.' She sniffed. 'Would you like some tea?'

'I wouldn't say no.' He liked the idea of being with her in the kitchen, knowing her as he did now. He got out of bed and began to pull on his clothes. Kathleen lit a cigarette and watched. 'Is this where you sleep with your husband?' he asked, and wasn't surprised when she said the room was a spare. There were no clothes around, no bits and pieces on the dressing table, just a glass tray on a lace mat. It reminded him of a room in a hotel, dull and unlived in. While he buttoned his shirt, she stubbed out the cigarette, reached for the robe and slipped it around her narrow shoulders. She stood in front of the mirror and tried to calm her untidy hair with her fingers.

'When can I see you again?' he asked. 'Tomorrow?'

She looked at him through the mirror and they shared another of those inexplicable moments. 'I'm on duty tomorrow. I run the Well Women Clinic in the Merryvale surgery every Monday, Wednesday, and Friday. Tuesday and Thursday mornings, I'm in court and Saturday, my husband will be home, but he plays golf on Sunday afternoons. Can you come then?'

He and Jean usually went to tea with one of the girls on Sunday. He'd make an excuse, he'd lie, cheat, do anything if it meant seeing Kathleen Quinn again. 'Sunday it is,' he said.

'Come after lunch.' Her eyes glowed, as if she could already imagine them in bed together. 'If the garage door is closed, it means Michael's still here, but I'll phone if he's not going – it would take something like an earthquake to make him miss his golf.'

'Don't phone,' Steve said quickly. 'Me wife always answers. No, I tell you what, let it ring twice, then put the receiver down. It'll be a signal not to come.'

Kathleen sighed rapturously. 'I can't wait till Sunday.'

'Neither can I.'

That was just the beginning of their life of deceit and lies.

He was working overtime, he told Jean, when he started coming home two or three hours late on Tuesday and Thursday afternoons.

'I hope they're paying you,' she said sourly. He gave her an extra ten quid a week as proof, leaving himself seriously short.

Sundays were more difficult to explain away. There were only so many times he could say he didn't feel up to it, that he had a headache, that there was something going on at the club. In the end, he just flatly refused to go, causing ructions. Tea with his daughters had become an institution. They took it in turns: Brenda was the first Sunday in the month, Maggie the second, and so on. Steve had never enjoyed them. His four sons-in-law, all in their twenties and with decent jobs, constantly offered him advice on how to turn his life around, make money, train for this and train for that, start up a business of his own, Jean nodding in the background, making derogatory remarks: 'He's just an old stick-in-the-mud. You'll never get our Steve to change his ways.'

He was fed up being the object of so many people's

attention, being told which way to jump. Kathleen liked him the way he was and she was the only one who mattered. Jean hardly spoke to him because of the Sunday tea business, but he didn't care. He sang under his breath as he pushed trolleys up and down the hospital corridors, began to use aftershave, showered every night, wore his best shirt for work every Tuesday and Thursday. It might look suspicious, but he didn't care about that, either.

'Michael knows about us,' Kathleen said on Easter Sunday afternoon after they'd made love. They'd been seeing each other for two months and it was getting better and better with each time.

'How?' Steve asked, startled.

'He just guessed. He said I looked different, that he'd never known me look so happy.' She nestled against him. 'I am too, so happy I could cry.'

'What'll happen now?' He'd die if he couldn't see her again.

He felt her shrug against him. 'Nothing.'

'Nothing!' The other way around, he would have killed the chap.

Her breath was warm on his shoulder when she spoke. 'Michael's upset, but he doesn't object to me having an affair.'

'Why not?' He felt confused. 'I don't understand, luv.'

'He's impotent,' she said flatly, 'has been for years, since not long after Conrad was born.'

'Flippin' heck, Kathleen.' He sat bolt upright on the bed. 'Why didn't you tell me before?'

She shrugged again. 'There was no point. It didn't matter. It still doesn't. Michael loves me in his own way, and I love him in mine, but he realizes he can't complain if I sleep with another man.'

'But you can still do things for him,' he said awkwardly.

'I know that and so does Michael, but it's not the same. He's too ashamed to accept second best.' She gently squeezed his arm. 'I'd sooner not go into detail, Steve, not right now. I just wanted to tell you that Michael knows and that he's not likely to come barging in and play the injured husband.'

'I'm surprised you didn't get divorced,' Steve muttered.

'It may surprise you even more to know that I've never met a man I loved as much as I love Michael, not until I met you. He said he'd divorce me if I want. I said I'd ask what you wanted first.'

'This is getting beyond me.' He got out of bed and began to drag on his clothes. 'I don't understand any of it. I don't want any part of it. It's unnatural.'

'Where are you going?' She was sitting up in bed, clutching her knees, as naked as the day she was born, her red-brown hair curled over her white shoulders and her grey eyes misted with love. She had never looked so desirable and he had never wanted her so much.

'Downstairs,' he gulped, resisting the urge to tear off his clothes and get back into bed. 'I need to think.'

He sat on the padded bench in the kitchen, stared at his folded hands. What the hell had he got himself into? He began to dissect Kathleen's words, split them up into ones and twos, until it eventually dawned on him that she'd just told him she loved him, that she would divorce her husband if that's what he, Steve, wanted. His heart began to race.

Was it what he wanted? Did he want to spend the rest of his life with Kathleen Quinn?

She was a strange woman, mysterious. He could never tell what she was thinking. She was different every time they met, warm and friendly one day, shy and diffident the next. Sometimes he found her in what he called her magistrate's mode, brisk and efficient, or she might be withdrawn, uncommunicative, or as giggly as a schoolgirl. Perhaps she wasn't sure who she was herself. Whatever her mood, when they made love, she was as passionate as ever.

'Have I shocked you?' She came into the kitchen fully dressed, face made up, hair combed.

'Yes,' he said bluntly.

'Not every family is as simple and straightforward as yours,' she said in her prim and proper voice. 'Same wife after thirty years, children grown up and living on the doorstep, in and out of each other's houses by the minute. Other families have stresses and strains you couldn't even guess about.'

'D'you think it wasn't stressful when I lost me job as a miner?' he said gruffly. 'You're talking like a bloody judge again, passing opinions on things you know nothing about.' He hadn't told her that he hadn't touched his wife for twenty-four whole years, not since Alice, the youngest, was born. Jean had had four children and that was enough. She didn't want another. For a while, she took the pill, but it made her sick and it could give you cancer, she said. Other sorts of birth control she didn't trust – lots of women she knew had got pregnant despite their men using condoms, so they were out, and she didn't fancy a cap, it was too messy.

'Anyroad, Steve, I was never very keen on that side of

things.' Although she'd been keen enough when they were courting, he remembered.

They'd slept in the same bed ever since, each on their own side, never trespassing on the other's territory. But, there you go, that was Jean for you. In her own way, she was ten times more complicated than Kathleen and his own life was hardly what you'd call normal.

'I'm sorry.' Kathleen sat down and laid her hands on his. They felt cool and soothing. 'Were you shocked when I told you I loved you? I didn't realize it had slipped out until after you'd gone. And it was stupid of me to talk about divorce, lay it on you so suddenly, without warning. You might only be coming for the sex – lots of men would. Love might be the furthest thing from your mind. I just hope I haven't frightened you off. I'd hate to lose you.'

'You'll never lose me.' He was conscious of his voice breaking slightly. He wrapped her small hands in his large, broad ones, and said huskily, 'I'd like us to be together, *living* together, though I don't know how we'll manage it. Come July, I'll be out of a job, me bank balance is in the red since I paid your bloody fine, and Jean's engagement ring's still in the pawnshop.' The whipround in the club had hardly raised a quarter.

'You'll soon find another job,' she said, grinning, 'a big, strong man like you. And I have plenty of money. I own half the house and Michael can well afford to give me my share. We'll be a partnership,' she said encouragingly when she saw him frown. 'Please don't be old-fashioned and say you can't live with a woman who earns more than you. This is the twenty-first century. Things like that don't matter any more.'

Steve felt as if he'd entered another, quite different,

world. His wife, his daughters, everyone apart from Kathleen, seemed to be speaking to him from somewhere else, their voices muffled and unreal. The things in his house, once so familiar, looked strange, as if he'd never seen them before. He no longer knew where the things were kept, and kept looking for them in the wrong places.

His relationship with Jean had sunk to its very lowest when the pit closed and hadn't improved since. Yet never once had he even faintly considered leaving. She was his wife and would stay his wife until death did them part.

But now everything had changed and it both excited and terrified him, the idea of leaving all the certainties behind and treading into the unknown with a woman he'd met only a few months ago.

He felt confident that Jean would never agree to a divorce, but that wasn't the end of the world. More importantly, his girls would never speak to him again, and he would lose all contact with his grandchildren. It was something he'd just have to put up with if it meant being with Kathleen.

They decided to leave things as they were until July when his job came to an end and he'd get his redundancy money. He'd give the lot to Jean. He didn't want to walk out and leave her penniless.

One Sunday afternoon in June, they went to Huddersfield in the Mercedes to view a site in the city centre where a block of flats was being built. It was a warm, summery day, the first time he and Kathleen had been out together. She wore a cream flowered frock and a pink velvet jacket that made her look more like a girl than a 42-year-old woman. He found her more desirable than ever.

'Would you like to live in a flat?' she asked. The car parked, they walked to the site that was partially hidden behind a high wooden fence. The builders had reached the third floor. There would be six by the time it was finished, Kathleen said.

'I dunno,' he said cautiously.

'We could reserve one right at the top. The view would be magnificent.'

'I dunno,' he said again. She'd got hold of the details and the prices shocked him. 'I just wish I could pay summat towards it.' He was aware he sounded a touch sulky.

She dug him playfully in the ribs. 'Don't be silly. You would if you could, I know that.'

'Yes, but I can't.' He hunched his shoulders uncomfortably. 'I feel like one of them gigolos, if you must know.'

'That's true enough. I only want you as my own, personal stud.' She giggled. 'Let's leave it for now. You're obviously not keen.' As they walked away, arm in arm, she said, 'Steve, we have to live somewhere. We can rent a place if you prefer.'

'That mightn't be a bad idea. Once I've got another job, I can pay my share.' He pulled her into a doorway and kissed her passionately.

'Oh, God! I love you, Steve Cartwright.' She flung her arms around his neck, saying recklessly, 'Let's do it here, in front of everyone.'

'I don't think that'd be such a good idea, luv.' Right now, it was what he wanted more than anything in the world.

'Why not?' She pressed herself against him and he felt his body stir.

'Well, someone might see us and we might get

arrested. We'd end up in front of a magistrate, and you know what I think about *them*.'

'Then let's find a hotel. I can't wait till we get home. Anyway, Michael will be back soon. I don't want to rub his nose in it.'

'OK, let's find a hotel.' He couldn't wait, either.

When he got home on Wednesday, an unsmiling Brenda was sitting in Jean's chair in the living room. 'Where's your mam?' he enquired.

'In bed,' she said curtly. His eldest daughter most resembled himself: big-boned, broad-faced, with long, wavy brown hair the same shade as his. She was the sort of woman people described as 'handsome'. Nowadays, Steve wasn't sure he liked her all that much. She had grown up a bit of a tyrant: with her kids, with Graham, her husband, and with her dad most of all. Only her mother, of whom Brenda was staunchly protective, saw her soft side.

'Isn't she well?'

'You could say that. I'm not sure how you'd describe someone who's just discovered her husband's having it off with another woman. Don't deny it, Dad,' she said brutally when Steve opened his mouth to speak, although he had no idea what he was about to say. 'Angie Curtis saw you in Huddersfield last Sunday, coming out of some cheap hotel, holding hands with a girl young enough to be your daughter.'

'And Angie came and told your mother?' He kicked the back of a chair. It was a nervous gesture rather than angry. 'I was going to tell her meself one day soon. Why couldn't the bitch keep her bloody gob shut?'

'Why should she? Mam has a right to know. And it weren't Mam she told, anyroad, it were me,' his daughter sneered. 'And it were *me* who told our Mam. And you might like to know that, yesterday, I rang the hospital and nobody knew anything about you working overtime, so I borrowed Graham's car and followed you home. It didn't surprise me when you turned into some dead posh house and didn't come out again for almost two hours.'

'You should get a job with MI5, girl. You'd make a good spy.' He was blustering, trying to cover his confusion. This was totally unexpected and he had no idea how to deal with it.

'That's not all I did.' Brenda's eyes were bright with spite. 'I went to the town hall this morning and looked up who lived in the house: Kathleen and Michael Quinn. Our Maggie said there's a Dr Kathleen Quinn at her surgery, so it seems you've picked a dead posh tart to screw, Dad.'

Steve's heart sank to his boots. 'Do your sisters know?'

'Of course. Why, would you have liked it kept a secret?'

'For now, yes. I told you, I was going to tell your mam soon.'

'When?' she demanded.

'When I left for good.'

'For good!' Her eyes bulged. 'You're leaving Mam – for *good*?'

'I would've thought she'd be pleased at the idea. I've been feeling a bit surplus to requirements over the last ten years.'

'Don't be daft, Dad. Mam's gutted. And don't you think it's about time you went upstairs to see her?' She jerked her head towards the stairs.

Jean was lying, fully dressed, on top of the bedclothes, her shoes on the floor, neatly side by side. She raised her head when he went in and he saw her eyes were puffy with tears. 'Steve. Oh, Steve! How could you do this to me?'

All he could feel was impatience. He had no intention of saying he was sorry, because he didn't regret a single thing. 'What did you expect, Jean? We've not been man and wife in a long while. I'm not exactly made of steel. All I can say is, it's a wonder it didn't happen sooner.'

'You should've said summat, luv,' she cried. 'We could have worked things out between us.' Her nose was running, badly. He gave her his hanky and she wiped it with a trembling hand.

'I remember saying quite a lot when you turned away from me, refused to let me touch you, but you've forgotten.'

She turned, buried her face in the pillow, and said in a muffled voice, 'I'm nearly through the change, so there's no chance of me falling pregnant. We could do it now, Steve. We could do it tonight. I wouldn't mind.'

He stared at the crumpled figure on the bed. It was years since Jean had given any thought to her appearance. Her thick tights were wrinkled around her ankles, her swollen hips encased in a shapeless skirt, her blouse torn under the arms. The hair that had once gleamed a pretty blonde had turned to dull grey and was cut sensibly short. There was no style to it and she only wore make-up when she left the house. He'd grown so used to it that he no longer gave it any thought. She was his wife. She was Jean, and this was the way she was.

'It's a bit late for that,' he said gruffly. 'I can't turn meself on and off like a bloody tap.'

'Brenda said Angie told her the girl you were with only looked half your age,' she whispered into the pillow. 'I can't compete with someone like that.'

'She's forty-two, only seven years younger than you.'
Despite himself, he was beginning to feel sorry for her.
He would sooner she ranted and raged, attacked him,
than face him with her tears.

'I want to die,' she sobbed. 'If you don't stop seeing
this woman, Steve, I'll kill meself.'

A few days later, Steve's supervisor called him into his
office. Ken Crook was an ex-sergeant major in the
Marines, a hearty, red-faced man in his sixties whose job
would also shortly disappear. Lately, Steve had spent
most of his time loading equipment and furniture into
vans, there being hardly any patients left to push around.

'Sit down, son, close the door,' Ken said when Steve
entered the room that was hardly bigger than a cupboard.
He grinned amiably. 'Seems like you've been a naughty
boy. Either that, or someone's got it in for you.' He
threw a letter across the desk. 'That came this morning.'

'Dear Sir,' Steve read, 'This is to inform you that Mr
Steve Cartwright is having an affair with a married
woman. Yours faithfully.' There was no signature,
nothing to say where it had come from, although he
recognized Brenda's sharp, pointed writing and felt a
flood of bitter anger.

'Short and to the point, eh!' Ken guffawed. 'Well, all I
can say is, good luck to you, son. What people do out of
working hours is none of the hospital's business.
Anyroad, there won't be a bloody hospital by the end of
the month. We'll all be out of a job.' He gave Steve a
lewd wink. 'I only wish it were me having the affair.'

Kathleen's husband and one of the doctors in the
surgery where she worked had received similar letters.
'Michael already knows and Dennis Burke asked if I was
sleeping with a patient. Once he realized I wasn't, he

didn't care.' She shuddered delicately. 'But it's horrible, Steve. Last night, the phone went twice, but there was no one there.' She went on to say she'd taken the opportunity of giving in her notice. 'It might be best if we moved away from Huddersfield and lived somewhere else. If we stay, I doubt if that malevolent daughter of yours will give us any peace. What do you think?'

He didn't tell Jean what Brenda had done. Jean was a broken woman. Day after day he would come home and find her in bed, her face haggard with weeping, telling him that she loved him, pleading with him to stay. She'd had her hair permed, bought a couple of nice frocks, but it only made her seem even more pathetic as she tried to compete with his beautiful Kathleen.

He wanted to leave, find himself lodgings of some sort, while he waited for his job to come to an end and his life with Kathleen to start, but it seemed cowardly to shirk the small amount of responsibility he had left.

For some reason, the girls kept well out of the way. Perhaps they thought that, left alone with their heart-broken mother, his own heart would be touched and he'd stay. Although the guilt was piling on him, choking him, the idea of staying with this sad, weeping woman didn't enter his head. He was too much looking forward to being with Kathleen, although when they were together, his mind would be pre-occupied with Jean, who'd make herself ill if she didn't pull herself together. It reminded him of the business with the new house. She hadn't wanted one when the money was there, but all hell was let loose when she demanded a house and it was too late. Now she was doing the same thing with her husband.

Kathleen had been writing after vacancies advertised in the medical press. There was, as always, a shortage of doctors, and replies usually arrived by return of post inviting her for interview.

'Where would you like to live?' she asked. 'Brighton, Broadstairs, the Isle of Wight or Liverpool?'

'Liverpool,' Steve said instantly. It was a working-class city and he'd prefer to live amongst his own kind, not in some toffee-nosed, middle-class area where he'd feel out of place.

'Good.' She looked pleased. 'There's a job in the maternity department at the general hospital. I've worked with mothers and babies before and I loved it. I'll ring them later, arrange an interview.'

Steve's hospital was now a ghostly place, empty of patients and beds. He spent his last day playing cards and drinking with a group of men who, like him, had been made redundant. The atmosphere was a mixture of gloom and bravado, as they discussed what they do with themselves on Monday when they would normally have gone to work. Most were off to the Job Centre that they'd been haunting for weeks without success.

'What about you, Steve?' someone asked.

'It'll be the same for me,' he said. He didn't mention the Job Centre would be in Liverpool. Kathleen had got the position she was after, starting the beginning of August. They would stay in a hotel while looking for somewhere to live. He'd booked a taxi to take him to Threshers' End first thing in the morning – he didn't want Kathleen collecting him from the house.

But before any of these things happened, he had to say goodbye to Jean, something that he was dreading.

She was downstairs for a change when he got home, wearing one of her new frocks. The red-rimmed eyes in the waxen face made her look a bit like a clown and he felt a surge of pity. He could smell something delicious baking in the oven. 'I'm making a steak and kidney pie,' she said.

'Ta, luv.' He sat in his old chair, while she stood in the kitchen doorway, looking at him, wiping her flour-covered hands on her apron.

'You're a very good-looking man, Steve.' Her voice was low and tired. 'I remember how proud I felt when we got married. I only noticed recently that you've hardly changed a bit. No wonder that woman fell in love with you.' Her hands dropped to her sides. 'I've let meself go, haven't I? I stopped making meself pretty. It's just that I felt so sure of you. I didn't think it mattered how I looked.'

'It wasn't that, Jean,' he muttered.

'I know what it was and I'm sorry. I didn't think that mattered either.'

He didn't reply, worried that he'd say too much and it'd end up in a row. Later, he ate the pie, said how nice it was, and stayed in that night, saying little because there was little left to say, watching telly, when he'd meant to go the club for a last drink with Bert and Fudge and the other lads. It was just that he didn't like to desert Jean on their last night together.

At ten o'clock, when she was engrossed in something on the telly, or pretending to be, he went upstairs and put a few clothes in a bag; a spare pair of jeans, underwear, and a couple of shirts. Jean could take the rest to one of them charity shops. There were enough around these days. As an afterthought, he included his best suit. He'd need it when he went after jobs. He put the bag, out of sight, in one of the unused bedrooms.

When he returned downstairs, Jean was making

cocoa. 'Would you like a snack of some sort, a sandwich?'

'No, ta.'

'I'll turn in after I've drunk this.'

'I'll be up later,' he lied. He had no intention of going to bed. He'd sleep in the chair. Jean had started turning to him during the night, putting her arms around him, whispering his name, while he pretended to be asleep. It was much too late for that, and he didn't want it to happen again on his last night.

When he woke, aching all over, bright sunlight was pouring through the window and the birds were singing outside. The clock on the mantelpiece showed ten past seven. The taxi would arrive in fifty minutes. He stood, stretched his arms, and gave himself a good wash in the kitchen, shaving in front of the tiny mirror on the window sill. When he looked, it was only half past seven. Opening the kitchen door, he strolled down the narrow strip of lawn and imagined his girls playing on the grass when they were just kids, four pretty frilly figures batting balls to one another. He remembered putting up a length of rope, turning the grass into a tennis court, pretending it was Wimbledon.

There was a shed at the bottom where he'd occasionally gone for a bit of peace and quiet when the girls got older and had their boyfriends round and the house been turned into a disco.

'There you are, skiving again,' Jean would say in a bitter voice when she found him. He thought she'd hated him, but it turned out she'd loved him all the time, just not bothered to show it.

The shed door creaked when he opened it and the sun scorching on the corrugated roof had turned it into a hot house. It smelled of paint and turps, dirt and dust. The windows were draped with cobwebs. He should've cleaned it before he left, but it was too late now. It was too late for an awful lot of things.

Indoors, the clock showed quarter to eight. He went upstairs for his bag, peeked round the bedroom door and saw that Jean was fast asleep. She wore the nightie she'd bought when she went into hospital to have Alice, the pattern washed away over the years. He couldn't have described the colour it was now. Perhaps he should've bought her things like pretty nighties, except, he thought ruefully, she was bound to have found something wrong with them, because nothing he could ever do was right.

He wouldn't wake her: he'd had enough of tears. He visualized her running after him down the path, screaming, trying to drag him back. Once she woke and found him gone all she had to do was pick up the phone and the girls would be around in a jiffy.

Picking up the bag, he crept downstairs and decided to wait outside, so there'd be no need for the taxi driver to sound his horn. He stood by the gate in the brilliant July sunshine. It didn't feel right to be leaving the village where he'd been born, where he'd always lived, without a soul around to wave him off, wish him luck.

The taxi turned the corner. When it got nearer, he recognized Jim Brogan, an ex-miner behind the wheel. According to Jean, Jim was someone who, unlike him, hadn't gone under when the pit closed. 'Why don't you do summat like that?' she'd demanded and didn't want to know when he explained Jim barely scraped a living from his taxi and had two other jobs on the go.

'Hiya, Steve.' Jim opened the passenger door. 'Where are you off to?'

'Threshers' End, it's a big house at the bottom of Coopers' Hill.' He threw his bag on to the back seat, climbed inside, and turned to take one last look at the house where he no longer lived. It might have been his imagination, but he could have sworn the net curtain on the bedroom window twitched slightly. Perhaps Jean had been pretending to be asleep when he'd looked in.

'Is there summat wrong with your own car?' Jim asked.

'No, it's just that I won't be needing it any more.'

He stopped thinking about Jean and thought about Kathleen instead.

Sunday

8 JULY 2001

Chapter 3

'Steve!' Kathleen cried when she woke on Sunday morning and saw she was alone in bed. She rubbed her eyes and found them wet with tears.

'Morning, luv.' He came in, feet bare, wearing only jeans and carrying tea in the pretty china mugs they'd bought the day before. 'The sun's splitting the flags outside. It's a grand day. Shall we drive into the countryside later and have a pub meal?'

'I thought you'd left me.'

He hurriedly put the teas on the floor and took her in his arms. 'Left you! As if I would.' He looked at her indignantly. 'You can't think much of me, Kath, to say summat like that.'

'I had this dream,' she said. 'I was in this horrible dark house, feeling terribly alone.' The feeling had weighed down on her until she could hardly breathe. It was still there, the feeling, just a little.

'Well, you're not alone. You've got me, and you'll never be alone again.'

'I know.' She relaxed against him. Everything had been going so well since they'd come to Liverpool. She was already in a state of euphoria when a secretary from the hospital had phoned the hotel where they were staying to say she'd discovered a new house that was available to rent. 'Actually, it's a bungalow, detached, on a tiny estate in a very nice area.'

They'd gone to see it immediately and taken it on the spot. It was less than a quarter of the size of Threshers' End, but Kathleen didn't care. As long as she was with Steve, nothing else mattered.

Then, yesterday, she discovered he'd rung Brenda because he was worried about his wife. It wasn't *exactly* a betrayal, but felt like one. He was such a soft old thing, worried he'd hurt Jean, forgetting how much she'd hurt him in the past. But how could he and Kathleen start a new life together when he was still clinging to the old?

When Ernest Burrows woke that Sunday morning, it took him a while to work out where he was. He looked at his wife, sleeping peacefully in the twin bed, and for the briefest of seconds, *he couldn't remember her name.*

Anna. Her name was Anna.

The hairs prickled ominously on Ernest's taut neck. It had been happening a lot lately, forgetting the obvious, like Anna's name. The other day, he couldn't think what the things were called he was putting on his feet. 'They're me . . . *shoes.*' It had taken more time than it should have for the word to come.

While his body remained in perfect condition, he was beginning to lose his mind. And what would happen to Anna then?

Victoria Macara had been up since six, clearing out drawers. There were dozens of them: sideboard drawers, chests of drawers, huge drawers at the bottom of wardrobes. The kitchen was full of drawers and so far she had only managed to empty two. The contents were spread on the table. What was she supposed to do with the neat balls of string Gran had collected over the years, the odd shoelaces, half-used notebooks, the enormous number of perfectly good ballpoint pens, boxes of matches, key rings galore, some with keys attached that she didn't recognize but it seemed wrong to chuck away?

The house was to be let, fully furnished, while she was in America. The developer had wanted to buy it and put another house, or two, in its place. She'd said 'no', because it would have felt traitorous to sell the house where generations of Macaras had lived – and she'd have had nowhere to live when she came back. *If* she came back. It depended on how things went. Either way, the drawers and cupboards still had to be cleared.

Perhaps she could put all this stuff in the loft, out of people's way. She looked at the dresser, full of plates at the top, more drawers in the middle, cupboards underneath. The loft would be full to bursting if everything went up there. No, she'd give the good things to a charity shop and chuck the rest away.

The items on the table were ruthlessly swept into a black plastic bag although, a few moments later, she retrieved the pens. Someone, somewhere, could make use of them.

Three Farthings' doorbell rang at more or less the same time as it had the previous morning. In her smart, white kitchen, Rachel Williams was watching the tiny flecks of dust and what looked like minuscule threads of cotton that were dancing in the shaft of sunlight pouring through the window. It looked so pretty, if you forgot you were breathing in all this stuff. The particles were dancing up her nose, into her ears, and would dance into her mouth when she opened it.

She sighed deeply when she went to answer the door. Kirsty had got up very early, saying she was going to Wales with some friends and wouldn't be back till late.

Frank and James were still in bed. Frank was tired after his exertions the day before, putting up Sarah Rees-James's curtains, hanging pictures, helping her unpack. Rachel's lips twisted bitterly. There were plenty of things in their own house still to do.

She opened the door. Tiffany was outside, carrying her teddy bear, but wearing a nightdress instead of yesterday's vest and pants.

'Mummy's dead again,' she said brightly.

'I don't think she is, darling. Mummy's just fast asleep and she'll wake up when she's ready.'

'Can I have some milk then? I'm thirsty.'

'Of course you can. Come in.'

With a regal gesture, Tiffany lifted the hem of her nightdress and stepped inside. She followed Rachel into the kitchen and hoisted her small body on to a chair. 'He's called Oliver,' she said.

'Who is?' Rachel asked, perplexed.

'Him.' The girl held up the teddy bear. 'You can kiss him if you like.'

Rachel obligingly kissed Oliver's furry cheek. 'He's very handsome,' she said.

'I'm going to marry him when I grow up.'

'I'm sure you'll be very happy together.'

'I shan't let him slap me the way daddy used to slap mummy.'

Oh, Lord! Rachel was taking a carton of milk out of the fridge. She let it close with an unintentional bang. 'Did he do it often?'

'Often enough,' Tiffany said darkly.

She wanted to ask more questions, but it seemed wrong to pry. 'How do you like your new house?' she asked instead, sliding a glass of milk in front of the child.

'It's nice, nicer than our old one. And I like Frank. He's much nicer than Daddy.'

Rachel didn't know whether to be pleased or sorry that Sarah's children were forming an attachment to her husband. It would only give him more reason to visit the house, which was an awfully mean thought to have. Tiffany was such a dear little girl and Jack was clearly disturbed, the way he clung to that scrap of blanket. It could only be a good thing for them to have a kindly father figure in their lives – for all his faults, Frank adored children. On the other hand, Rachel couldn't be expected to endorse her husband spending half his time in another woman's house, a woman who hadn't exactly discouraged Frank's advances the day before.

'I'm hungry,' Tiffany announced.

'Would you like some cornflakes?'

'Scrambled eggs on toast would do nicely, thank you.'

'Would they now.' Rachel smiled. She was a cheeky little madam, but quite charming. 'All right, I'll make some for us both. Did Alastair keep Mummy awake last night?'

'Only for a bit. Jack cried the most. He's . . .' she struggled for the word, '. . . homesick,' she finished triumphantly. 'He's missing Jason.'

'And who is Jason?' Rachel enquired.

'Mummy's boyfriend,' Tiffany replied.

The egg Rachel was breaking nearly missed the bowl it was intended for. She rather hoped Jason would turn up soon. *That'd* certainly put Frank in his place.

Tabitha was curled in a striped ball on the kitchen window sill when Gareth went in. It was very un-hygienic because he must have jumped on to the draining board to get there. One of Debbie's sisters,

Kelly, had done the dishes when she'd come the night before. 'How can you live in this mess?' she'd asked, casting an aggrieved glance at Gareth for some reason.

He hadn't bothered to say it wasn't his turn, that he'd been working all morning while Debbie had been out, using her credit card in every shop in Liverpool it would seem. When they'd met in Bluecoat Chambers' restaurant, he'd found her sitting in a sea of plastic bags.

Which worried him somewhat. Debbie behaved as if money grew on trees, yet their finances were already stretched to the limit, what with the mortgage and the hire purchase on the furniture that had been bought from the very best shops, no expense spared.

The Hamiltons had always lived on the edge. Joyce Hamilton, his fearsome mother-in-law, whom Gareth didn't like very much, had a row of jam jars on the sideboard labelled 'Gas', 'Electricity', 'Rates', 'HP' (which stood for hire purchase), 'HE' (household expenses), 'Car', (she didn't have one at the moment), 'Flowers' (for the church), into which she slipped a few quid every week. Last night, Debbie had come up with the brilliant idea of handing over his cherished Escort to her mother when it could easily raise a few hundred useful quid towards the ridiculous Prairie Dog vehicle she yearned for. In no time, his prized car would be as filthy as the old banger Joyce used to have: full of rotten apple cores, empty burger boxes, sweet papers, old clothes, and enough dust to stuff a cushion.

Gareth gave Tabitha a nudge. The kitten raised its head and yawned. 'Talk to me,' Gareth demanded, but the little bugger just went back to sleep.

'Well, if that's how you feel,' he told it huffily, 'I'm going for a walk to clear me head.' Debbie was still in bed, watching some pop programme on television –

they'd had digital installed straight away because she couldn't live without it.

He yelled, 'I'm just going out for a while. Be back in time for twelve o'clock Mass,' and didn't wait for a reply in case she tried to stop him.

This is a great place to live, he thought, when he went outside and surveyed the new houses. I think I'll like it here, but I wish we were in one of the bungalows or the semis that hadn't cost an arm and a leg. Damn Debbie. He was beginning to feel just a little bit cross with her. At the rate she was going, they'd be bankrupt.

The woman in Clematis Cottage banged on the window and gave him a friendly wave. She'd seemed a nice old bird when he'd met her yesterday. He waved back and gave the thumbs up sign for some reason.

As he strolled towards the exit, already feeling slightly better now that he was out of the house where all he seemed to think about was money and how much he owed, he spied a small boy also on the point of leaving the square. He was clutching a tatty blanket and wore pyjamas that were much too small, exposing half his bottom to the world. Gareth hurried after the faintly familiar figure. A paedophile's dream, the child should definitely not be allowed out on his own.

'Hey, kid,' he called. 'Where are you off to?'

The little boy turned, his eyes moist with tears. 'Home,' he hiccupped. 'Want Jason.'

'I've got a feeling your home's back there.' He belonged to that cracking blonde, Gareth remembered. But which house did she live in? He picked up the child, just as the back gate of the old house in the corner opened and a girl came out.

'Oh, you've got him,' she said. 'That's good. I went upstairs for something and saw through the window he was about to wander away. His name's Jack, and you're Gareth Moran, aren't you? I'm Victoria Macara.'

'How do you do. I'd shake hands, but they're otherwise engaged.' He jiggled the child in his arms. 'Jack told me he's going home.'

'He probably hasn't got used to living here yet, have you, Jack?' Victoria chucked the little boy under his chin. 'His mum mustn't be up yet. The baby's teething and she doesn't get much sleep. Shall we take him back? He lives at number one.'

'We'd better had.' As they walked towards the house, Gareth said, 'Rachel Williams told me you were something to do with computers.'

'She told me about you too. I design websites and you're a database developer.'

'And you're going to work in New York next week?' He rather liked Victoria Macara. She wasn't exactly pretty, she was a bit too boyish for that, but she had a guileless, open face and lovely brown eyes that he found very appealing.

'Good morning.' They turned and saw Rachel coming towards them leading Tiffany by the hand. 'It's a good job the baby can't crawl otherwise he'd be wandering off too. Here, let me have Jack and I'll wake Sarah up.' She lifted the boy out of Gareth's arms. 'Perhaps the square should club together and buy her an alarm clock before one of the children is abducted.'

'That mightn't be a bad idea.' Gareth chuckled. 'Jack was on his way home.'

At this, Rachel rolled her eyes and took the children into Sarah's house – the front door was wide open. Gareth and Victoria smiled at each other. 'Would you like a coffee?' Victoria asked. 'I was just about to make one for meself.'

'I'd love one, thanks,' he said.

'The house is in a mess, I've been clearing drawers all morning and haven't even done half yet.'

Gareth said he didn't mind, he was used to houses being in a mess, not strictly true as Hamilton Lodge could have featured in an ideal homes magazine if it hadn't been for the kitchen. He followed Victoria into her own quaintly old-fashioned kitchen where the table was piled with bundles of cutlery tied with string, dishes, cookery books, pans, heaps of tablecloths and embroidered serviettes.

'This is all going to a charity shop, so if there's anything you fancy, just take it,' Victoria said generously as she put the kettle on.

'I'd like the eggcups.' There was one shaped like a train, the other a car. 'I used to have some like that when I was little, but they were different colours.' He picked up the eggcups and fondled them. 'These bring back memories.'

Victoria smiled, rather sadly. 'For me too. They were mine when *I* was little.'

'I'll look after them for you. You can have them back when you come home from New York, that's if you're coming home. Otherwise, I'll keep them. Who will you be working for out there?' he asked, genuinely interested.

'A firm of economists, Parker Inc. They predict trends all over the world, anything to do with finance: pensions, house prices, how much people in China will be paying for rice in two thousand and fifty, that sort of thing. It's not what I'm used to, but I'm sure I'll soon get the hang of it.'

'Sounds fascinating.'

'Doesn't it!' Her face glowed and all of a sudden she looked almost beautiful. 'Who do you work for?'

'A place called Ace Designs. It's in Duke Street. There's just me and these three other guys. Damien's the boss. He's only a year older than me. But I'm just marking time,' Gareth explained, his own face glowing. 'I'm designing this really comprehensive site of me own. I do it at home. If there's anything you want to know about football, like who was Tranmere Rover's inside right in nineteen twenty-three, you'll find it on Footy info.co.uk – when it's finished, that is,' he added hastily. 'The research is taking ages.'

'Wow!' Victoria looked impressed. 'There's some footy books upstairs that belonged to me granddad. They're awfully old. You can have them if you like. I'll look them out later.'

'Thanks – you won't tell anyone about my site, will you?' He realized he'd told her something that no one else in the world knew. If Debbie knew he was designing something that might make them very rich one day, she'd see it as a reason to spend even more.

Victoria put her finger to her lips. 'I won't tell a soul. Would you like that coffee put in the microwave, Gareth? You've let it go cold.'

'You haven't touched yours, either.'

'I forgot all about it. We've been too busy talking, that's why.'

The Jordan boys had gone for a ride on their bikes. 'Watch out for the traffic lights,' Marie had warned them. 'Don't dare budge until they're green.'

'We already know that, Ma,' Patrick said impatiently. 'You'd think I was seven years old, not seventeen.'

'I'm sorry, lad,' Marie said apologetically. 'It's just me,

being daft, but you know I worry meself sick about you whenever you're out of me sight.'

'I know, Ma.' Patrick's voice was gentle now. He understood his mother's fears. Hadn't his brother, Danny, seen one of the people they loved most in the world shot dead in front of his eyes?

'Have you got your mobiles now?'

'Yes, Ma,' they said together.

'Well then, don't hesitate to give us a ring if you're in trouble.'

'No, Ma.' They both grinned and Danny said, 'We're not going to the North Pole, Ma.'

'Just stop making fun of me. Have a nice time now.' She watched until they turned out of the square and disappeared. When she went indoors, Liam was reading the Sunday paper. She wondered how he could remain so calm. 'I miss going to Mass,' she said. 'I feel on edge.'

He gave her one of his gentle smiles. 'Sit down, Marie, stop wringing your hands, try to relax. You're full of nervous tension and it does you no good at all.'

'In a minute.' She couldn't imagine feeling relaxed. Later, she'd go up to the privacy of her bedroom and say the rosary. She kept the beads in their own little purse under her pillow. 'The boys have gone to look at the docks. Is that far?'

'Not on a bike, though I didn't think Liverpool had any docks left.'

'It's a new one called Albert's Dock. There's an art gallery there, the Tate. You know how mad our Danny is on painting.'

'And how good he is at it too. He'll make a fine artist one day.'

'Yes.' She sat down and began to bite her nails.

'Marie.' He looked at her from over the paper.

'Sorry.' She folded her hands on her lap. Very soon, she'd have no nails left. 'Did you hear that baby next door? It screamed its little head off until gone two, then another child took over. It sounded like a boy. Their poor mother must be done in.'

'Why don't you go round, offer to take the baby for a walk or something? Give the mother a break.'

She raised a smile. 'Are you wanting to be rid of me, Father?'

'*Marie!*'

'Oh, Jaysus. I'm sorry – Liam. I'll go next door, like you said.' She fled from the house.

'Hello,' their neighbour said listlessly when she opened the door. She wore tight jeans and a skimpy white T-shirt. Her midriff was bare. Despite her heavy eyes, she still managed to look desperately attractive. The baby was crying again. It sounded very weary.

'I'm from next door,' Marie began, but before she could finish, the woman said in a tired voice, 'If you've come to complain about the noise, I'm sorry, but there's nothing I can do about it. Alastair just cries and cries and now Jack's started. He wants to go home.'

'Ah, no. I haven't come to complain, not at all. I've come to offer a hand. I thought you might like a wee rest while I took the baby for a walk or something. Is he teething? Our Danny had terrible trouble with his teeth.'

The woman looked relieved. 'That's awfully kind of you. Alastair's teething for England. Oh, does that sound silly? I hardly know what I'm saying these days. Come in. My name's Sarah. What's yours?'

'Marie. I've got two boys, Patrick and Danny, they're

seventeen and fourteen, although Patrick will be eighteen on Saturday. They've gone out on their bikes and I can't stop worrying they'll be run over.'

The house was moderately tidy when she went in. A little boy lay fast asleep on a rug in front of the fireplace, and a girl was equally dead to the world on the settee. The whole house must be worn out.

'I thought children got easier as they got older,' Sarah remarked drily.

'Don't you believe it, girl. You worry about them at school, then you worry about drugs and them getting beaten up in a club or marrying some woman who'll make them miserable. You'll be worrying about your children until the day you die. I know I will.'

'I love them to bits,' Sarah said tearfully. 'But I'm a hopeless mother. You see, I never had to look after them on their own until now.'

'You'll soon get used to it, Sarah,' Marie said sympathetically. 'Sit down while I see to the wee baby.' He sounded as if he was upstairs. 'Once he's calmed down, I'll make us a cup of tea.'

A red-faced Alastair lay in his cot in a tangle of blankets looking as weary as he sounded. He was kicking his legs and waving his arms in a half-hearted way. 'You'll be sending your poor mam to an early grave, so you will,' Marie told him. He had on one of those stretchy towelling suits her own lads used to wear. He felt very hot when she picked him up.

'You don't need all that bedding when it's such a warm day,' she chided, as if Alastair had put the clothes on himself. 'And I think we'll get this outfit off you too.' She undid the snappers and unpeeled the suit away from his clammy limbs, then removed his nappy and rubber pants. He was sweating cobs, poor little lamb.

She stood, laid the baby on her shoulder, and put her cool hand on his back. 'When Irish eyes are smiling,' she crooned, and Alastair stopped crying immediately, peed all down her frock, and fell asleep. She was wondering where to lay him, when Sarah came upstairs.

'I thought you'd murdered him,' she whispered. 'I've thought of murdering him myself a few times over the last few days.'

'No, he went out like a light,' Marie whispered back. 'He was far too hot. Have you got some clean cot sheets? Those are all damp. And I'd take them blankets away if I were you. Just put a few towels and a nappy under him in case he pees again and a single sheet on top should be enough in this weather. Next time you nurse him, do it standing up. Me own mammy told me that and it seems to work. And press your hand against his flesh. He'll feel closer to you than through his clothes.'

'You're a miracle worker.' Sarah was looking through drawers. All the furniture was that nice yellow pine stuff. The walls were painted pale blue and the curtains were white cotton with a broderie anglaise frill. 'I can't remember where his bedding is.'

'There's no hurry, girl. Don't get yourself in a state,' Marie said calmly, when she herself had been busy biting her nails to the quick less than half an hour before. There was nothing like other people's problems to take your mind off your own, or so her dear, darling mammy was fond of saying.

Victoria had invited her friend Carrie to lunch. They had met at school and were still close. Carrie had married at twenty-two and divorced four years later. There were no children. John had been 'playing around', and she'd hated men ever since, which was a pity, Victoria thought, because Carrie, with her little snub nose, pouting pink lips, and baby-blonde hair, oozed sex appeal and could have married half a dozen men instead of John.

'I sometimes wish I were a lesbian,' she said over the curried chicken and rice that had come out of a packet and been heated up in the microwave. 'Trouble is, I don't fancy women, not sexually.'

'That is a bit of a drawback,' Victoria admitted.

'Women are so much more trustworthy and dependable.'

'A bet a lot of men don't think like that, the ones whose wives have been unfaithful.'

'They probably deserved it.' Carrie sniffed disdainfully. 'Hey, this wine's the gear. What sort is it?'

'I've no idea. I just picked the cheapest.' Victoria looked just a touch shamefaced. 'I keep forgetting I've got money. Perhaps I should have bought champagne. This is the last Sunday lunch we'll have together in a long time.'

'Miser,' Carrie said affectionately. She gave her friend an appraising look. 'You're remarkably unbitter, considering what that Philip chap did to you.'

'Is there such a word as unbitter?'

Carrie wrinkled her cute nose. 'What does it matter as long as you understand what I mean?'

'It matters if you're a teacher. I hope you're not teaching the children words that don't exist. Anyroad, as regards Philip, he didn't do anything except forget to mention he had a wife who was expecting his child. If the wife had found out about us, she'd have been hurt far more than I was.' Victoria somehow doubted this. Her heart felt as broken now – well, almost – as it had done three months ago when she'd seen Philip in Marks &

Spencer linking arms with a very pregnant young woman. They were looking at baby clothes.

'Huh!' Carrie said scathingly. 'I just hope that's not the reason you're going to America, as a way of getting over the louse.'

Victoria thought that might well be the case, but wasn't prepared to admit it. And, anyroad, just because Philip had turned out to be such a louse, it didn't mean all men were. Gareth Moran, for instance, she'd trust with her life. They'd got on like a house on fire and she could have talked to him all day. Trouble was, he was already married and had made no secret of the fact.

'A woman in one of the new houses is holding a barby on Saturday,' she told Carrie. 'I can bring a friend – would you like to come?'

Carrie's face went bright red. 'Sorry, Vic, I can't.'

'Why not? Since you got rid of John, you've never had anywhere to go on Saturday nights.'

'I've met this chap,' Carrie muttered, her face turning redder. 'He's taking me out to dinner.'

Victoria shrieked with laughter. 'You hypocrite, Carrie Clarkson. All that guff about hating men. You didn't mean a word of it.'

'Yes, I did. This one's bound to turn out to be a louse just like the rest.'

Earlier, Kathleen had gone next door to introduce herself to the people in Clematis Cottage. 'They'll think we're terribly unsociable,' she said to Steve before she went. 'Ever since we moved in, we've behaved as if the rest of the world didn't exist. It's about time we remembered there are other people on the planet or it'll come as a shock when we start work.'

She was starting at the hospital on 1 August and,

tomorrow, Steve was going for a job interview, only as a security guard – they wouldn't see much of each other when he was on nights – but it would do until he found something more convenient. She knew how anxious he was to contribute towards their living expenses.

'Shall I introduce myself as Kathleen Quinn or Kathleen Cartwright?' she asked. 'Shall I say you're my husband or my partner?'

'Husband,' he said quickly, as she'd guessed he would. He was terribly old-fashioned. He probably still hadn't come to terms with the fact that people lived together quite openly these days.

'I love you,' she said, kissing his nose. 'Don't touch me,' she yelped and dodged out of his way when he made a grab for her. If they made love again, she'd never get out of the house.

Kathleen still had her hand on the knocker of Clematis Cottage when the door opened, so suddenly, that she was taken by surprise. A tall, extremely fit-looking, white-haired man smiled at her.

'I'm just fixing a bell,' he explained. 'I was right behind the door. It plays *The Minute Waltz* by Chopin. Me wife picked it out.'

'It's one of my favourites,' Kathleen said.

'Who's there?' a sweet voice called. 'Whoever it is, come in. Ernie's sulking. He wanted *The Red Flag*, but I talked him out of it.'

'You bullied me out of it, Anna,' Ernie said. 'And I'm not sulking. I'm doing as I'm told like I always do. Go on in, luv. Anna's in the parlour.'

The geography was exactly the same as their own bungalow: the living room and main bedroom at the front, kitchen and second bedroom to the rear with a small bathroom and toilet squeezed between. She went into the room that Steve – and the white-haired man – referred to as 'the parlour'. It was hard to believe that people had only recently moved in. The furniture looked as if it had been there for years: a china cabinet full of dishes and ornaments, a sideboard, statues on the mantelpiece, Impressionist prints on the walls. Carpet with an intense whirly design had been laid on the wood-laminated floor. A petite, silver-haired woman was sitting in a straight-back, padded chair, her feet on a footstool. She wore a yellow cotton sweatshirt and white trousers. Oversized gypsy earrings dangled from her tiny ears. She seemed delighted to have a visitor.

'I'm Kathleen Cartwright from next door.' She extended her hand and the woman seized it, although her grip was surprisingly limp. Kathleen knew immediately she had something wrong with her. 'How do you do?'

'I'm very well, dear. I'm Anna Burrows and my sourpuss of a husband is called Ernie.'

'He seemed very charming to me.'

Anna's blue eyes danced with mischief. 'He's just putting it on. He's a monster when there's no one else around to protect me.'

'I'm sure that isn't true,' Kathleen protested.

'Of course it isn't true. He's an old darling. I adore him, but I didn't think *The Red Flag* was right for a doorbell. I don't want all and sundry knowing our politics.'

'You should be proud of your beliefs,' Ernie shouted from the hall.

'Now you're eavesdropping, Ernie. Make Kathleen and I some tea, there's a dear. Or would you prefer coffee, Kathleen? And we've got sherry: medium, I think it is.'

'Tea would be fine, thanks.' She must be ill. She wasn't the sort of woman who would ask her husband to do things if she was able to do them herself.

'You're not from Liverpool, are you, dear? I can detect a trace of an accent, but not from round here. I'd say Yorkshire. Am I right?'

Kathleen gasped. 'You're quite remarkable. I didn't think I had any sort of accent, but I was born in Yorkshire and lived there all my life, until now, that is.'

'I'm good at accents.' She looked very pleased with herself. 'I was on the stage when I was young. I even made a film once,' she said proudly, 'but I've never met anyone who's seen it.'

'What was it called?' Kathleen had belonged to a film society in Huddersfield where obscure films were sometimes shown.

'*The Fatal Hour*, but it's not the one with Boris Karloff. Mine was made in Hungary before the war. I was only eighteen. I'm not sure if it was ever released. Ernie's tried to track it down, but no luck, I'm afraid.'

'I'd love to see it,' Kathleen said sincerely. She found Anna Burrows quite delightful. Then Ernie came in with the tea, and she saw the way he glanced at his sparkling wife, the way she looked back at him, her blue eyes full of love. He put the thin, china cup in her hands. 'Can you manage it, luv?' he said gruffly.

Is this what Steve and I will be like when we're this old? she wondered. If Anna had made a film before the war, she must be in her eighties.

'Now, Kathleen,' Anna said firmly when Ernie had returned to fixing the doorbell. 'All I've done since you came is talk about myself. Tell me, dear, what do you do? I wouldn't be surprised if you told me you were a film star or a model. You're beautiful enough.'

It was almost an hour later when Kathleen returned home. Steve was coming out of the bathroom, rubbing his wet hair with a towel.

'I thought you'd left *me*,' he grumbled. 'What took you so long?'

'I just met this marvellous couple,' she enthused. 'Anna's had multiple sclerosis for years, but it doesn't get her down, not a bit. And Ernie's wonderful. He waits on her hand and foot and it's obvious they love each other very much.' She paused for breath. 'Anyway, you'll be pleased to know we're taking them to lunch.'

Steve didn't look even faintly pleased. 'Are they posh?' he asked.

'Anna is, Ernie isn't. He was very impressed when I said you'd been a miner. Anna asked us to lunch first, but we decided we couldn't all fit in their little car. The boot isn't big enough for her wheelchair and it usually goes on the back seat, so I said I'd take them in ours.' The Mercedes was actually hers, but she wanted Steve to think of it as belonging to them both.

'I suppose it wouldn't hurt,' he sighed. 'I just want you to meself, that's all.'

'I know, darling. But you'll like Anna and Ernie, I promise. Oh, and I told them we'd only just got married, that we were both divorced. Anna wanted to know my life history – later, she'll probably want to know yours. I couldn't very well pretend Michael and Jean had never existed.' She glanced at the phone and wondered if he'd rung Brenda while she'd been out.

★

Marie had asked Sarah and her children to lunch. 'It'll give you a wee break. It's only salad with trifle for afters.'

'I'm sorry,' Sarah said apologetically, 'but the children won't eat salad. All they like is beans or spaghetti rings on toast.'

'Ah, so did my lads when they were little. I was forgetting how finicky little children are. I can do beans on toast no problem. Have you tried them with fish fingers?'

Liam said he was glad she'd made a friend, but when Patrick and Danny arrived, they were more than a bit put out to discover they'd be sharing the meal with strangers. 'Oh, Ma, you shouldn't have asked them,' Danny complained, although when Sarah and the children arrived, Marie noticed Patrick couldn't keep his eyes off Sarah's bare, brown midriff, and Tiffany formed an instant crush on Danny. Danny pretended not to care, but Marie could tell he was flattered.

From the window, Rachel had seen Sarah and the children come trooping out of number one and go next door to the Jordans'. As far as she knew, they were still there. They must be having lunch. Sarah must have done something to make Mrs Jordan feel sorry for her. What she didn't realize was, given half a chance, Sarah would put on her 'helpless little me' act, and make off with her husband.

'It can't go on like this,' Rachel had sternly told a blurry-eyed Sarah that morning when she'd taken the children home and found their mother fast asleep in bed. 'You must get new locks on the doors, the sort that can be locked inside as well as out and hide the key in a place where the children can't find it. Jack was about to wander into the road until Gareth Moran captured him.'

It had genuinely frightened Rachel, who knew to her cost what could happen to small children when they were out on their own.

'I'm sorry,' Sarah had replied in a voice as blurry as her eyes. 'It's just that I'm so tired.'

'I've gone through the same sort of thing, being kept awake all night by a crying baby. You'll just have to learn to cope, as other mothers do.'

Sarah had looked at her oddly, as if she was wondering why the woman who had been so obliging the day before, had even offered to babysit, had so quickly changed. It was all Frank's fault. He shouldn't have started flirting with the girl. She'd wanted to be Sarah's friend, but he'd spoilt it.

Frank had taken James for a drink. Neither had thought to invite her. Perhaps they'd only gone to get away from her, the inadequate wife, the useless mother.

Rachel went into the kitchen to get the dinner ready. It would have to be something that could easily be warmed up later when her husband and son came home and that could be any time. She was peeling potatoes, wondering what to have with them, when she heard laughter outside, and immediately went to see who it was. Victoria was having a friend round for a meal, Carrie. Perhaps she was bringing Carrie to meet her, she thought hopefully. She felt badly in need of company.

Instead, the laughter was coming from Anna and Ernie Burrows and the people from next door, the Cartwrights, who were all slowly making their way towards the garages. Anna was leaning on Mrs Cartwright's arm. Rachel had only glimpsed her once and she really was quite lovely. She wore a scarlet dress with no sleeves that fitted her slim figure perfectly. And that hair – so thick and smooth and shiny, it looked like silk, the way it fell forward when she bent to speak to Anna. Rachel fingered her own lifeless brown hair, lying flat against her head, and felt deeply envious.

She wondered how the couples had become friendly enough to go out together – almost certainly to lunch. Mr Cartwright, who reminded her of a younger Sean Connery, rolled up the garage door, revealing a gleaming black Mercedes. He backed the car out, everyone got in, Anna with some difficulty and a great amount of giggling. Ernie Burrows transferred a wheelchair from his own car into the boot of the other, and they drove away.

Tears pricked Rachel's eyes. Four of the families in the square were lunching with each other and no one had thought to ask *her*, yet she'd tried her hardest to be friendly, arranging a barbecue so everyone could get to know each other. Perhaps she'd tried too hard and it had put them off.

She felt even worse when a crowd of people arrived and made for Hamilton Lodge, and she realized she was the only one in Victoria Square who was in the house by herself.

Gareth was becoming paranoid. Was this going to be a regular event, having the Hamiltons for Sunday dinner, the whole tribe of them – the widow Joyce (Debbie's mother), Kelly and Tracy (Debbie's elder sisters), Grant and Luke (Debbie's younger brothers), and Keith and Ivor (Debbie's elder sisters' boyfriends)? It hadn't happened when they'd lived in the flat in Woolton, because there hadn't been the room or the chairs for them to sit on or a table big enough for them to sit around. In those days, they'd come surreptitiously in their twos and threes.

When they'd moved, he'd argued with Debbie when

she'd insisted on buying a table that, when opened, could seat twelve, little realizing that the Hamiltons were about to descend upon them every Sunday *en masse*, and no doubt at Christmas and on Bank Holidays too.

The girls helped cook the meal, while the men sat in the front room drinking beer, can after can. To Gareth's horror, he began to count them, working out how much they'd cost. He reckoned, between them, they'd drunk about twenty quid's worth before everyone sat down to the joint of beef that had set him back . . . He tried not to think how much the meat had cost, or the wine, or the massive cream and peach gateau for afters, or whether Debbie had bought one or two.

As well as paranoid, he was beginning to feel like a milch cow kept soley to provide milk. He was now a milch man, kept to provide food for his wife's family, plus various hangers-on.

'You're awfully quiet, Gar,' Debbie said. 'Is something wrong?'

'No,' he muttered. 'I'm thinking.' He glanced at her and his heart melted. She looked good enough to eat herself, her dark hair in plaits, and wearing a shell pink top he'd never seen before and pale blue matador pants he'd never seen before either. The blue sandals with impossibly high heels were strangers to him too. No doubt they'd been in the bags she'd been surrounded by in Bluecoat Chambers the day before. The make-up on her small, elf-like face was a work of art, which wasn't surprising, seeing as she was a beautician.

Kelly's frilly blue top, he recognized. He'd actually been with Debbie when she'd bought it a few weeks ago, wincing at the price. He'd only seen it on her a few times and it would seem she'd passed it on to her sister. Kelly couldn't have afforded the top out of a shop assistant's wages. Not only were they feeding the Hamiltons, but it would appear they were clothing them too.

It was midnight in Victoria Square. Ernest was in bed, listening to Anna's quiet breathing and saying his nine times table under his breath – he'd always found it the most difficult. He felt triumphant when he reached nine times twelve without a pause. Maybe his mind wasn't going, after all. He counted down from a hundred, just to make sure, and managed it successfully.

Before going to bed, while Steve was still in the bathroom, Kathleen picked up the phone and found there was a message on voicemail. She felt slightly sick when she pressed seven and the message began to play.

'It's Brenda,' announced a hard, brittle voice. 'Just thought you'd like to know, Dad, that Mam's not stopped crying all day and it's all your fault. How could you do this to her? How could you be so cruel? If she carries on much longer, she's going to be really ill and you'll have *that* on your conscience for the rest of your days – and that tart of a doctor you've taken up with . . .'

Kathleen wasn't prepared to listen to any more. She pressed three for delete, then pulled the plug out of the phone. Tomorrow, while Steve was at his job interview, she'd change the number and ask to go ex-directory.

Victoria was still emptying drawers. Her back ached from bending down. 'What am I supposed to do with all this lot, Gran?' she asked when she opened the drawer in her grandmother's wardrobe and found it full of bedding. Normal bedding, she could have left for whoever rented the place, but nowadays people would turn up their noses at flannelette sheets full of darns, no matter how sparklingly white they were or how neat the darns. There were also loads of blankets, the hard, thick sort that itched your skin if they happened to touch you during the night.

'I wish you'd used a duvet, Gran, like everyone else,' Victoria complained.

The bedding took up four big plastic bags. 'I suppose someone, somewhere will make use of it,' she muttered, as she had done a dozen times that day when faced with drawers full of thick, lisle stockings, silky bloomers that reached the knees, lock-knit petticoats. One of Gran's nighties actually had a Utility label inside and must have been bought during the war. Victoria had never known her wear it. Unlike the other, more practical nighties, this was plain black crêpe, long and slinky, with narrow shoulder straps.

'I bet she got this for when Granddad came home from India.' Granddad had been in the Army and had spent four long years away from home. She had pressed the nightie to her breast. 'I can't possibly give it away.' Later, she put it with the 'things to keep' pile, which was growing ominously large.

Victoria stretched her arms. She felt tired and it was time to go to bed, but first she'd make some cocoa. The football books she'd promised Gareth Moran were on the kitchen table. Most were very old and she hoped he'd find them useful.

'I liked him, Gran,' she murmured wistfully. 'I liked him an awful lot. And I'm sure he liked me.'

If only he wasn't married. If only, if only . . .

Gareth was thinking about Victoria at the same moment as she was thinking about him. The Hamiltons were still downstairs where they'd been watching television for the last – he looked at his watch – seven hours – seven very noisy hours – and he'd been thinking how nice it would be to live in a quiet house where people didn't scream with laughter at every damn thing the telly threw up. Even the news could send the widow Joyce into convulsions. He wondered what his late father-in-law had died of and reckoned his brain had probably exploded from the noise made by his charmless wife. He must ask Debbie sometime.

Shit, it had been an awful day. He'd been hoping to get further on with his footy site over the weekend, but hadn't had a minute, not until a few hours ago, when he couldn't stand watching another old comedy programme on telly – it was on some digital channel that showed them one after the other, and even the ones he liked, *Seinfeld*, for instance, he'd already seen before – so he'd gone upstairs and switched on the computer. It was ages before anyone had noticed that he'd gone. Debbie came, hours later, and told him he was rude just to disappear, and he told her, rudely, that he was busy.

'I don't have a nine to five job like most people. I have work to do at home.'

'Well, if that's how you feel,' Debbie had pouted, 'I'll leave you in peace to get on with it.'

'Gee, *thanks*,' he'd said sarcastically. Peace was at a premium in Hamilton Lodge. He couldn't remember when he'd last experienced it. Then he remembered that morning, talking to Victoria Macara in her comfy old house with its comfy old furniture. It had been peaceful there. The time had flown by. He looked out the window and saw there was a light on upstairs in Victoria's and wondered if she had finished emptying drawers. There'd been something awfully brave and honest about her. She was tough, yet at the same time fragile. He hoped she would manage, all on her own, in New York. Perhaps they could email each other. He felt he didn't want to lose all contact with Victoria Macara.

Rachel Williams was in bed on the verge of sleep. She'd taken a sleeping tablet. It had been a truly horrible day and the sooner it was over the better. Frank and James had come home and announced they'd had a pub meal and didn't want anything to eat. Neither seemed to care she'd already made them dinner. Then James had gone out again and Frank had spent the afternoon watching a football match on television and Rachel watching for the Burrows and the Cartwrights to come back – it was ages before they did and they looked as if they'd had a great time. Sarah Rees-James and the children had spent virtually all afternoon in the Jordans. The younger Jordan boy had taken Tiffany for a ride around the square on the crossbar of his bike.

'I'm being left out,' Rachel whispered. 'No one wants to know me.'

In number two Victoria Square, Marie Jordan was saying the rosary under the bedclothes, her fingers touching the beads lovingly before moving to the next. When she finished, she kissed the crucifix, and slid the rosary under the pillow.

She'd really enjoyed today. It was a long time since she'd felt like a normal human being. There'd been no need to look over her shoulder every few minutes, worried someone might be watching, wondering where they'd seen her before.

At around ten o'clock, she'd gone to Sarah's to make sure the children had settled down for the night. The two older ones were asleep and Alastair was grizzling pathetically in his cot. Marie had dosed him with Calpol and changed his soaking nappy – she wished she could have afforded the disposable sort when Patrick and Danny had been babies. It was something his mother should have done, but the girl had looked dead on her feet. Besides which, she didn't have much idea how to look after children. Until recently, she'd had a nanny who'd done everything, she'd explained earlier. There was a mountain of clothes in the kitchen waiting to be washed. Tomorrow, Marie would give her a hand, bring some of the washing home and do it in her own machine. Helping Sarah could well occupy her until Patrick and Danny started school when she intended to look for a job. She'd never been a lady of leisure and didn't fancy it a bit. By then, Sarah would surely be able to cope on her own.

Marie was curious to know what had happened. Why had Sarah dispensed with the nanny? Why had she moved to Victoria Square? Where was the children's father? She would never ask. She hated it when questioned about her own life. Even so, she felt curious . . .

Sarah

Chapter 4

Sarah's mother was a timid little thing. She went around with a helpless look on her pretty face, which didn't matter, because Daddy was the most capable man in the entire world. It was Daddy who paid the bills, told Mrs Wesley, the housekeeper, what they should have for dinner, went with Mummy to the supermarket to make sure she bought the right groceries. Daddy had interviewed the au pairs who'd looked after Sarah and her sister, Julia, when they were small, and he organized their schooling – they went to private schools, naturally, as there was no question of Robin Fitzgerald's daughters being educated by the State.

Daddy didn't go to work like most girls' daddies. He had an office upstairs with a word processor and a telephone and he invested in things, bought stocks and shares and property. He'd once tried to explain what he did to Sarah, but she didn't understand.

'I'll have to make sure you marry a rich husband,' he'd chortled. 'You're not likely to get very far with your brains.'

Sarah was glad she took after her father, physically, at least. He was tall and blond, with the features of a Greek god – she wasn't the only person to think that. Quite a few girls at school had a crush on him.

'He looks like a film star,' they would say admiringly when he came to collect her and Julia in his vintage

Bentley. Somehow, even in old jeans and a crumpled jacket, he managed to look smarter and more elegant than most other girls' fathers.

While Julia was small and delicately pretty like their mother, Sarah was tall, fair-haired and striking. She was also very athletic, always winning at least half a dozen medals on Sports Day, Daddy watching from the side and frantically cheering her on. He bought a frame to put the medals in, adding more each year. When Sarah grew older, she captained the hockey team and twice won a cup when she represented the school in a tennis tournament.

When she looked back on her childhood, Sarah couldn't remember a single unpleasant thing happening. The Fitzgeralds lived in a big old house that had once been a vicarage and was situated in the countryside halfway between Knowsley and St Helens. Daddy would take them shopping for new clothes in Liverpool or Southport. Anything they wanted, they could have, no expense spared. 'We'll be a long time dead,' Daddy would say when he wrote the cheques, signing them with an arrogant squiggle, though she knew he was short of money sometimes when investments failed or stocks and shares fell when he thought they would go up. Or something like that.

But it didn't get Daddy down. Nothing did. He just laughed his way through life, adoring his girls, loving his quiet little wife, enjoying himself to the full. In summer, the Fitzgeralds went on holiday to the South of France, always staying in the best hotels. Every so often, they threw a party and, when the girls were small, they went around with trays of drinks and refreshments and everyone said how very sweet they were. Dinner parties were held regularly and, as Sarah and Julia grew older, they sat with the guests and Daddy started inviting scores of eligible young men. Although quite a few asked the girls out, they always refused a second date.

There was an insurmountable problem with all the young men: they weren't Daddy. They were nothing like Daddy. They giggled, told silly jokes, were unsure of themselves, didn't know how to treat waiters – Daddy was always firm, but charming, because that way you got the best service. It was the same in banks and shops. Daddy, with his wicked smile and engaging manner, always got his way. People rushed to serve him, whereas the young men had no idea how to behave and were either rude or servile.

Sarah and Julia decided it could only be because they were young, though they felt sure Daddy hadn't been so callow in his youth and, as they couldn't marry him, they couldn't imagine marrying anyone.

At sixteen, Julia left school with three GCEs and went to work in an antique shop owned by a friend of Daddy's. When Sarah left two years later with a GCE in Art and *nearly* one in History, he found her an equally nice job in a big hotel owned by another friend. She was never quite sure what she was supposed to do there. She had her own office and people came to her with problems that she was never able to solve, often guests who wanted to complain about something. Sarah just gave them a big smile and said she was terribly sorry and they went away, apparently satisfied.

One day, quite out of the blue, when Julia was twenty-one, she fell in love. Gary Moss was small, very pale, with mousy brown hair and, although he had an interesting face and a lovely smile, he wasn't remotely like their big, sunburned, outgoing Daddy.

'How on earth did you manage it?' Sarah asked her sister.

'Manage what?'

'Manage to fall in love with Gary?'

'I don't know,' Julia replied, shrugging helplessly. 'It just happened.'

Gary wasn't remotely eligible. He and Julia had met at a party – someone else's party where Daddy wasn't able to choose the guests. A social worker, he earned scarcely enough to live on, let alone buy a decent house.

'We'll just have to buy an indecent one,' Gary said with a grin when Daddy felt bound to point this out. He wasn't the least bit over-awed by his future father-in-law.

'I'm not in a position, at the moment, to help you out with a few grand,' Daddy said stiffly.

'I don't wish to be rude, Mr Fitzgerald, but I wouldn't have taken it if you were. I'd sooner provide for me wife meself, thanks all the same.' Gary came from Liverpool and had a truly horrid accent.

'Call me Robin.'

'I know my wages don't sound much to someone in your position, Robin, but they're pretty average. Lots of people have to manage on much less.'

Daddy looked as if he didn't believe it.

Julia's wedding wasn't as grand as her father would have liked. He was in one of his downward spirals, he explained. But things would soon buck up, he added, as cheerful as ever. By the time Sarah married he would be flush again, but for now they couldn't afford to invite more than a hundred guests and would Julia mind if they had a buffet meal instead of a sit down one?

Twenty-five of the guests were from Gary's family. Daddy was fearful they'd be frightfully badly dressed, drink too much, swear, and throw food at each other, but Gary's relatives turned out to be eminently respectable. His father was a toolmaker, whatever that meant, and his mother a social worker, just like her son. Mrs Moss wore a lovely blue bouclé coat and a feathered hat that Sarah admired very much, until Mrs Moss took them off at the reception and she noticed they'd come from C&A and went right off them. She'd never been inside C&A, but understood it was frightfully common.

Julia and Gary went to live in a titchy little terraced house in an area of Liverpool called Fazakerley – such an awful name. 'It's like a dolls' house,' Sarah commented when she first went in. It was in terrible condition. The people they'd bought it from had been very old and it looked as if it hadn't seen a lick of paint since the year dot.

'You'll have to get people in to decorate,' Sarah said.

Julia just laughed. 'No way, we couldn't possibly afford it. We're going to decorate the place ourselves.'

Sarah looked at her, shocked to the core. 'You can't *paint* things!' Daddy always got a man in, or sometimes a whole gang of men, whenever anything needed doing on the house.

'Oh, sis. You can do anything if you try.'

Sarah had no intention of trying. She vowed she would only marry someone who earned more than a hundred grand a year and that she would never so much look at a paintbrush.

Daddy's fortunes didn't improve as he'd predicted. Sometimes, unusually for him, he got quite tetchy, and Sarah guessed his fortunes were getting worse. He had to sell the Bentley and bought a silly little Mini that looked more like a toy than a real car. When she came home from work at the hotel, she always went into his office to say hello, and would find him buried in papers or totting up figures on the calculator, too busy to speak. He might be on the telephone, his voice strange, wheedling almost, as if he wanted something badly off the person at the other end.

One day when she went in and he was on the phone, he sounded terribly cross. 'For Chrissake, Alex,' he shouted. 'It was you who told me that the damn place was a surefire investment, a goldmine, I think you said. I put everything I had into it. I notice you got out quickly enough,' he added bitterly. 'You might have told me what was going on. I thought we were supposed to be friends, partners.' He slammed down the receiver, noticed Sarah, and said, 'Hello, Poppet,' a trifle half-heartedly. 'Daddy's busy at the moment. I'll talk to you later at tea.'

It must have been Alex Rees-James he'd been speaking to. Sarah had always assumed he *was* Daddy's best friend and partner. They spent hours in the office upstairs studying the *Financial Times* and talking business. Until a few months ago, Alex and his incredibly skinny wife, Midge, had dined with her parents at least once a week. One year, they'd all gone on holiday together to the South of France. The Rees-Jameses had no children and seemed terribly fond of one another. It had come as quite a shock when, after Christmas, Alex announced he and Midge were getting divorced. Nobody could understand why and Alex and Midge weren't prepared to tell them.

Alex was a few years older than Sarah's father. He wasn't quite so tall, so brown, or so handsome, but he was an attractive man all the same. Powerfully built, the nose on his flat, tough face was slightly crooked, which Daddy said was because he'd been a boxer in his youth and it had been broken. 'Alex was born in the East End of London and his name then was Alex James,' he said a trifle spitefully, adding, 'It's marvellous the way he's hauled himself out of the gutter.' Alex always wore beautifully cut Italian suits – he must have had a whole wardrobe of them – and Sarah had always admired his forceful personality and abundant energy.

He lived in a big house called The Grange only a mile from their own. Alex had designed it himself. It had acres and acres of garden. Mummy, who rarely passed an opinion on anything, had called it a monstrosity of a place, but Sarah liked the big, arched porch, the floor-length windows, the little turrets on each corner, the stone eagles perched at each side of the massive, iron gates.

Most of all, she liked the horses that Alex bred in the brand-new stables – he was hoping to produce a Derby winner one day. Daddy used to take her and Julia to see them and feed them carrots. Sarah loved the feel of the soft, velvety noses nuzzling her hand, although horse riding was one sport that didn't interest her because she was scared of heights.

She was still standing outside Daddy's office when the phone rang. 'I'm sorry I lost my rag, Alex,' she heard him say, so humbly that she squirmed. 'It's just that Spanish thing virtually cleaned me out. I'm desperate.' Another pause, then, 'Of course you can come tomorrow. What time? After breakfast? That's fine. Look forward to seeing you, Alex, old friend.'

'Alex rang earlier,' he remarked over tea. 'There was something in his voice. I think he might have decided to bale me out.'

'So he should, darling,' Mummy said in her little-girl

voice. 'You wouldn't be in this mess if it weren't for him.'

Three days after this conversation, Alex Rees-James invited Sarah to dinner. A month later, he presented her with a diamond ring as big as a walnut and proposed. Sarah didn't say yes straight away. She wanted to ask her father's opinion first. If he thought it a bad idea, she would turn Alex down.

But Daddy seemed hugely pleased. 'He's a fine chap, Alex,' he said, but there was something in his expression, a funny look, almost as if he was embarrassed as well as pleased. 'He'll make a fine husband. You have my blessing, Poppet.' He fondly patted her head. 'You may as well go ahead with the wedding as soon as possible. There's no point in hanging around. Why not ring Alex now, tell him you've accepted his proposal? He's probably on tenterhooks, waiting to hear.'

For some reason, her parents weren't speaking to each other, something that Sarah had never known happen before. Mummy had been as mad as hell when she was told that Sarah was going to marry Alex Rees-James. Mummy being mad about anything was another thing that had never happened before.

'He's too old,' she snapped, 'and he's not a very nice man. He swears like a trooper and those suits he wears are atrocious.'

'I don't mind him being old,' Sarah said defensively. 'In fact, I prefer it. Anyway, I like him. And I like his suits.'

'Yes, but do you love him? That's what matters.'

'I'll grow to love him.' It would be like marrying a slightly inferior Daddy. She couldn't marry the real one and the young men she met were quite beyond the pale.

Alex would be *almost* perfect. It also helped that he was immensely rich. Sarah had no intention of ending up, like Julia, in a miniature house having to do her own cleaning and go into hospital to have a baby in a ward with hundreds of other women, as Julia would do in three months' time when she gave birth to her first. The fact that Julia seemed blissfully happy meant nothing. Perhaps falling in love rotted the brain. It certainly hadn't done Julia any good.

Sarah's wedding dress was a strapless, skin-tight silver affair that clung to her shapely figure like a second skin, making her look like Venus di Milo according to Daddy, or a mermaid, Julia said. For something borrowed, she wore Mummy's diamond necklace and for something new, Alex bought her a tiara. For the blue thing, she wore a garter that rather spoilt the line of the dress, so she took it off before leaving for church, and for something old, she put on a pair of bikini panties that she'd bought a whole year ago, but hadn't worn much. She left her hair loose and wild and wore the minimum amount of make-up because she didn't really need it.

Alex's eyes popped when she came down the aisle of the crowded church to where he was waiting. 'It's like marrying Miss World,' he whispered. He'd had to slip the vicar a hefty donation so the wedding could be held there. Not only did he never go near a church, he'd only recently been divorced.

'Cor, blimey,' he muttered that night when they made love for the first time in a sumptuous hotel in Monaco. 'I never dreamed you were still a virgin.' Normally he spoke terribly well, but occasionally his cockney roots showed if he was surprised by something.

'I was saving myself,' Sarah said.

'What for?'

'Tonight.'

He kissed her. 'You're a sweet girl, Sarah. I'll try to be a good husband. Just don't take any notice if I lose my temper. I don't mean it.'

She hoped the kiss wasn't a signal that he was going to make love again because the first time had hurt rather, though had got quite nice towards the end. She felt sure she would eventually come to like it.

Sarah's first child, a girl, was born in a Southport nursing home. There were frilly curtains on the window of her private room, a thick cream carpet on the floor, and the walls were painted a slightly lighter cream. She'd been so heavily drugged during labour that she'd hardly felt a thing.

The baby was born exactly nine months after she'd married Alex and he was incredibly pleased with both Sarah and his daughter. The room was full of flowers that had arrived that morning, only moments before Alex himself.

'She's a stunner,' he said in an awed voice when he looked down at the baby in the cot beside her mother's bed. 'God, she's beautiful.'

'You can pick her up if you like,' Sarah said generously.

'Can I?' He looked different, much softer, almost gentle, as held his daughter for the first time. 'I wish I'd been here when she was born.'

'I tried to track you down, but no one knew where you were.'

'I was having dinner with someone in a hotel. There was a meeting afterwards that went on until the early hours and I thought I might as well stay the night. I

forgot to tell Charlie where I was going.' Charlie was his assistant. He did virtually everything for Alex except dress him.

'Why didn't you and Midge have children?' Sarah asked curiously.

'She couldn't have 'em,' Alex said abruptly.

'You could have adopted some.'

'It wouldn't have been the same.' His eyes hardened, the way they always did when she brought up a subject he didn't like. 'What are we going to call our little girl?' His face changed again and he rubbed his cheek against the baby's smooth white one.

'Tiffany's my favourite girl's name,' she said. 'It's what I wanted to be called when I was little. Sarah seems so dull and plain.'

'Sarah's all right, but Tiffany's better.'

The following night he came in armed with a video camera and filmed Tiffany awake, Tiffany asleep, Tiffany having her nappy changed and being breastfed by her beautiful mother.

'I'll do this every year on her birthday,' he vowed, 'and give it to her when she gets married.'

Just then, Julia arrived. Her little boy, Kevin, had been born the day after Sarah's wedding. Now she was expecting again and looked terribly tired and bedraggled.

'I'm fine,' she cried when Sarah remarked on the fact. 'I just didn't get much sleep last night. Kevin's teething. I've left him with Gary. I wasn't sure if the nursing home would allow a National Health baby on the premises. I suppose,' Julia went on, 'you've got a whole team of nannies at home to look after Tiffany.'

'Only two,' Sarah said stiffly. 'A permanent one and a maternity nanny who's only staying for three months.'

'Is that all?' Julia hooted.

Daddy was up with the stars again. The Spanish thing had been sorted out somehow and he'd made some good investments since. Property was the thing, he claimed, but he was sticking to his own country from now on. He managed to buy a piece of land that Liverpool Corporation wanted for a school and had made a 1,000 per cent profit when he sold it. Sarah wasn't quite sure what this meant, but it sounded awfully clever.

Although his situation had improved out of all proportion for the better, Sarah could tell her father wasn't very happy. He badly missed his girls. His favourite day was Sunday when they came to tea: Julia with Gary, Kevin and Dorothy, the new baby, who cried all the time, and Sarah with Tiffany, who was a little angel. Sarah had never known her cry, but then, as Julia said tartly, she didn't see her all that much, so wouldn't really know. Daddy's eyes would mist over when he looked at his growing family and remark he wished they could come every day.

Perhaps he would be happier if he'd been getting on better with Mummy. There'd been a distinct coldness between them ever since Sarah had announced her engagement to Alex. And he wasn't even all that friendly with Alex, who refused to come to tea, saying he had more important things to do with his time.

She was deeply shocked when, one Sunday, she overheard Gary say to Julia that he felt sorry for the old chap.

Old! Daddy! Sarah looked at her father and could have cried when she noticed, for the first time, the deep lines under his eyes, the sharp crevices running from mouth to jaw, his thinning hair. Then she blinked, and when she looked, he was his old self again, her youthful, virile

Daddy, who would never change, not in her eyes, until the day he died.

Three years later, Daddy did die. Mummy found him in his office, his head buried in the *Financial Times*. He'd had a heart attack and had been dead for two hours.

Sarah was inconsolable. It didn't help that she was pregnant for the third time and was having dreadful morning sickness. What made it worse was that no one seemed as upset as she was. Julia cried a lot at first, but her life was so busy, what with three small children to look after, Gary working all hours, she didn't have time to mourn. She got over losing Daddy in no time.

Mummy was very calm about things. Sarah had expected her to wither away with a broken heart without Daddy to support her, but she seemed to be holding up surprisingly well. She'd actually remained dry-eyed at the funeral, to which very few people came, when Sarah had thought her father had had loads of friends.

In Sarah's opinion, the house was put on the market with indecent haste. 'There's no point in hanging on to it, darling,' Mummy said gently, 'not now that your father's gone. It's cold and draughty and costs a small fortune to keep up.'

'Are you short of money?' Sarah asked, concerned.

'Oh, no, there's pots of money. Robin died at the height of one of his upward spirals, so I'm more than all right. He left everything to me in his Will but, darling, I shall put large sums aside for you and Julia.'

'Julia needs it, but I don't, Mummy. Alex is rich, far richer than Daddy ever was.'

'You might need it one day, Sarah, possibly more than Julia. I'll let you have the details once it's sorted but I'd prefer you didn't mention it to Alex.'

'Why on earth not?' Sarah cried.

'Because a woman needs money of her own that her husband knows nothing about. I only wish *I'd* had some put away. Daddy got us into some terrible scrapes over the years.'

'I'm sure he didn't,' Sarah protested.

Mummy laughed. 'Darling, you don't know the half of it. There were times when we didn't have enough to buy groceries or pay Mrs Wesley's wages. If I'd had money, I could have bought food and paid the wages and Daddy would never have known.'

Sarah sighed. 'Where are you going to live when the house is sold?'

'Paris. I shall buy myself a flat there.'

'But you can't speak French.'

'Sarah, darling, I speak perfectly good French. Didn't you notice when we were on holiday that it was always me who asked for things?'

'I thought it was Daddy.'

'No, it was me.'

Despite learning that her father hadn't been the perfect human being she'd always thought, six months later, Sarah still couldn't stop crying over his loss. Alex got quite cross with her – he'd already begun to get quite cross before Daddy died. It appeared she got on his nerves rather a lot. She was stupid, never read a book or a newspaper or watched anything on television that was even faintly serious. She didn't have a hobby, didn't knit or sew or paint. She couldn't type or use a computer. He couldn't talk to her about anything and neither could his friends. He felt embarrassed taking her out. 'You're so bloody ignorant, people laugh,' he sneered one night when Sarah was eight months pregnant. 'I bet you can't name a single politician.'

'I know the Prime Minister is Tony Blair,' she said defensively. Alex and most of the people she knew regarded him as the devil incarnate.

'Who's the Chancellor of the Exchequer?' Alex countered.

Sarah shook her head. She didn't know.

'You stupid cow!' To her intense horror, he slapped her face! The blow stung rather than hurt. Then he went down to the basement to play snooker, muttering, 'I'll get more sense out of the balls than I do from you.'

Sarah was left on her own, nursing her face, in the big, terribly depressing living room, the sort that you'd expect in an ancient manor house, not one that had only been built about twenty years ago. The walls were panelled in dark oak and there was a stag's head on the wall over the gigantic sideboard. The poor thing looked awfully unhappy, which was understandable under the circumstances. Sarah knew how it felt because she was very unhappy too. It was the first time in her life anyone had laid a finger on her and she could hardly believe it had happened.

Sniffing, she went upstairs to her own little sitting room. She had chosen the furniture and the curtains herself and the paper for the walls. She'd managed to do *that* on her own. Perhaps she could take up interior decorating as a hobby. She sat on a pretty, armless chair, put her hands on her swollen stomach, and could feel the baby trying to kick his or her way out. Tears ran silently down her cheeks. She hadn't thought it possible to be so miserable. If only Daddy was around to buck her up. 'Come on, Poppet. There's no need to cry,' he would say in his big, booming voice. He'd remarked, more than once, that she was a trifle short of brains, but he hadn't said it in a nasty way like Alex. He'd said it fondly, as if it only made him love her more. She reckoned he would have thrashed Alex to within an inch of his life had he known he'd struck her.

Sarah thought about ringing her sister for a little chat, but she'd be in the middle of something. Julia was always in the middle of something: the washing, or putting the children to bed, or making a meal. Mummy had gone to Paris for the umpteenth time to look at flats and there was no way of getting in touch with her, although she'd promised to come home as soon as the baby was born.

'I need someone of my *own* to talk to,' Sarah sobbed. She had friends, but none were the sort you called on in a crisis.

It dawned on her that she had two children – Jack had been born a year before Daddy died. Alex had been over the moon. He'd always wanted a son. She recalled her father had never once mentioned wanting a son. He'd been perfectly content with his two little girls.

She left the sitting room and lumbered along the corridor to the nursery. Julia had been right when she said Sarah saw little of her children. Her mornings were taken up with shopping or having coffee with friends, followed by lunch with more friends. In the afternoons, she went to fashion shows or a matinée at the theatre, played Bridge, although she still hadn't got the hang of it. If she wasn't pregnant, she played tennis – *that* was something she was good at. She wished she'd mentioned it to Alex. Occasionally, a group of them went down to London for a few days to see a show and shop at Harrods. They held coffee mornings to raise money for things like blind children in Africa or victims of avalanches. Or was it earthquakes? One or the other.

Once, they'd made over two hundred pounds for Battered Wives – she never dreamed that one day she'd become one.

All these things, important though they were, left little time for children. Sarah played with them when she was home, took them for walks around the garden, pushed them on their little swings when they were old enough. Tiffany was a bundle of energy and Sarah found her rather tiring. Jack insisted on being carried, which was also rather tiring. He was a quiet, nervous little boy who refused to be parted from a scrap of blanket that he took everywhere with him. She had an awful feeling that *he* was also beginning to get Alex's nerves.

Nanny Harper catered for all her children's needs. Sarah had tried, but was hopeless at changing nappies. She was staggered when she discovered Julia used towelling ones that might well be monumentally cheaper, but were even more difficult to put on. Not only that, they had to be washed.

She opened the nursery door and went in. It was something she did every night to make sure her children were fast asleep, although Nanny Harper slept in the next room and could hear the least sound.

A dim lamp illuminated the room just enough to see by. The lace-covered crib had been brought down from the loft and was in the corner, waiting for the new arrival. Eighteen-month-old Jack was lying in his little white bed with a thing on the side to stop him from falling out. His blanket was stuffed in his mouth and he looked terribly pale. She touched his cheek and it felt icy cold. A wave of panic swept over her. Her little boy was dead! She was about to lift him up, when she noticed the sheet over him was rising and falling, ever so slightly. She sniffed. The room wasn't exactly warm. A heap of bedding was folded on a chair and she carefully laid an extra blanket over her son, then stood watching him for ages. When she touched his cheek again, it felt slightly warmer.

Like Alex, Tiffany was a restless sleeper and the bedclothes were in a mess. As Sarah was straightening them, Tiffany sleepily opened her eyes and murmured, 'Hello, Mummy,' then fell asleep again.

'Hello, darling.' For some reason, Sarah wanted to cry. These were her children, yet she hardly knew them. She felt tempted to wake Tiffany so they could have a little talk. A forward child, she was old well beyond her three and a half years, and carried on quite adult conversations with Oliver, her faithful teddy bear. More tears welled up in Sarah's eyes when she remembered how much Daddy had loved his dear little Tiff.

For quite a while, she sat in a low chair listening to the soft breathing of her children. She hadn't realized she loved them quite so much. She could actually feel the love flowing from her body and surrounding them in a misty cloud.

Getting up from the chair proved difficult. It creaked like mad when she tried to stand, disturbing the children. Jack coughed, Tiffany turned over, and the door to Nanny Harper's room opened and she came in.

'What are you doing here?' she said in an undertone, as if Sarah had no right to be in the same room as her own children.

'Just saying goodnight.'

Nanny Harper beckoned. 'Come in here a moment.'

Sarah shuffled into the large bedsitting room. Nanny was still fully dressed, though minus her white overall, and had been reading a book that had been placed face down on a table. Very quietly, she closed the door. She was a tall, well-built woman with muscular arms and never smiled except at Tiffany and Jack, with whom she was extremely caring.

'I had a job getting Jack settled tonight, Mrs Rees-James,' she said haughtily. 'I'd prefer it if you didn't disturb them.'

'But I always come and say goodnight.'

'Yes, but you usually just pop your head around the door.'

'Well, tonight I didn't.' She felt defiant. Nanny Harper was far too possessive with the children. Sarah had actually been banned from being present when they were being bathed because they played up in front of their mother.

'Well, I hope you won't do it again, Mrs Rees-James. Jack is such a fidgety, anxious little boy. I have terrible trouble getting him to sleep.' She opened the door to the corridor. 'Goodnight, Mrs Rees-James. Please leave this way just in case you disturb the children again.'

That night, Sarah cried herself to sleep.

Alastair was a huge baby, over ten pounds. The labour took for ever and Sarah had to have five stitches when it was over. She felt exhausted and very sore. The soreness quickly went, but not the exhaustion.

Back home, she lay in bed, day after day, too lethargic to get up. A doctor came and told her to stay there until she felt better. 'You're an exceptionally healthy young woman, but you've just had a ten-pound baby and it's taken a lot out of you. You're a bit run down, that's all.'

Nanny Harper or the maternity nurse brought Alastair along for his feeds, although they had to be supplemented with a bottle – Sarah didn't have as much milk as she'd had for her other children. Mummy came to see her and told her she'd be fine and Julia said the same. Tiffany popped in regularly and climbed all over the bed and Jack fell asleep beside her, much to Nanny Harper's annoyance. Everyone was very sympathetic, apart from Alex, who complained that, when people came to see the new baby, there was no sign of his mother.

'Are you going to stay in bed for the rest of your life?' he asked contemptuously. These days, he hardly ever spoke to her nicely.

'I'll get up as soon as I feel better,' she promised.

'Huh!' was all Alex said.

One morning, Sarah managed to drag herself out of bed and have a shower. She felt slightly stronger today. In the nursery, Alastair could be heard crying and she realized how little she'd seen of her new son who'd been born a whole month ago. She put on a pair of jeans and a loose top, slipped her feet into a pair of flip-flops, and made her way, rather unsteadily, along the corridor. Alastair had stopped crying, but she still longed to see him.

Her heart nearly turned over when she went in the nursery and found Tiffany putting Oliver to bed, Jack playing with a train and being seriously hampered by his blanket, and a strange woman giving Alastair his bottle. The woman looked up and she wasn't strange after all. It was Midge, Alex's first wife, who looked very much at home. Midge was all sharp knobs and angles, like a skeleton with a very fine layer of skin.

'Hello, Sarah,' she said serenely.

'What are you doing here?' Sarah asked in a cracked voice.

'I used to live here, remember?'

'Yes, but you don't now. I'll take over, if you don't mind.' She plucked Alastair off Midge's knee. He cried briefly, but stopped as soon as the bottle was put back in his mouth. 'Please don't come in here again,' she said to Midge.

'I think I'd better be going.' Midge looked very calm. 'Bye, kids.'

'How long has she been coming?' Sarah asked when the door closed.

Nanny Harper looked uncomfortable. 'Only for a while. It wasn't my place to stop her.'

'You should have told me.'

'She said I wasn't to. I assumed Mr Rees-James knew all about it.'

'I don't like her,' Tiffany put in. 'She kisses me all the time.' She wiped her mouth with her hand. 'Ugh!'

Sarah was still angry when she laid Alastair in his crib, the bottle empty. How had Midge got in, not just in the nursery, but the house? She felt certain Alex couldn't have known. She could understand it being possible for men to stay friendly with their first wives, but not allow them free rein of the house where they lived with the second. She'd have a word with him about it. In fact, she'd have it right now, she thought, when the nursery door opened and Alex came in.

Before Sarah had a chance to open her mouth, Alex snarled, 'Who the hell do you think you are? How dare you tell Midge to go away? This is *my* house and I'm the one to say who comes and goes.'

Sarah could hardly believe what she was hearing. 'But she was feeding Alastair!'

'So fucking what?' Alex asked belligerently. 'You've not exactly been in a state to do much for Alastair yourself.'

Nanny Harper gasped. 'Mr Rees-James! Please don't swear in front of the children.'

'But I've been ill,' Sarah protested. 'The doctor said I was run down.'

'Run down! Run down!' he hooted. 'You're a lazy bitch, that's all.' With that, he slapped her face, much harder than the first time.

Tiffany, who rarely cried, burst into tears. She ran across to her mother and clutched her leg. Jack looked up to see what all the fuss was about and clutched the other leg.

Nanny Harper said in a shocked voice, 'How dare you, Mr Rees-James. The girl's only just had a baby.'

'Mind your own fucking business, Nanny,' Alex snarled. 'And just remember this, both of you, Midge is welcome in this house, in this room, any time she wants.'

'But I don't want her near my children!' Sarah cried hysterically.

'The children are mine as well as yours, and what I say goes. Just remember that, Sarah, before you start throwing your weight around again.' Alex left, slamming the door loudly behind him.

Tiffany said in a shaky voice. 'I don't like Daddy any more.'

'What am I going to do?' Sarah looked appealingly at Nanny Harper.

Nanny shook her head helplessly. There was pity in her eyes. 'I don't know, Mrs Rees-James. I just don't know.'

Sarah felt frightened. Alex was hitting her regularly. Every time they were together, she would say or do something that irritated him and he would lash out. Midge came to the house quite openly now. Sarah often found her with the children and didn't dare tell her to leave. One night, she actually sat down with them to dinner. Sarah pointedly picked up her own meal and took it to the kitchen to eat, but Alex came storming out, slapped her face, and dragged her back to the dining room.

'There's no need for that, darling,' Midge said.

'She needs to be shown who's boss,' Alex growled.

Sarah was too ashamed to tell her mother or Julia. Mummy had been against her marrying Alex. For the first time, she felt envious of her sister being married to Gary, who was so sweet and helpful and wouldn't dream of raising a hand to her. Really, when you thought about it, money wasn't terribly important if you were married to someone you loved. Sarah had only loved Daddy and, to a lesser degree, Mummy. She'd never actually *fallen* in love.

Not until she met Jason Bridge, that is.

Alex wanted Jack to learn to ride. Sarah wanted to say he was too young, too nervous, but was too scared. Tiffany was a fearless rider. She had her own little pony, Boots, and rode him around the paddock a few times every day under the watchful eye of one of the stable boys who could be anything up to eighty years old.

'There's a new stable boy,' Alex was saying. 'He's younger than the rest and a genius with horses. His name's Jason. Tomorrow, I want you to take Jack to the stables for his first lesson. I'm off to London on business and won't be back for a few days.' He looked at her threateningly, as if to say that if Jack wasn't a first-class rider by then there'd be trouble.

Next day, Sarah led a fearful, snivelling Jack, clutching his blanket, to the stables that smelled earthily of a mixture of leather and manure. Jason was in the end stall with Petra, she was told, a mare that had been sired by a successful flat racer, nowadays let out to stud. Alex had high hopes of Petra becoming a winner in her own right one day.

At the end stall, Sarah stood for a moment, entranced by the sight of the sleek, beautiful horse being groomed by a sleek, beautiful young man in jodhpurs and a sleeveless T-shirt. Jason was slim and brown – she learned later that his mother was Sri Lankan – with straight black hair that shone as brilliantly as Petra's smooth coat. She could have watched for ever, the way the muscles in his arms rippled as he wielded the brush, the way his neck went taut, looking twice as long as a normal neck, when he stretched upwards. Then Jack started to cry and Jason turned to him, his brown eyes soft and gentle.

'Ah,' he said in a voice as soft and gentle as his eyes, 'so, this is Jack. I've been looking forward to meeting you. And you must be Mrs Rees-James. How do you do?'

They shook hands and, at the touch of the long, slim fingers, Sarah fell in love. And so did Jack.

Boots was brought out for Jack to make friends with. Jason encouraged him to stroke her silky mane, which Jack did willingly, and just as willingly allowed himself to be lifted up and placed on Boots's bare back. Jason held him firmly while they walked a few steps, then trotted a few steps more, murmuring encouragement, telling him what a clever boy he was, and how very brave. A saddle was fetched and fitted. Jack managed to cling to the reins without letting go of his blanket. Then, wonder of wonders, Jason was able to persuade him to give up the wretched thing. 'I'll take care of it, I promise.'

An hour later, Jack and Boots were able to trot quite

confidently around the paddock, Jason running along-side, while a mesmerized Sarah looked on. She smiled when they trotted towards her.

'I think that's enough for one day, Mrs Rees-James.' There was just a trace of perspiration on his brow. Sarah longed to wipe it away – no *lick* it away with her tongue.

'You've done marvellously. Alex will be terribly pleased. And call me Sarah, please.'

'It's been a pleasure, Sarah. I'll see you both the same time tomorrow.'

She looked into his brown eyes. 'I'm sure Jack can't wait.'

A few days later, something truly awful happened, followed by something truly wonderful. It was a day that changed Sarah's life for ever.

It was April and the first warm, sunny day of the year. She fed Alastair while sitting up in bed. The maternity nurse had left a few weeks ago and Nanny Harper would come for him in a minute. Once the baby had consumed all the milk available, she laid him on the bed and got dressed. At nine, Jack was due for another riding lesson and Sarah felt almost happy. She knew the happiness would last only as long as she was with Jason, but it was better than not being happy at all.

Dressed, hair brushed, she wondered why Nanny hadn't arrived, so picked up the baby, told him he was getting fat, and carried him to the nursery. Jack might be being difficult. He wanted to live in the stables with Jason and refused to listen when it was explained to him that he couldn't.

Nanny was in the nursery alone. She looked very tearful.

'What's the matter?' Sarah enquired, alarmed. 'Where are Tiffany and Jack?'

'Mr Rees-James and that woman, I don't know what to call her – I suppose she's Mrs Rees-James, same as you – they've taken them out for the day to Chester Zoo. I couldn't very well refuse to let them and Mr Rees-James said to mind my own business when I asked if you knew.'

'What?' Sarah screamed.

'They've only just gone. You might catch them.'

Sarah put Alastair in his cot, ran down the stairs and out of the front door to find Alex backing the Rolls out of the garage. A bewildered Tiffany and Jack were sitting in the back. Midge was in the front beside her ex-husband. Sarah seized the rear door and opened it and Tiffany tumbled out yelling, 'Mummy!' Alex got out and punched Sarah in the jaw with a terse, 'Fuck off', shoved Tiffany inside, clicked the locks, got back behind the wheel and the car drove away, Tiffany beating her fists on the rear window, still yelling, 'Mummy', and a helpless Sarah nursing her throbbing jaw.

'I saw that,' said a voice. She turned and found Jason watching her. 'I was told he hit you, but didn't believe it until I saw it with my own eyes.'

'Everyone knows!' Sarah burst into tears. 'I don't know what to do,' she cried. 'I don't know which way to turn.'

'Come inside,' Jason said softly, taking her hand. They went into the house and he asked where there was a bathroom so he could bathe her now swollen jaw.

She took him up to her own bathroom and he dabbed her chin with a flannel, said she would soon have a bruise. Then he kissed the place where the bruise would be and Sarah led him into the bedroom and they made love very tenderly, holding back the passion for another time.

That afternoon, Sarah went to a solicitor and said she wanted to divorce Alex Rees-James.

'I don't know why I didn't think of it before,' she said to the solicitor, a woman called Mrs Carey who wasn't much older than herself. 'I've been in a daze. I couldn't imagine leading a different sort of life.'

'You say he did that to you this morning in front of a witness?' Mrs Carey nodded at the bruise.

'Yes,' Sarah whispered, feeling terribly ashamed for some reason.

'Well, in that case, there'll be no contest, and he'll stand no chance of getting the children.'

'You mean there was a chance that he would?' Sarah felt a rush of fear.

'Under some circumstances the father is allowed custody, but not in yours, not in view of the way he's treated you.'

It dawned on Sarah that Alex would never, *never* let her have the children. He'd employ the top lawyers in the country, claim she was an unfit mother, that he'd been goaded into hitting her – or the witnesses would be bribed or threatened to say he'd never laid a finger on her. Even Jason might not be immune. She jumped to her feet. 'I've changed my mind. I don't want a divorce. Alex would kill me before he'd let me take the children.'

'Please sit down, Mrs Rees-James,' the solicitor said sternly. 'Your husband can't take the law into his own hands.'

'Yes, he can. You don't know him.' Sarah shuddered. 'There's nothing on earth he can't do.'

'There's all sorts of things he can't do and one is keep

the children when a court has decreed they should live with their mother.' She looked at her client sympathetically. 'You're exaggerating, but only because he's got you into such a frightful state. It's up to you, but do you really want to live with this man any longer? It must be awful for you.'

'It is.' Sarah thought for a moment. 'Look, I've acted too hastily. I'd still like to put things off for a bit. It would be best if I found somewhere to live before I left. *Then* divorce him.' She didn't like to think what Alex's reaction would be if the divorce papers came while she was still living with him.

'Good idea. Will you be buying a property or renting?'

'Buying.' She hadn't touched the money Mummy had given her after Daddy died. It was in a secret account that Alex knew nothing about. She'd never dreamed she'd need it, but she did now.

'Then why not call in at a few estate agents before you go home and ask for details of properties in your price range?'

'I'll do that.'

'But don't let them have your address in case your husband sees the post and guesses what you're up to. Do you have a mobile phone?' Sarah nodded. 'Use that number in future. You don't want personal calls getting through to the house.'

Amongst the particulars Sarah collected there was a brochure for a tiny estate called Victoria Square, still in the course of construction, but would be ready to move into by July. According to the description, it was 'a peaceful oasis in a busy, bustling part of Liverpool'. The drawings made it look terribly pretty. She went to view that very day. The bungalows were too small and, although she would have preferred one of the big, detached houses, they were much too expensive. She settled on a semi, number one.

It would do for now. She felt pleased that she was actually taking charge of her own life for once and didn't much care where she went as long as she and the children escaped from Alex. In July, he was going to Saudi Arabia. There were horses he wanted to see and perhaps buy. She'd leave then.

Alex had stopped sleeping with her while she was pregnant with Alastair. She'd felt relieved when he didn't come to her bed again, having rather gone off sex since he'd been making her do things she found quite repugnant. Perhaps he was doing the things with Midge, who seemed to be there all the time.

Now she had Jason, with whom making love was absolute bliss. They couldn't manage to see each other every day – apart from when Jack had a riding lesson. If Alex was out, Jason would sneak into the house and they'd go up to her bedroom. At night, there was always a stable boy in attendance in case one of the animals became upset and, if it was Jason, they would lie in each other's arms in the alcove off the tackroom where there was a bed.

They never spoke about the future. Sarah didn't tell him about the house she was buying in Victoria Square. There was plenty of time for that. The builders telephoned and asked what colours she would like on the walls, what sort of tiles on the kitchen floor? She bought curtains, chose furniture and left it in storage ready for the day when the house would be ready to move into. Her heart was always in her mouth, worried that Alex would find out what she was doing. She suspected he would be glad to see the back of her, but he would never willingly give up his children.

July, and Alastair, seven months old, was teething badly. Sarah was woken more than once in the middle of the night by the sound of his screams along the corridor. Nanny Harper had been quite discouraging when she'd offered to help. In less than a week, she would have to manage Alastair, and the other children, on her own, and prayed she'd cope – if Julia could then so could she.

Alex was taking Jason with him to Saudi Arabia and Jason was quite excited about it. She still didn't mention she was leaving, just in case he let it slip. She'd telephone when he got back. The house was ready for her, the furniture in place. All that had to happen was for Alex to go away.

He went on Thursday morning. To her surprise, he handed her a video before he left. 'I'd like you to watch this straight away, Sarah. I found it very entertaining. I'm sure you will too.'

The house already felt peaceful without him. Sarah went up to her sitting room, slid the video into the machine and pressed play. After a series of flashes and a flurry of white spots, a couple appeared on the screen. They were making love and enjoying it immensely. Was this some sort of sick joke? She was about to press the off button, when it struck her that there was something familiar about the couple and, horror mounting, realized it was herself and Jason.

She couldn't bear to watch. She put her hands over her eyes and a few minutes later, nearly jumped out of her skin when she heard Alex's voice. He'd come back! But when she looked, the voice was coming from the television and his smiling face was on the screen, although the smile was awfully sinister and made the blood curdle in her veins.

'Thank you, Sarah,' he said. 'You're stupid enough to have forgotten there are cameras in the stables. Midge and I had a good laugh when we watched. Anyway, dear girl, you've given me perfect grounds for divorce: adultery. I've already begun proceedings and you can expect a Writ any minute. By the way, I'll be back on Monday and I'd like you out of the house by then. The children will be quite safe with Nanny Harper, they don't need you. See you in court, Sarah.' He waved, smiled again, there were more flashes and dots, and Sarah turned the video off.

She couldn't stop shaking. Had Jason deliberately seduced her? Or was he just an innocent party? And because she'd committed adultery, did it mean Alex would be allowed custody of the children?

Well, she wasn't going to sit there all day, moping and shivering. She had planned on leaving in stages over the space of a few days, taking her own clothes first and some of the children's things that Nanny Harper wouldn't notice were missing such as the bikes and the bigger toys that were kept in the garage. Another trip would have to be made with towels and bedding and Alastair's push-chair. How she would get the children's clothes from under Nanny's nose, she had no idea. If necessary, she'd just have to buy more. There was still plenty of money left.

There was a cry from the garden and when she looked, Midge was forcing a reluctant Tiffany on to the swing. The little girl sat there mutinously when Midge began to push. Jack trailed over the grass, looking frightfully despondent.

She'd forgotten about Midge. And now she could hear Alastair crying again. Oh, this was too much!

Sarah threw back her shoulders and marched along to the nursery. Nanny was trying to soothe the baby, her eyes red with tiredness.

'I'll take him off your hands for the day, shall I?' Sarah offered. 'I thought I'd take all three to the beach in Southport.'

'You'll never manage on your own, Mrs Rees-James. Would you like me to come with you?'

'No, thank you, Nanny,' Sarah said curtly. 'Alastair can go on the back seat in that carrycot thing.'

Nanny looked at her oddly. 'You sound different,' she said slowly. 'You're leaving, aren't you? I don't blame you. I've wanted to leave for a long time. The atmosphere here is horrible, what with the way your husband behaves and two wives on the premises.' She looked tenderly at Alastair. 'But I hated the idea of leaving the children.'

'*I'm* not leaving the children. I'm taking them with me.'

'When?'

'Now, this minute,' Sarah said impulsively. 'I can't stand being in this house another minute.'

'You're not the only one.' Suddenly, Nanny Harper no longer looked tired. Alastair, perhaps aware of the seriousness of the situation, had stopped crying. 'Shall I help you pack?'

'Everything won't fit in the car. I'll have to make several journeys.'

'Then hire a van and driver. It'll be less trouble. I'll call a few numbers out of Yellow Pages and find someone who can come straight away.'

'Thank you, Nanny, you're being terribly kind. You

know, Alex will get in a terrible rage when he comes back and finds us gone. He'll almost certainly take it out on you.'

'He won't have the opportunity. I'll be gone too. I shall leave straight after you. My sister lives in High Barnet. I'll stay with her while I look for a new position.' She made a face. 'I won't be able to ask Mr Rees-James for a reference.'

'*I'll* give you a reference. You've been a wonderful nanny. I just wish we could have become friends.'

'So do I. I shouldn't have been so brusque with you. I've been in trouble before for getting too impatient with mothers.'

'Well, that's water under the bridge now.'

'What about the other Mrs Rees-James?'

'She might object, but I'm sure we're much stronger than she is.' They both laughed.

It had all proved incredibly easy. Midge left, she had an appointment at the hairdressers. As soon as she'd gone, Sarah and Nanny Harper loaded the Renault with as much stuff as it would take, a van arrived and took the rest, and everything was dumped on the floor of number one Victoria Square.

Sarah's feeling of elation diminished considerably as soon as the van had driven away. The pram, the bikes, and the bigger toys had been left in the hall – she should have asked the man to put them in the garage, but she'd forgotten she had one and now it was too late. The lounge and kitchen were so full of cardboard boxes and plastic bags there was literally no room to move. Alastair's carrycot with the baby in it had been dumped on the floor. The curtains she'd bought were still in plastic bags, there were pictures and a mirror to be hung.

137

She had no idea where to start. The bedding and nightclothes would have to be found before they went to bed. She remembered she hadn't got an electric kettle. Where did you switch on the hot water?

Then Alastair started to scream, Jack demanded Jason, Tiffany had mislaid her precious Oliver and bags and boxes had to be emptied until he was found, leaving the floor in an even worse mess.

Sarah limply reached for the nearest box. It contained all the things off her dressing table. Leaving Alastair to scream, she took it upstairs and put it in the big bedroom where she would sleep on the new double bed and felt a sense of achievement. One thing done! Downstairs again, she picked up another box: the children's books. She carried them up to Tiffany's room to sort out later.

Alastair was getting on her nerves. Tiffany was jumping up and down on the new pale lemon settee and Sarah wondered if it perhaps wasn't an impractical colour to have bought. Jack was grizzling.

Perhaps Alastair was hungry. She went cold. Where on earth were his bottle, the tin of formula, and the little jars of baby food?

She collapsed on to a pale lemon armchair, determined not to cry or lose her temper, not to give in and somehow, *somehow* to manage.

Monday

9 JULY 2001

Chapter 5

When Sarah opened her eyes and looked at her watch she was astonished to see it was almost eight o'clock. She'd slept the whole night through, Alastair too. She got up immediately to make sure Tiffany and Jack hadn't gone wandering off, but both were fast asleep. Alastair looked quite content, his chubby legs splayed and the soles of his feet pressed together, making a perfect diamond. She felt a rush of love that almost choked her and was confident that she would enjoy having the children to herself, get to know them properly, and be a good mother.

Downstairs, she made tea and sank on to the settee, already full of smudges from the children's dirty fingers, but she didn't care. The sun was shining in a perfectly blue sky, the room looked relatively tidy, and she felt at one with the world.

I've done it, she thought. I've had an awful lot of help, but I've still done it. Despite the upset, the chaos, the lack of sleep, she hadn't once considered giving up. Yesterday, the Irishwoman from next door, Marie, had invited them to lunch and shown her how to stop Alastair from crying. It didn't always work, she'd said, but it was worth a try. Today, Marie was going to give a hand with the washing and explain how to use the machine. On Saturday, Frank Williams from Three Farthings had taken her shopping, while his wife,

Rachel, had looked after the children. Then Frank helped put up the curtains and other stuff. The next day, Rachel had been rather horrid. Sarah couldn't understand why. She'd seemed so nice and kind before.

For the first time since moving, she thought about Jason – Jack had cried for him a few times, but the name had barely registered on her brain before it vanished because she'd had so much to do. Now she thought about him properly and was surprised that she hadn't missed him at all, as if he was part of the life she'd left behind and he didn't belong in this one.

Thinking of Jason reminded her that Alex was coming home today and would find the children had gone. Sarah felt uneasy. Although he didn't know her address, he would eventually find it, of that she felt convinced. But he couldn't just come and take the children away. Could he?

The sun seemed to dim slightly, as Sarah realized she hadn't done with Alex Rees-James, not yet.

When Gareth came downstairs, he found his in-laws hadn't bothered to clean up before they'd left the night before – actually, it had been early morning, well past midnight. The kitchen was heaped with dirty dishes, there were lager bottles, mugs, and plates of half-eaten snacks on the living-room floor. Debbie had already left for work, having made no attempt to clear up. Well, she needn't think *he* was going to touch it. He glared at Tabitha, who was licking greasy gravy off a plate that had been left on the kitchen table and poured him a saucer of leftover lager.

Why the hell had they moved? he thought bitterly. Things had been going quite smoothly when they'd lived in the flat. Debbie had always been extravagant, but since they'd come to Victoria Square, she'd been spending money as if there was no tomorrow and her relatives seemed determined to eat him out of house and home.

The phone rang. He considered not answering, but picked it up in case it was important, and was glad that he had when the caller turned out to be his mother.

'Hello, son, I was just wondering if you were all right. You didn't ring yesterday . . .' Her voice trailed away.

'Oh, hell, Mum, I forgot.' He always rang his mum on Sundays. 'It's just that the Hamiltons were here and it completely slipped me mind.'

'Never mind, son. As long as you're all right. It's just that you know I always worry about you.'

'I know, Mum, and I'm dead sorry.' He imagined her sitting in the little terraced house in Wallasey where he'd grown up, a look of anxiety on her tired face. She'd never been in very good health. There was something wrong with her heart, but it hadn't stopped her from working all the hours God sent to help him through university. His father had died when Gareth, an only child, was ten. 'How are you, Mum?' he asked.

'Fine, son, absolutely fine.' She would swear she felt fine on her deathbed. 'How's Debbie?'

'OK.' He didn't want to talk about Debbie. 'Why don't you come over for the day next Sunday? You still haven't seen the new house.'

'I don't know, luv,' she said cautiously. 'Will Debbie's family be there?'

'I'm not sure.' He understood her caution. The widow Joyce and her tribe ignored her. They weren't being rude, it was just that they only had time for each other. Gareth, having married into the clan, had been vetted, judged acceptable, and was now considered a Hamilton, while his mother was regarded as an outsider.

'Joyce Hamilton always makes me feel as if I'm not your mother any more, that she's taken over. I feel in the way.'

'I'm sorry, Mum.' He felt like crying.

'Oh, I shouldn't moan. Anyroad, son, I'll let you get on, otherwise you'll be late for work. Tara, Gareth. Look after yourself.'

She always said that. 'Bye, Mum. I love you,' he said with a catch in his voice.

'I love you too, son.'

Gareth slowly put down the receiver. He was neglecting his mum and it wasn't fair. He was earning pots of money, but none of it was spent on her, yet it was she who'd been responsible for him getting a degree, which made earning pots of money possible. Mind you, he'd need to earn mountains to pay back all he owed and keep Debbie in the manner to which she had so quickly become accustomed.

He searched through the Yellow Pages for a florist and ordered two dozen red roses to be sent to Mrs Ellen Moran, and felt a bit better. Only a bit. It was *him* his mother wanted, not flowers.

The post had come while he'd been on the phone. He picked up the pile of envelopes and began to sift through them. They were either circulars wanting to sell him something, or bills, some marked with a stern 'Overdue'. He paused over one envelope addressed to Mrs D. Moran. He hadn't known Debbie had a Goldfish card. He tore open the envelope and saw that, in June, she had purchased goods to the value of £754.13. It wasn't quite as bad as he'd expected, until he noticed that the amount still outstanding was nearly four thousand pounds. He wanted to kill her.

Victoria had just started emptying the last of the drawers when she remembered Anna Burrows had invited her for coffee at eleven o'clock. She wallowed in the ancient bathtub for half an hour, washed her hair, dried it, and looked for something nice to wear. Anna was always beautifully dressed and mightn't appreciate her visitor turning up in jeans and one of Granddad's old shirts.

She put on a navy-blue blouse, a white skirt, and high-heeled sandals. Normally, Victoria never wore high heels because they made her fall over, but these had been bought for a wedding when she'd wanted to look smart, although she'd had to take them off when the dancing started. She should be able to get as far as Clematis Cottage without falling flat on her face.

Before leaving, she turned on the computer to see if there were any emails and found one from Parker Inc, asking if she'd let them know what time her plane would land on Sunday so someone could meet her at Kennedy airport. The same someone, whose name was Nancy Tucker, would put her up in her apartment until she found a place of her own. It finished by saying how much they were looking forward to having her work with them.

They sounded incredibly friendly. She emailed back immediately, giving the time of her arrival and thanking them for their help, then made her way to Clematis Cottage, wobbling slightly on the high heels.

Mr Burrows let her in after the doorbell had played a racy little tune she didn't recognize. 'That's nice,' she remarked. 'The tune, that is.'

'So everyone ses,' he grumbled. 'Although it's not the one I'd've chosen meself.'

'What would you have chosen?'

'*The Red Flag*.'

'I know that. "*Though cowards flinch and traitors sneer, we'll keep the red flag flying here*" ' Victoria sang, not very tunefully.

Mr Burrows looked at her with respect. 'How come you know that?'

'Me granddad used to sing it, much to Gran's annoyance. She was a Conservative and he was Labour and they argued all the time, although she was terribly sad he wasn't alive when Labour got elected in nineteen ninety-seven.'

'And what's your own politics, luv? That's if you don't mind me asking.'

'I don't mind a bit. I'm a Green,' Victoria said proudly.

He gave her another look of respect. 'Well, at least you thought for yourself. I like that.'

'Ernie,' Mrs Burrows called from somewhere inside. 'Are you going to keep Victoria to yourself all morning?'

'Sorry, luv. Go on in the parlour, Victoria. I've been ordered to make coffee. Do you take milk and sugar?'

'Both, please, two sugars.'

'I never used to worry about my figure when I was young,' Anna said when Victoria went in. 'You look just right, neither fat nor thin.' She patted the chair beside her. 'Sit down, dear. Now, I want you to tell me all about yourself, from the day you were born, until you got out of bed this morning. I won't interrupt once, I promise.'

I must stop this, Rachel told herself as she stood by the

window of Three Farthings on yet another glorious day, and saw Victoria enter the Burrows's bungalow. People will start to notice I'm always in the window, spying on them, a sort of female Peeping Tom. She had intended to call on Victoria herself later that morning to invite her back for coffee, but now it was too late.

If only she hadn't been so unpleasant to Sarah Rees-James the day before! When she'd woken that morning, very early, she'd realized she must be mad to think a girl like that would have an affair with a paunchy, balding man more than twice her age. She'd been hoping Tiffany would come demanding a drink as she'd done the last two days, and she could take her home and patch things up with Sarah, apologize for being short-tempered, claim she'd had a bad headache or something.

But Tiffany hadn't come and now she and Danny Jordan were kicking a football against the garage doors and Sarah and Danny's mother had been in and out of each other's houses all morning. It looked as if Mrs Jordan was helping Sarah with the washing.

I could have done that, Rachel thought, if I hadn't been such a fool. Now she was stuck in the house by herself, Frank and James having gone to work, and Kirsty to see friends. The beds were made, the breakfast dishes washed, the house tidied, and she had nothing to do except stand by the window and watch other people lead their lives.

Perhaps she should go into town, buy something: a new frock, for instance. It was ages since she'd had a new frock. But it wouldn't help her find friends and, at this moment in time, a desperately unhappy Rachel needed friends more than anything else on earth.

Five minutes later, she was knocking on the door of number seven Victoria Square, having remembered she hadn't introduced herself to the Cartwrights. She'd ask if they were coming to the barbecue, it was a perfect excuse.

The door was opened by Mrs Cartwright. She wore a red, satin dressing gown, the belt pulled tightly around her slim waist. Her face was flushed, her dark hair tousled, and she was smiling, as if something marvellous had just had happened.

'Oh, dear!' Rachel said in a voice that sounded too loud and terribly false. 'I hope I didn't get you out of bed. My name is Rachel Williams. I live over there.' She vaguely waved her hand. 'I thought you'd like this.' She pushed a pot plant at the woman, so suddenly that she didn't take it quickly enough, and the pot fell, smashing to pieces and spilling soil all over the step.

'Oh, dear!' Rachel said again. She knelt on the path and began to collect the soil with her hands. 'I'm so sorry. I'll see to this, don't worry. You go back to bed. I wish I hadn't disturbed you.'

'You didn't disturb me,' Mrs Cartwright said. 'And I wasn't in bed. Steve, that's my husband, has just left for a job interview and I was about to have a shower. Rachel,' she said in a soft voice, 'why are you crying?'

'Am I crying?'

'Well, it's not raining, yet the step is getting very wet.' Mrs Cartwright knelt and took hold of her dirty hands. 'Come inside, Rachel, and tell me what's wrong.'

Rachel didn't know how to describe what was wrong. Mrs Cartwright took her into the kitchen, sat her at the table, and made tea. To say she badly wanted a friend sounded awfully childish.

'I feel depressed,' she said, which was true. And, 'I want to cry all the time.' Which was also true.

'Is it the menopause?' Mrs Cartwright asked.

'I don't know. I've been feeling like this for months and months, more than a year, ever since . . .'

'Ever since what?'

'Ever since something awful happened. I'd sooner not go into it, if you don't mind.'

'Of course I don't mind. How old are you? I hope *you* don't mind my asking that, but I'm a doctor and back in Huddersfield I saw a lot of women of about your age with the same symptoms.'

'You don't look remotely like a doctor.'

Mrs Cartwright smiled. 'Well, I am.'

'I'm fifty-one,' Rachel sighed.

'You really should go and see your own doctor. It might possibly be the menopause and he or she will give you something for it.'

'Thank you very much.' Rachel knew darn well her 'symptoms' as Mrs Cartwright put it, were nothing to do with the menopause. She pushed back the chair and got to her feet. 'I won't disturb you any longer.'

Mrs Cartwright looked disappointed. 'Oh, you're not going already. I was hoping you'd stay and we could have a little chat. Apart from the Burrows next door, I don't know anyone here. I'm Kathleen, by the way.'

A sensation of warmth spread through Rachel's body, making it tingle. This lovely woman actually wanted to talk to *her*. 'I'd love to stay,' she gulped.

'Good,' Kathleen beamed. 'Now you must excuse me for a minute while I get dressed. Perhaps you'd like to make another cup of tea while I'm gone, then we'll go in the front room where it's more comfortable. You can tell me about the other people who live in the square. I'm dying to know.'

★

Steve had gone for the interview wearing the suit he'd had on when he had first met Kathleen. The cheap material held no warmth in winter and clung clammily to his skin when it was hot. He returned home, perspiring mightily, and looking very glum. Kathleen assumed the interview hadn't been successful, but he announced he'd got the job and would start on Monday.

'Then why the miserable face?' she asked.

'It's the minimum wage, the hours are disgraceful, and I've got to wear a poncy uniform,' he grunted.

'Poor Steve.' She kissed him. 'Still, it won't be for long. I'm sure you'll get a much better job soon.'

'Huh!' he snorted.

'I had a visitor while you were out,' she told him. 'This poor woman from across the way, Rachel, came and burst into tears on our doorstep. I felt so sorry for her, I persuaded her to stay for the whole morning. She badly needed someone to talk to. Tomorrow, I'm taking her to lunch.'

His face took on a set expression and she knew he was thinking about Jean, who was an entirely different case to Rachel Williams. Jean had four daughters and hordes of neighbours to pour out her troubles to. Rachel appeared to have no one.

She remembered she'd meant to contact British Telecom and ask for a new, unlisted number. Meanwhile, the phone remained unplugged. It was hard luck on Brenda if she was trying to get through.

'I think I'll have a shower,' he muttered.

She kissed him again and pulled him into the bedroom by the lapels of his horrible suit. 'Why don't we . . .'

Before she could finish the sentence, Steve whooped, lifted her up and threw her on to the bed.

★

Patrick Jordan was practising on his guitar, the bedroom window open, the music sounding faintly subdued, as if it was being smothered under the heat of the afternoon, and Sarah was hanging the last of the washing on the whirly thing in the garden that Marie said was called a rotating clothes line. Marie, who was sitting on the back step, watching, had loaned her the pegs.

'You'll never believe this,' Sarah cried, 'but I've never hung out washing until today.' She could hardly believe it herself. It seemed an awfully satisfying thing to do, washing. There was a huge pile of clean stuff indoors and just looking at it made Sarah's heart swell with pride.

'I've never met a woman before who didn't do her own washing,' Marie said with a grin. 'Apart from the Mother Superior of the convent I went to, and she probably did enough when she was a novice. Don't hang that frock by the hem, Sarah, it'll stretch and make it droop. Peg it under the arms. Same with them T-shirts.'

'I've never dusted before, or used a vacuum cleaner either,' Sarah confessed, adjusting the frock. 'Daddy expected Julia and me to tidy our rooms when we were little, but not clean them. Julia's my sister,' she explained. 'She lives in a place called Fazakerley. I'm not sure how to get there from here. I think it's on the other side of Liverpool.'

'We've got an A to Z,' Marie said helpfully. 'I'll look it up for you.'

'Julia doesn't know I've moved. She's gone to the Lake District on a camping holiday with her husband and children.' Sarah shuddered at the idea of looking after three young children in a tent. 'I'll phone on Saturday and tell her. She'll be back by then. Mummy doesn't know either. She's staying in Monte Carlo with friends. I'll ring her on Saturday too. She'll be terribly surprised.'

She wasn't sure if Mummy would be all *that* surprised that she'd left Alex. She'd never liked him from the start.

'I've got eight sisters and three brothers, me,' Marie said proudly.

'You mean there are *twelve* of you?' Sarah was impressed.

'And fifty-eight cousins.'

'Fifty-eight!' Sarah squeaked. 'I have just one and she lives in New Zealand. We've never met.' She sighed happily. 'Shall we go and see how Danny, Tiffany, and Jack are getting on at Victoria's?' Victoria had seemed terribly sweet and she'd liked her straight away. 'I'll take Alastair. He's actually awake and not crying. Oh, isn't this nice?' she cried. 'Going from house to house and doing so much washing! It's like a game.' She had never enjoyed herself quite so much.

'I'm awfully sorry,' said Victoria, 'but Tiffany's been rooting through the stuff I'd put aside for charity and she's found loads of things she fancies. I hope you don't mind.'

'Mummy!' Tiffany appeared clad in a straw picture hat, a long winceyette nightdress, a gold belt around her waist, fur slippers as big as cats, and carrying a crocheted handbag. 'Don't I look lovely?'

'Adorable, darling.'

'Victoria said I could have them, but only if you'll let me.'

'If you want them, Tiff, then you shall have them.'

'I'm afraid that's not all. She's got a whole bag full of stuff,' Victoria said apologetically. 'And Jack's taken a fancy to a harmonium that belonged to me granddad. It doesn't work very well.'

'What's a harmonium?' Sarah enquired. 'Where is Jack, by the way?'

'It's like a concertina,' explained Victoria, 'And Jack's upstairs watching Danny on the computer, quite enthralled.

'I hope Danny's not being a nuisance,' Marie said.

'No one's being a nuisance. I've loved having them. I almost wish I wasn't going to America now that you've all come to live here.'

If Gareth Moran hadn't been married, she would have almost certainly stayed.

'Ernie, will you help me up, darling?'

'Coming, luv.' Ernie abandoned the *Sporting Life* he was studying, lifted Anna's feather-light frame out of the chair, and set her on her feet. She swayed and he caught her just in time.

'I'm afraid you're going to have to carry me to the bathroom, Ernie. I feel desperately tired.'

'You're doing too much, luv,' he said accusingly. 'We went out two days in a row and you entertained Victoria all morning. You're wearing yourself out.'

'Victoria entertained *me*. She told me her life story, and such an interesting one too. She's such a sensible, admirable young woman. She reminded me of myself when I was young.'

'You were admirable, Anna, but I can't remember you being exactly sensible.'

'Fiddlesticks!' she replied. 'Did you know there used to be a removal and storage company on this site? The horses used to live where our bungalow is now.'

'I know, luv,' I heard.' He carried her into the bathroom. 'Do you want me to stay, or can you manage on your own?'

'I'd sooner try and manage myself.' She didn't like him doing intimate things for her.

He waited outside the door, counting down from a hundred just to pass the time. The chain flushed. 'You can come in now, darling,' she shouted.

She was sitting on the toilet seat, her clothes adjusted. 'I was just thinking, can we have a computer? Victoria made them sound awfully interesting. She said we could play games on it together.'

'I'll look into it,' Ernie promised. He carried her back and sat her tenderly in her chair. 'You just sit there quietly,' he commanded in a no-nonsense voice. 'No more visitors today. If anyone comes, I'll tell them you're not well.'

'You'll do no such thing, Ernie Burrows. People will stop coming if they think they're disturbing me. Just fetch me a glass of wine and I'll be fine.'

'You can't have wine. It interferes with your medication.'

'Bring me some wine, Ernie, or I'll scream the house down. And put a video on. Something nice and cheerful, a musical – *Kiss me Kate*, it's one of my favourites. And stop looking so downhearted, it makes me feel downhearted too.' She paused for breath. Her voice was becoming fainter and slightly slurred, but she wasn't giving up. 'Have a glass of whisky. Let's get drunk, Ernie. We haven't got long to go, either of us. Let's make the best of things before it's too late.'

He bent and kissed her full on the lips. He felt young again and the face he kissed was smooth and unlined. 'Jaysus, Anna Kosztolanyi, whatever would I have done without you!'

'I didn't realize I'd spent that much,' Debbie said that

night when Gareth showed her the Goldfish statement. 'Anyroad,' she added indignantly, 'what gave you the right to open my mail? It's personal.'

'If it's personal, does that mean you'll be paying this back out of your own pocket?' He waved the statement at her.

'I have been doing so far,' she said haughtily.

'Oh, yeah!' he snorted. 'Last month, you paid back twenty-five quid. It didn't even cover the interest. Then you went and spent over seven hundred. At that rate, you'd never clear the debt in a million years.'

'Then you can pay it for me.' She pouted her lips in a way that Gareth normally found irresistible, but didn't tonight.

'In your dreams, Debbie,' he said tightly. He flung the statement at her, slammed out of the house, and went to see Victoria Macara.

'Hello,' Victoria said brightly when she let him in. She looked very smart, in a navy blouse and white skirt. Her brown feet were bare, her toes short and stubby, the nails unpainted. The house was beginning to look rather empty without any ornaments or dishes on show. She said, 'I've never had so many visitors in one day.'

Was that a hint? Did it mean she didn't want any more? 'I'll go if you like,' he offered. 'I don't want to be a nuisance.'

'Don't be ridiculous. Sit down immediately.' She'd taken him into a living room that looked more like a museum and shoved him into an elderly, extremely comfortable armchair. 'I'm dead pleased to see you,' she said forcefully, and he realized she wasn't capable of dropping hints and was genuinely glad he'd come. 'Are you all right?' she asked. 'You look a bit down. Would you like some wine, by the way? I've just opened a bottle.'

'I'd love a glass of wine and, yes, I do feel down – more than bit. Me wife's become a shopaholic and I don't know what to do.' He'd told someone at last! He already felt better, having got it off his chest.

She curled up in an identical chair on the other side of the iron fireplace, tucking her feet underneath her. 'Really?'

Gareth nodded. 'She's hooked, good and proper.'

'Oh, dear.' Victoria looked dismayed. 'Can't you stop her?'

'Only if I lock her in a room and put bars on the windows so she can't get out,' he replied gloomily. 'Nowadays, there's nothing to stop people from having half a dozen credit cards and spending to the limit on every one. The entire country is in debt. It said so in the paper the other day.'

'*I'm* not, but only because I got loads of money for the land. I had to use some of that to finish off the debts Granddad left years ago when he died. Gran and I had been trying to do it for years.'

'I don't know why,' Gareth said with a sigh, 'but that only makes me feel even more down. I've got nothing to sell. Apart from my wages, there's no prospect of any money coming from anywhere.' It could be ages before his footy site got off the ground.

'Maybe your wife could get counselling. It seems to be all the rage these days,' Victoria suggested helpfully.

'Half an hour with Debbie and the counsellor would end up a shopaholic.' He didn't particularly like talking about Debbie in such a detrimental way to someone he hardly knew. But then Victoria didn't feel like a stranger, more as if he'd known her all his life. Nevertheless, he was glad when she changed the subject.

'I've got those footy books for you,' she said, 'the ones that belonged to Granddad. Don't forget to take them when you go.'

'Ta.' They sat in comfortable silence for a while, sipping wine, the only sounds the loud ticking of a clock with a pearly face on the sideboard – his mum had one just the same that had belonged to his grandmother – and the faint cries of children playing in the square. 'Are you selling this place or letting it?' he asked. She must be doing one or the other or she wouldn't be getting rid of so much stuff.

'Letting it. An agency will see to it after I've gone. I didn't want people wandering around while I was still here, pointing out the flaws.' She gave the room a worried glance. 'Although I'm not sure if people will want to live with such rackety old furniture.'

'I think it's charming.' He wriggled further into the chair, feeling as if he could stay there for ever. 'It's like being in a time warp.'

'That's what Rachel Williams said the other day. It mightn't look so bad, the furniture, once I've given it a good polishing. That's next on my "things to do" list. Then I shall buy a few rugs to replace the rag ones that Gran made during the war and refused to be parted from. They're probably full of germs and fleas and all sorts of other unmentionable things.'

'If you don't manage to do everything before you go, I'll finish it off for you,' Gareth offered.

'I'll remember that. It's very kind of you.'

They looked at each other and smiled. Their glances held for a very long time and Gareth found himself wishing all sorts of things that, as a decent, married man, he knew he shouldn't. He lowered his eyes at the same time as Victoria did and when he looked again she was blushing. He wondered if she'd been wishing the same things.

Patrick was still playing the guitar. He was practising for the barbecue on Saturday, singing under his breath at the same time. Downstairs, Liam and Danny were watching a holiday programme on television.

Marie was sitting on her bed, the rosary beads lying idle in her red, hardworking hands. At some time during the day – it was when she'd told Sarah that she had three brothers and eight sisters – she'd been overcome by a feeling of nostalgia for the green fields of Donegal and the farm where she'd been born and raised.

None of her brothers and sisters knew where she was. As far as they were concerned, Marie and her lads had just vanished off the face of the earth, although she'd sent a note to her mother to say she was all right, just in case they started looking for her. They'd been so close, not exactly one big happy family, there'd been too many rows for that, but always knew that they could rely on one another if they were in trouble. She wondered if she'd ever see them again.

There was a knock on the bedroom door. It could only be Liam, the lads always barged straight in. 'Come in,' she called.

'You're being very quiet tonight, girl,' Liam said. His slight frame, clad in jeans and a short-sleeved check shirt, looked larger in the cramped room: the lads slept in the biggest bedroom, Liam and Marie had a smaller one each. He came and sat on the bed beside her. He'd been out all day, as he was most days. Today it had been Blackpool. He was now a salesman for a company that made a special sort of security lock, which must be proving very popular as he was never short of money and gave her far more than she needed for the housekeeping.

'I was just thinking.' Marie was almost incapable of coherent thought with his knee touching hers, ever so slightly, sending a series of electric shocks through her body. She had a strong urge to make the Sign of the Cross, absolve herself of the carnal thoughts that she had whenever he was near. She lowered her head in case her eyes reflected how she felt.

'Sad things, you're thinking sad things. I can tell.' He put a finger under her chin and tipped her face towards him. 'I've been thinking too, why don't we go to the pictures, you and me?'

'Tonight?' Her heart somersaulted in her chest.

'Tonight,' he said firmly. 'There's one of those multiplex cinemas in town – London Road. I brought the *Liverpool Echo* home with me. All the films are listed and you can take your pick.'

'But what about Patrick and Danny?'

'They'll be quite safe on their own.'

'Are you sure?' she asked doubtfully. Although she knew her lads would be perfectly all right, she didn't want Liam to think she could so easily be persuaded to leave them.

'Sure I'm sure,' he said easily. 'Put your glad rags on, Marie. If we hurry, there might be time for a drink an' all.'

He left, and Marie hurriedly made the Sign of the Cross and said three quick Hail Marys. But it didn't change how she felt.

'I see you decided to make yourself beautiful for your

husband's homecoming,' Frank said sarcastically when he came in.

'You're early. I wasn't expecting you yet.' Rachel tore the rollers out of her hair. That morning, Kathleen had suggested she pamper herself.

'Have a warm, scented bath when you get home,' she had advised. 'Have you got a face pack?'

When Rachel said that she hadn't, Kathleen had given her one of her own. It smelled of peaches.

For almost an hour, she had lain in the bath with the face pack on, cotton wool pads on her eyes, letting in more hot water when it began to go cold. She had felt much better when she emerged and even better after she had rubbed some of Kirsty's body lotion all over herself. Then she had put her lifeless, freshly washed hair in rollers.

Everyone would be surprised when they came home and found her looking half-decent for a change. But then Frank had arrived early and told her she looked a sight. 'But not for sore eyes,' he added contemptuously.

And now her hair was ruined, the damp curls having fallen flat against her scalp when she'd hastily removed the rollers and she could hear Frank in the dining room joking with the children, saying he'd nearly had a heart attack when he'd come in and found a monster in the kitchen, but it had turned out to be their mother.

'Stop it, Dad,' Kirsty had protested. 'You're being horrible.'

Rachel wanted to rush in and kiss her daughter, but it was a long time since she'd done anything like that.

'Kathleen,' Steve said when he was closing the curtains, 'the plug's come out of the phone. That's why the damn thing wouldn't work when I tried to use it earlier. Who pulled the curtains back this morning?'

'I think it was me,' Kathleen replied. 'I must have done it then. I'm sorry.' She bit her lip. It was awful, being deceitful, pretending it was an accident, when she'd quite deliberately pulled out the plug.

'I actually used the Burrows's phone to complain ours was out of order,' Steve went on. He'd wanted to tell the security company his National Insurance number as he'd forgotten to take it with him to the interview. 'We'll have to be careful in future. It's easy to dislodge it with your foot when you reach for the curtains.'

'Did you want to use it now?' she asked casually.

'What?'

'The phone.'

'No.' He picked up the receiver, listened, and put it back. Was he checking to see if there were any messages on voicemail or merely making sure it was working properly? He gave her a knowing look. 'I can tell what you're thinking,' he said.

'And I can tell what *you're* thinking, at least some of the time.'

'Most of the time I'm thinking about you. Occasionally, I think about Jean. I worry about her. Don't you ever worry about Michael?' His voice was as cold as his face and it scared her.

'Of course I do. As you say, it's only natural, but I haven't telephoned to see how he is. I wouldn't be prepared to go rushing back to Huddersfield if I discovered he was unhappy.' She had to struggle to find the words. 'I . . . I *knew* he would be unhappy if I left him. He loves me in his own way and I love him. Did you think you could just walk out on Jean and she would let you go without a murmur?'

'I didn't expect her to carry on the way she did,' he muttered. 'If I shut me eyes, I can still hear her crying.'

'She refused to sleep with you for all those years. She had no right to make a scene because you'd found someone else.'

'That's what Jean's like.'

'If you knew what she was like, then you shouldn't have left her,' Kathleen said heatedly.

He raised his eyebrows. 'And what would you have had to say about that?'

'I would have been upset. No, more than upset, it would have broken my heart. But I'd rather that had happened than be haunted by the thought of you rushing back to stroke her brow whenever your conscience pricks.'

To her relief, he reached for her hand and pulled her on to his knee. 'I love you,' he said fervently. 'I love you more than I've ever loved anyone in me life before. I can't promise not to think about Jean any more than you can stop thinking about Michael, but from now on, there'll only be you and me.'

'Then do you mind if I change our phone number? I'd sooner you didn't get any more calls from Brenda.'

'All right, luv,' he said after a pause that went on for far too long. 'Whatever you want.'

She could sense the reluctance in his voice. She wouldn't change the number. If he was all that worried about Jean, he could always ring one of his daughters from somewhere else – there was bound to be a telephone he could use in the place where he was going to work. Oh, how horrible it was that she didn't trust him!

They went to bed early as usual. Used to getting up at the crack of dawn, Steve started to feel sleepy at around ten o'clock. They made love and it was as tender and passionate as ever, but a little, dark cloud was poised in the corner of Kathleen's brain and she was unable to let herself go as wholeheartedly as she usually did.

After Steve had been asleep for over an hour and she still felt wide awake, she got up, went into the living room, picked up the phone and dialled a number. Michael answered. Like her, he rarely went to bed before midnight.

'It's me, Kathleen,' she said.

'Darling! Are you all right?' He sounded concerned. 'I didn't expect to hear from you for a long time.'

'I just wanted to hear a familiar voice. We're still friends, Michael.' How could she explain that to Steve? She'd deliberately downgraded her relationship with Michael, not wanting Steve to know how close they would always be. But they weren't dependent on each other. Unlike Jean, Michael would never pretend to be ill or upset in order to get her back. 'I'm fine,' she said. 'How are you, Michael?'

'Missing you, as you can imagine. I miss you not being here when I come home. I miss hearing your key in the door. I suppose I just miss your company, Kath.'

Kathleen recalled the young man she'd fallen in love with in her final year at university. They were both twenty-three. Slimly built, incredibly handsome, he'd worn old-fashioned grey flannels and an Airtex shirt, so different from the other students. His manners and bearing were old-fashioned too. He was the only one who hadn't tried to get her to bed at the first opportunity.

'Kath,' he said gently, 'what's wrong?'

'Nothing's wrong, Michael. I just wanted to talk to you.'

'You've hardly been gone a fortnight. It sounds to me as if there's something badly wrong.'

'OK, something's wrong, but it's not all that bad, I promise.'

'If things get worse, you can always come home,' he said warmly. 'I know it was all very unsatisfactory, but it's better than nothing.'

'Thank you, Michael. I'm sorry if I disturbed you. Do you mind if I ring again?'

'Any time, Kath.'

'Bye.' Kathleen sat on a chair nursing the phone. Perhaps she was making a mountain out of a molehill, but the fact that Steve could have seriously contemplated going to see Jean suggested otherwise.

Ernest Burrows was sitting at the table in the parlour studying *Sporting Life* and making notes in a spiralbound pad. Anna had fallen asleep in the chair. In a minute, he'd wake her with a cup of warm milk.

Ernest was a professional gambler. In the years after the war when he and Anna had lived in Cairo, he'd worked in a small office for a group of English newspapers, sending home items of local news and gossip. King Farouk of Egypt was pursuing an increasingly flamboyant lifestyle and it was all quite fascinating. Then the King ordered the British to leave Egypt, Britain retaliated by occupying the Suez Canal, and the papers sent over their star reporters to deal with such a major story. Ernest found himself sidelined during this critical stage in world history. He handed in his notice feeling deeply hurt.

For a long time, Anna had been longing to travel and see the world; now was the ideal opportunity. They sold all their possessions and flew to Monte Carlo, meaning only to stay a few weeks before moving on – at some point soon he'd have to get another job. Anna, who couldn't wait to see the inside of a casino, had virtually to drag him along, and he watched men and women with manic faces gamble away huge sums of money on roulette. Ernest, cautious to his bones, was astounded. There were thirty-seven slots that the ball could land in and the odds against winning were exceptionally low.

He continued to watch over the heads of the crowd around one of the tables and saw it was possible to bet on the colour the ball would land in, red or black, which meant the chance of winning was a mere two to one. Anna had already lost fourteen of the twenty chips she'd bought. He cadged the remaining six off her and placed one on the black. He lost. He tried again, two chips this time, the ball landed in the black, and he doubled his money. It wasn't a way of making a fortune but, by the end of the evening, Ernest left the casino with more than twice the francs they'd started with. Next day, they rented an apartment and stayed in Monte Carlo for ten years.

Ernest's cautious method of gambling still provided him and Anna with a more than satisfactory living. These days, he bet on horses, scorning hunches, spur of the moment inspirations that a particular horse would win a particular race. If a horse had been called Anna Kosztolanyi, he wouldn't have put money on it without first studying its form, the track it was about to race on, and how well it had performed on the same track before. How successful had the animal's trainer been with other horses? How many winners had the jockey had in the past? What would the track be like on the day: good, firm, or soft? This meant waiting until the very last minute before putting a bet on and the odds might have shortened, but Ernest wasn't prepared to take the risk there wouldn't be a thunderstorm overnight and the course would turn to mud or the horse would be injured or ill and be withdrawn.

He had accounts with four of the leading bookmakers, sharing out his custom so it would become less obvious when he won more often than he lost. He supposed he could have become a rich man, but it didn't do to be greedy. Rarely did he wager a really large amount, only when he went to a race meeting, although it was a long time since that had happened because he didn't want to go without Anna.

He smiled, remembering how much she'd loved the races. At Ascot, she'd get dressed up to the nines wearing hats that she'd decorated herself with flowers and ribbon and bits of net, a different style every year. She'd looked far smarter, far prettier, than the women in the Royal Enclosure whose outfits had cost ten, twenty times as much. Still, those days were over, and now Ernie did his betting by phone.

In the past, people had frequently asked what he did for a living. 'Insurance,' Ernie always replied. 'I'm in insurance.' If he'd told them the truth, he'd be badgered for tips by all and sundry. No one had asked what he did for a long time. They assumed he'd retired.

He made a list of the horses he'd back tomorrow. All the bets were slightly higher than usual. Anna had asked for a computer, and a computer she would have.

'I love you, Marie,' Liam whispered. 'I've loved you for a long time.'

'Why didn't you say before?' Marie whispered back. She couldn't stop shaking. Whey they'd arrived home from the cinema, Patrick and Danny were fast asleep, having left the living room in quite a state: books, videos, clothes, and magazines all over the place. She had immediately set to and tidied up the mess. Marie couldn't stand untidiness. Her fingers would itch until everything had been put away and the room was itself again.

Liam had stood in the doorway, leaning against the frame, watching her with a smile on his face. They'd been to see *Gladiator* with Russell Crowe. She didn't like it a bit, it was too violent, but Liam seemed to enjoy it.

She had just finished straightening the living room when Liam had told her that he loved her. 'Why didn't you say before?' she'd asked for want of something to say and because she couldn't think of anything more sensible or fitting to the occasion.

'I didn't say anything before,' Liam said gently, 'because our lives were so insecure, too upside down. But I reckon we're going to be happy in Liverpool, make a good life here. You've made friends – you've never done before. The lads are settling in, particularly Danny, and Patrick's agreed to sing at the barbecue.' He reached for her arm and stroked it. 'Everyone thinks we're a couple, so why don't we become a proper one? I love you, Marie,' he repeated. His long fingers curled around the soft flesh on her arm and he led her upstairs and lay on the bed with her, kissed her trembling lips, caressed her trembling body, and would have made love to her, but Marie, with a supreme effort, managed to push him away.

'No,' she gasped. 'No!'

'Why not?' Liam pleaded, kissing her neck.

'You know why not.'

'That doesn't matter any more, Marie.'

'It does to me.' She pushed herself into a sitting position and sat on the pillow, clutching her knees, as far away from him as she could get.

After Liam had gone reluctantly back to his room, Marie reached for her rosary and sat up half the night saying all five decades over and over again, knowing it was a waste of time because the good Lord would never forgive her for having nearly made love to a priest.

The grandfather clock in the hall struck midnight and Gareth realized with a shock that he and Victoria had been talking for five whole hours. The time had flown by. They had so much in common. Computers apart, they read the same books, liked the same films, watched the same programmes on television. Gareth had never had much interest in politics, but always voted for the Green party, as did Victoria. 'At least they want to make the world a better place,' he said. 'The other parties only make it worse,' and Victoria said they were her sentiments exactly.

'I didn't know it was so late.' He got to his feet after the clock had finished striking. 'I'd better be getting home.'

'Your wife will be wondering where you've got to. Don't forget to take those books with you. They're on the table in the kitchen.'

'I won't. Well, thank you for an enjoyable evening – and the books,' he said politely.

'It's been nice having you,' Victoria replied, just as politely.

Gareth contemplated kissing her, politely, on the cheek, but didn't trust himself not to kiss her lips, not all that politely, once they were in such close contact.

'Do you mind if I come and see you again?' he asked.

'Come whenever you want. I won't be here for much longer.'

'I know you won't,' he said sadly.

When Gareth returned to Hamilton Lodge, he found a note on the fridge. 'Gone to see Mum,' it said in big, black, angry letters. Debbie often ran back to her mother if she was cross with him, usually staying the night as an extra punishment. Gareth's own night would then be spent tossing and turning, worried she wouldn't come back, although that night he slept like a log and dreamed about Victoria.

In Three Farthings, Rachel Williams was also dreaming. She was alone in an empty place in the dark and mist of a winter night. Every now and then, the mist would drift away, like smoke, to reveal an angry mass of black clouds overhead. Then the clouds would disappear, exposing a weak, yellow moon like an eye, watching her accusingly. Rachel wondered what she had done to make the moon look at her in such a horrible way. She was grateful when the clouds closed over and the moon was no longer there.

Then, all of a sudden, she was swimming in water that smelled strongly of oil and tasted filthy, and a ship, huge and menacing, was coming slowly towards her, its black shape barely visible through the mist. Someone on board must have seen her as they were shouting furiously, 'Get out of the way!'

But all Rachel could do was tread water, feeling her feet sink into mud, tugging her downwards, while the ship approached, relentlessly, unable to stop. As was the way with dreams, she was able to see the water after both she and the ship had gone. It looked flat and undisturbed, the surface broken only by swirls of darkly coloured oil, and she had to assume that she had drowned.

Rachel

Chapter 6

Rachel Paige was born in June 1950. It had come as an unpleasant surprise to her mother, Martha, to discover she was pregnant again at forty-seven. Her husband, Reg, was in his early sixties and they already had two grown-up sons. The eldest, Christopher, was a bachelor making a career for himself in the Army, and Peter had a wife and two children, so Rachel came into the world already an aunt.

The Paiges lived in a little, cramped cottage in Maghull on the outskirts of Liverpool. Their once-isolated home had gradually been surrounded by new estates that they very much disapproved of, even if it meant there were lots of new shops and other facilities.

Martha and Reg felt too tired to care for another baby at their ages. Rachel was well fed, well dressed but, although nothing was said, she soon learned it was a waste of time to expect them to play with her. Even making childish conversation with their little girl required too much effort − every night, her father fell asleep in the chair as soon as he'd had his tea, while her mother sat in gloomy silence, not bothering to switch on the light until it was almost dark.

From the age of three, Rachel attended a day nursery. A quiet, solitary child, she found it hard to mix with other children and her mother never encouraged her to invite a child back to play − she found it difficult enough caring for her own. The thought of having two children in the house appalled her.

With few social skills and an inability to carry on a conversation with her peers, Rachel had a hard time at infant and junior school. It didn't help that she was conscious of her isolation. She badly wanted to make friends and often tried to talk to other girls, but found herself saying the stupidest things and the words that came out sounded stilted and unreal. Most of the girls just laughed and ran away. A few were kind enough to tolerate her for a while, but Rachel could sense their pity, knew she was being a nuisance, and left these girls alone.

It didn't help that her parents were so old and the source of much merriment among the other pupils. By now, her father was almost seventy and looked it with his straggly grey hair and elderly gait and Martha Paige seemed much older than her already advancing years.

'Your mum and dad look like Mr and Mrs Rip Van Winkle,' Rachel's classmates taunted. Sometimes, it was assumed they were her grandparents and Rachel didn't contradict anyone who made this assumption.

The best times of her life were when her brother, Christopher, came home on leave – Peter lived in Plymouth and she rarely saw him. Christopher was immensely tall and sporty looking with the build of a heavyweight boxer. He gave her piggybacks in the garden, wrestled with her on the grass, and took her to the pictures. Rachel would never forget the first time they went and saw a film called *The Shaggy Dog* with Fred MacMurray. She sat with a box of chocolates on her knee and entered a completely different, magical world. A few days later, he took her to see *Sleeping Beauty*. She could hardly wait for Christopher to come home so they could go again. He would send her postcards and presents from faraway places like Cyprus and Berlin.

'You've led a pretty lousy life so far, haven't you, Titch?' Christopher said one day when Rachel was about nine.

'Have I?' She couldn't imagine life being any different to the way it was and always had been.

'Well, Mum and Dad aren't exactly the liveliest of souls and they've got worse with the years. I always said they were born under-fuelled. Perhaps that's what attracted them to each other. They really should start the day with a double whisky each and top up every few hours. At least Peter and I had each other. You've got no one. Poor little Titch.' He picked her up and threw her over his shoulder and she squealed with delight.

When Rachel was eleven and went to comprehensive school, things got very much better. First of all, she discovered she was clever. She had an 'aptitude for figures' according to the maths teacher, Mrs Hubbard, and 'a way with words', Mr Newley, the English teacher claimed. She also discovered she was quite good at art, found geography fascinating and history absorbing. None of these talents had been obvious at her previous school where shyness had been mistaken for a lack of intelligence.

She made friends with several girls and a few boys who shared her interest in lessons. Her best friends of all were Eileen McNichol and Grace Parry. As the girls grew older, they would go into Liverpool together, to the theatre or the pictures, sometimes to discos, which Rachel didn't like as she was rarely asked to dance. Her mirror had already told her she wasn't even faintly attractive. Her face was very flat, her eyes very small, her mouth very thin, and she could never do anything with her fine hair – the only colour she could think to describe it was khaki.

'But you've got an incredibly kind face,' Grace would insist whenever Rachel complained about her looks. Grace was small, blonde, and pretty.

'It's got loads of character,' claimed Eileen, who was tall, dark, and equally pretty. 'You look terribly brainy. Me,' she said disparagingly in order to make Rachel feel better, 'I look as thick as two short planks.'

The three girls went to each other's houses, sat in their respective bedrooms and talked about what they would do when it was time to leave school. Mrs Paige didn't mind them coming to the cottage: they were out of sight and out of hearing and didn't disturb her and Reg at all. It was Rachel who made any drinks that were required.

Grace and Eileen intended going to university: Grace to become a teacher and Eileen, who was good at languages, to travel the world as an interpreter. 'I want to visit as many countries as possible,' she breathed excitedly. They were dismayed that all Rachel wanted to do was get married and have children.

'But you're so clever,' they said together when Rachel first expressed this rather limited ambition.

'Then I'll be a clever wife and a clever mother,' Rachel said with a smile.

'It's such a waste,' Eileen cried.

'Such a shame,' said Grace.

But Rachel longed to be a wife and mother. She was determined to play with her children every minute of every day and never stop showing how much she loved them. She would have long conversations with her husband about the weightier aspects of life, and the house would be filled with music, bright lights, and the scent of flowers. Despite her plain looks, she just knew that somewhere in the world there was a man who'd been made especially for her and she for him.

'You can still get a degree,' Grace insisted. 'Let's all go to the same university. We'll have a marvellous time.'

It was a hard invitation to resist. The idea of living away from home with her two best friends was very appealing. Rachel agreed, but said she'd leave immediately if she met her future husband while she was there. 'I don't believe in long engagements.' She sighed happily. She couldn't wait.

In 1968, the girls left school with three top grade A levels each, easily enough to admit them to Manchester University to which they had applied and been accepted on condition of achieving their predicted grades. Rachel planned to take English Literature, her favourite subject of all. They discussed what they would take with them.

'I'll take my hairdryer and an electric kettle,' Grace offered.

Eileen said she'd bring her curling tongs and a travelling clock that also had an alarm.

'I'll fetch that portable wireless our Christopher bought me for Christmas and an electric iron,' Rachel promised. Christopher, his Army service over, had bought an apartment in Cyprus that had a stunning view of the Mediterranean, so it said in his letters. To occupy his time, he had bought into a small travel agency.

Their bags were ready, except for clothes that would crease and couldn't be packed until the last minute when, one night, only days before they were due to leave, Rachel's father died peacefully in his sleep.

'You'll come as soon as the funeral's over, won't you?' Eileen asked anxiously.

'The very minute,' Rachel promised. It would have been a lie to say she was terribly upset. Neither of her parents had shown much fondness for her and she'd never grown to love them as a daughter should. Despite the changed circumstances, it didn't cross her mind to stay at home. She felt quite confident her mother would prefer to be left alone rather than have Rachel cluttering up the place, disturbing her solitude.

Christopher flew home for the funeral. Peter, her other brother, whom Rachel had only seen about half a dozen times, also came, but didn't stay overnight. 'I have a business to run,' he said crisply. 'I can't possibly spare the time.'

The funeral was terribly sad, if only because nobody seemed the least bit upset about her father's passing: Peter kept glancing at his watch, Christopher looked inscrutable, her mother's face bore no expression at all, and Rachel found herself wondering how Grace and Eileen were getting on in Manchester without an iron and the wireless she had promised to bring.

Two days later, Christopher returned to Cyprus. Rachel gave him her address in Manchester to write to. 'You girls must come and stay with me sometime, Titch,' he said heartily. 'I can get you cheap flights and I've a spare bedroom, but it'd have to be sleeping bags on the floor.'

Rachel said she'd love to and was certain Grace and Eileen would too.

'When are you off?' Christopher asked.

'The day after tomorrow, Monday.'

'Have a great time, Titch. See you!' He plonked a wet kiss on her cheek, got into the taxi waiting outside, and waved to her until he was out of sight.

On Sunday night, Mrs Paige had a stroke and Rachel's

plans of going to university were shattered beyond repair.

'Rachel, my friend, you can't stay in this miserable place looking after your mother for ever,' Grace cried. 'You've already stuck it out for five years. You're twenty-three, for God's sake, and you've had no life at all. Oh, do be quiet, Sally.' She gave the little girl tugging at her knee and demanding a drink an impatient shove. 'I can't hear myself speak.'

'I'll give her some cordial. Come along, Sal, into the kitchen, and you can help me pour it.'

'Well, if you want it all over your shoes,' Grace said petulantly.

Rachel picked up eighteen-month old Sally and carried her outside. Sally helped hold the bottle of cordial and together they tipped some into the glass. Rachel filled it up with water.

'See, dry shoes!' she said cheerfully when she went back, depositing the child on the floor. 'I'll be glad when you've had that baby, Grace. You're nothing but an old sourpuss these days. Poor Sal doesn't know whether she's coming or going.'

'I know, Rach. I'm sorry,' Grace said abjectly. She held out her arms. 'Come to Mummy, sweetheart, and I'll give you a nice big hug.'

Sally stumbled into her mother's arms, spilling drink on the way, and Rachel watched enviously as her slim arms slid around her mother's neck. Grace had got married straight from university, her career as a teacher thrown to the winds when she'd fallen in love with Tom Ogilvie whom she'd met at a Manchester disco.

Grace had noticed the envious look. 'I wish you'd leave, Rach. It's just not fair. Your mum's being awfully selfish. *Make* her go into hospital if she's not prepared to go of her own accord.'

'I couldn't possibly,' Rachel said stubbornly. She'd had the same argument with Grace before, and with Eileen, though only in letters. Eileen was finding jobs in all sorts of out-of-the-way places, just as she'd always wanted, and meeting loads of attractive men. Christopher had also tried to persuade his little sister to leave.

'You know how unsociable my mother is,' Rachel said to Grace. 'She couldn't stand being in a ward with other women, being cared for by strange nurses.'

'But she won't even go for therapy!' Grace wailed. 'She doesn't *want* to get better. She's perfectly content to lie upstairs and be looked after by her long-suffering daughter.'

'I'm not long-suffering,' Rachel protested. 'I'm quite happy most of the time. I love my job.' She worked for Liverpool Corporation in the Tourist Office, promoting the attractions of the city to the world at large. Work wouldn't have been possible if Christopher hadn't sent money to pay for a nurse to look after her mother during the day. Nights and weekends, Rachel did it herself. It left no time for a social life. She didn't tell Grace how boring and tedious these times were, or how much she disliked helping her ungrateful mother with bedpans and having to empty them afterwards. 'And I've got you and Tom and Sally, haven't I?' she said instead, smiling. 'Now there's a new baby on the way and I'll have him or her too.'

Grace bent her head and began to pleat and unpleat the material of her voluminous maternity frock with her fingers. This was something her friend always did when she was about to convey bad news. With a sense of foreboding, Rachel waited for her to speak.

'Actually, Rach, Tom has applied for a job in Canada – Vancouver. Lab technicians earn at least twice as much over there. We can buy a bigger house and it will be a much better life for the children.'

'When will you be going?'

'If Tom gets the job, in a couple of months.'

'Tell Tom I wish him all the luck in the world, but I can't say how much I'll miss you all.'

Mrs Paige lived for another two years. Rachel was working in her office in the Town Hall when the nurse phoned to say her mother had suffered another stroke and been taken into hospital. 'It's really serious this time, Rachel. I think you should prepare for the worst,' she said.

Three days later, her mother died, and Rachel was ashamed that all she could feel was a sense of enormous relief. Christopher paid for the funeral, but didn't come, and neither did Peter, who sent a wreath: Rachel and the nurse were the only mourners.

When she went to bed that night, she knew she wouldn't be living in the cottage for much longer. Peter's letter had arrived at the same time as the wreath. He had reminded her that the cottage belonged to the three of them and, just now, his business wasn't doing terribly well. 'I'm desperately in need of a new van and my house could do with a few improvements. Would you kindly have the property valued and put on the market as soon as possible?' He felt sure that she, a single woman with no dependents, would easily find somewhere else to live. 'Anyway, Rachel, a nice bedsitting room close to town would be far more convenient than the wilds of Maghull,' he finished.

The estate agent quoted an unbelievable figure for

what he reckoned the cottage would sell for. The original sale documents had been with her mother's papers and fifty years ago, the place had cost ninety-five pounds. Now it was worth almost five hundred times that much.

Christopher wrote and said she could have his share of the proceeds – he was so angry with Peter that his normally steady handwriting literally shivered with anger. 'That should be enough for you to buy a flat of your own, my dear Titch.'

Rachel was glad to escape from the cramped house and start afresh somewhere new. As soon as the cottage was sold, she bought a pleasant little one-bedroom flat in Waterloo less than half a mile from the River Mersey and only a short distance from the station.

She was twenty-five, free to lead her own life at last.

Over the years, Rachel had grown in confidence. She would never be an extrovert, but had lost her shyness and made quite a few friends, mostly women. She had joined a chess club, gone to night school for a variety of subjects, visited the theatre and the cinema at least once a week with her female friends, was invited to parties and even threw the occasional one herself, although found this something of an ordeal. Every September, she spent a fortnight in Cyprus with Christopher.

Her ambition remained the same as it had always been: to get married and have children. However, as the years passed and she approached her thirtieth birthday, having this ambition realized seemed less and less likely. Among the women she knew, she was the only one not married. She was quite resigned to the fact she was no oil painting, but always dressed smartly, wore make-up, and had her hair set every Saturday morning in George Henry Lee's.

Occasionally, a man would invite her out, but he rarely asked for a second date. Perhaps her anxiety showed – the longing for this to be *the* man, the one she'd been waiting for all her life, and her disappointment would be obvious as soon as she realized that this man wouldn't do at all. Still, she remained convinced that he existed, somewhere, and all they had to do was meet and recognize straight away that they were made for each other.

It didn't exactly happen like that, but on her thirtieth birthday, she met Frank Williams and fell in love. She was never entirely sure if Frank felt the same, but he *needed* her and that would do.

One of her friends had arranged a dinner party on her birthday. There were twelve of them altogether: five couples, Rachel, and a tall, slim, very presentable man with sandy hair and light blue eyes about the same age as herself. It often happened that an extra man was invited for Rachel. The man was introduced as Frank Williams and they were placed next to each other at the table.

'What do you do?' was Rachel's first question. It always seemed the obvious thing to ask.

'I'm a car salesman. I work for Warwick Cars in town. We only sell the most expensive makes.'

'I imagine you'd be good at that.' He had a brash, open charm and an easy manner. 'I bet you could easily persuade me to buy a Ferrari or something.'

It was the right thing to have said. He proceeded to tell her that he was very good at his job, sold almost twice as many cars as the other salesman, and the manager thought very highly of him. He continued to boast throughout the first and second courses. Rachel realized he was trying to impress her and there was something in his eyes, a lost sort of look, almost frantic at times, which told her that, deep down, he was desperately unhappy and the boasting was a cover for his inadequacy or lack of confidence, something she completely understood.

It wasn't until the sweet arrived that he asked a question about herself. 'I'm sorry,' he said, looking embarrassed. 'I've been rattling on about myself all this time. I always do that.'

'It doesn't matter. It was all very interesting.' She went on to describe her job and where she lived, told him about Christopher in Cyprus and Peter in Plymouth, that she visited Christopher once a year, but hadn't heard from Peter in ages. 'I send him a Christmas card every year, but he never sends one back.'

He looked shocked. 'That's awful. Families should stick together. I had a brother and sister but, when my father walked out, my mother put us all into care. I've never seen either of them – or my mother – since.' His mouth trembled slightly as if the memory upset him.

'You poor thing,' Rachel said sympathetically. 'That's even more awful.'

He shrugged. 'I'm always envious of people with close families.'

At the end of the evening, he asked her out the following Saturday.

'I'm afraid I can't,' Rachel began, but before she could continue, Frank burst out with, 'You found me boring, didn't you? I'm hopeless at parties. I never know what to say and all I do is talk about myself. I'm sorry you had such an awful evening.'

'I had a lovely evening,' she cried. 'What I was going to say was, I can't see you Saturday, I'm going to the theatre, but I'd love to go out with you another day.'

Six months later, on a freezing cold day in December 1980, Rachel Paige and Frank Williams became man and wife.

'What's this?' Frank picked up the daily paper and waved it at her.

'It's a newspaper,' Rachel replied.

'I know that,' he said impatiently. 'But you've finished the crossword. I was going to do it later.'

'I'm sorry, love, but we're about to go to bed. It would have been thrown away in the morning.'

'Still . . .' He shrugged and looked sulky, and Rachel realized she must never finish the crossword again until the paper was ready to go in the dustbin and Frank wouldn't know, just as she never read a certain sort of book in front of him, or watched programmes on television that he couldn't understand. She stuck to light romantic novels and only turned on the television for games shows, soaps, and films that couldn't possibly be described as 'heavy'.

They'd been married for ten months. Frank wanted them to have a perfect marriage and perfection meant not having a wife who was cleverer than he was. Rachel didn't object. She was quite happy to play along because she loved him. He'd been badly damaged as a child, moved from one foster home to another, and had an idea in his head of what married life should be – him as the head of the household, a submissive wife, a nice home, children. In another two months, their first child would be born and he'd spent months turning the second bedroom into a nursery fit for a prince or princess.

The baby in her womb gave a couple of sharp kicks and she uttered a little cry. 'It's very active tonight,' she gasped.

Frank was kneeling beside her in an instant, his irritation over the crossword forgotten. 'Are you all right, darling?'

'Yes, but I think I'd like to go to bed. I'm rather tired.'

'I'll give you a hand upstairs.'

She went up and down the stairs a dozen times a day unaided, but let him help her to the bedroom, feeling the comfort of his arm around her waist.

'Would you like some warm milk?' he asked.

'That would be nice,' she said gratefully, knowing how much he enjoyed being an attentive husband. It was how a perfect husband in a perfect marriage should behave.

James arrived seven days before Christmas, a beautiful, healthy baby, very content. Rachel felt almost dizzy with love when she first held him in her arms.

Frank was the proudest of fathers. He took champagne and an expensive box of cigars into work. Margot, the receptionist at the showroom, brought Rachel a lovely basket of flowers. The staff had taken a collection and she'd delivered them herself so she could take a look at James.

'According to Frank, there's never been a baby like him before.' She smiled at Rachel. 'I've never known him so happy as since he married you. All we hear from him is, "my wife this", or "my wife that", and now you've got a baby, there'll be no standing him. I understand the next one's going to be a girl, at least so Frank ses.'

As Frank had predicted, Rachel's second baby was a girl: Kirsty, born a year and a day after her brother. She was smaller, paler, less content with life than James, but just as beautiful.

Rachel's family was complete. She felt like an actress who had slogged away for years before becoming a star. Now she was putting everything she had into her role as a wife and mother and was happy beyond her wildest dreams.

Frank had felt uneasy, even a touch resentful, that the sale of Rachel's flat had provided more than half the money for their house. She'd wanted to tell him not to be silly, but had quickly learned that Frank couldn't stand criticism, at least not from her. 'Don't be silly' was one of the worst things she could say.

'It means we won't have a huge mortgage to repay,' she said gently, and he'd had to accept the fact, albeit grudgingly, that she was bringing more wealth into the marriage than him, when he considered it should be the other way around. He wasn't quite as good a salesman as he'd claimed the night they'd met: some weeks the commission he earned was quite small and money would be tight.

They'd bought a new semi-detached house in a village called Lydiate, not far from Maghull. They had to pass the cottage where she'd been born to reach it and the first time Rachel had been astonished to see that it had been demolished and a large, detached, Tudor-style house had been built in its place. It had a name on the door, Three Farthings.

'We'll live in a house like that one day,' Frank promised when she pointed it out.

He wouldn't let her do anything in the new house, apart from watch while he laid carpets, put up tiles in the kitchen and bathroom, began to turn over the black soil in the garden in readiness for a lawn. Like her, he got an enormous amount of pleasure out of simple things, like seeing the washing blow on the new clothesline for the first time, or admiring a picture that had just been hung on the wall.

Everyone on the new estate was very friendly. Almost every morning, Rachel was invited to a neighbour's house for coffee or she invited them to hers. They babysat for each other, so Rachel and Frank often managed to see the latest films once they considered the children were old enough to be left.

Frank was the most popular of men, particularly with women. When they were in company, he would single out the most attractive one and flirt with her outrageously, compliment her fulsomely, until he had the woman eating out of his hand. It didn't bother Rachel. It was *her* who Frank would hold in his arms that night, *her* whom he needed. She was his prop, the mother of the children he adored, the person who had given him the self-confidence to flirt, who was responsible for banishing the hurt, frantic look in his eyes that had been there when they'd met on her thirtieth birthday.

James started school, then Kirsty. Rachel joined the Parent-Teacher Association and helped raise funds for various school causes. She was in her element, organizing fêtes, Christmas bazaars, cheese and wine evenings. Grace wrote from Canada and asked if she'd become a cabbage.

Have you stopped using your brain? Are you still the same person who read Proust and Goethe at school? The one who dragged Eileen and me to the Playhouse whenever there was a Shakespeare play on? Your letters

are full of Frank and the children, nothing about you.
Has Rachel Williams become an entirely different person
to Rachel Paige? Me, I did a refresher course and have
started teaching at last. Sally loves drama school and
Kim still wants to be an astronaut. I don't see much of
Tom since the divorce – the kids go round to his place
these days. There's a new man in my life, but I don't
know yet if he'll become a permanent feature. His name's
Joe and he teaches at my school. I suppose you know
Eileen's in Brazil living with an American journalist
who's got a wife back home . . .

Perhaps she *had* become a cabbage. She no longer
wanted to read Proust or watch Shakespeare. Frank and
the children were enough and she couldn't think of a
single other thing she wanted. Once, she would have
been envious of Eileen, but now felt only pity for a
woman nearing forty who was still wandering the world,
unable to settle, sleeping with married men. If Eileen
wasn't careful, she would soon be too old to have
children. As for Grace and Tom getting divorced, words
failed her. 'We just grew apart,' Grace had said in one of
her previous letters.

'No commitment, that's what it is,' Frank said, shaking
his head, when she'd shown the letter to him. 'Not like
us, eh?'

The children were growing up so rapidly it scared her.
James started comprehensive school – in another few
months he would be twelve. Another year, and he
would become a teenager. Kirsty was ten, double figures,
but already behaving more like an eighteen-year-old
with her clumpy shoes, short skirts, and skimpy T-shirts.
She was nagging her parents to have her ears pierced, but

Frank put his foot down. 'Over my dead body, Kirsty,' he threatened. Rachel found lipstick and mascara hidden in her dressing-table drawer, but didn't say anything.

She missed having babies, missed their dependency, teaching them to talk and walk, running into her arms when she collected them from school, helping to tie their shoelaces and myriad other things.

Although James and Kirsty could still make her heart turn over: James, for instance, when he'd been presented with two prizes on the final speech day at Junior school, looking incredibly serious and proud when he marched up to the front to take them from the headmistress; Kirsty for just being herself, tall and gawky, atrociously dressed, pretending to swoon during *Top of the Pops* when Take That came on the screen, promising herself that one day she would marry Robbie Williams. 'Then I won't have to change my name, will I, Mum?'

'No, sweetheart,' Rachel assured her.

The day Kirsty started senior school, Frank telephoned from the showroom. Did she get off OK?' he asked.

'She hates the uniform, but we already knew that. I've promised to take the skirt up a few inches tonight.' Rachel sighed. She felt terribly sad.

'I suppose you don't know what to do with yourself.'

'Well, there's plenty of washing and Kirsty's room is a tip, but I know what you mean. I wish we'd had more children, Frank.'

'It's a bit late in the day to think that, love. We thought two was all we could afford.'

'I know.' She sighed again. She was unlikely to conceive again at forty-four. 'But, Frank,' she said, 'it wouldn't hurt to try. Hang the expense.'

Perhaps God had been eavesdropping, because a few months after her conversation with Frank, Rachel found herself pregnant. 'If it's a girl,' she said, 'let's call her Alice – Alice in Wonderland.'

Some women actually said they felt sorry for her, having a baby at her age. Rachel was aghast. 'But I'm thrilled to pieces,' she exclaimed, 'and so is Frank.' James and Kirsty pretended to be embarrassed by the growing evidence that their parents, whom they'd thought well past it, had actually engaged in sex, but Rachel could tell they were secretly pleased.

Alice burst into the world on the first day of June after a long and excruciatingly painful delivery that left Rachel too weary to nurse her straight away.

'She's a little smasher,' Frank whispered. He'd been present throughout the birth and his cheeks were streaked with tears. 'I hope you haven't been having it off with the milkman, love, because she's nothing like us or our other two.'

Rachel glanced at the baby in the cot beside her bed, struggling to free herself from the sheet wrapped tightly around her tiny body. 'It was the chimney sweep,' she said. Alice's curly hair was as black as soot. 'Christopher told me our father had black hair when he was young.' She gave a dry smile. 'I can't imagine my father being young.'

'I can't even remember what mine looked like.' Frank made a face. 'But we've come through, haven't we, Rach, despite our lousy childhoods?' He laid his head beside her on the pillow. 'Our kids have always known how much we wanted them. They've never been shown anything but love.'

Within a few months, Alice's eyes had turned from blue to brown and her black hair had grown into a tangle of waves and curls. She reminded Rachel of a Victorian doll with her tiny snub nose and little pink mouth. She had the sweetest of natures, never stopped smiling and clearly found the world a delightful place. Even the women who'd felt sorry for Rachel when she was pregnant had to concede she was an exceptionally lovely child. 'If I'd been in your place,' one woman said, 'I'd've had an abortion – but just imagine if you'd got rid of Alice! It hardly bears thinking about.'

Rachel shuddered. 'Such an idea never entered my head.'

James and Kirsty adored her. When Alice caught a mild cold, James walked all the way home from school in his lunch hour to make sure she was all right. Kirsty was her willing slave and brought her friends back home to admire her baby sister. Several times a day, Frank would ring to ask what Alice was up to.

'She's just crawled across the room,' Rachel would tell him or, later, 'She's just walked a few steps,' and, later still, 'She said "Dada" this morning.'

When Alice was three, Rachel was reluctant to let her go to playgroup, wanting to keep her precious daughter all to herself, but common sense told her it was best for her to mix with other children. The first morning, alone, the house felt unnaturally quiet without Alice's joyous presence, but she was determined not to mope. At an age when most women's children were adults, she'd been blessed with a beautiful little girl and it was ridiculous to resent her growing up. One day, her children would get married and have children of their own. Best look forward to that day, not dread it.

Frank telephoned in the afternoon. 'How did playgroup go?' he asked anxiously.

'She loved it. She did a drawing of a teddy bear.' Rachel giggled. 'It looks a bit like you. I've stuck it on the fridge.'

'I can't wait to see it.'

That Christmas, Kirsty brought home her first boyfriend – at least, the first her parents knew about. His name was Whiz, he was seventeen, and had a gold stud in his eyebrow. Rachel glanced at Frank's horrified face. She could tell that, like her, he was praying it wasn't serious.

'What's Whiz short for?' she asked her daughter when Whiz had gone.

'Nothing, Mum, it's just his name.'

'He wasn't christened Whiz, surely?'

Kirsty shrugged. 'It seems a perfectly OK name to me.'

Frank, playing the heavy father, asked what Whiz did for a living.

'He's still in the sixth form at school. Next year, he's going to university. He wants to be a doctor.'

Rachel and Frank looked at each other, stunned, and Frank muttered he wouldn't have much confidence in a doctor with a stud in his eyebrow.

Whiz was soon replaced by Chas, who was replaced by Ian. From then on, Kirsty seemed to have a new boyfriend every month.

And James, who had seemed such a sensible, respectable young man, always neatly dressed, arrived home one day with his head shaved.

'Ronnie Bannerman did it with clippers in the lunch hour,' he said, looking terribly pleased with himself. 'What d'you think, Mum? If we buy clippers of our own, it'll save a fortune at the barber's. Dad could use them too.'

'You look like a skinhead,' his appalled mother gasped. 'Lord knows what your father will say.'

An equally appalled Frank said much the same as his wife. James was hurt. 'The leader of the Conservative

Party, William Hague, has a haircut like this. I thought you'd be pleased.'

'I can't recall doing anything even faintly shocking when I was sixteen,' Frank said that night when James was upstairs doing his homework.

'Neither can I,' Rachel replied. 'I was incredibly well behaved.' She smiled. 'Although I'm glad they feel they can be themselves. I'd rather that than they be a pair of goody-goodies.'

After some consideration, Frank said he felt the same.

James commenced his final year at school on the same day that Alice started her first. On a beautiful September day with a faint hint of autumn in the air, Rachel walked along the towpath of the Liverpool Canal, Alice dancing beside her, a furry haversack on her back in the shape of a panda that held a new pack of felt pens, two pencils, a rubber, and a spare hankie. She wore a blue and white check frock and a navy-blue cardigan and looked terribly self-important. The canal sparkled like a silver ribbon. It was a slightly longer way to school, but made a pleasanter walk than the main Southport road.

'Can I paddle on the way home?' Alice asked.

'No, sweetheart, the water may look nice, but it's filthy. Not only that, you might drown.'

'I *am* coming home, aren't I, Mummy?' She looked at Rachel nervously with her huge, brown eyes. 'I'm not going to stay at school for ever?'

'Of course not.' Rachel laughed. 'You'll have lunch there, then I'll collect you in the afternoon and we'll be home well in time for tea.'

'Will I like the lunch, Mummy? Will I have to eat carrots?'

'I'll tell the teacher you hate carrots and, if you don't like the lunch, tomorrow I'll make you sandwiches.'

'Thank you, Mummy,' Alice said gravely. 'You're very kind.'

'And you, Alice Williams, are the funniest little girl in the whole world. Come here and let me give you a kiss.'

Unlike James, who'd always claimed to find school boring, and Kirsty, who continued to hate every minute because she couldn't stand people telling her what to do, Alice quickly settled into the routine of lessons. She really enjoyed being taught how to read and write. Rachel made a set of cards with a three-letter word written on each: CAT, MAT, BIG, DOG ... James and Kirsty fought over who would give Alice her reading lesson that night.

Rachel, who'd already started knitting for the Christmas Bazaar the school was having on the Saturday before Christmas, sat in a chair in front of the fire, watching and listening, thinking what loving, perfectly adorable children she had. In a few months, the new millennium would arrive. In the past, she'd often wondered where she would be, whom she would be with on the eve of the twenty-first century and had never dreamed she would spend it in such perfect company.

On the final day of the autumn term, Rachel woke up with a throbbing headache. She didn't mention it to Frank or the children, but after she'd taken Alice to school, she took two tablets and lay on the settee, mentally ticking off the things she still had to do.

The bazaar was tomorrow and it would be Christmas next week. The decorations were up and there were already a few parcels under the tree – her brother,

Christopher, always sent expensive presents for the nieces and nephew he'd never met, although Rachel sent him loads of photographs – they could never afford to take the whole family to Cyprus and Christopher was at first too busy, then too frail to come home – he'd recently had his seventy-sixth birthday. The cake and the puddings had been made weeks ago, but she still had mince pies to do and shortbread for Frank – he loved homemade shortbread – and had promised to make a couple of sponges for the cake stall at the bazaar. There were buttons to sew on the matinée jackets she'd knitted and, of course, ordinary, everyday things, like washing, cleaning, and preparing that night's meal. As soon as the headache had gone, she'd get started.

An hour later, the headache had got worse, not better, and the pain had spread to her limbs. She was shivering, yet felt much too hot. Twice during the morning the doorbell rang, but she felt too sick to answer. At around noon, she managed to stagger as far as the kitchen and take more tablets but, almost straight away, she vomited them up in the downstairs lavatory. She collapsed on to the settee and drifted into a restless sleep.

When she came to, it was quarter past two. In an hour, it would be time to collect Alice from school. Rachel tried to stand, but fell back when a wave of dizziness mixed with nausea washed over her. She'd never make it as far as school. She wondered who to call and ask to fetch Alice home? Some of her close friends had moved away and the ones left no longer had children at infant school. She was about to ring the school, but remembered Frank had promised to come home early that afternoon. He would be only too pleased to collect Alice. Once again she drifted into sleep, this time full of bizarre dreams featuring giant spiders and trees with eyes that stared at her balefully.

It was Kirsty who woke her. 'Are you all right, Mum? You look awful,' she said when Rachel struggled to sit up.

'What time is it?' She rubbed her eyes. They felt sticky and would hardly open. She saw it was pitch dark outside.

'Nearly five o'clock. Where's Alice?'

'Isn't she home?' It was a stupid question to ask. As if Alice would have come home and not woken her mummy! Rachel had the first feeling of dread.

'She's being awfully quiet if she is.' Kirsty went to the bottom of the stairs. 'Alice,' she called, 'are you up there?' There was no reply. Kirsty said, 'I'll just make sure,' and ran upstairs. 'She's not there,' she said, white-faced, when she came down.

'Then where is she?' Rachel screamed. She stood, but had to sit down again when her head swam. 'Is your dad's car outside?'

'No.'

'He said he was coming home early. I expected him to pick Alice up.'

'Don't panic, Mum,' Kirsty said sensibly, although she looked about to panic herself. 'If you weren't there to collect her, maybe she's gone to someone's house. You shouldn't have relied on Dad, you know. He often promises to come home early, but can't if a customer turns up.'

'Yes, but . . .'

'But what, Mum?'

'Never mind. I'll ring the school. Maybe she's still there.' It seemed most unlikely at this hour. She tried to stand again, but it was impossible. Her legs refused to support her. 'Kirsty, you'll have to do it for me, love. I think I've got the flu.'

'OK, Mum.' A few minutes later, she came back. 'I spoke to the secretary and she said all the pupils had gone, but Alice's teacher, Mrs Burgess was still there and she called her to the phone. Apparently, it was late when Alice left. She'd been making a Christmas card for the family and the glue hadn't dried. Mrs Burgess said she was dancing around the classroom, waving the card to dry it. Next time she looked, Alice had gone and she thought you'd taken her. Why didn't you call the school, Mum, and tell them you were ill?'

'I don't know,' Rachel muttered.

James arrived, dumped his satchel as soon as he heard the news, and left to search the streets for his sister. Kirsty called every number she could think of to see if anyone knew Alice's whereabouts, but no one had seen her. She called the showroom to ask her father to come, but he'd already left. 'Mum,' she said in a frightened voice, 'I think we'd better call the police.'

Rachel nodded. By now, fear had entered her soul. She just knew, could feel in her aching bones that something terrible had happened to her darling Alice.

Neighbours knocked to ask if Alice had been found. They stood outside, looking grim, telling each other they couldn't imagine how they'd feel if it had happened to them, and what a lovely child Alice was.

Time passed very slowly: seven o'clock, eight o'clock, nine, and with it came the certainty that by now there was no chance of Alice coming home of her own accord. Someone must have taken her. Either that, or she'd had an accident.

No one had thought to close the curtains on the Williams's house, so gaily decorated for Christmas. Frank could be seen, pacing the room like a crazy man, while Rachel lay on the settee, her mind full of nightmares and her body shaking with fever. James had long since returned from his search of the streets, having shouted his sister's name, the shouts becoming louder and more desperate when Alice didn't appear. There was no sign of Kirsty, who was in her room trying not to imagine the unimaginable horror of Alice never coming back.

It was just before midnight when a police car drew up outside the house. By then, the small crowd had gone, although quite a few curtains moved when the car was heard to arrive.

Alice's body had been found floating in the canal. Rachel couldn't think what it was that made her come home that way. Perhaps, knowing it was Mummy's favourite walk, she'd thought they were more likely to meet.

'I'm sorry,' the oldest of the policeman said soberly. 'It looks as if she just slipped, but there'll be an inquest, naturally, to see if there's any sign of foul play.'

Frank's eyes were two black holes of horror. His face seemed to collapse, as if the bones were coming apart and Rachel realized how fragile he was inside. His wife and children had made him strong, but now that one of the children had been tragically taken away, he could no longer hold himself together. Rachel knew that, from now on, he would need her more than ever. Her blood seemed to turn to water when he turned to her and said in a voice she'd never heard before, 'It's your fault. If it weren't for you, Alice would still be alive. I'll never forgive you for this, Rachel. Never!'

Christmas was forgotten. No one left the house. Endless

cups of tea and coffee were drunk and Frank was never seen without a glass of something in his hand: whisky, rum, gin, bought to offer visitors over Christmas.

Rachel's flu persisted for a few days, but she did her best to rise above it. Her grief was fourfold. She had her own to deal with while at the same time her heart ached for James and Kirsty who were gutted. And Frank, poor Frank, who refused to let her comfort him the times he collapsed, sobbing in despair. 'Don't touch me,' he would roar when she tried to put her arm around him.

Inevitably, once the new millennium arrived, life acquired a semblance of normality. The children returned to school and Frank to work, although he continued to use his wife as a sort of mental punchbag to help him cope with his despair. He looked on the edge of a nervous breakdown, so Rachel just bowed her head and let him get on with it in the hope he would eventually come to his senses.

'It was all your fault,' he would insist contemptuously. 'Alice would still be alive if you'd used your brains and asked someone to collect her.'

'But you promised to be home from work early,' Rachel protested more than once, knowing how weak it sounded, knowing what his reply would be.

'I didn't promise. I said I might. You're a fool to have relied on that. The manager called a meeting and I had to stay.'

'I felt ill, Frank.'

'Nobody's that ill.' He turned away, not realizing that she was more necessary to him now than she'd ever been. Without Rachel, he would have had no one to blame, no one to vent his frustration on.

James and Kirsty were growing away from her. They also

blamed their mother, although hadn't said it openly. Whole days would pass and they'd hardly talk. In the main, Frank ignored her, but when he spoke, he made her feel very small and very stupid and told her she was letting herself go, which was true. She no longer bothered to have her hair set, didn't care what she wore, was putting on weight, although had no idea why because she ate very little. Perhaps it was the lack of exercise, of sitting in a chair for hours on end, thinking about Alice, torturing herself, wondering if she'd suffered and cried for her mummy as her head sank under the dirty water of the canal.

She didn't want to see the few friends she had left. Their eyes were full of blame, although they pretended to be sympathetic. She longed for new friends, people to talk to who didn't know about Alice, about how she'd died and why.

That summer, James left school and went to work for a firm of accountants in Liverpool – and Frank had an affair. A divorcee in her forties had moved into a house across the road. Her name was Bella and she was the very opposite of his wife, with her long brown hair and short skirts and dazzling, inviting smile. As soon as James and Kirsty were in bed, Frank would slink out of the house and not return for hours, not caring what Rachel thought. She didn't protest. She told herself he was getting things out of his system. One of these days, everything would return to normal – or as normal as they would ever be without Alice.

Another New Year and nothing had changed. Bella and Frank had parted, but his clothes still smelled of perfume and he often arrived home late from work, offering no excuse and refusing the meal she'd made him. He didn't care what Rachel thought. All he felt for his wife was contempt, and the confidence, the sense of her own worth that she had acquired over the years drained away, drop by drop, until she felt like a little girl again, the one who'd gone to infant school and found it agony to speak.

In February, Christopher died in his sleep as his father had done before him. When Rachel was born, he'd been twenty-seven years old and, as far as she knew, had led a happy, contented life in the Army and his beloved Cyprus. It was many years since she'd seen him, but they'd corresponded regularly and often spoken on the phone. She felt too dispirited to go to his funeral, too exhausted to weep, too disillusioned to pray for his kind soul.

She knew Christopher had left her everything in his Will, but was surprised by the amount of savings he'd accumulated. Added to the proceeds from the sale of his apartment and his share of the travel agency, it came to quite a hefty sum.

'I don't want anything to do with it,' Frank said churlishly when she told him. 'It's your money, you do with it what you like.'

'I'd like us to buy another house, get away from here.' Memories haunted her. She kept expecting Alice's curly head to pop round from the behind the settee, her favourite hiding place. There were nights when she could have sworn she could hear a childish voice shouting for a glass of water. She would never forget Alice for as long as she lived, but wanted to live in a place where her ghost wasn't around every corner, reminding her of her loss, where she could make new friends and start to feel normal again.

Frank looked ready to dismiss the idea, but Kirsty said

immediately, 'I'd love for us to move. I think it's a really cool idea.'

'What about school?' Frank growled.

'I'll be leaving in July. We might not even have moved by then.'

'We could live closer to Liverpool,' James suggested. 'It'd be more convenient for my job.'

'Yeah,' Kirsty agreed, 'and more convenient for clubs and stuff.'

Frank just shrugged and didn't speak. Rachel took this as a signal to proceed and contacted a number of estate agents. She was inundated with details of houses, although none were the sort she had in mind.

'What exactly *did* you have in mind?' Frank demanded irritably.

'I don't know,' Rachel said vaguely. 'All the ones we've seen so far look too *lived* in. People might have died there. There might be a horrid atmosphere. I want a house that's ours and ours alone.'

When a brochure arrived for Victoria Square, she knew immediately that one of the detached houses was exactly what she wanted. They were very similar to the one built where the cottage in Maghull had once stood: it had been called Three Farthings, she remembered. The properties hadn't been built yet: the brochure showed only drawings, skeletons of houses with empty rooms set around an oval of little dots that would be a lawn. The small estate was adjacent to a park and close to a lively shopping area in one of the nicest parts of Liverpool, only a short bus ride away from town.

Frank drove them to the site that weekend. The foundations had been dug, the coffee-coloured brick walls of the two detached houses were only a few feet high, the floors just stretches of smooth concrete.

James and Kirsty examined the plans and discussed which bedrooms they would have. For the first time since Alice had died, there was excitement in their voices. The move would do them good, Rachel thought gratefully. She even felt a tiny surge of excitement herself.

'What do you think, Frank?' she asked cautiously, expecting to have her head bitten off, but it was much worse than that.

'I like the fact it's got four bedrooms,' he said pleasantly. 'It means I won't have to sleep with my stupid wife any more.'

Rachel took a step backwards. She felt herself go icily cold as the meaning, the sheer nastiness of his words sank in. Frank pushed his hands in his pockets and went over to speak to the children. She looked at him, seeing for the first time how stout he had become, that his shoulders were no longer square, but round and heavy, and his hair had receded, exposing his red, heavily freckled scalp. Why hadn't she noticed before? It must have happened overnight. Perhaps it was because she loved him that she'd only seen the handsome man she'd married.

And did it mean she no longer loved him now that she could see him for the man he had become?

Rachel wasn't sure.

Tuesday

10 JULY 2001

Chapter 7

It was another brilliantly sunny day. Kirsty shouted, 'Tara, Mum. I'll see you when I see you,' and slammed the door. She didn't kiss her, as once she would have done. Rachel watched her walk across the oval of grass – everyone did it. In no time at all there would be bare patches criss-crossing it. Perhaps they should start a Residents' Association and suggest everyone use the path. She could have the first meeting in her house – she'd raise the matter at the barbecue.

With her long, slim legs and short skirt, Kirsty reminded her of a stork. She and James liked living in Victoria Square, so close to town compared with Lydiate. Today, she was starting a four-day course in scriptwriting. As soon as the holidays were over, she would begin to look for a job, but had no idea what she wanted to do.

The eldest of the Jordan boys had come out of his house, a pile of books under his arm, and Kirsty stopped and spoke to him. They started laughing and left the square together. Rachel felt envious. At nineteen, she wouldn't have had the nerve to approach a boy like that and was pleased her daughter had no such inhibitions.

'What was I doing then?' she asked herself. Looking after her mother, she remembered. Grace and Eileen were at Manchester University. More than thirty years later, they still wrote to each other, but the letters had become less frequent. Eileen was in America, having married a widower with three grown-up children and Grace was living alone, her own children married and living far away from Vancouver. In the last of her letters, she had talked about returning to Liverpool. 'There's not much left to keep me in Canada now.'

Rachel attacked the breakfast dishes and quickly made the beds. At midday, she and Kathleen Cartwright were going into town to have lunch. Kathleen wanted to do some shopping. She badly needed a new outfit and had suggested they eat first and shop later. Before then, Rachel wanted to make herself look nice, or rather, as nice as humanly possible.

'Ceiling,' Ernest murmured the very second he opened his eyes. 'Dressing table, hairbrush, mirror, duvet, slippers.' But what were the damn things he was wearing called? 'Pyjamas!' It took at least ten seconds for the word to come. A knot of worry formed in his brain. He was convinced his memory was going.

'Are you having a conversation with yourself, darling?' Anna enquired from the other bed. He detested having twin beds, but Anna slept better on her own, able to turn over at will and not feel guilty about disturbing him.

'I didn't realize you were awake, luv.'

'I've been awake for ages. I was thinking of getting up, bringing you tea for a change, but I seem to be stuck here. I can see it's a fine day outside.'

Ernest got out of bed, lifted her tiny frame into a sitting position and stacked the pillows behind her. 'I'll make us a cup of tea. Where's me . . .' He paused.

'Where is your what, darling?'

'Dressing gown,' Ernest gulped.

'You left it in the parlour last night. You said you felt too hot.'

'Ta, luv. Won't be a mo.'

'Take as long as you like, Ernie,' Anna said graciously.

After they'd eaten – all Anna could manage was a piece of toast – Ernie carried her into the bathroom where she insisted on washing herself. He helped her put on a pretty, shell pink frock. 'Tighter, tighter,' she urged when he buckled the belt. 'It usually goes in the last hole.'

'You won't be able to breathe, luv.'

'I'd sooner not breathe than have a fat waist.'

'Anna, Anna,' he groaned, 'vanity is a sin.'

'I've always been vain, Ernie. I would've thought you'd got used to it by now. I'd like to wear my gold sandals, please. They're under my bed.'

He fetched the sandals and put them on her feet, tenderly kissing each foot before placing it gently on to the carpet.

'I adore you, Ernie Burrows,' Anna said softly.

Ernie wasn't comfortable with words like 'adore'. 'And I love you, Anna Kosztolanyi.' They told each other that at least dozen times a day. 'Now,' he said in a business-like way, 'I've got a few telephone calls to make, then I'll give the windows a good clean.' He was a far more efficient and thorough housewife than Anna had ever been.

Half an hour later, he was giving the inside of the parlour windows a final polish while enjoying the heat of the morning sun – Anna was watching one of them daft chat shows hosted by a dead smarmy geezer with a permanent suntan dealing with topics like 'I slept with my husband's granddad', or 'I killed my sister's cat' –

when he said in an awed voice, 'Cor! There's a roller just driven in.'

'What's a roller?' Anna enquired.

'A Rolls-Royce, it's silver.'

'Turn the chair around, Ernie,' she said eagerly, 'so I can see.'

'You need one of them swivel chairs, luv, one that never stops turning. You could watch telly and look through the window at the same time.'

She ignored him. 'The driver looks most unpleasant. Look at the way he's scowling! And what a perfectly frightful suit. I can't stand chalk stripes. He's either a member of the Mafia or a bookie. I hope he's not coming to see you, Ernie.'

'He's hammering on the door of number one.'

'That's where that pretty Sarah girl and her children live. I wonder what he wants?'

'Alex!' Sarah said weakly when she opened the door.

'Sarah!' he sneered. He pushed the door, throwing her against the wall, and stormed into the house. 'Where're my children?'

She ran after him, shouting, 'They're *my* children too, Alex.'

He turned, lashing out with his fist and catching her on the side of her face. 'You're not fit to be a mother. I want my kids. I'm taking them abroad and you'll never see them again.'

'I won't let you, Alex.' She pulled his arm, but he viciously jerked his elbow back into her ribs. Sarah screamed and doubled up in agony. He was so big and strong and possessed with such brutal rage that she was no match for him. She had known he'd want the children, but hadn't expected him to take them by force.

How had he found her so quickly? She'd hoped to have consulted her solicitor and acquired one of those injunction things before he turned up.

Tiffany came in the back door carrying Oliver and wearing only a pair of frilly pants. 'Did you shout for me, Mummy? Daddy!' she said sternly when she saw her father. 'Leave Mummy alone and go away.'

'Put your clothes on,' Alex commanded. 'It's obvious your mother isn't capable of dressing you.'

'I'm playing with water. Nanny always made me wear my swimming costume when I played with water, but Mummy doesn't know where it is. She's going to buy me a new one. Jack won't play with water, because it gets his blanket wet. Oliver quite likes getting wet, don't you, darling?' Tiffany kissed Oliver and stamped her bare foot. 'Daddy,' she said haughtily, 'didn't I tell you to go away?'

'And I told you to get fucking dressed.'

'Only bad men swear. Nanny said.'

Alex picked up his daughter, placed her none too gently at the foot of the stairs, and gave her a push. 'Put your clothes on, Tiffany,' he said threateningly, 'or else I'll punch your mother so hard it'll send her to kingdom come.'

Tiffany rolled her eyes and marched upstairs, slapping her feet unwillingly on each step. She looked back at Sarah when she reached the top, her blue eyes full of fear. Sarah gave her a little nod that didn't mean anything.

By now, Alex was in the little back garden where a fully-dressed Jack was holding his blanket with one hand and trying to catch a butterfly with the other – he'd acquired an obsession with butterflies and wanted one as a pet. 'Where Jason?' he asked when he saw his father.

'In a place called Saudi Arabia, son,' Alex said pleasantly. 'Somehow or other, I'm not quite sure how it happened, but he managed to lose his passport. Christ knows when the poor chap will get away – if ever,' he finished with a chuckle.

'You bastard,' Sarah cried. 'You did that deliberately.'

'Well, I certainly didn't do it accidentally, my dear.' He smiled a smile that sent shivers of ice up and down her spine. 'Now, Sarah, when Tiffany comes down, I intend to take my children home. If you try making a scene, all I have to do is pick up the phone and there'll be people along to help me within minutes.' He smiled again. 'Either that, or I'll knock you senseless.'

'How did you find out where we lived?' She only asked in order to stall him in the hope that help would arrive, though she couldn't imagine anything or anyone stopping Alex from doing whatever he wanted while he was in his present mood.

'That van you hired, it had the name of the firm on the side, didn't it? One of the stable lads made a note of it. I called and asked where the driver had taken you. That was stupid of you, Sarah, but I've always known you were dead from the neck up.'

'Then why on earth did you marry me?' she cried. 'Daddy would have a fit if he were alive and knew how horrid you'd turned out to be.'

He burst out laughing, showing two rows of yellow teeth and looking like a wild animal about to devour a tiny, defenceless baby. 'Daddy wouldn't have given a damn. What you've never realized, Sarah, is that I *bought* you off your father. I put down a deposit when we got engaged and paid the balance in full on the day of the wedding. It was all my idea and Robin jumped at the chance. Anything, even selling his precious daughter, was better than going bankrupt.'

'That can't be true! Daddy would never have done such a thing.' But Sarah remembered how eager he'd been for her to marry Alex and to do it quickly. 'There's no point in hanging around,' he'd said. He'd been in a terrible pickle at the time, having lost everything on some investment in Spain. Had Mummy known what he'd done? She'd done her best to put Sarah off Alex, but Sarah had taken no notice.

'Why did you want to marry me?' she asked in a defeated voice.

Alex glanced at Jack. 'I wanted kids,' he said bluntly. 'That's why Midge divorced me, so I could have kids.'

'And you just used me! Alex, how could you possibly be so cruel?' she said, appalled.

He shrugged. 'It wasn't like that. I just didn't realize you'd turn out to be such a brainless bitch. It came to the pitch where I couldn't stand us being in the same room together. All I wanted was to be rid of you.'

'And where does Midge come into this?'

'Midge has never been out of it. She'd have still been there even if you and me had got on like a house on fire. She just loves them kids and you'd've got used to her eventually. Now she can have them all to herself.'

Would Daddy have still been so agreeable to her getting married had he known Alex intended hanging on to his first wife when he took a second? Sarah daren't think what the answer would be. She wanted to run upstairs, throw herself on the bed, and have a good cry, but now wasn't the time.

'Where's Alastair?' Alex demanded. He yanked Jack by his arm towards the back door. Startled, the little boy dropped his blanket and began to scream.

'Asleep in the front room.'

'Blanket!' Jack yelled, struggling to reach it.

'You can forget about your bloody blanket, son. It's about time you learned to live without it.' He shoved Sarah into the house. 'Tiffany!' he yelled. 'Are you dressed yet?'

A haughty Tiffany was coming downstairs wearing the nightdress and picture hat she'd found in Victoria's. She looked for all the world like a miniature Scarlett O'Hara. Alex cursed, but didn't comment.

He went into the front room and scooped up Alastair in one arm. 'Tiffany, hold Jack's hand,' he commanded. '*Hold your brother's fucking hand,*' he yelled when the girl held back, 'else I'll chuck your bloody mother through the window.' He nodded at Sarah. 'Open the front door.'

'No.'

'Tiffany, you open the door. You know what'll happen to your mother if you don't.'

Tiffany visibly suppressed a sob as she reached for the latch and turned it. Alex stepped outside, a still sleeping Alastair in one arm, a distraught Jack demanding his blanket hanging on to the other, and Tiffany hanging on to Jack.

'*No!*' Sarah screamed, lunging at her husband. 'You're not taking my children away.'

'Well, well, well, what's going on here?' said a voice and Alex came face to face with the tall figure of Ernest Burrows, who was standing outside, arms folded, legs apart, looking as if nothing on earth would move him.

'Fuck off!' Alex spat.

'I heard noises. What's happening?' A curious Marie Jordan emerged from the house next door.

Rachel Williams came hurrying out of Three Farthings. 'Is everything all right? I could hear Jack screaming. Oh, the poor dear, he's lost his blanket.'

'Get out the way, the lot of you,' Alex snarled.

'If you're not careful, you'll drop that baby,' Rachel warned. Alastair had woken and begun to cry.

'Look,' Alex said reasonably. 'These are my kids. If I don't take them now, I'll only take them another time.'

'That's funny,' Ernest said reasonably. 'I thought they were Sarah's.'

'So did I,' agreed Rachel.

'And so did I,' Marie echoed.

'They are, they are,' Sarah cried.

'In that case,' Ernest said to Alex, 'I don't think I can let you take them.'

'Who the hell d'you think you are?' demanded an incensed Alex.

'A concerned citizen,' replied Ernest gravely. 'Someone who doesn't approve of men who hit their wives. I saw the way you pushed your way in and thumped her. By the way, me own wife's rung the police. They should be along any minute – in fact, that'll be them now.'

The wail of a police siren could be heard in the distance. Everyone stood very still as it got closer and closer, then Rachel leaped forward and snatched Alastair from his father's arms, Tiffany released Jack's hand, Sarah pulled him away, and Alex was left, childless, a look of panic on his face as the siren got louder. He jumped into the Rolls – no one tried to prevent him – and was backing out of the square when the police car drove in, stopping with a shriek of brakes and blocking his way.

After everyone had given statements and the police had taken Alex away, they gathered in the Jordans' house for a cup of tea, including a stunned Victoria, who had missed all the drama and had only been alerted by the siren, and a jubilant Anna who had been making her slow way, unnoticed, across to the scene of Ernie's triumph – everyone agreed it was Ernie who was the hero of the hour.

'You were wonderful, darling,' Anna cooed, kissing him.

An embarrassed Ernest stayed only a few minutes and returned to cleaning the windows, leaving the women and children to themselves.

'He's always been exceptionally brave,' Anna told the assembled company.

'After today, your husband won't try to take the children away again,' Rachel assured Sarah.

Sarah shuddered. She was still shaking and her ribs were hurting badly. 'I still don't trust him. He said he was going to take them abroad.'

'Don't want to go abroad with Daddy,' Tiffany announced.

'I don't blame you, darling,' Anna said sympathetically. 'Such an awful person, terribly uncouth. I've always said, never trust a man who wears chalk-striped suits.'

'I used to admire them.' Sarah sniffed. 'They're Italian and cost the earth. He's got dozens more at home.'

'How on earth did a man like that acquire a hyphenated name?' Marie enquired.

'He used to be Alex James,' Sarah explained. 'The "Rees" was added when he started to make money.'

'It should be "Creep",' Victoria said disgustedly. 'Alex Creep-James.'

At that, everyone started to laugh. They laughed till

they cried, although it wasn't remotely funny, but it helped release the tension.

'I'm amazed you didn't hear anything,' Rachel said over lunch with Kathleen. Earlier, Anna had recommended a very nice, very regal restaurant in Bold Street that had once been the Atheneum Club. 'The police siren was very loud.'

Kathleen turned faintly pink. 'We heard the siren, but we were busy with something and didn't realize it was actually in the square.'

'It was like a film.' Rachel still felt imbued with the excitement of the morning that had ended with all the women in Marie Jordan's kitchen. She was friends again with Sarah, which was a relief. 'Ernie Burrows was Clint Eastwood and Sarah's husband was the villain. It ended with good triumphing over evil.'

'As Clint Eastwood's films always do. Steve will be cross when I tell him. He should have been outside, supporting Ernie – not that it sounds as if he needed it.'

'No, he was marvellous. Someone came later and took the Rolls away. I wonder,' Rachel said thoughtfully, 'why on earth Sarah married such a revolting individual?'

'Perhaps he wasn't revolting when she married him, or at least was pretending not to be.'

Rachel sighed. 'I don't suppose anyone really knows what the person they marry will be like until they're actually married to them.'

'That's an argument for living together,' Kathleen said thoughtfully. 'So many people do it nowadays. Would you like afters, Rachel?'

'No thank you. The lasagne was lovely, but very filling, and I really must lose weight. It's not so much the amount I eat, but the lack of exercise.'

'Shall we have another glass of wine? There's enough left in the bottle. I'll order coffee in a minute.'

'It's awfully nice of you to treat me. It'll be my turn next time.'

'I'm already looking forward to it,' Kathleen twinkled. 'I wish I'd known what was going on this morning. It would have been an opportunity to meet everyone. The only people in the square I've spoken to are Anna and Ernie Burrows and you.'

'You and Steve seem to keep a very low profile.'

Kathleen went pink again. 'We're still sorting out the house, wondering where to put things. Can we have two coffees, please,' she said when the waitress came to remove their plates. 'What sort would you like, Rachel?'

'A cappuccino.'

'And I'll have a latte. Now,' she said when the waitress had gone, 'as soon as we've finished, I'd like to go to George Henry Lee's and look at clothes.'

'I wouldn't mind buying something new,' Rachel remarked. There was still plenty of Christopher's money left. 'About what you said earlier, would you like me to invite everyone round to our house in the morning so you can meet them?'

'That's a wonderful idea. I'd love it.'

Kathleen bought a long, flowing black skirt patterned with red cabbage roses and a red cotton top to match. Rachel, rooting through rows of dresses, was beginning to feel like a normal person for a change.

'This would suit you,' Kathleen pulled out a dark green silky dress that was long and straight with splits in the side. 'It's very slimming. It would look great with strappy sandals.'

'Except I haven't got any.'

'Well, buy some. Have you noticed Anna Burrows often wears gold sandals? They look terribly exotic and smart. I wouldn't mind a pair myself.'

'I'd better try the dress on first, then we'll look at sandals.' She was actually enjoying herself. Perhaps she could buy gold earrings too, although it was so long since she'd worn them, the holes could well have closed up.

Kathleen waited outside while Rachel went into a cubicle to try on the dress. She removed the rather tired cotton thing she was wearing, slipped the new one over her head, and looked at the result in the mirror. Kathleen was right, it was very slimming and would suit being worn with gold sandals. She stared critically at her reflection. The problem was that her hair badly let her down. She recalled that in the days when she'd cared about her appearance she'd used to have it cut very short and casual and it hadn't looked so flat. There might be time to have it cut that afternoon.

She was about to remove the dress when she became conscious of voices in the next cubicle.

'What do you think, pet, the pink one or the blue one?'

'I like the pink one best, Mummy,' a childish voice replied.

'I knew you'd say that, Emma. You've got a thing about pink.'

'You look beautiful in both, Mummy. You look beautiful in everything.'

Ten minutes later, when Kathleen peeked around the curtain to ask why Rachel was taking such a long time to make up her mind, she found her sitting on a stool, weeping uncontrollably. 'My little girl is dead,' she sobbed. 'I don't care about dresses. It doesn't matter what I look like any more. It doesn't matter about anything.'

★

It was almost six o'clock when Kathleen arrived home. 'That was a long lunch,' Steve complained sulkily.

'I'm sorry, darling, have you been feeling neglected?' She kissed him. 'Actually, I was back by four. I've been in Rachel's house. She's in a terrible state, poor thing, so mixed up. Her little girl died eighteen months ago and she still hasn't got over it – not that anyone ever gets over losing a child – but she hasn't learned to live with it, put it that way. I got the impression her husband isn't very sympathetic and her other children aren't much help. I think that's why she's having this barbecue, in order to make friends. Shall we go out for a meal? I helped Rachel with dinner, so I've had enough of cooking.' She became aware that Steve was still looking sulky. 'What's the matter?' she asked.

'I didn't know you made a habit of picking up stray dogs,' he said coldly. 'If you're so concerned about this woman, why can't you understand the way I feel about Jean?'

Wordlessly, Kathleen went into the bedroom, put her new skirt and top on a hanger, and hung them in the wardrobe. Steve watched from the door. 'I bought these today,' she said.

'Good for you.' He folded his arms. 'I just asked you a question.'

'Which I'm not prepared to answer because it's so stupid,' she said scathingly. 'If you can't see the difference between a woman whose five-year-old daughter drowned and your whinging bitch of a wife, then I feel sorry for you.' She pushed past him. 'And kindly don't *ever* again refer to Rachel as a stray dog, or I'll walk out of this house and never come back.'

She was sitting in the kitchen with a cup of tea and a cigarette, when Steve appeared, looking contrite.

'I'm sorry. It was a daft thing to say. I suppose I just wanted you to understand how I feel.' He sat at the table and looked at her beseechingly. 'I've known Jean all me life. We lived in the same street. She were in the class after me at school, and only sixteen when we first went out together. Three years later, we got married. Until I met you, she's the only woman I ever loved. I suppose you could say she's become part of me, and now that part's hurting and it makes me feel as guilty as hell.'

'Would you feel any less guilty if you went to see her?'

'I dunno,' he sighed.

'Don't you think she'll only cry even more when you leave a second time?'

'I suppose.' He sighed again.

'And if you decided to stay,' Kathleen said levelly, although she seriously wanted to scream, 'she'll be all lovey dovey for a few weeks, then the fact you walked out, had an affair, will be added to your list of crimes, and your life will be even worse than it was before.'

'I wouldn't dream of staying.' He looked hurt at the very idea.

'Then I don't see the point of you going in the first place. Actually,' she angrily stubbed out the cigarette, 'I don't know why we're having this crazy conversation. We came away together and all you can think of is the bloody wife you left behind — although she's not really left behind, is she, Steve? You brought her with you. She's in your head and in your heart. I don't think there's room for another woman in your life, only Jean.'

Gareth had only been home a few minutes and was

nursing a delighted Tabitha, who was furiously licking his face, when his mobile rang. It was Debbie.

'I've been waiting all day for you to call,' she said. 'I thought you might want to apologize.'

'For what?'

'For the things you said last night, for opening my letters.'

'Are you going to apologize for secretly acquiring a credit card and spending so much on it?' he asked frostily.

'Only if you apologize first.'

'I've no intention of apologizing for anything.'

'In that case, I'm not coming home. I'm going to stay the night at my mum's again.'

'Suits me, Deb,' he said laconically and rang off. He had a wash, changed his T-shirt for a fresh one, combed his hair, and was on his way to the old house on the corner when he remembered Tabitha's ecstatic welcome. The poor little thing must feel lonely. He returned for the kitten and took him to Victoria's.

'Oh, hello,' Victoria said, beaming at him. 'I've got company: Danny and Tiffany are upstairs. Danny's playing on the computer and Tiffany's watching. She's only four, but madly in love with him. Come in, I was just about to make meself a cheese omelette. D'you fancy one? I've loads of eggs.'

Gareth realized he was starving. He'd been so anxious to see her it hadn't crossed his mind to have something to eat before he left. 'I'd love a cheese omelette. I hope you don't mind, but I've brought someone with me. This is Tabitha. She's a he, despite the name.'

'Hello, Tabitha. Oh, aren't you gorgeous?' Victoria reached for the kitten and cuddled him to her chest. 'We used to have a cat, his name was Blizzard – please don't ask why. He was nearly twenty when he died and Gran was so upset, she vowed never to have another. I'm glad in a way. I couldn't have gone to America and left a cat behind.'

They went into the kitchen. Victoria explained she'd put the frying pan in one of the plastic bags to be given away and it had taken ages to find it again. 'I spent most of today cleaning and polishing. I never realized there were so many cobwebs on the ceilings – I had to unearth the feather duster too.'

'There's not much left to do now, is there?'

Victoria shrugged and wrinkled her nose. 'The whole place could do with decorating from top to bottom. The wallpaper's older than I am. I've had to leave the pictures up because the wall's a completely different colour behind them.'

'I was only thinking last night how much I liked your pictures,' Gareth remarked. 'All we have are modern prints in stainless steel frames. They're dead uninspiring to look at.'

'Then why on earth did you buy them?'

'Debbie did. She thought they went with the house.'

'You should have chosen them together. I thought that's what married couples did.'

Gareth recalled that, in fact, this was roughly what had happened; he just hadn't made a squeak of protest when Debbie had picked the miserable daubs that pretended to be paintings. Either he was too easygoing by a mile, or a craven coward, the sort of man who was perfectly content to let his wife wear the trousers. He changed the subject, not wanting Victoria to know he'd had as much say about what went into Hamilton Lodge as Tabitha. 'I've been looking forward to this,' he said impulsively.

'What, the omelette?'

'No . . .' There was a long pause. 'Seeing you again,' he said softly.

Victoria put Tabitha on the floor. She turned away and began to break eggs into a bowl. 'Do you want two eggs or three?'

'Three, please.'

She broke another egg and whisked them madly with a fork. 'I was hoping you'd come tonight.' Her voice was very low and he could only just make out the words.

'I like you very much,' Gareth said even more softly than before.

'And I like you,' Victoria whispered.

'I wish you weren't going away.'

'So do I, but it's a good thing that I am, under the circumstances.'

'Victoria?'

'Yes, Gareth?' She turned towards him, smiling, but her eyes were bright with unshed tears.

'Come here.' He put his hands on her shoulders and was about to kiss her smiling lips when an unearthly scream came from upstairs.

'A kitten! I didn't know you had a kitten, Victoria. Mummy's going to buy us a kitten, and a puppy too.' Tiffany came scrambling downstairs, Tabitha in her arms. 'Is it a boy cat or a girl?'

'It's a boy,' Gareth told her. 'His name's Tabitha and he belongs to me.'

'He jumped on my knee.' Tiffany looked immensely flattered.

'He must have liked you straight away.'

'Can I take him home to show Mummy?'

'I don't think that's such a good idea. He wriggles like mad when he wants to get down and he might escape and not know where to go – he's a bit too young yet to know which house he lives in.'

'Then can't *you* bring him to show Mummy?' Tiffany persisted.

'But Victoria's just about to make us something to eat.'

'The omelettes can wait a few minutes,' Victoria said. They looked at each other, the spell between them broken.

'Oh, all right then,' Gareth said reluctantly. 'Come on, Tabitha. You're very popular tonight.'

At the Rees-Jameses, Tabitha was duly admired and petted. The delectable Sarah showed him to the baby, who chuckled and waved his arms in delight, and the little boy, Jack, demanded that they keep him.

'We'll get one of our own soon,' Sarah promised. 'You must think of a name for our kitten, Jack.'

'Jason,' Jack said promptly.

Gareth was a bit dismayed when Tiffany returned with him to Victoria's. 'Isn't it time you went to bed,' he said sternly when they were outside. Tabitha had fallen asleep against his neck.

'But I left Oliver behind, he'll be terribly upset, and I haven't said goodnight to Danny,' she said as she trotted along beside him. 'I'm going to marry Danny when I grow up. I was going to marry Oliver, but I've changed my mind. He can be me and Danny's little boy instead.'

'I find that very confusing,' Gareth admitted.

'I don't know what confusing means.'

They went through the back door. In the kitchen, Victoria was grating cheese. There was a bottle of red wine and two glasses on the table, a bowl of mixed salad, and a plate of bread and butter.

Tiffany regarded the miniature feast with interest. 'If

you're Victoria's husband,' she said to Gareth, 'why do you live in another house?'

'But I'm not Victoria's husband.'

'Then why is she making your dinner?'

'It doesn't automatically follow that if you share a meal with someone that you're married to them.'

'I don't know what that big word means,' Tiffany said gravely.

Gareth mouthed 'help' at Victoria and she giggled. 'I think you'd better say goodnight to Danny and go home, Tiff. You've struck Gareth speechless.'

'I didn't touch him,' Tiffany protested.

'Jaysus, Mary and Joseph,' Gareth groaned, letting his head drop on to the table with a thud, waking Tabitha who scuttled upstairs, just as Danny Jordan came marching down.

'Mam'll have the tea ready by now,' he announced. 'I'd better be going.' He was a heavily freckled boy with flaming red hair and looked about fifteen.

Victoria introduced them. 'Danny, this is Gareth. He's a whiz on computers, miles better than I am.'

The two shook hands. Danny said he'd brought Oliver down with him and would take Tiffany home. The little girl took his hand and regarded him adoringly.

'Things are getting clearer,' Gareth said after the pair had gone.

'What do you mean?'

'Oliver's a teddy bear. I thought he was a live human being.'

Victoria grinned. 'Can I make the omelettes now?'

'Unless there are more people likely to come down-stairs, why not?'

'Ma,' Danny said excitedly when he went into number

two, 'Victoria said I can have her computer when she leaves on Sunday.'

'How much does she want for it, son?'

'Nothing. She said I can have it for nothing. Our Patrick can have our old one for himself.'

Patrick frowned. 'But that's not fair.'

'I don't see why,' Danny said reasonably. 'You've only met Victoria the once and then you were rude to her. I've been there every day and she's my friend.'

'It's a waste of time arguing about it,' Marie pointed out. 'There's only room for one computer in the bedroom. The old one'll have to go.'

'*That's* not fair!' Danny argued. 'Why should our Patrick use the new one when it's mine?'

'Because Patrick plays on the computer just as much as you and he can't be denied the use of the only one we have. What do you think, Liam?'

Liam had been listening to the argument while half-watching the television news. 'I think your mammy's right. Tomorrow, perhaps Patrick could go and thank Victoria for such an expensive gift. Take her something, a little bunch of flowers, for instance. I'm sure she'll be very pleased.'

Patrick looked at Marie. He was a much shyer, far more withdrawn lad than his brother. 'Do I have to, Ma?'

'It would be a nice gesture, son.'

'I would call it a condition, not a gesture,' Liam said evenly, 'if you want to use the computer that Victoria is giving to Danny.'

It was rare that either of her lads lost their tempers, Marie was shocked to the core when Patrick's face bulged with anger and went very red. 'Who the shit do you think you are, laying down conditions?' he demanded thickly. 'You're not me da.'

'Don't swear, son,' she said weakly. 'And don't speak to Liam in that way.'

'I'll speak to Liam in whatever way I like,' Patrick said contemptuously. 'He's nothing to do with me. He's in no position to talk to us about conditions.'

Marie noticed Danny edge closer to his brother. They might fight between themselves, but they always stuck together if the situation called for it. 'I wouldn't want to keep the computer to meself, not really,' Danny said. He looked quite shaken by the argument. 'Victoria surely meant it to be for Patrick too. I'm sorry about what I said before, Paddy.' He nudged Patrick's shoulder with his own and Patrick managed to raise a half-smile.

'Ah, well, so that's settled,' Liam said easily. 'I think I'll go upstairs and have a wee read where it's quiet.'

'Are you all right now, Patrick?' Marie asked after Liam had gone and the ensuing silence seemed to go on for far too long.

'I'm OK.' He didn't look it. His face was still red and he was trembling with anger. 'Can we go on the Internet d'you think, Ma? Me and Danny could log on to all sorts of interesting sites — it'd help with our homework. Someone has to come and fix it to the phone line.'

Danny's eyes lit up. 'Crazee! Oh, Ma, that would be great.'

'If you want, son.' Marie was surprised, not so much by the request, but that Patrick should make it now when he was so wired up and angry over Liam.

'I've got all the stuff about it in our room. Danny, will you go and fetch it, please? It's on the bookcase or the desk, I'm not sure which. I think it might be in a brown envelope.'

'Sure thing.' Danny sped eagerly upstairs.

'I'll be having a word with Liam,' Marie promised when she and Patrick were left alone. 'I don't suppose he realises you're almost a man. He . . .'

Before she could continue, Patrick broke in. 'I think you could do with having more than a word, Ma. I think you could do with bolting your bedroom door an'all.'

Marie felt a blush spread from the roots of her hair down to the soles of her feet. 'I don't know what you mean, son,' she gasped.

'I think you do, Mam. I heard you with the priest last night. Our dad's hardly been in his grave a year. If I were you, I'd be desperately ashamed.' He looked at her sadly, his face no longer red, his eyes accusing.

'We didn't do anything, son, I told him to go away.'

'Then you took a long enough time telling him: a good ten or fifteen minutes by my reckoning.'

'I don't know what got into me,' Marie breathed, which was the God's honest truth. 'I do feel ashamed for letting him go as far as he did. I've felt so ever since. Everyone thinks he's me husband, yet he's a priest.' The words tied themselves in knots in her throat. For months now, she hadn't known if she were coming or going, her head a muddle of mad thoughts that she couldn't make sense of, yet refused to go away.

Patrick was looking at her as if indeed she was completely mad. 'When I was a girl,' she continued, 'there was this priest, Father Murphy. He was only young and as handsome as a film star. All the girls were madly in love with him – not just the girls, but the married women too. If he'd wanted, all he'd have had to do was snap his fingers and he could have had any one of us. He made us go weak at the knees. There's nothing in this world we wouldn't have done for him.'

'Because he was a man or because he was a priest?' Patrick asked.

'A priest.' Marie hung her head. It didn't seem right to be talking to her son in this way. Upstairs, Danny could be heard searching the room for the Internet stuff that she suspected wasn't there. Patrick had just used it as an excuse to get him out the way.

'Priests are only flesh and blood like other men,' Patrick stated. 'It's daft to put them on pedestals, invest them with some sort of magic and look up to them as if they were God Himself, vastly superior to everyone else. I'm surprised at you, Ma. This is the twenty-first century, you're not a teenager, and I'd have thought you'd have grown out of it by now.'

'I know I should have,' Marie conceded, shamefaced. 'I won't do it again, lad, I promise.' She felt as if a tremendous load had been taken off her mind. Like a silly little schoolgirl, she'd been blinded by the fact that Liam was a holy man and it had taken her seventeen-year-old son to make her see the light. 'Your daddy'll never be dead while you're alive, Patrick. He was full of common sense, just like you.'

'Tonight,' Patrick said authoritatively, 'you're to bolt your door, just in case Liam has another try.'

'The door doesn't have a bolt.'

'I know. I bought one this morning. I'll put it on in a minute.'

The conversation had been stilted all night. They were both inhibited by what had happened before – had *nearly* happened before – that they didn't feel easy with each other any more.

It was early when Gareth announced it was time he

went home. 'I haven't done anything on me footy site for days.'

'Don't forget to take Tabitha with you,' Victoria reminded him.

'Where is he?'

'On my bed, asleep.'

'I'll fetch him.'

'It's the room on the left at the top of the stairs.'

Her room had windows at each end. The big double bed with ornate wooden boards at the top and bottom, sat beneath the window overlooking the square. There was an old-fashioned wardrobe and a chest of drawers to match, and a piece of furniture that was a cupboard with drawers underneath. His mother had one and he tried to remember what it was called – a tallboy, that was it. He wasn't sure if you could still get them nowadays. The floorboards were badly in need of a fresh coat of varnish and there was a rag rug beside the bed.

If there'd been anything on top of the dressing table and tallboy then it had been removed and the room looked very bare apart from one corner where, in stark contrast to all this antiquity, a computer stood on a metal desk that was heaped with books and files and paper. More papers had spilled on to the floor.

This was where Victoria slept. Gareth went over to the bed – Tabitha was asleep in the centre of the rose-sprigged duvet. He knelt on the floor. 'Time to go home, young man,' he said, but Tabitha didn't hear and slept on. He looked so vulnerable, Gareth thought, so tiny and isolated in the big stretch of flowered cotton, completely oblivious to the dangers that existed in the world outside.

Just like Victoria. All her relatives had died or gone

missing like her father. She had no one, yet she faced life with such cheerfulness and courage and innocence that it made him want to weep. In a few days, she was about to fly to a strange country where she didn't know a single soul. A lump formed in his throat when he thought of all the terrible things that could happen to her in New York. He bent his head and laid it on the pillow where Victoria's lay at night when she was asleep. 'Please don't go, darling,' he whispered. 'Stay here with me.'

'I'm afraid that's not possible, Gareth,' Victoria said softly from the door. She came and sat on the bed. 'I thought you'd fallen asleep.'

'I was just thinking about how much I loved you.'

'Don't think it. Don't say it. Don't let it enter your head again.' She looked terribly sad and terribly wise.

'I can't help it,' Gareth groaned. He got to his feet, sat beside her, and took her in his arms.

Victoria sighed and lifted her face to his. This is very wrong. If I wasn't going away, I wouldn't be doing it.'

'Say you love me, Victoria.'

'I love you,' Victoria said, just as Gareth's mobile rang.

He groaned again, pulled it out of his pocket, and was about to switch it off when he saw Debbie's name on the screen, but Victoria stopped him. 'Answer it. It might be important.'

'Gareth,' Debbie said in a frightened voice. 'Where are you?'

'At a mate's house.' He did his best to sound considerate because she really did sound upset. 'What's the matter?'

'I've just come home and there's no sign of Tabitha. I've looked everywhere, but he's disappeared. I thought you'd be here. I came back especially.'

'I brought Tabitha with me. Don't worry. I'll be home in a minute.' He rang off and made a face at Victoria. 'I've got to go. Can I see you tomorrow?'

'I should say no,' she shrugged helplessly, 'but I can't.'

When he entered Hamilton Lodge, Debbie flew into his arms. 'I'm sorry,' she cried tearfully, 'sorry for everything. I couldn't find Tabitha and I wanted to die when I saw you weren't here either. Oh, Gareth! It was horrible.'

Gareth patted her back and murmured, 'There, there,' in a kindly way, although all he could feel was irritation that the wife whom, until recently, he'd loved to bits, had interrupted him when he was about to make love to Victoria. He felt even more irritated when he noticed the two Per Una carrier bags on the floor. Debbie had been shopping again.

'What's the house like?' Michael asked.

'Very small, very modern, rather nondescript,' Kathleen replied. 'You'd hate it. The neighbours are nice, the ones I've met, that is.'

'Well, at least it'll be warm in winter. This place is like a fridge.'

'We used to spend most of our time in the kitchen, didn't we? I miss that kitchen, not that I've done much cooking so far.'

'Do you miss *me*, Kath?'

Kathleen could imagine the sweet smile on her husband's face as he spoke, the way his lips curled around the words in a way she'd always found very appealing. She reached for an ashtray and put it beside her on the floor. Steve was asleep, it was nearly midnight, and she'd

got up and phoned Michael because she needed someone to talk to and he was the only one she could confide
in.

'I think I must do. I miss the certainty of you. Steve
said today that his wife had become part of him, so I
suppose you've become part of me – and me of you.'

'That's a rather odd thing for Steve to say,' Michael
remarked drily. 'Funny conversations you two are
having.'

'He feels guilty for leaving her. Apparently, she's not
stopped crying since he went.' For the very first time, she
wondered if she would have given Steve a second glance
if Michael had been able to make love to her like a
normal man. 'I'm terribly mixed up,' she told him.

'You're not the only one. By the way, our son rang
this evening. He wants his mum and dad to come to
Denmark in September for the weekend.'

'Did you tell him about us?'

'No, I thought you could do that, Kath. You can
explain it better than me. Will we go together, or is that
just not on?'

'Oh, Lord, Michael, I've no idea.' She doubted if
Steve would take lightly to her going away with her
husband when she was making such a fuss about him
seeing his supposedly sick wife.

Michael was speaking again, but she had to break in.
'I'm sorry, I have to go.' She put the receiver down with
a crash. Steve had come into the room. If he'd noticed
she'd been on the phone, he didn't say, or perhaps didn't
care. He just grabbed her hands, pulled her feet, and
carried her into the bedroom.

'I'm going to make love to you all night long,' he said
in a voice husky with passion. His big hands caressed her

breasts and almost met around her waist when he squeezed it. She shuddered with ecstasy and just lay there while he touched every part of her then did the same with his lips, bringing her body to the very peak of trembling delight until everything exploded and she tumbled back to earth with a rapturous cry.

Then she did the same to him.

The Burrows had been watching a video. Anna liked musicals best, or anything that made her laugh or cry. Tonight they'd seen *Once Upon a Time in America*, a film so hauntingly beautiful that even the cynical Ernest had felt moved. Almost four hours long, it was past midnight when he realized the curtains hadn't been drawn.

'The lights are on in the empty bungalow,' he announced. 'There's a woman putting up the curtains.'

Anna immediately demanded he turn her chair around so she could see. 'She looks quite young. Go over there, Ernie,' she said imperiously, 'introduce yourself and ask if she'd like a cup of tea. You never know, the gas and electricity mightn't be turned on yet.'

'There aren't many things I wouldn't do for you, luv, but that's one of 'em. I've no intention of introducing meself to anyone at half past twelve in the morning. If she wants a drink, she'll have brought a flask.' He drew their own curtains quickly before the woman noticed them staring.

'Sometimes, Ernie,' Anna complained, 'you can be not very nice. The poor woman might not have anywhere to sleep. I haven't seen a furniture van arrive.'

'Are you suggesting I go and offer her a bed for the night?' Ernie smiled and raised his bushy white eyebrows. 'I might end up in jail like that Rees-James geezer. "Eighty-one-year-old man accused of propositioning woman young enough to be his daughter." Might even be granddaughter.'

'Talking about that Rees-James creature, you were awfully brave this morning, Ernie.'

Ernest wriggled uncomfortably. 'You said that before, luv, at least half a dozen times.' Sarah Rees-James had come over in the afternoon with the children to thank him profusely. He'd had to kiss the little girl's teddy bear and Anna had made a show of herself the way she drooled over the baby. He'd been thankful to see the back of them.

'Made quite a few quid today on the horses,' he said.

'Did you, darling?'

'Thought we could go out tomorrow and buy one of them computers you're after.'

'Oh, Ernie,' Anna cried. 'You are an absolutely perfect husband.'

He grinned. 'Your wish is my command.'

'But will we know what sort to buy, darling?'

'I wondered if we could take Victoria with us? She's not working at the moment. She'll advise us and we can treat her to a meal.'

Anna clapped her hands. 'I'm already looking forward to it.'

So was Ernie. It would make a pleasant change to their rather dull, uneventful lives.

Not long afterwards they went to bed. He fell asleep immediately and began to dream about the time when their lives had been anything but dull . . .

Anna and Ernie

Chapter 8

It was a long time, years later, when Ernest realized that the man was his dad. His name was Desmond Whitely and he was tall, slim, and very handsome, with straight, white-blond hair and dazzling blue eyes. He came to see Mam every Friday on his way home from work. Mam called him 'Des' and used to cry when he left. Des was better dressed than all the other men Ernest knew. He wore a suit and a collar and tie. The suit had frayed cuffs and his well-polished shoes were worn down at the heels, but he still looked dead posh. The first finger of his right hand had a dark blue stain that Mam said was ink.

'He's a bookkeeper,' she said proudly.

Des always came with a little gift for Ernest: a magic painting book, a drawing pad, a box of crayons, a wind-up toy. He would give Mam money before he said tara, always using exactly the same words, 'I only wish it were more, Peggy, but I've got three more mouths to feed.'

'It's all right, Des,' Mam would say. 'I know you do your best.'

Every now and then, Des would turn up with a paper bag that contained clothes for Ernest. 'Our George has grown out of these, I thought they'd do for the little chap.'

Ernest was always referred to as 'the little chap'.

When he was very small, Des would jiggle him up and down on his knee and say what a fine little chap he was. 'Just like his dad,' he would chuckle.

'Just like his dad,' Mam would echo.

Mam and Ernest lived in a small upstairs room at the back of a terraced house in Chaucer Street, Bootle, only a stone's throw from the docks and the River Mersey. It had a gas fire, a gas ring, and a gas mantle on the ceiling, and was so full of furniture there was hardly room to turn around – the little table they ate on had to be moved to open the door and there was only one chair, so Ernest always sat on the bed. The window overlooked a dirty backyard where the lavatory was. Mam and Ernie hardly ever used the lavvy, preferring the po that was kept under the bed. Every morning, very early, before the O'Briens who lived downstairs were up, Mam would empty the po in the lavvy and at the same time fetch a huge pan of water from the kitchen that would last all day – the O'Briens resented having to let out their back bedroom and weren't very polite to their lodgers so Mam always made herself as invisible as possible.

On the occasions when there was no money for the meter and it was cold as well as dark, they would cuddle up in bed together and Mam would tell Ernest stories about when she was young – not that she was all that old now. She'd had Ernest when she was only seventeen.

She'd been born in a big house in Merton Road, only a mile away. Her mother had been the live-in cook and her father a seaman in the Merchant Navy who her mam had met one Christmas when she'd gone to the music hall.

'They sat next to each other and it was love at first

sight,' Mam said. 'His name was Charlie Burrows and they got married the next time his ship came in.' Her mam had managed to stick it out as a cook until a second child was born when she'd felt obliged to leave and had rented the bottom half of a house in Clifford Street.

'Me dad didn't exactly earn a fortune, but we had enough to eat and he brought us home lovely things from places like Turkey and Persia.'

'What sort of lovely things?' Ernest would ask, although he already knew the answer.

'Sweets and dried fruit, scarves and stuff.'

Mam was eleven when the Great War started and twelve when her dad's ship was sunk with the loss of all hands in a storm in the Black Sea.

'Is the water really black, Mam?'

'Yes, Ernie,' Mam replied with conviction, 'as black as night.'

According to Mam, Ernest's own dad had died in the final year of the Great War. Ernie wasn't old enough to know this couldn't be true. He was born in 1920 and the war had ended two years before. It wasn't until he was about ten that the penny dropped – three pennies to be precise: he was too young for his father to have died in the war; if Mam had been married then her name would have changed from Burrows to something else; Ernest had the same coloured hair and eyes as Des Whitely, who was almost certainly his dad. Hadn't Des remarked how alike they were on more than one occasion?

None of this seemed the least bit strange to Ernest. He didn't wonder why Mam never went to see her own mam and the five brothers and sisters who only lived a few streets away.

While he wasn't perfectly happy, he was happy enough. He loved his mam with all his heart and didn't doubt that she loved him back. She never smacked him or raised her voice and they would roll their eyes at each other whenever the O'Briens downstairs had one of their frequent rows and the whole street would echo to their screams.

'Some people!' she would say exasperatedly, her head bent over a knitting pattern. Mam knitted for a living – or, as Des put it, she was a professional knitter, which sounded terribly grand. People would place their orders at Martha's, the little wool shop in Marsh Lane, buying the wool and the pattern at the same time, and Mam would deliver the finished garment within a few days if she wasn't busy and the pattern was a plain one. It would take longer if she already had several orders or the customer wanted a Fair Isle jumper making or something in a complicated stitch and her charges would go up accordingly.

One of Ernest's abiding memories would be of winter evenings, the curtains drawn, him lying on the bed drawing or reading, while his pretty mam sat in front of the gas fire, needles flashing, whatever she was knitting having grown magically longer every time he looked.

Apart from various pennies dropping, another important thing happened when Ernest was ten. Mam got a job as a housekeeper and they left the room in Chaucer Street and went to live around the corner in Sea View Road where the houses were much bigger and Ernest had a room of his own.

The house belonged to Cuthbert Burtonshaw, who had a chandler's shop in Marsh Lane that sold not only hardware, but things like animal food and firewood, crockery, and dusty, secondhand books that were in boxes outside and hastily brought in if it started to rain. The shop was a little gold mine and recently Cuthbert had bought a second-hand car: a Model A Ford.

Cuthbert was a widower approaching sixty. His face was very fat and red, contrasting oddly with the rest of him, as he was quite thin and his big head made him look top heavy. He had a bush of wiry grey hair, mutton chop whiskers, and a grown-up son and daughter, Vernon and Hilda, both married, who resented Ernest's mam right from the start.

'She's not dusted the sideboard properly,' Hilda said one Sunday when she came to visit her father – she found something to complain about every time she came. Ernest used to sit on the stairs and listen. 'See, Dad, there's dust underneath the clock.'

'Peggy's all right,' Cuthbert replied good-naturedly – he was a good-natured man all round and Ernest liked him tremendously. 'She looks after me fine and she's a decent cook. That nipper of hers, Ernie, is dead bright. He can read and write better than I can.'

'Our Dicky can read and write an' all, Dad.'

'Yes, but not as good as Ernie.'

Mam cooked the meals, did the washing and shopping, and kept the house sufficiently clean and tidy to suit Cuthbert. He was a lonely man and liked her and Ernest to keep him company of an evening. They would listen to the wireless or Cuthbert would teach Ernest to play chess or they'd just read, although Mam couldn't read very well and usually got on with the knitting that she still did in her spare time. Cuthbert was dead chuffed when she made him a Fair Isle pullover.

It wasn't long after the pullover that Ernest was

woken up in the middle of the night by a shrill scream followed by, 'Get off me! How dare you! I'll be leaving this house first thing in the morning.'

He jumped out of bed and raced into his mother's room, where Cuthbert, wearing striped pyjamas buttoned to the neck, was standing at the foot of the bed almost in tears.

'I'm sorry, Peg,' he stammered. 'I thought . . . I thought . . . I don't know what I thought.'

'Whatever you thought, you were dead wrong. Go away, Cuthbert. I'm going to start packing right now. Look, you've woken our Ernie. Come here, luv. Did you get a fright?'

Eventually, Ernest went back to bed, satisfied that Mam was no longer in danger. He was never sure what happened between him falling asleep and waking up, but Mam never left the house in Sea View Road and a month later she and Cuthbert Burtonshaw got married, much to the ire of Vernon and Hilda who refused to come to the wedding.

Within a year, Ernest's half-sister, Gaynor, was born, and Charlie arrived eighteen months later. Cuthbert claimed to have never been so happy as he was with Mam and his new family – including Ernest, of course.

Unfortunately, Cuthbert wasn't to enjoy his happiness for long. Charlie was barely a year old when his father fell off the ladder in the shop while reaching for something off the top shelf and knocked himself out. Sadly, he never regained consciousness and died the following day.

Mam was upset, naturally. She'd liked Cuthbert, although she'd never loved him. She feared for her children. 'What's going to happen to us now?' she asked Ernest.

Ernest had no idea. Life was full of ups and downs and people had to cope as best they could.

Vernon and Hilda came back to the house after the funeral. 'We'd like you out of here forthwith,' Hilda said crisply.

Mam looked at Ernest. 'What does that mean, son?'

'It means straight away.' He'd never heard of the word 'forthwith' before, but got the meaning. He was struck by a brilliant idea. 'Why can't me mam just rent the house like Cuthbert did?' he asked. They could afford it. In a few months, he was due to leave school and start work, the house was big enough to let out a couple of rooms, and Mam could start knitting full-time again.

'Because it's a bought house, that's why, and now it belongs to me and our Hilda,' Vernon sneered. 'We're going to sell it, the shop an' all.'

When Ernest thought about this later, it hardly seemed fair. Surely Cuthbert's wife, in other words Mam, had more right to the house than Vernon and Hilda? And, after all, Gaynor and Charlie were Cuthbert's children too. It seemed to Ernest that he was urgently in need of advice. But where could he get it?

He called in the police station, but the copper on duty told him to go and piss up his kilt and stop bothering him. He asked the teacher at school, but she seemed unable to understand what he was getting at. 'It all sounds terribly complicated, boy. You need to see a solicitor.'

Before seeking out one of these mysterious individuals, Ernest had one last try at the library where he was well known as a keen borrower of books. He explained the situation to the woman behind the counter where the books where stamped. She was very old, with neatly waved grey hair and wire-rimmed glasses. She listened attentively, then said to a young man, also behind the counter, 'Will you take over for a while, Mr Bright? I have to see to something.'

Ernest was taken into a little office and asked to explain everything again. When he'd finished, the woman asked if Mr Burtonshaw had left a Will. 'It's a document saying who would inherit things when he died,' she explained in response to Ernest's puzzled look.

'Not as far as I know,' he replied.

'Well, in that case, the property automatically goes to his wife. His son and daughter are just trying it on. Tell your mother under no circumstances to move out. The house belongs to her. Is this the Mr Burtonshaw who ran the chandler's in Marsh Lane?'

'Yes,' Ernest acknowledged.

'Well, in that case, the shop belongs to your mother too.'

For weeks, his mam kept walking around the house touching the walls, stroking the furniture. 'Is it really ours?' she would ask Ernest, seeking reassurance.

'Yes, Mam. The shop an' all.' The shop was being temporarily looked after by Tom Quigley, an old mate of Cuthbert's.

'You're dead clever, Ernie. Me, I'd have just walked out and let them two have it.'

'Them two' had been round a few times, raising hell when Mam, Ernest standing staunchly at her side, stubbornly refused to move, claiming the property was hers by rights. They hadn't been for a while. Perhaps they'd been to see one of them solicitor people who'd told them they were flogging a dead horse.

Thelma O'Neill sidled into the chandler's, fluttered her long lashes, and said in a cloying voice, 'Can I have a firelighter, please, Ernie?'

Ernest put the firelighter on the counter, wrapped it in brown paper, and grunted, 'That'll be a halfpenny.'

'*Thank* you,' Thelma said in the same cloying tone. She came into the shop most days, asking for things like a single cup hook, a dishcloth, a couple of nails, stuff that never cost more than a penny. Ernest knew darn well she was after him – the firelighter was a pretty poor excuse, as it was midsummer and only someone who was stark raving mad would light a fire. 'Are you going to the dance at the Town Hall on Saturday?' she asked.

'I might,' Ernest said carelessly. He was eighteen, six-foot-two-inches tall, fair-haired, and a 'catch', according to Mam, because not only was he incredibly handsome, but he had his own shop and his own car – he'd learned to drive the Ford.

Ernest quite enjoyed girls chasing after him, although wouldn't have admitted it for the world. Pretty, buxom Thelma was just one of half a dozen who came into the chandlers for a variety of reasons. Molly Regan always came to ask the time – 'You're the only one I know who's got a watch,' she would brazenly claim – and Magdalene Eaves would enquire after things he didn't stock, always pretending to be astonished when he said that no, he didn't have any Kellogg's cornflakes or that week's *Dandy*.

'Have you seen the picture on at the Palace?' Thelma enquired pertly.

'Haven't been to the Palace in a while.'

'It's called *Wings of the Navy* with George Brent and Olivia de Havilland. I haven't seen it meself,' she hastily assured him, 'but me friend said it's dead good.'

'I might go and see it if I can spare the time.' If he took a girl, it would be Magdalene Eaves, who was small and dark and prettier than Thelma by a mile. Thelma was wasting her time and money buying things from his shop.

A year later, Ernest and Magdalene were going steady and marriage was on the cards, but it was 1939 and such a major decision would have to be left until the war that was about to start was over and done with. Ernest had already received his call-up papers, had passed the medical with flying colours, and been assigned to the Royal Tank Regiment. No one doubted that the war would see Britain emerge victorious in six months' time, possibly less.

'We'll get engaged when I come back,' Ernest promised a tearful Magdalene when he bade her tara. His mam, Gaynor, and Charlie were even more tearful to see him go, although he felt sure they would manage without him – Desmond Whitely had come back into his mother's life after the death of Cuthbert and spent a lot of time in the house in Sea View Road.

Ernest was secretly looking forward to the war. Managing a chandler's wasn't exactly an exciting occupation for a young man of nineteen and he quite fancied being a soldier and having all sorts of thrilling adventures. In the years to come, once he and Magdalene were married and had children, the chances were he would never leave Bootle again.

Six months later, there was no sign of the war being over and Ernest hadn't used a weapon in anger or left the shores of the British Isles. It wasn't until the spring of 1940 that his particular section of the Royal Tank Regiment set sail on the 14,000-mile journey around the Cape of Good Hope bound for North Africa and a place called Cyrenaica.

Their first battle against the Italians was a doddle: 130,000 of the enemy were taken prisoner, along with most of their guns and 400 tanks. As Ernest's best mate, Ronnie Beale, put it colourfully, 'We tore them bastards up for arse paper.'

Within a few months, Ernest was perfectly attuned to desert life. He felt almost as if he'd been born for it. The scorching heat didn't bother him. Despite his fair colouring, his tough skin soaked up the sun, turning it a golden bronze. He enjoyed living under canvas, knowing that everything could be moved at the drop of a hat to another site, that it was only temporary. He liked the feel of the silky sand undulating beneath his bare feet. There was something strangely liberating about being able to see from one flat horizon to the other, the sky just acres of blue and not a single cloud in sight, the sun a brilliant burning ball of fire.

Ronnie Beale wasn't so cockily triumphant when General Rommel appeared on the scene at the head of the mighty German Army and the British were driven back until all of Cyrenaica was in enemy hands. Over the next two years, thousands of men were killed in action as the battle raged back and forth, the British and their Allies advancing one minute, the Germans forcing them back and predominantly in control, until on 23 October 1942, under the leadership of General

Montgomery, British forces attacked at El Alamein and Rommel was routed.

Ernest, an old hand by now, felt lucky to be alive, having lost quite a few of his mates in the fighting, Ronnie Beale among them. By now, he had forsaken tanks for a staff car and become driver to Colonel Turlough McBride. The colonel had taken a shine to him when the company had been holed up in Tobruk. One evening, a sergeant had stuck his head into the tent where the lower ranks were eating and hollered, 'Can any bugger here play chess?' Ernest had put up his hand and been taken to the colonel's tent where he was sitting staring miserably at a chessboard, the black and white figures standing idly at each side as if raring to have a go at each other.

What the colonel liked about him, he said rather stiffly after losing the first two games – Cuthbert had been a good teacher – was that Ernest, a mere private, hadn't felt obliged to let his superior officer win.

'Can you drive, Burrows?' he asked after losing another two games.

'Yes, sir.'

'In that case, from now on, you can drive me. It'll make a change to have someone to talk to who isn't as servile as hell.'

Driving the colonel to and from the base camp and the scene of battle could be more dangerous than taking part in the fighting. On several occasions shots were fired at the car from a stray German tank that had inadvertently crossed enemy lines. Fortunately, they missed every time and Ernest and the colonel pretended to ignore them, Ernest merely pressing his foot on the accelerator and driving even faster, so the car was submerged in a huge cloud of powdery sand. It didn't make them less of a target, but they felt safer.

The colonel was forty-five and had been a soldier all his life. He had fought in the Great War to end all wars. Around his neck, he wore a purple silk scarf that had been given to him by his fiancée, now his wife, in 1917. It was his lucky mascot and had kept him safe in two world wars. Educated at Eton, Harrow, and Sandhurst, he had a cut-glass accent and the coarsest sense of humour Ernest had ever encountered. Short and tubby with a perfectly round face and a slight squint, he always wore a heavy-weight suede jacket, despite the sweltering heat, and consumed whisky by the bottle, at least one a day, though he managed to remain in control of all his faculties.

He and Ernest got on well. They argued a lot, mainly about politics. Ernest was a solid Labour man, while the colonel was a right-wing Conservative who considered Churchill a woolly Liberal.

In the jubilation and chaos following the Allies' magnificent victory at El Alamein, one morning Ernest was commanded to take the colonel into Cairo so he could buy another supply of whisky. Ernest loved Cairo, having spent a few days leave there a year ago and been captivated by the mysterious atmosphere, the narrow streets, the dirt and the strange smells. He'd already taken the colonel there numerous times for fresh supplies of spirits, when all he'd had to do was wait in the staff car, then carry the crates to the boot.

The same thing happened that morning and they were on their way back to base camp, the colonel already halfway through a bottle of whisky that usually lasted all day, when Ernest was startled by a shot that sounded alarmingly close, followed by another and another. When he turned, the colonel was firing his pistol out of the rear window with a dangerously unsteady hand, an empty bottle on the seat beside him.

'Got you, you bastard,' he roared at the empty desert.

Ernest stopped the car. 'Will you put that gun away, please, sir?'

The colonel laughed maniacally. 'I'm the one who gives the orders round here, Burrows.'

'I wouldn't dream of giving an order, sir, I'm just asking you nicely.'

'Oh, all right,' the colonel said grudgingly. He withdrew his hand, dropped the pistol, bent to retrieve it, another shot rang out, and the colonel said disbelievingly, 'I've shot myself in the ruddy foot!'

'Don't worry, sir. I'll get you to hospital straight away.' Calmly, Ernest started up the car and sped in the direction of base camp.

'Turn around, you numbskull,' the colonel screamed. 'Take me back to Cairo.'

'But what you need is a hospital, sir!'

'I need medical treatment, but not in a ruddy Army hospital. I've just shot myself in my own ruddy foot, man. It's not what soldiers are supposed to do. If the Army find out, I'll be in very deep shit. Turn the ruddy car around and take me back to Cairo – that's an order, Burrows, and if you don't obey it, I'll shoot you in the back of your ruddy head.'

Three hours later, the colonel was ensconced in a bed with gold brocade drapes in a sumptuous bedroom in an apartment belonging to friends whose current whereabouts were unknown – the woman who looked after the place obviously knew the colonel and had let him and Ernest in without a murmur. Her name was Leila.

A doctor was sent for who spoke excellent English. He removed the bullet – the colonel didn't even grimace while this was done – dressed the wound, and said he would call again tomorrow. The patient was given tablets to reduce the pain and help him sleep – he immediately took four when he'd been advised to take two, and washed them down with whisky. Minutes later, he was snoring.

Ernest left him to it and investigated the apartment that comprised the entire third floor of a magnificently gaudy building on the island of Gezira on the Nile, set like a jewel in the very heart of Cairo. There were three more bedrooms, a living room at least thirty feet long, two bathrooms – one black marble, the other cream – a dining room and a study. The door to the kitchen was open, but he didn't venture inside: he could glimpse Leila sitting patiently at the table, probably wondering what had hit her. She was very old, her brown face a cobweb of creases.

The place was like a miniature palace: the furniture exquisitely carved, the walls covered with richly embroidered hangings and erotic paintings, the curtains made from thick ornamental silks and brocades. Giant fans rotated on the ceilings and the patterns on the mosaic floors made him dizzy if he looked at them too long. He reckoned the contents of the apartment had cost more money than he would earn in his lifetime.

Who did the place belong to? Whoever they were, they must be as rich as Croesus. The big room was full of photographs in silver frames. The same couple appeared in every one, a man and woman very alike, middle-aged and elegantly dressed, accompanied by other couples who were never the same. He found one of the colonel with a stout woman wearing layers of floating lace, the elegantly dressed couple either side of them. All four were linking arms.

What was he supposed to do with himself now? He couldn't very well abandon the colonel and return to base on his own – not that he felt the faintest inclination to do so. He liked being where he was and decided to go for a walk around Cairo. After a double dose of sleeping tablets, it would be ages before the colonel returned to the land of the living.

He went into the black bathroom, ran a lukewarm bath, and scrubbed himself with a loofah and a block of highly scented soap. When he finished, the bottom of the bath held a layer of sand that had collected between his toes, under his arms, in his hair, his ears, and in a fine layer all over his body. He dried himself, saw in the mirror that there were too many crinkles around his eyes for a chap of twenty-two, which had come from squinting too much at the sun and the glistening sand. With an expression of distaste, he eyed the baggy, sweat-stained shorts, rancid socks, and run-down boots that he'd recently removed and now felt reluctant to touch, let alone put back on. He hadn't been wearing a shirt and his beret looked as if it had been used as a football – he vaguely remembered that it had.

Ernest didn't hesitate. He went into one of the opulent bedrooms and examined the contents of the wardrobe. It contained only women's clothing – he wasn't *that* desperate. In the next room, the wardrobe was empty except for a row of ruched velvet hangers, but the third was crammed with men's stuff. He picked out a short-sleeved white shirt, white shorts and white pumps. He'd have everything cleaned before he left and no one would know they'd been used. All he had with him in money was a few piastres, enough to buy a couple of beers.

This was the life! The sun was going down, the sky was purple with dramatic slashes of blue and green, and a few faint stars had appeared. Ernest jingled the coins in his pocket as he walked slowly along a narrow, lantern-lit street with shops and stalls on both sides and smelling to high heaven, mainly of dung. Within the space of ten minutes, he'd been offered dirty postcards, women, a small, pathetic looking boy, flash jewellery, and some foul looking meat that he wouldn't have touched had he been about to die of starvation. With every step he took, he was tempted with more women, more postcards, temptations he had no difficulty in turning down.

There were plenty of servicemen about, not just British, but Australians, Indian troops wearing turbans, the French in their kepis, a couple of New Zealanders. Like Ernest, not everyone was in uniform, but were recognizably fighting men. They nodded at each other or smiled, still buoyed after their recent victory over the Jerries.

Somewhere in the region there was a British pub run by an ancient geezer called Reuben who'd served in the Boer War. He found it around the next corner. It was called the Queen Victoria and sold beer like no beer he'd ever tasted before and a selection of Egyptian wines that could take the roof off your mouth.

Inside, the long tables and benches were packed to capacity and there was little room even to stand. The noise was deafening and the smell of dung had been replaced by one of sweat and musty socks and boots. To whet the appetite, a poster advertising Guinness adorned the clay walls, although it hadn't been in stock on Ernest's previous visit and wasn't now and probably wouldn't be again until the war was over.

He bought a pint of watery beer and spent the next couple of hours explaining to fellow soldiers why he looked so clean and smelled so fresh and, no, he wasn't wearing scent, he said indignantly, it was the soap he'd washed with. When describing the course of his unusual day, he left out the real reason for the colonel's accident and said he'd tripped getting out of the car and broken his ankle. It wouldn't do for the truth to get back to those on high.

When he returned to the apartment, the colonel was still asleep, still snoring, and Leila was still sitting patiently in the kitchen.

'Bed.' Ernest pressed his hands together and put them against his cheek. 'You go bed now.'

She seemed to understand, nodded tiredly, and went through a door at the other end of the kitchen, giving him a little nod as if to wish him goodnight.

'Goodnight,' Ernest said, and went to bed himself.

Next morning, the colonel woke in a foul temper. He churlishly refused the ta'amiyya – beans and spices fried in a patty – that Leila brought him, although gulped down the bitter black coffee, then commanded Ernest to give him a hand as far as the bathroom.

'Get me a glass of water,' he said after he'd been helped back to bed, 'and put a slug of whisky in it.'

'How much is a slug, sir?'

'An inch or two. And where's them ruddy tablets the doctor left? My foot's hurting like blazes.'

'Not surprising, sir, seeing as how you shot it.'

The colonel gave him a suspicious glare. 'You're looking remarkably fit this morning, Burrows. Where did those clothes come from?'

'One of the wardrobes, sir. I hope the owner won't mind, but me own stuff's not fit to wear. I didn't think,' he added innocently, 'that I'd need a change of gear when I came to Cairo yesterday. I've no money, either, although I suppose I could always drive back to camp and collect me wallet.'

'You'll do no such thing. If they see you, they might make you stay and I don't want to be stuck here on my own.' He pouted childishly. 'It wouldn't be a bad idea if you got a message through. Tell them I've had an accident, that I've . . .' He paused.

'Broken your ankle, sir?'

'That'll do fine, Burrows. Thank you. Help yourself to a few quid from my trouser pocket, it's English and you'll have to change it – I want it back, mind.' With that, the colonel took another four tablets with the whisky and water and was fast asleep within minutes.

Ernest took two pounds out of the trousers, ate his own breakfast, and left the apartment. He remembered that the doctor was coming back today, but Leila could see to him.

This certainly *was* the life, Ernest crowed as he strolled across the Qasr el-Nil Bridge, the Nile gleaming beneath him, the air sparkling and as fresh as it could ever be in Cairo.

He reached the mainland and continued to stroll, passing the British and American embassies, through the Garden City. He'd walked a couple of miles by the time he reached Old Cairo with its narrow streets, bazaars, stalls, tiny coffee houses, and offers of postcards, women, and untouchable food. A goat wandered across his path, he had to move out of the way of a donkey and cart. This was the part he liked most, throbbing with life, noise, music, crime, even depravity – he'd already had two small boys pushed under his nose.

He was about to enter the Queen Victoria, aching for a pint to quench his thirst, when a woman approached.

'Sir,' she began, but Ernest interrupted with a curt, 'Sorry, luv. I'm not interested,' but the woman persisted.

'Sir, I look for Anna Kosztolanyi, if you please.'

Ernest shrugged. 'Never heard of her, sorry. I'm a stranger round here.'

'She live by here, sir.' She grabbed his bare arm and Ernest, irritated, was about to shake her hand away, when he realized she was holding him for support. Her eyes half closed, her knees buckled, and he managed to catch her just in time, laying her gently on to the ground outside the entrance to the pub.

He looked at her properly for the first time and was surprised to see she wasn't a native, but European, about fifty, dressed in black, her head covered with a black scarf. From the well-preserved face he could tell that she was a woman of means, or had been until recently. Now her clothes were thick with dust and the nails on her smooth hands were broken.

'*Nana est morte!*' a plaintive voice cried and Ernest suddenly found himself surrounded by children, the biggest, a girl holding a baby in her arms. They were pale-skinned, dark-eyed, and their faces were tight with exhaustion and fear.

He only knew a few French words and one was *morte*. It meant dead. 'Not *morte*,' he said in a loud voice. 'Your nana's just fainted.'

Two Australian servicemen were about to enter the Queen Victoria. 'Do us a favour, mate,' Ernest called, 'ask Reuben if he knows a woman called Anna something. She lives around here and might be French.'

One of the Australians returned within a few minutes. 'She's Hungarian and she lives in the flat upstairs, the stairs to your right. D'you need a hand, mate?'

'It's all right, I think she's coming round.' The woman's eyes were flickering open. She groaned, saw Ernest bending over her, and struggled to a sitting position. '*Pardonnez-moi, monsieur*,' she stammered, followed by a string of French he didn't understand.

'The woman you want's up there.' He pulled her to her feet and took her to a narrow, stone stairway at the side of the pub, and supposed he'd better help her up. The children trailed after them and he could hear their feet dragging tiredly on the steep, stone stairs.

Ernest knocked on the single door at the top. A young woman opened it, almost too pretty to be true, with a cloud of golden curls, blue eyes, and rosy lips. Her skin had the lustre of the finest china and he immediately wanted to stroke it, imagining it to be cool and firm underneath his tough, coarse fingers. She was tiny, hardly coming up to his shoulder, and wore a white caftan with embroidery around the neck and hem. Through the thin cotton, he could make out her white brassiere and pants and tried not to stare too openly.

'Anna Kosto . . . ?' He struggled to get the name out, but couldn't remember the rest. 'This lady's been looking for you.'

'I am Anna Kosztolanyi, yes.'

The woman burst into tears and, as if this was some sort of signal, the children also began to cry, the baby included. Anna smiled, and the smile almost took Ernest's breath away. It was so sweet, so welcoming, as if it came from the very bottom of her heart. She reached for the woman's hand and drew her inside. The children stumbled after her, and Ernest, who had intended making a run for it at this point, found himself following into a large, low-ceilinged room with windows on three sides and furnished with an assortment of chairs, none of which matched, and scraps of faded carpet. Everyone found seats and the woman began to speak in a stream of lilting French, waving her arms dramatically, rolling her eyes, twice even baring her teeth – Ernest assumed she was describing her reasons for being there.

Anna had seated herself at a table piled with papers and books and an elderly typewriter. She was taking notes and, when the woman had finished, she turned to Ernest and said in a high, bell-like voice with only a trace of foreign accent, 'Madame Montand has come all the way from Algeria with her six grandchildren. They started off with a car and plenty of money, but first the car was stolen, then the money. They have been walking for weeks, begging for food, sleeping in the desert or in doorways. They are all very tired. I have been asked to tell you that Madame very much appreciates your help, but now you must go. She doesn't want to take up any more of your time.'

'Why have they come to Cairo?' Ernest enquired. He didn't want to go, preferring to stay in the presence of the breathtaking Anna.

'Because Madame Montand and her family are Jewish,' Anna said a trifle impatiently. 'Her daughter-in-law, the children's mother, recently died of blood poisoning and her son is away, fighting the war on the side of the Free French. She is aware of how Jews are being treated in Germany, she has heard of the death camps, she knew Rommel was winning the war in the desert, and was expecting the whole of North Africa to end up in German hands. She wants to get the children to the safety of Palestine before it is too late. Trains go from Cairo to Palestine and I shall arrange the paperwork for her.'

'But the Germans have been beaten good and sound,' Ernest argued. 'From now on, she'll be quite safe in Cairo with the kids.'

'The British won the last battle, but the Germans won many before,' Anna replied, even more impatiently. 'Who's to say there won't be more battles and their side won't win next time? They are desperate for control of the Suez Canal; they might try again. Besides, Madame Montand has no money and nowhere to live in Cairo. She has a sister in Palestine she can stay with.'

Ernest didn't try to argue with her logic. His heart was racing and he was sweating as he desperately tried to think up reasons not to go. He felt drawn to Anna Kosztolanyi in a way he'd never been to a woman before. He didn't want to leave, even though she was making it obvious she wanted rid of him.

'Would you like me to fetch something to eat?' he offered hopefully.

'Thank you, but no. I have plenty of food. In a minute, I shall make some coffee. I think everyone is too tired to eat just now.' She indicated the children who had all fallen asleep.

He thought of saying he wouldn't have minded a cup, but it would only delay his departure a few minutes. 'Where will they sleep tonight?' he asked.

'Here, on the floor or the chairs. Madame Montand can have my bed. It will be only for one night.'

'There's plenty of room in the place I'm staying,' Ernest said recklessly. 'They can sleep there.'

They arrived in a taxi at about six o'clock. To his relief, Anna was with them, probably wanting to make sure her charges were being delivered into safe hands. She had changed out of the caftan into a silky blue frock. Gold earrings jangled in her ears and she wore high-heeled gold sandals on her tiny feet. She reminded him of a fairy off the top of a Christmas tree.

Ernest had spent the afternoon in the apartment, Cairo having lost its charm now that he'd met Anna. The patient had woken in the afternoon, demanding to play chess. It was one of the few times Ernest lost, too worked up to concentrate on a piddling board game. The colonel was encouraged to take more tablets with more whisky and was asleep again when the visitors arrived. The children had cheered up considerably since morning, but were still tired, and their grandmother was finding it hard to remain on her feet. A mystified Leila made everyone a drink and they retired to the three bedrooms – each held a double bed so there would be enough room. Earlier, Ernest had thoughtfully removed a drawer from the wardrobe for the baby, lining it with pillows.

At last Ernest had Anna to himself. The first thing she said when they sat in the big room full of photographs was, 'You've been so kind, yet I've never asked your name.'

'Ernest Burrows. Call me Ernie, everyone does.' His heart was beating so fast and so loud he half expected his chest to explode.

'Does the apartment belong to you, Ernie?'

'Jaysus, no!' He explained the reason for his being there, getting the words all jumbled, stammering now and then when he lost the thread, yet he was a man normally in perfect control of himself, never flustered. Anna seemed to have dislodged something in his brain. He couldn't think straight any more.

'Does the colonel know the Montands are here?'

'No.' He grinned, not caring if he knew or not, then asked how she spoke such perfect English.

'Back in Hungary, I was an actress,' she said proudly. 'When I was seventeen, I actually made a film. Before the war, our company toured Europe many times. We performed in London, Paris, Berlin, Rome, as well as Budapest. My father was a language teacher and he taught me to read in English so that's what I'm best at, the others not so good.'

'And what are you doing in Cairo?' His heart had slowed down a bit. He felt more relaxed now that he was *real* to her, no longer the anonymous person who had turned up that morning and been unwilling to go away.

'Helping Jews get to Palestine,' she said simply. 'Not everyone in Egypt wants the British to win. There have actually been demonstrations in favour of the

Germans. Jews who want to go to Palestine are finding it difficult to get visas. The British embassy is besieged with applicants and it can take days, even weeks before the application is processed and then you can't be certain of success. That's what I do, supply the necessary visas. In fact, someone is making them for the Montands at this very minute.'

'*Making* them? You mean forging them?'

Anna nodded. 'My friend, Omar, does them.'

'But isn't what you're doing dangerous?' Ernest gasped, worried for her. 'What would the authorities do if they found out?'

'I don't know.' She shrugged carelessly. 'Throw me in prison, I suppose, if only for the forgeries. But if you do dangerous things, you must be prepared to face the consequences. It's dangerous to fight, but it didn't stop you from fighting the Germans, knowing that you could be killed at any time.'

'I had no choice,' Ernest pointed out. 'You have.'

'No, I haven't.' All of a sudden, her voice was bleak. Her face was devoid of all expression as she said, 'Back in Hungary, I returned from the theatre one night and found the Nazis had taken away my parents and two young sisters. I have never seen them since and have no idea where they are, whether they are alive or dead. I am doing this for them, for my family, helping to save other Jews if I can.'

Ernest was too horrified to reply. Anyroad, what could he say? Tell her she was brave? Say how sorry he was about her family? He was surprised when she gave a tinkling little laugh.

'I'm sorry, Ernie. I've depressed you, haven't I? The trouble is you ask too many questions and the only answers I can give are the truth.' She got to her feet. 'I must hurry. I am meeting someone and we are going to the cinema: *Boom Town*, with Clark Gable and Spencer Tracy. Have you seen it?'

'No,' said Ernest, although he had, but hoped she'd invite him along and was bitterly disappointed when she didn't. He'd been on the point of asking her out for a meal and it meant his disappointment was twofold.

Every time the colonel woke, he was in a worse mood than before. Just after midnight Ernest was alerted by a series of groans and felt obliged to rise from his uncomfortable bed on an elegant sofa that hadn't been designed to sleep on, to discover the reason for the groans.

'What time is it, Burrows?' the colonel snapped when he went in.

'About a quarter past twelve, sir.'

'Is that night or day?'

'Night, sir,' Ernest replied, adding pointedly, 'It's dark outside.'

'How the hell am I supposed to know that when the ruddy blinds are drawn?' the man snarled. 'I'm bored, Burrows, bored out of my skull. Tomorrow, I'll ask the doctor if I can get up and you can drive me to Shepherd's for afternoon tea.'

'Good idea, sir,' Ernest said tonelessly. As a mere private, he wouldn't be allowed inside Shepherd's Hotel. It would mean waiting outside until the colonel had had his tea, his dinner, and no doubt his supper, before condescending to emerge in a state of acute inebriation. 'We'll just have to see what the doctor has to say tomorrow.' He prayed the doctor would merely hand out more tablets and order the patient to stay in bed.

The door swung open and the colonel nearly jumped out of his skin when a small boy entered and said something in French that Ernest didn't understand.

'What was that, son?'

'He wants to wee-wee, Burrows,' the colonel shrieked. 'Show him where the bathroom is, then come back and tell me exactly what he's doing here.'

Anna arrived in a taxi next morning on the dot of ten, as promised. The Montands' papers were ready and she was taking them straight to Ramses Station to put them on the train to Palestine.

'I'll come with you,' Ernest said, determined not to take no for an answer. 'Madame Montand isn't a bit well. She'll need helping on to the train.' This wasn't a lie. Madame had vomited up her breakfast and was having a job keeping upright. 'She seems to have some sort of fever.'

'Oh, dear,' Anna exclaimed. 'Thank you, Ernie. What is it they say in English? I bet you'll be glad to see the back of us.'

'No. Oh, no,' he assured her. 'In fact, I was wondering if we couldn't see each other again: tonight, maybe, or tomorrow.'

'That would be nice.'

Was she only being polite or did she mean it? His stomach was in turmoil, his head was aching, he didn't know what to do with his hands. He *had* to see her again. He *had* to. He couldn't just let her disappear out of his life. If necessary, he'd just have to *tell* her how he

266

felt, lay his love out before her like a blanket and invite her to sit.

Ramses Station was in a state of utter confusion: everyone bumping into each other and no two people seeming to want to walk in the same direction. The noise was deafening, the smoke-filled heat hardly bearable. Anna carried the baby, Ernest virtually carried Madame Montand, and the children were ordered to hold each other's hands and not let go for any reason. At least Anna seemed to know which platform the train was leaving from. The further towards the front of the crowded train they walked, the thicker the smoke became.

'I'm afraid I could only afford third-class,' she said. 'Funds come from sympathizers in Palestine and I hadn't enough for first-class seats.'

Ernest grimaced. The third-class carriages were dirty and what seats were left looked hard and uncomfortable. 'There's two empty in there,' he said, pointing through the grubby window. 'At least Madame can sit down and one of the kids can sit beside her with the baby. We'd better grab them before they're taken.'

Two days later, Ernest entered the apartment on the island of Gezira. 'Is that you, Burrows?' the colonel roared from the bedroom.

Ernest threw open the door, marched inside, and stood stiffly to attention. 'Yes, sir,' he said, saluting.

'You said you were just going to the station. I've been going off my ruddy rocker here, nothing to do, no one to talk to for two whole days. Where the ruddy hell have you been, man?'

'I'm sorry, sir. I'm afraid it was unavoidable, but I've been to Palestine.'

Madame had been close to fainting when she was helped to the seat on the train. Eva, the eldest girl, who was in charge of the baby, seemed nervous at the idea of the ten-hour journey spent looking after her grandmother and an infant at the same time, the other children had nowhere to sit, drinks would have to be bought on the way, food. Anna wondered aloud if they shouldn't all go back to her flat. 'But there isn't another train until the day after tomorrow and Madame might still be sick – she could be for days. I think it best if they go now. It'll be hellish, but to-night they'll be with their aunt and they'll think it was worth it.'

The little boy who'd given the colonel such a fright the night before was trying to climb on to his grandmother's knee, the baby smelled to high heaven, everyone else in the compartment was smoking highly perfumed Turkish cigarettes and regarding the new-comers with some hostility. The window was closed and Ernest knew a minor war would have to be fought to open it.

'I'll go with them,' he said impulsively. 'I can look after the children and I'll catch the same train back tomorrow.'

'But you haven't got a ticket!' Anna cried.

'I'll bluff my way along. I'm a British soldier. They won't chuck me off.' He'd noticed a couple of British officers further back in a first-class carriage. If neces-sary, he'd throw himself on their mercy.

They were trying to pitch him off the train as it rushed through the night. The door was open and someone was holding him by the shoulders, pushing him towards the gaping black hole. Ernest tried to resist, hands on the doorframe, but they were too strong for him and he was flung into the blackness and his heart stopped as he waited to land, knowing it could mean death.

He woke up just in time and found Leila shaking him by the shoulder. She stopped when she saw his eyes had opened and began to gesture towards the door, wanting him to come. If it was the colonel eager for a game of chess, Ernest swore he'd shoot him in the other foot. The white clothes he'd been wearing had disappeared and been replaced with his Army shorts, washed and carefully pressed, socks folded on top. His boots were beside them, well polished, the laces neatly threaded. He pulled on the shorts and went barefoot into the hallway. Voices were coming from the big room, one of them Anna's followed by the colonel's jovial laugh.

'Ah, here he is,' the colonel chuckled when Ernest went in. 'The sleeper awaketh. You've got company, Burrows, extremely delightful company, I must say. Well, I'll leave you two to it.' He got to his feet – he'd acquired a stick from somewhere – and hobbled towards the door, pausing on the way to slap Ernest on the shoulder. 'I shall dine out on this for a long time once this ruddy war is over: my driver goes for a walk and returns with seven refugees. He takes them to the station, but doesn't come back for two ruddy days having accompanied said refugees all the way to ruddy Palestine. On top of all this, he meets an incredibly pretty girl.' He gave Anna a lewd wink. 'I'd like all the details later, Burrows, tonight, when I take you and Anna to dinner.'

The door closed. Ernest stared at Anna. 'Why are you here?'

'I came to thank you for what you did, to see how you got on.' She smiled. Dimples appeared in her smooth cheeks and her blue eyes twinkled like stars. 'There's another reason. You must know what it is, Ernie. I came for you.'

Ernest held out his arms and she ran into them. He held her very tightly, knowing that he would never, ever let her go.

Ernest spent only another seven days in Cairo: magical, thrilling days that would always remain the high point of his life. Barring death, an intolerable thought, he and Anna knew they would spend the rest of their lives together, as soon as the war, which was to last another two and a half years, was over.

Ernest fought with the victorious Eighth Army in Tripoli and Tunisia, then was conveyed in an armada of more than 3,000 ships to Sicily, upwards through Italy where the retreating German Army fought with a harsh, audacious obduracy, despite knowing that the war was lost.

By a strange quirk of coincidence, it was three years to the day that Ernest had first climbed the stairs to Anna's flat in Cairo accompanied by Madame Montand and her charges, that he climbed them again, a civilian now, and knocked on her door.

She opened it and she was as beautiful as he remembered if not more. 'Ernie!' she breathed. 'I wasn't expecting you for days yet.'

'I came straight away. I didn't even go to see me family.' He picked her up and carried her inside to start the rest of their lives together.

Wednesday

11 JULY 2001

Chapter 9

The kettle was on for the first cup of tea of the day and gentle sunshine fell through the window, setting the kitchen alight.

'It's going to be another scorcher,' Ernest muttered. He was arranging the tray for Anna's breakfast when she appeared in the doorway, looking very pleased with herself.

'I got up by myself,' she crowed. 'I feel terribly well today, darling. Shall we go somewhere exciting?'

'We're going to buy a computer this afternoon,' he reminded her. 'Isn't that exciting enough? I'll ask Victoria later if she'll come with us.'

She clapped her hands, thrilled. 'Of course we are, I'd forgotten. I was going to suggest we went up the Eiffel Tower to look at the view or had a few games of roulette at our favourite casino in Monte Carlo, but buying a computer is much better.'

He pulled one of the chairs from under the little table for her to sit on, made the tea, and sat down with her. 'Do you miss those days, luv?' he asked gruffly.

'I miss being young, Ernie.' She sighed and her lips twisted in a smile so sad it made Ernest want to weep, but then she surprised him with a laugh, as she had so often done in the past. 'What a fool I am! I'm lucky to have lived so long, lucky to have had you. We've had a wonderful life, darling.'

'I had a funny dream last night. It started in that little room I told you about where I lived with me mam, and finished after the war when I came back to Cairo and carried you into your flat.'

'And we made love! Oh, we made love for days and days. It must have been at least a week before we came up for air.'

'We did stop now'n again for a drink and a bite to eat,' Ernest conceded.

'I'd like those days back,' Anna said, her face young again as she remembered.

'Now all we can do is dream about them.'

'At least we have some marvellous things to dream about, darling.' She put her hand over his and squeezed it. 'Not everyone has.'

Victoria hadn't talked to her gran for two whole days. She usually told her every little thing, but couldn't very well tell her that last night she'd nearly made love with Gareth Moran – if his mobile hadn't rung, there would be no 'nearly' about it. What's more, Victoria didn't feel even faintly ashamed. It wouldn't harm Gareth's marriage as it wasn't exactly perfect, and she was going away on Sunday and wouldn't see him again.

Anyroad, Gran had probably been watching the whole time, tut-tutting loudly, shaking her head, and saying, even more loudly, 'That *girl*!' which she always did whenever Victoria had done something naughty, looking at her straight in the face, yet speaking as if she wasn't there.

'Are you there, Gran?' she asked. 'Are you watch-ing? Can you see the state of the house? It's disgusting. We both just sat and let the place rot around us. At least you kept it clean. You should have seen the cobwebs on the ceiling. I was covered in them by the time I'd finished, but you probably saw that an' all. You used to be able to see around corners when you were alive.'

She wondered if Gran had met Mum during the time she'd been in heaven. 'Say hello to her for me. Tell her I miss her, I always have, just like I miss you and Granddad and I'll miss the house once I'm gone.' It was hard to imagine living anywhere else.

'I must be going mad,' Victoria said, to herself this time, 'sending a message from one dead person to another. It's time I did something useful for a change, like sponging down the wallpaper. That should keep me busy for a few days.'

She prepared a bucket of warm, soapy water and had washed half the hall – to little effect – when Rachel Williams called and invited her for coffee at eleven o'clock. 'It's for Kathleen Cartwright really. She wants to meet everyone. Sarah Rees-James and Marie Jordan are coming. I'm just off to ask Anna Burrows and I'd better remind Kathleen in case she's forgotten.'

Victoria had almost finished another wall when Ernest Burrows came and asked if she could spare the time to go shopping with him and Anna for a computer that afternoon and she said she'd love to, particularly when Ernie said they would have lunch first.

'I hadn't forgotten, not at all,' Kathleen said, 'but I thought you might not feel up to it. You look a bit . . . harassed.'

'I feel fine today,' Rachel professed, although her

eyes were wild and her face red and shiny with perspiration.

'Would you like to come in for a minute?'

'No, thank you. I only came to remind you.'

Kathleen offered to come early and help get things ready, but Rachel said she could manage on her own. 'It's only coffee and I made some fairy cakes first thing this morning.' She dropped her eyes and ran her fingers through her untidy hair. 'I'm sorry about yesterday. It was just when I heard that little girl in the next cubicle. She reminded me of Alice. She used to tell me how beautiful I was. So did Kirsty and James when they were little, but now they think I'm just a mess.'

'I'm sure that's not true,' Kathleen protested.

'It is,' Rachel said flatly. 'Well, I won't hold you up any longer. I'll see you later, shall I?'

'I'm looking forward to it.'

'Who was that?' Steve asked when Kathleen closed the door and went into the kitchen where they'd been having a late breakfast.

'Rachel. She's invited me for coffee.' She looked at him, eyes narrowed, daring him to say something offensive about her new friend, but he didn't speak. 'I won't be gone long,' she added, resenting that she felt slightly guilty for leaving a grown man by himself.

'Take as long as you like. I shouldn't have said anything yesterday. I suppose I was just worried about you – and I missed you.'

'Anna will be at the coffee morning. Why don't you go round and see Ernie?' she suggested. 'He'll be on his own too.'

Steve smiled. 'There's no need to find me a

playmate, luv. I'll go for a walk, buy meself a newspaper. D'you know we're not far from Penny Lane? The girls'll be tickled pink when I tell them I've been there.' He groaned and made a face. 'Sorry, I didn't mean that. It just slipped out without me thinking. For the moment, I'd forgotten they'd grown up.'

'That's all right.'

'Who was that on the phone last night?' he asked casually. 'I seem to remember you were speaking to someone when I came in.'

She wasn't prepared to lie. 'It was Michael.'

'I see.' He nodded and looked grim.

'I doubt if you do,' she said shortly. 'After the things you'd said earlier, I needed someone to talk to. There was no one else but him.'

'What happens if *I* need someone to talk to?'

'Oh, don't be so childish, Steve.' She went over to the sink and began to wash the breakfast dishes when there was a crash behind her. When she looked, startled, Steve had swept the milk jug off the table with a single sweep of his big hand.

'Don't you dare call me childish!' he said in a low, grating voice she'd never heard before, his face ugly with rage. 'I'm fed up being treated like a kid. Last night, I was just trying to explain how I felt. I was being honest with you. I thought you'd understand.'

'Understand?' Kathleen cried. 'Understand when you tell me that Jean's part of you? How do you think that makes me feel? *I* want to be part of you. I want . . . oh, I don't know *what* I want.' She burst into tears, hating herself for it, knowing how easily he was moved by tears – it was Jean's tears that were calling him back home and she didn't want to play his wife's game. 'I'm so mixed up. I don't know what *you* want either. Perhaps we should never have come away together.'

'Don't say that!' His rage vanished as quickly as it had come and he pulled her on to his knee. 'I'm mixed up too.' He buried his head in her shoulder. 'I don't know whether I'm coming or going,' he said in a muffled voice. 'I'm sick of us fighting.'

Kathleen sniffed. 'So am I.'

'I love you.'

'And I love you.'

He stroked her face. 'Let's not fight any more. I promise never to mention Jean again.'

'And I promise not to ring Michael.' She remembered that, in September, their son had invited them to Denmark for the weekend, but September was a long way off. She'd cross that bridge when she came to it.

'Did you notice,' Anna said to the assembled women, 'that the curtains are up in the empty bungalow?'

Everyone said they hadn't, apart from Rachel who told them a woman had come round the night before to borrow a torch.

'She'd forgotten to bring one and it was dark and she couldn't find where to switch the electricity on. Her name's Donna Moon and the house isn't hers, but her mother-in-law's – she's moving in tomorrow. The furniture's coming this morning and Donna will be back to see to it. I invited her for coffee, but she said she'd be too busy.'

The conversation turned to mothers-in-law. Sarah Rees-James had never met hers. 'Alex had a big family somewhere in London, but they never saw each other.

Maybe he was ashamed of them – or they were ashamed of him. Now I'll never know.'

Rachel told them Frank's mother had put him into care and had had nothing to do with him since. 'I wouldn't have wanted to meet her,' she said with a little shudder.

'My first husband's mother was a really charming person,' Kathleen said, feeling obliged to contribute towards the discussion. 'She died two years ago and I was terribly upset. Steve's mother was already dead when I met him. Steve and I only recently married,' she added for the benefit of anyone who hadn't already heard the lie she'd told.

Marie Jordan didn't contribute towards the conversation, Kathleen noticed. She seemed very uptight, as if something was troubling her. Victoria wasn't married and didn't have a mother-in-law, and Anna said she hadn't met hers either. 'Though I would have loved to. According to Ernie, she was a wonderful person, but they lost touch during the war.'

'Is that when you met Ernie, in the war?' Rachel enquired.

'Yes, in Cairo.' Anna's eyes glowed. 'We stayed in Cairo for years afterwards, and then moved to the South of France. We also spent time in Paris and Rome – we even lived for a while in Las Vegas. Ernie used to be an inveterate gambler.'

'He doesn't look like a gambler,' Kathleen remarked. 'He gives the impression of being a very cautious man.'

'Oh, he is, he is,' Anna trilled. 'He's a very cautious gambler. Have any of you ever been in a casino?' Everyone shook their heads, enthralled by the turn the conversation had taken. 'Well,' Anna went on, 'you probably don't know that in roulette you can bet on a number the ball lands in, or you can bet on the colour. Ernie always put his chips on the black, knowing the ball was bound to end up on black eventually. If it didn't, he'd double his stake, then double it again if he lost. One night,' Anna paused for a dramatic breath, 'one night, the ball landed on red nine times in a row. Now Ernie's not the sort to get all hot and bothered, but that night his hands were shaking. He'd started off with a thousand francs, but now he'd have to stake – I can't work out how much it would be,' she said, fretful all of a sudden.

'Just over five hundred thousand.' Kathleen was good at mental arithmetic.

'Half a million francs,' Sarah gasped. 'How much is that in English money?'

'I don't know,' Anna confessed. 'The exchange rate was very different in those days; there were hundreds and hundreds of francs to the pound. Anyway, all our money had gone, every penny. Poor Ernie was shattered, so I did no more than turn to the woman next to me and offer to exchange my ruby necklace for her chips. She didn't hesitate – she knew she was getting a bargain – so I threw the chips on the black square and we won.'

The women uttered a relieved sigh, and Victoria said in wonder, 'You actually had a ruby necklace?'

'I did indeed,' Anna said boastfully.

'I bet Ernie never went near a casino again for a long time,' Rachel commented.

'Oh, no, dear. We just went to the bar and had a drink – champagne, if I remember rightly – and he was back at the tables within an hour.'

'Wow!' Sarah gasped. 'We used to spend holidays in

the South of France when I was little. Daddy loved casinos, but he always lost. Mummy used to get terribly cross with him. What a fantastic life you've led, Anna!'

Anna preened herself and Kathleen said, 'And that's not all. Before the war, she was an actress. Tell them about the film you made, Anna.'

'Well,' Anna began, only too willing, 'I was only seventeen . . .'

By rights, Ernest's ears should have been burning considering the amount of personal information his wife was conveying to the women across the way. Instead, inspired by the dream, he was thinking about his mother sitting in front of the fire in Chaucer Street, knitting needles moving backwards and forwards like pistons on an engine. He hadn't 'lost touch', as Anna had put it. When he'd first got to North Africa, he'd written regularly to his mother, but his letters had got fewer and fewer and had stopped altogether when he met Anna. There was only room for one woman in his life and she was all he could think of.

By then, Ernest had changed, no longer the same naive, inexperienced nineteen-year-old who'd left Bootle what seemed like a hundred years ago. No way could he see himself going back, marrying Magdalene, and working in a chandler's shop for the rest of his life – he wrote to Magdalene and told her. She didn't reply and Mam's painfully written, badly-spelt letters continued to arrive, but stopped after a while when he didn't answer – she probably thought they weren't reaching him.

He didn't even go to see his family when he was demobbed at a base in Kent, not prepared to waste days of his time when all he wanted was to get back to Anna and their future together.

'I was a bastard,' Ernest told himself. 'A selfish, unthinking bastard.' He hadn't even thought to contact Gaynor or Charlie when he returned to Liverpool with Anna ten years ago. Liverpool had been her idea, not his.

'Let's retire,' she'd said. 'Properly retire, go somewhere completely different and make new friends.' Their old friends were dead or had retired themselves and the disease she had was getting worse. She was having more bad periods and fewer remissions. 'I don't want you pushing me around Monte Carlo or Paris in a wheelchair, Ernie. It would be too sad for words.'

He'd never forget the day Anna was told she had Multiple Sclerosis. It was like a death sentence. Ernest had thought he wouldn't have her for much longer. Nearly thirty years later, she was still alive to entertain him every minute of every day.

They'd moved to Liverpool and it had taken ten years and a vivid dream to prompt Ernest into thinking about Mam and the brother and sister he'd left behind when he was barely out of his teens.

Gaynor and Charlie would be well into their sixties by now and could be anywhere in the world – Gaynor was likely to have married and changed her name. On impulse, he picked up the telephone directory and looked for Burtonshaw. There were only two and one had the initial 'C'. Now all he had to do was pick up the phone and dial, but Ernest, usually a man of courage, couldn't bring himself to do it. What would he say if he established that the C. Burtonshaw was his half-brother, Charlie? 'Hello, this is Ernie. Nice talking to you again after sixty years. Sorry I didn't get in touch sooner.'

He'd discuss it with Anna. She'd know what to do, she always did.

There was a loud, rumbling noise outside and when he looked a furniture van had driven into the square. It stopped outside the bungalow where curtains had been put up the night before. A row of curious faces appeared in the window of Rachel Williams's house where the women were having coffee. Ernest grinned. What interest people found in other people's furniture would always be a mystery to him.

After they'd tired of watching the removal men carry in Mrs Moon's strangely painted furniture – apart from Kathleen who considered it degrading and had remained in her seat – Rachel refilled everyone's coffee cups and brought in another plate of fairy cakes. Anna had exhausted herself and was listening for a change. She was a remarkable woman, Kathleen thought, very old and very ill, but with no intention of sinking into the background as other women in the same position might. She thrust herself forward, determined not to go unnoticed.

Having dealt with television and their favourite programmes, dismissed politics as dull and unworthy of discussion, and swapped their favourite recipes, Victoria was now telling them what the square used to look like before the houses had been built.

'We just called it "the yard", and it was an eyesore. Granddad had no head for business and the company just went down and down until it fizzled out altogether. I've photographs at home showing the place in all its glory, when it looked very smart, and an even earlier one when it was green and countrified. If I'd known you'd be interested, I'd've brought them with me.'

'Perhaps we could have another coffee morning next week and you can show us then,' Sarah Rees-James suggested. 'We could have it in my house if you like, make it a regular event.'

'I shall be starting work at the hospital in August,' Kathleen told her. 'I won't be able to come then, but it would be nice to meet again next week.'

'I'll be looking for work as soon as the children go back to school,' said Marie Jordan, 'but I could come next week an' all.'

'I won't be here next week,' Victoria reminded them. 'I'll be in New York, having already started my new job. But don't forget the barbecue on Saturday. I'll be here for that.'

'I'd forgotten you were leaving.' Sarah looked at her glumly. 'Tiffany will miss you terribly. And so will I, which is silly, because I hardly know you – *that's* silly too, because I feel as if I've known you for ages.'

'Our Danny will miss you too, Victoria,' Marie put in, 'me as well.'

'We all will,' said Rachel.

Anna remarked how sad she also would be to see Victoria go.

Victoria blushed. 'There's been times this week when I've wished I wasn't leaving, but it's too late to back out now. I might come home, you never know the way things will turn out, and I'm not selling the house, it'll still be mine. If I *do* return, I wonder if you'll all still be here by then?'

Gareth couldn't concentrate on work that morning.

His head was all over the place: one minute he was thinking about Victoria, next it was Debbie with whom he'd had a terrible row all to do with the planned holiday in Barbados. The travel agent had written wanting the balance in full – so far Gareth had only paid a deposit. He'd blanched when he saw the amount required.

'We can't afford this, Deb,' he told her. 'I'm not prepared to take on any more debts.'

'Why not?' Debbie tossed the pigtails that looked ludicrous on a 25-year-old: until now he'd considered them cute and sexy. 'We can afford to pay it back.'

'No, we can't, Deb,' he said patiently. 'I did a calculation the other night. After I've paid instalments on all the loans, there's hardly enough left for us to live on. The interest on top is horrendous and a complete waste of money. It would be madness to go on holiday. We'd need spending money: we'd get even deeper into debt. I'm going to ring the travel agent and cancel. It means losing the deposit, but that's just too bad.'

'You'll do no such thing, Gareth Moran.' Debbie stamped her foot and Tabitha, who'd been listening, his head going from one to the other as if he was watching a tennis match, turned in fright and ran upstairs. 'I'm really looking forward to that holiday. I *need* a holiday. I've been working dead hard lately.'

'If you need it all that much, then why don't *you* pay for it.'

'You know I don't earn enough.'

'Well, now you know that *I* don't earn enough, not to pay for holidays in Barbados and fancy golf carts,' Gareth responded angrily.

'It's not a golf cart, it's a Prairie Dog.' The little

pointed jaw that he'd kissed so tenderly in the past dropped an inch. 'Does that mean we're not getting the Prairie Dog either?'

'Not unless you buy it yourself, Deb.'

On the way to work in the Escort, he'd regretted saying that, just in case she went out and bought the damn thing with her Goldfish card. She might even pay for the holiday as well. He thought of ringing Goldfish and telling them he wouldn't be held responsible for his wife's debts, but it seemed an awfully traitorous thing to do.

'Have you gone deaf, man?' Kevin enquired from the next desk. Kevin was the same age as him, earned the same wages, was married and had two kids, lived in a perfectly nice house with perfectly nice furniture, drove a newish car, and the only money he owed was to the Halifax for his mortgage. Gareth envied him tremendously. He was beginning to regret marrying Debbie. If they'd just continued to live together, everything would have been fine. It was getting a joint account that had been his undoing.

'I'm sorry,' he said to Kevin. 'Did you say something?'

'I said, "Are you going deaf?" and before that I asked if you'd like some posh nosh at lunchtime. It's me birthday and I'm treating all youse guys to a meal.'

'Count me in,' Gavin said with a sigh. It might take his mind off things for a while.

Alastair, who'd been asleep in his pram outside Rachel's back door, woke and began to cry. Sarah took him home for his midday meal, saying, 'Danny's babysitting Tiffany and Jack. He'll have had enough by now.'

Marie said, 'I'll come with you,' and Victoria announced she and Anna were going into town to buy a computer. 'We're having lunch first and Ernie will probably want to leave in about half an hour.' She took Anna home, the older woman clinging to her arm. Only Rachel and Kathleen were left. Having the coffee morning was Rachel's way of bravely trying to regain some normality in her life, but the effort had left her nervous wreck.

'I think that went very well,' Kathleen said warmly.

'Do you? Frank says I'm a hopeless hostess. I force things on people and they feel obliged to take them just to please me.'

'You were perfect,' Kathleen assured her. 'Everyone enjoyed themselves, I could tell, and I know I did. Isn't Victoria sweet? I really liked her. I liked Sarah and Marie too,' she added hastily, 'and Anna is a real character.'

'Would you like another cup of coffee?' Rachel asked. She probably didn't realize how much her eyes were pleading for Kathleen to say 'yes'.

'I'd love one, thank you, and one of your delicious fairy cakes.' She should really be getting back to Steve, but Rachel's need seemed so much greater.

Anna had recovered her voice. In the restaurant, she had a loud argument with Ernest as to whether he should order a whole bottle of wine. 'It's much cheaper than buying it by the glass,' she said.

'It depends how many glasses you buy. *You're* only allowed one. Unless Victoria can drink the rest of the bottle, it'll go to waste. I'm having beer. She shouldn't really drink at all, it interferes with her medication,' he said to Victoria.

Victoria assured them she couldn't possibly drink three-quarters of a bottle unless they stayed all afternoon, so Ernest ordered two glasses and Anna made a face at him. 'Meanie!'

Ernest grinned. 'I'm just looking after your best interests, luv.'

'You're still a meanie.'

They were in the Life Café in Bold Street where Kathleen and Rachel had lunched the day before on Anna's recommendation. It was her favourite restaurant. 'This room's so gracious,' she remarked when they went into the circular dining area that had an elegant balcony where more people could be seen having lunch.

'I've always wanted to eat up there,' Anna said, 'but I can't manage the stairs.'

'I've offered to carry her up, but she's not having it.'

'I still have some dignity left, Ernie Burrows. You can carry me in private, but not in public. What would you like to eat, Victoria, dear? I'm having chicken salad.'

'I'll have curried anything. I love curry.'

The waitress came and Ernest gave their order. They began to talk about computers. 'Can either of you type?' Victoria asked.

'I used to be able to type quite fast,' Anna said. 'I learned during the war, but these days my fingers aren't what they used to be. Ernest can manage quite well with just two.'

From the balcony of the Life Café, Gareth was watching Victoria eat. He'd been hoping for a stress-free hour enjoying the food and the company of his mates, but he'd barely started on his steak and chips

288

when Victoria had walked in with the old couple from the house next door to Hamilton Lodge. They seated themselves at a table directly beneath him. All he could see was the top of Victoria's dark curly head. He sent half a dozen thought messages telling her to look up, but they mustn't have arrived because she didn't.

'What's down there, man?' asked Kevin.

Gareth jumped guiltily. 'Down where?'

'Down there where you keep looking?'

'I don't know what you're on about, Kev.'

'Every time I speak to you, your eyes are somewhere else. You must be getting a squint.'

Gareth ignored this. Earlier, Kevin had told him he was going deaf. He must be giving an awfully odd impression to people. He continued to look down and saw the old guy, Ernie, signal to the waitress and, worried he might be calling for the bill, he leapt to his feet, muttering, 'Won't be a mo,' and hurtled downstairs.

'Fancy seeing you here!' he gasped when he reached the table where his neighbours and Victoria were sitting.

'Oh, hello.' Victoria blushed.

'Hello.' Anna seemed delighted to see him, as if he were a long-lost friend. 'Sit down a minute, dear. Gareth, isn't it? We're leaving soon.'

Gareth sat in the chair next to Ernest. 'I was upstairs, on the balcony,' he gulped. 'I thought I'd just come and say hello.'

'Hello,' Victoria said again.

'Do you work near here, son?' Ernest asked.

'In Duke Street, it's no distance away.' He liked the old couple, they were the gear, but Gareth wished they would go away and leave him with Victoria.

He'd be happy for the whole world to disappear as long as she was left behind, the only two people on the planet, with no one to talk to but each other. He loved her! He loved her in a way that he'd never loved Debbie: deep down, with his heart and his soul and his mind and his body. He longed to tell her now, say it aloud, shout, 'I LOVE YOU, VICTORIA MACARA,' so the whole restaurant would know.

The old guy, Ernie, was saying something to him, asking if he'd like a drink. 'No, ta. I won't keep you,' he stammered. Anna had been chuntering on, saying something about computers and being about to buy their first. He said, 'If you need any help setting it up, let me know.'

'Victoria's going to do it, but I'm sure another pair of hands will prove useful. Come tonight if you're free. We'll open some wine, won't we, Ernie? Make an evening of it.'

Gareth glanced at Victoria who was carefully examining her nails. 'I'll be there,' he said in a choked voice.

'Isn't he married?' Ernest said a few minutes later as he helped Anna into her wheelchair. Victoria had gone to the Ladies. 'You should've invited his wife if we're going to make an evening of it.'

'Don't be an idiot, Ernie,' she snapped. 'Can't you see those two young people are madly in love? The last person Gareth wants there tonight is his wife.'

'You shouldn't really be encouraging them, luv.'

'Don't be such a misery guts. They've only got a few days left together. 'I'll encourage them all I like.' She sighed dreamily. 'It must have been love at first sight, just like you and me, Ernie.'

'When we first met, you couldn't wait to get shot of me,' Ernest grumbled.

'I was only pretending. I knew for certain we'd meet again, just like that song. "*We'll meet again*",' she warbled in a shaky voice and everyone turned to look, making Ernest feel hugely embarrassed yet strangely proud of his incorrigible little wife.

In Allerton Road, the tall, luscious figure of Sarah Rees-James, clad in white – stretch T-shirt and stretch jeans – was causing a similar distraction as she pushed the pram along the crowded pavement with a sleeping Alastair inside, Jack crouched at the foot, and Tiffany clutching the handle with one hand and Oliver in the other. Sarah was remarking at the top of her voice on the 'dear little shops', saying, 'How quaint,' when she saw a beauty parlour.

'What's quaint about it?' Marie asked. She wasn't even faintly pretty, but usually drew admiring glances with her long red hair. Not today though. All eyes, particularly those of the men, were drawn only to Sarah and, in particular, her shapely breasts.

'I didn't think there were places like that out in the sticks.'

'We're hardly out in the sticks, Sarah. We're not far from the centre of Liverpool.'

'I wouldn't have expected the people from around here to have facials and leg waxes and stuff,' Sarah said, much to the annoyance of a passing woman, who turned and glowered at her back.

'Shush!' Marie had noticed the woman's black stare. 'Don't talk so loud or someone's likely to give you a thump.'

'Well, I've never been shopping in a place like this before. It's almost Victorian.'

'There's a Tesco's over there. Did they have them in Victorian times?'

'They might have, I wouldn't know. There's a hairdressers. It looks quite respectable. I'll go there and have my streaks done. Hold the pram a minute, Marie, while I buy the children some chocolate.'

'It'll melt all over their clothes.'

'I don't mind. I *love* washing things.' Sarah breathed ecstatically. 'I feel like a magician when I take them out of the machine and they're all clean again.' She disappeared into a sweet and tobacconists called O'Connor's. Marie held the pram and glanced idly at the cards in the window advertising things for sale.

Sarah reappeared. 'Isn't this a super adventure, kids?' she remarked, giving Tiffany and Jack each a Cadbury's Flake. 'Oh, look! There's a shop where you can have keys made and shoes repaired at the same time.' She looked puzzled. 'That's a strange combination. They engrave things too.'

'There's thousands of shops the same all over the country, girl. I suppose you threw your shoes away as soon as the heels wore down a bit,' Marie added caustically.

'I did no such thing! Mummy used to give them to Mrs Wesley, the housekeeper. She had a daughter who took the same size. Anyway, by that time, they were out of fashion and I wouldn't have dreamed of wearing them again.'

Marie rolled her eyes. 'Lucky old you.'

Sarah slowed down the pram and looked at her. 'Am I getting on your nerves?'

'A bit. You'd think everyone around here lived in the Dark Ages.'

'All this is new to me. I'm not used to buying groceries and stuff. All I bought were clothes for myself and occasionally for the children. Nanny always bought their shoes. It was such a bore, having to have their feet measured. Jack always cried, I can't think why.'

'He thought they were going to cut his feet off, Mummy,' Tiffany said.

'Poor little angel.' Sarah kissed the top of Jack's head. 'Next time, Mummy will take you to buy shoes, darling, and no one will cut off your feet, I promise.'

They walked on. When they passed a small W.H. Smith, Sarah asked Marie if she would hold the pram again while she went to buy a book.

'What sort of book?'

'I don't know,' Sarah said vaguely. 'Any sort, really. Alex said one of the worst things about me was I never read books.'

She wandered inside and emerged about ten minutes later with a book in a plastic bag. 'I told the woman I'd never read a book before and she recommended this one. It's called *Harry Potter and the Goblet of Fire*. Isn't that an interesting title? Oh, look, Marie!' she shrilled. 'There's a dear little café across the road. Shall we go and have coffee?'

'OK,' Marie said weakly.

'I used to get on Alex's nerves terribly,' Sarah confessed when they were having the drinks. She lowered her head and her thick, blonde hair fell forward, shadowing her face, making her blue eyes seem darker. In a low voice, she said tremulously, 'I'm awfully worried about him, Marie.'

293

'There's no need to worry, surely? The police took him away.'

'I rang the station this morning and they'd let him off with a caution. My solicitor has applied to have a restraining order put on him, but nothing will stop Alex from getting what he wants. He told me he was going to take the children abroad, that I'd never see them again.'

'Can he do that without your permission?'

'He wouldn't ask for my permission.' She glanced to see if Tiffany was listening, but she was busy trying to make Oliver drink through a straw. In an even lower voice, Sarah said, 'I wouldn't put it past him to come with a gang of thugs who'd snatch them off me and put them straight on to a plane.'

'I wouldn't go, Mummy.' Tiffany had been listening all the time. 'I'd scream and scream and Ernie would come and save us again.'

'I know you would, darling,' her mother said tearfully, 'but Ernie won't always be around to save you. I wonder if we shouldn't move again to a place where Alex will never find us,' she whispered to Marie.

'If he's the sort of man you say he is, there's nowhere on earth where he won't find you,' Marie whispered back.

'I envy you, Marie.' Sarah sighed. 'Your husband, Liam, seems awfully nice. You never complain, nothing bothers you. I wish my life was as calm and trouble free as yours.'

Marie wanted to say, 'Don't you believe it.' Instead, she just shrugged and said nothing.

Victoria had advised getting a proper desk for the

computer, 'With a shelf at the back for the monitor, otherwise you'd have to balance it on books or something to save getting a pain in the neck having to look down all the time.'

Ernie said everything could go in the spare bedroom. 'It's still a mess. I haven't had time to sort it yet.'

'We could call it the office, Ernie,' Anna said importantly. 'Or does the study sound better?'

'Call it anything you like, luv.'

Desks only came in flat packs, but Victoria said she'd put her own desk together and, anyroad, Gareth would be there to help.

Ernie's idea of a mess differed wildly from Victoria's. When they got to Clematis Cottage, she went into the spare bedroom where cardboard boxes, as yet unpacked, had been neatly placed on top of one another. There was a single armchair and a bookcase full of books: in alphabetical order by author, she noticed. Most of the books were thrillers, but there were a few military histories and political tomes on a separate shelf.

Ernie said that, once they were settled, it was where he intended to come and have a quiet read when Anna was watching a film he didn't like or had a visitor. He was carefully opening the box that held the desk with a Stanley knife.

'I see you've got *The Ragged Trousered Philanthropist*,' Victoria remarked. 'That was Granddad's favourite book. He read it over and over. I only put it out the other day for a charity shop.'

'I'd've liked to have met your granddad,' Ernie said. 'He sounds like a man after me own heart.'

'You'd have got on well together.'

'That copy you've got,' Ernest said thoughtfully,

'Steve next door might like it. He's a Socialist, same as me.'

'I'll take it round sometime. I met Steve's wife this morning. She seems awfully nice.'

The doorbell rang and Ernest went to answer it. Seconds later, Gareth entered the room. 'Hi,' he said. 'Ernie's gone to make us some tea.'

'Hi.' Victoria didn't look up, her head bent over the diagram showing how the desk should be erected.

'I understand we've got a desk to put up.'

Victoria nodded, still not looking at him. 'It was my idea that they buy it. It's quite straightforward, there are no drawers or extending bits. I hope you don't mind.'

'Of course I don't mind. I'd do anything, build a house, let alone a desk, if it meant being with you,' Gareth said simply.

She looked at him then. 'Don't say things like that. What about Debbie? What excuse did you give her for leaving? Where does she think you are?'

'She hasn't come home. She's probably gone to her mother's again. I'm being punished because we had a row this morning. I'm very much in Debbie's bad books.' He stuffed his thumbs in his jeans' pockets and shrugged. 'It was about money again. She can't understand why I'm not willing to get even more overdrawn.'

'I'm sorry, Gareth.'

'Not half as sorry as I am,' Gareth said with a sigh, just as Ernie came in with three cups of tea on a tray.

'Anna's got wine, but I thought it'd best if we kept our heads clear until this thing has been put together.'

'You're very wise, Ernie,' Victoria told him.

'It comes with growing old, luv,' Ernie said gruffly.

'I wasn't wise when I was your age else I might have done all sorts of things differently, but then I wouldn't have had nearly such a good time. Too much wisdom can make life awful dull.'

'Lord, Ernie! Now you sound even wiser.' Victoria gulped down the tea. 'Shall we get started? The sooner it's finished the better.'

Victoria was kneeling on the bed, looking out of the window at the still and soundless square, and breathing in the heady scent of lavender. She would have gone downstairs and made a drink, but it meant climbing over Gareth who was fast asleep, disturbing him. She'd been unable to sleep herself, although she usually dropped off the minute her head touched the pillow. The last time she'd looked at her watch it had been ten past two.

They'd had a marvellous time at Clematis Cottage – not that anything even faintly exciting or interesting had happened – but just being in the same room as Gareth, knowing how he felt about her and she about him, eyes meeting, hands touching every now and then when they'd put the desk together, sharing Anna and Ernie's astonishment when the computer had been connected and the logo appeared on the screen.

'It's a bloody miracle,' Ernie had gasped.

'Don't swear, darling,' Anna chided, nudging him.

'I bet Victoria and Gareth have heard worse words than that in their time,' Ernie said, not at all apologetic. 'Now, how d'you play them card games you told us about?'

'I thought the computer was bought for me?' Anna complained.

'You can have a turn in a minute, luv.'

It was almost ten by the time Ernie could be parted from the computer and into the front room to drink the wine and eat the biscuits Anna had provided. Victoria had refused wine, preferring tea and, as soon as she'd drunk it, said she had to be going home. 'I've loads to do tomorrow, walls to wash, that sort of thing.' Gareth remembered he had work to do on his own computer and it was time he went too.

They'd left together, running hand in hand towards Victoria's house, knowing what would happen when they got there.

And it had. And it had been wonderful, far better than Victoria had ever known before, even with Philip with whom, until days ago, she'd thought she'd been in love. Gareth had said the same, and she'd told him that he shouldn't, not when he was married to Debbie, but he said he couldn't help it. It was the truth.

'We were made for each other,' he said softly. 'It's another bloody miracle.'

Victoria had sobbed into his shoulder, knowing that what he said was true, but things had all gone wildly wrong because he already had a wife and it wasn't a miracle, it was a bloody tragedy.

She'd fetched a bottle of wine and they'd drunk it in bed, leaning against the headboard, telling each other tender things, their voices sad because they knew theirs would only be a very fleeting affair.

They made love again and it was even better than before, and then Gareth had made sure no lights were on in Hamilton Lodge indicating that Debbie had come home. It meant that he and Victoria could spend the night together. It might be the only night they ever would. Soon afterwards, he'd fallen asleep, and she had lain watching him, wishing things could be different, knowing it was a waste of time.

She looked at her watch again: quarter to three. A car door slammed in the main road and she was surprised when two men walked into the square. They could be seen quite clearly in the light of the moon and the lamps that cast a soft glow over the silent houses. They stopped in front of the first house where Sarah Rees-James and her children slept. Although the men had their backs to her, Victoria could tell they were giving Sarah's house a good look over. Their voices were audible through the open window, though she couldn't make out the words. One of the men approached the front door and she held her breath, wondering if she should shout and order them to go away, but the man merely examined the lock and returned to join his companion.

'Gareth.' She shook his shoulder.

'Wha?' muttered a sleepy voice, followed by a wide-awake one saying, 'Victoria, what a cracking surprise! I'd forgotten where I was for the minute.' He tried to drag her back into bed, but she said urgently, 'There's these men outside Sarah's house, casing the joint.'

'Casing the joint!' He laughed out loud.

'Shush! The window's open and they might hear. Come and look.'

When Gareth looked, the men were walking away. Soon afterwards, a car door slammed and she said quickly, 'Look through the other window, quickly, see if they came in a silver Rolls-Royce.'

Gareth leaped out of bed, as naked as the day he was born, and ran to the end room. 'It's a Rolls,' he said. 'I couldn't tell what colour in the streetlights, but I'd guess silver.'

'That's Sarah's husband's car. I told you what happened yesterday, didn't I? He tried to take the children, but Ernie stopped him. I missed everything,' she said regretfully. 'I was covered in cobwebs at the time. He must be intending to come back again. I'd better tell Sarah tomorrow. Oh!' She put her hand to her mouth.

'Oh, what?'

'Say if they come back tonight?'

'We'll just have to stay awake in case they do, then sound the alarm.'

'Stay awake all night!'

'That's easily done.' Gareth got into bed and took her in his arms. 'Very easily done,' he said, kissing her.

Tonight was the second time that Liam had tried to open her bedroom door, but had found it bolted on the inside. He knocked softly and whispered, 'Marie,' but Marie merely buried her head in the pillow, the rosary in her hand.

'Hail Mary, full of grace,' she whispered. 'Blessed art thou amongst women. Blessed is the fruit of thy womb, Jesus . . .'

Liam whispered her name and knocked again, but must have decided to give up when there was no response. The floorboards creaked as he crept back to his room, the bed creaked when he got into it, and Marie prayed faster and faster until the words ran into each other and no longer made any sense.

They hadn't been able to have a private word with each other all day – in a way it had been a relief as she had no idea what she would say. Patrick had been in when Liam had gone to work and was there when he came home. He had followed Liam into the kitchen when Marie was making the tea, and trailed after him into the garden where she'd gone to fetch the washing off the line. Quite clearly, Patrick had no intention of leaving her alone with Liam again. She wondered if her son had been awake when Liam had knocked and didn't like to think what would have happened if she'd let him in.

Things couldn't be allowed to go on in this way, living in such a horrible atmosphere – Danny had noticed and been unusually quiet all night. He probably thought it was all to do with the row the night before. He didn't know what Patrick knew, that his mammy had nearly had carnal knowledge of a priest.

'What am I to do?' Marie asked piteously. Her hand gripped the rosary so tightly that the crucifix pressed painfully into her palm. She gripped it harder, wanting to draw blood in order to pay for her sins, but the thought of blood brought back the memory of the house in Belfast with its blood-soaked room and the man with half his face blown away.

Who had done it?

And why?

Marie

Chapter 10

'Marie Clare Brennan, have you been wearing my black frock again?' Theresa screamed. 'I saw you sneak out last night, your coat buttoned to your neck, when you went to that dance at the Holy Spirit.'

'I did *not* sneak out,' Marie screamed back. 'My coat was buttoned because it happened to be snowing outside and I wore me very own blue dress underneath, the one *you* wore last week when you went out with Calum O'Reilly.'

'Then why is my black frock full of stains?'

'Don't ask me, Theresa. They're someone else's stains, not mine.'

'Mam!' Theresa continued to scream. 'D'you know who's been *borrowing* my best black frock?' The 'borrowing' was said in a tone of extreme sarcasm.

'Haven't I got more to do than keep me eye on whatever youse girls are wearing?' Mam shouted from the kitchen.

'Holy Mary, Mother of God.' Dad came to the bottom of the stairs and said wearily, 'Is it not possible for the women in this house to speak to each other like ordinary civilized human beings? You're like flamin' foghorns, the lot of you. You'd think we lived in different parts of the village, not under the same flamin' roof. Gerry, will you turn that flamin' music down,' he went on. 'I can't hear the telly and me nose is only six inches away from the flamin' thing.'

'I'm sorry, Daddy,' Theresa and Marie said together, but the noise in the next room – a marching band in full throttle – continued at the same level. Gerry hadn't heard. The two girls glared at each other over the crumpled bed that Mam refused to make unless the room was tidied first. As none of the four girls whose room it was were prepared to do it, the beds stayed unmade.

'I didn't touch your black frock, Theresa, honest,' Marie said sincerely, though she had – she crossed her fingers behind her back to excuse the lie. The stains had come from Tommy Costello's coke tin – he'd been hurling it into the air and when it was opened the liquid had spurted out, like a firework spraying sparks, all over Theresa's frock. At least the stains weren't quite as noticeable on black as they'd have been on blue – she'd have worn the blue if the armpits hadn't stunk to high heaven from when Theresa had 'borrowed' it the week before. It meant she'd have to wash it herself: no one trusted Mam with anything even faintly delicate as she just bundled everything into the machine, regardless of colour, never thinking to alter the temperature from the very hottest, so the whole wash was boiled and the clothes that emerged were unrecognizable: colours faded or a different colour altogether and only half the size they'd been when they went in.

'Where are you going tonight?' Theresa asked.

'Round Rita Kelly's house,' Marie replied. 'What about you?'

'I'm going to Donegal with Calum to see *Raging Bull* with Robert de Niro.'

'Is it getting serious with Calum, Tess?' The girls were

the best of friends again. The rows they had meant nothing.

Theresa went slightly pink. 'Pretty serious.' She sat at the dressing table and began to make up her face. The top was a jumble of bottles and jars, lipsticks, blushers, eye shadows and holy statues – three rosaries were draped over the mirror. More fights were fought over the contents of the dressing table than over clothes.

'Can I be your bridesmaid when you and Calum get married?'

'Aw, I dunno, Marie. If I say yes, I'd have to say it to everyone and Calum has three sisters. I'd feel daft having eleven bridesmaids. I mean we're not exactly royalty, are we? Anyroad, no way could we afford to pay for the frocks, you'd all have to buy your own, except our Sheila only earns a pittance at the art centre, and Orla and Kitty are still at school and Colette hasn't even started, so it seems bit much to expect Mam and Dad to shell out for them – it's less than a year since our Caitlin got wed—'

'And six months since she had their Darren,' Marie interrupted with a knowing laugh.

'Well, the less said about that the better,' Theresa said with a grin. 'There's a Brennan got married every year for the last four and Mam and Dad must be sick to the teeth of buying bridesmaid's frocks. First Clodagh, and then Siobhan, followed by Jimmy, and of course, Caitlin with the bulging belly that she tried to hide under a great bow. Did you ever know a bride before who had such a bow on the front of her dress and not the back?'

'Never!' Marie giggled. She lay on the bed in the chaotic room, as she had done thousands of times in the past, watching her elder sisters get made up and chatter about their boyfriends, and longing for the time to come when she'd have make-up and boyfriends of her own, one of whom she would eventually fall in love with and marry. Now the house was gradually emptying and, once Theresa married Calum, Marie, eighteen, would be the oldest Brennan girl left and have the double bed to herself. There were bunk beds at the far end of the room where Sheila and Orla slept, and Kitty and Colette were in the poky room that Dad had built in the loft. She hoped neither of them would want to sleep with her. She was looking forward to sleeping in the big bed alone.

'Anyroad, Tess,' she said, 'as regards the bridesmaid's frock, I'm willing to pay for me own as long it's something I can go dancing in afterwards and not some shiny taffeta creation I'll never wear again. By the way, that's *my* lippy you're about to put on. It's only Rimmel, but I'd prefer you didn't use it.'

Theresa scowled at the lipstick. 'Are you sure? I thought it was mine.'

'Since when have you worn russet brown?'

'You're right, mine's coral.' Theresa searched through the debris for the coral lipstick. 'Ah, here it is without the top. It's got hairs stuck to it. They're red.' She looked at her sister accusingly.

'I'm not the only one in this house with red hair, and I'd look a desperate freak in coral. It must have been our Orla using it, or it might have been Colette.'

'Colette's not even five yet.'

'Yes, but she's a forward little madam.'

Theresa sighed as she picked the hairs off the lipstick, a look of distaste on her face. 'I need to keep all me personal possessions under lock and key.'

'You're not the only one,' said Marie, thinking of her blue frock. She said casually, 'You'll never guess who was at the dance last night.' She paused for effect, 'Father Murphy!'

'He never was!' Theresa gasped.

'He was an' all. And he wasn't in priest's gear, either. He wore a polo-necked jumper and jeans.'

Theresa took in a long, ecstatic breath. 'What colour was the jumper?'

'White.'

'I bet he looked dead gorgeous.'

'He looked like Robert Redford in *Three Days of the Condor*. Remember we went to Donegal to see it last year?'

'I remember. Did he ask anyone up to dance?'

'Only Mrs Shaugnessy who does the flowers in church. She's about a hundred and two. They did an old-fashioned waltz. All the girls' tongues were hanging out a foot and a half, praying he'd ask *them*.'

'Fancy dancing with a *priest*! It makes me go all funny, just thinking about it.' Theresa stood and smoothed down her grey tweed skirt, adjusted the collar of her blouse, and patted her brown hair. 'Do I look all right?'

'You look fantastic, sis.'

'Honest?'

'Honest. Calum will be wanting to rip your clothes off the minute he sets eyes on you.' Half the Brennans had their dad's red hair, the other half their mother's rich brown. Looks had been doled out in similar proportions: the brown-haired Brennans were pretty – or handsome in the case of Francis who was fifteen – and the freckle-faced, ginger-headed half wouldn't exactly set the world alight with their looks: only their flaming hair and dark green eyes made them stand out in a crowd.

Theresa left and Marie lay staring at the poster of Mick Jagger that Clodagh had pasted on the ceiling when she was fourteen. Mam had done her nut, but when she'd tried to pull the poster down, the ceiling had started to come with it and she'd had to paste it back again. She was wondering if Mam would notice if she covered Mick Jagger with Sting, when her sister, Orla, came barging in.

'Jaysus! It stinks in here,' she gasped.

'That's our Theresa's perfume. It cost a packet.'

'Well, she wasted her money. What is it, Canal Number Five?'

'I bet you've been waiting years for the opportunity to use that joke.'

'It was in an old film I saw on telly last Sunday afternoon. Will you be off out shortly, Marie? I was intending to do me homework on that bed. Our Francis has bagged the table in the kitchen and Dad's watching telly in the front room.'

'I'll go now.' Marie rolled off the bed. She was only going round Rita Kelly's, so didn't bother to put on more lippy or comb her hair or change out of the clothes she'd worn for work at Monaghan's bakers in the High Street, something she would deeply regret before the evening was over.

Rita Kelly, Ursula Adams and Marguerite Kelly – no relation to Rita – had all been in the same class at school as Marie. When she arrived, they were sitting on the floor in Rita's bedroom listening to a Police record.

'Hi, Marie,' Rita hollered. 'Fancy a coke?'

'Sure thing.' Rita threw her the tin and Marie opened it cautiously, just in case it squirted out like the night before. 'Ta, Rita.'

Ursula produced a bottle from behind her back. 'Fancy some rum in it?' she asked. 'I pinched it from our Clifford's room. I'm going to fill it with cold tea afterwards, see if he notices.'

'I reckon he will,' said Marguerite, tossing her long hair. She was the prettiest, most glamorous there – and knew it. Marie was already wishing she'd changed into something more respectable when she saw Marguerite was wearing a black T-shirt with lace inserts, jeans, and long, dangly diamanté earrings. Her father was a solicitor and she was never short of a few bob.

'It depends on how pissed he is when he goes to drink it,' Ursula said. 'He's got a drink problem, our Clifford.'

'It shouldn't be a problem for long if all he drinks is cold tea.'

At this, the girls shrieked with laughter. Their laughter gauge was set at its very highest whenever they visited each other's houses although they never went to Marie's as there wasn't an empty room.

'Did'ya see Father Murphy at the dance last night?' Marguerite breathed.

'He reminded me of Harrison Ford in them clothes.'

'No, Robert Redford,' Marie argued.

'He looked more like Richard Gere in *Yanks*,' said Rita. She was a big-boned, healthy-looking girl with white-blonde, dead straight hair that positively refused to curl, no matter what was done to it. One of the nuns at school, Sister St Mary, used to insist she was Swedish. 'Robert Redford's too old, at least forty.'

'Richard Gere didn't wear jeans in *Yanks*,' Ursula informed them. 'It was set during the war and he wore a uniform the whole way through. I don't know why you're all slobbering yourselves to death over a priest, anyroad. He's only a *priest*. He still goes to the lavvy and wipes his bottom like everyone else.'

The other three gasped. Marie shook her head, as if she was trying to get rid of the picture of Father Murphy wiping his bottom that had come into her mind. 'That's a sacrilegious thing to say, Urse. You should be ashamed of yourself,' she said primly.

'It's not sacrilegious because I'm not a religious person any more. I'm an atheist, I only decided the other day. I don't believe in anything, not even God.' Ursula folded her arms and looked at them challengingly, but nobody could be bothered arguing. Wasn't she always saying things like that and hoping to create a stir? And hadn't they stopped taking the bait whenever the delicate, waif-like Ursula, who only looked about fourteen, claimed to have thought something or done something that was completely at odds with what they thought and did themselves?

'Rita, your brother's home,' a voice called. It was Brigid, Rita's sister, who was going on for forty and had become a substitute mother since Mrs Kelly had died giving birth to Rita, her tenth child. Brigid had been courting Edward O'Connor for twenty-one whole years and the wedding was taking place in a fortnight's time, a week after Rita's eighteenth birthday, when Brigid felt her duty to her family had been done.

'Which brother?' Rita shouted.

'It's our Enda.'

'Send him up. Tell him the girls are here.'

Footsteps thundered up the stairs, the door was flung open, and Enda Kelly hurtled into the room. He was twenty-one and, like his sister, was tall and big-boned, his blond hair as flat as a pancake — quite literally, as it looked as if a pancake had been slapped on to his head and moulded to shape.

'Hiya, kids.' He beamed at them. 'I've brought someone to see you. This is Mickey Harrison, me best mate at Harland & Wolff.' Enda worked at the shipyards in Belfast and often came home for weekends.

A man came into the room, about the same age as Enda. He was tall and slim, with jet-black wavy hair, jet-black eyes, and a wide mouth curled in the wickedest, most enticing of smiles that Marie had ever seen. He looked the girls over critically and his eyes settled on Marguerite, who, noticing the look, stretched voluptuously, finishing with her hands folded behind her head so that her small breasts, encased in a sexy black bra, were pointing at the newcomer through the lace inserts of her T-shirt, as if to say, 'I dare you to touch them.'

Mickey Harrison appeared quite ready to take the dare. His wicked smile grew wider as he stared at Marguerite. When Rita said, 'Come in and join us, youse two. We've got coke and rum,' he bounded across the room and plonked himself beside the breasts, completely ignoring Marie on his other side. She felt like the most unattractive person in the entire world. Either that or she'd disappeared, become invisible, and Mickey Harrison couldn't see her with his black, mischievous eyes.

It was a good half-hour before he turned and noticed her. 'Sorry, luv. I'm being rude, aren't I? What's your name? I know Rita told us, but I've forgotten.'

'Marie Brennan,' she said coldly. 'And yes, you *are* rude, sitting with your back to me all this time.'

He looked taken aback, probably expecting her to fawn all over him, as Marguerite had been doing ever since he came in, or thrust her breasts in his face – they were bigger than Marguerite's by a mile. 'I said I was sorry,' he stammered.

She shrugged carelessly. 'OK, apology accepted – what's *your* name? I've forgotten too.'

'Mickey Harrison.' His eyes held a gleam of interest.

Marie could tell that she intrigued him. 'Have you got a boyfriend, Marie?'

She wasn't sure what to answer. If she said yes, he might run a mile and, although she never went short of dates, she'd never had a proper boyfriend, but didn't want Mickey to know that. She shrugged again and said, 'A sort of boyfriend. He's in England, at university,' she added, inspired. 'He keeps on at me to get married, but I'm not sure if I want to.' The others were busy talking and didn't hear the brazen lie.

He opened his mouth to reply, but Marguerite did no more than put her hand on his face, turn it towards her, and say in a silky, soft voice that Marie had never heard her use before, 'When was it you said you were coming back to Donegal again, Mickey?'

'The weekend after next,' he replied. 'Enda's invited me to their Brigid's wedding.'

Marie had also been invited to the wedding. She resolved to turn up looking like a million dollars – Mickey Harrison would notice her then – but this turned out to be easier said than done.

'You can borrow me black frock,' Theresa said generously. It was Sunday, and they were lying on the bed, waiting for Mam to shout it was time for Mass.

'You don't wear black at weddings.'

'Then what about your blue one?'

'It's too much like a dance frock. I want to impress him with my elegance and sophistication. I'd wear me grey one with the bolero if I hadn't already worn it a thousand times before,' Marie sniffed gloomily.

'Your grey one's smart enough, but it's a bit miserable.'

'I know. Whenever I wear it, I feel as if I want to take

the veil. The rest of me frocks are too summery and I don't want to wear a blouse and skirt.' What she needed was a really smart suit.

'This Mickey feller must've taken your fancy, Marie, if you're so dead set on impressing him,' Theresa remarked.

'Oh, he did,' Marie said simply. 'He's gorgeous, drop-down-dead gorgeous. I can't get him out of me mind, but Marguerite Kelly's already got her eye on him and she'll turn up to the wedding dressed like a film star and I won't stand a chance. I haven't even got a decent coat to wear. I don't suppose you could lend me some money?' she said coaxingly. 'I could buy something new.'

'You already owe me seven pounds,' Theresa pointed out. 'I wouldn't mind that back, by the way. I can't afford to lend any more. Any minute now and I'll be saving up for me bottom drawer. Why don't you ask our Clodagh if you can borrow her fur coat? It's not exactly new, I know.'

'It's not exactly fur, either. It looks like a mouldy old rug. Didn't she get it from a jumble sale?'

'There's a jumble sale at the Holy Spirit hall next Saturday – you might find something suitable there.'

Marie hit her sister with a pillow, just as Mam called to ask if they were ready, and Marie went to Mass with a heavy heart. It was three days since she'd met Mickey and he had haunted her ever since. She had no money – she was in debt to Mam and Sheila as well as Theresa, and next Friday's wages wouldn't be enough to pay everyone back, let alone buy a frock that would make her look like a hundred dollars, let alone a million.

In the end, she wore Theresa's black frock that had long tight sleeves, a fitted bodice, and a flared skirt. Mam said there was no harm in wearing black to a wedding – hadn't Auntie Agnes worn a black bouclé costume to Caitlin's last year? Mam let her borrow her long amber necklace and earrings set that Dad had given her on their twenty-fifth wedding anniversary and said she didn't need to pay back the money she owed until next week, so Marie bought a pair of black suede shoes with four-inch heels and gloves to match. Clodagh had her fur coat cleaned and it came up a lovely creamy colour and didn't look so bad at all and Caitlin lent her a hat that was merely a pompom with a bit of net attached and wouldn't hide her lovely hair.

On the morning of the wedding, Marie got up early to have a bath – essential if you wanted to soak in the water for more than half a minute when ten people shared the bathroom. She smeared an apricot face pack on her very ordinary face, half hoping it would work a miracle of some sorts, but when she peeled it off, her face looked no different, apart from the gooey bits still sticking to her chin. She washed her long, red wavy hair, dried it with extra care, and took half an hour doing her face, dabbing every single freckle between her eyes and on her nose with an extra layer of Golden Surrender moisturising make-up base. After she'd decked herself out in the borrowed clothes and jewellery, she went downstairs to show the finished result to Mam and Dad.

'Why, don't you look a picture?' Mam exclaimed. For a fifty-year-old woman who'd born twelve children she looked remarkably youthful. 'Your hair's come up a treat, Marie.'

'Come along, me darlin' girl,' Dad said, kissing her cheek, 'I'll give you a lift. That sky's rather threatening, as if it might snow again.' Marie wanted to cry because she loved him and her mammy so much, as well as her eight sisters and three brothers.

As the ancient van bumped over the frozen ruts in the path that led from the Brennan's tied farm cottage to the road ahead, she was glad about the lift. Walking, and she'd have ended up with a broken ankle or a broken heel, one or the other.

When Dad drew up outside the church, Marguerite Kelly was just climbing out of her father's flash red car. She wore black, thigh-length boots, a short red leather coat and a red leather cap to match, and gave Marie a little wave.

'Your mate's forgotten to put on a skirt,' Dad remarked.

'I don't think so, Dad. That's the latest fashion.'

'I thought mini-skirts went out years ago.'

'They did, but now they're back in again.' Marie sighed. She might have known it would be Marguerite who'd turn up looking like a million dollars, not her.

'Have a nice time, luv. Don't forget, give us a ring when you want to come home and I'll come and fetch you. It doesn't matter how late it is.'

'Ta, Dad.'

The church was crowded for the Nuptial Mass and she couldn't see hide nor hair of Mickey Harrison any way she looked. The first sight she had of him was outside the church when the photographs were being taken. Her heart turned a somersault: he looked handsomer than ever in a light grey suit with a pale blue tie, but her heart came back to land with a painful thump when she saw that Marguerite was already hanging on to his arm.

How had she managed that? Marie seethed. She must have Radar or something. She seethed even more when they transferred to the Holy Spirit hall for the reception and she saw Marguerite and Mickey sitting together at a table on the far side of the room. Her own name card was beside Ursula's – Rita, a bridesmaid, was on the top table.

'I thought Marguerite was sitting with us,' Ursula remarked. 'She must have moved the cards around. That's probably why I've got some ould auntie on me other side. The poor thing's as deaf as a post and can't hear a word I say. She's complaining she should've been put next to her sister.'

It was not until much later, after Brigid and Edward had left for the honeymoon in London, the tables had been cleared, the band had arrived, and the dancing began, that Marie came face to face with Mickey Harrison. It seemed almost inevitable that Marguerite would be clinging to his arm – they'd been inseparable all day.

'You look nice, Marie,' he said, his eyes smiling right into hers, not that it could possibly mean anything when he'd already been captured by a girl who could knock spots off Marie when it came to looks.

'Isn't that your Theresa's dress you're wearing?' Marguerite said in a penetrating voice.

Instead of wanting to sink through the floor, Marie said proudly, 'Yes, she loaned it me, and our Clodagh loaned me the fur coat she got from a jumble sale, and Mam this necklace and earrings, and me hat belongs to our Caitlin. The only things that I can call me own are me shoes.'

Mickey burst out laughing. 'Nice, generous family you've got, Marie.'

Marie was about to tell him how wonderful they were, when Marguerite shrieked, 'Oh, listen! They're playing "Children of the Revolution", me favourite.

Come on, Mickey, let's dance,' and Mickey was dragged away, leaving Marie to wonder since when had Marguerite liked anything by T. Rex, a group that normally she claimed to loathe? Tommy Costello, who'd splashed Coca-Cola over Theresa's frock a fortnight ago, asked Marie up. She didn't like him, but went willingly because she didn't want to be seen sitting the dance out.

'Mickey Harrison's not the only man in the world,' she told herself, although had to concede he was the only one that mattered.

At ten o'clock, she decided to go home. Ursula had already gone and Tommy was as drunk as a lord and making a nuisance of himself. There was no sign of Mickey – he was probably outside with Marguerite, necking against the Presbytery wall. She'd ring Dad from the pay phone in the porch and ask him to come and fetch her, but when she tried to use it, the coin box was jammed and she couldn't get the money in. She cursed, loudly.

'What's the matter?' asked an achingly familiar voice and Marie turned and saw Mickey Harrison standing behind her.

'You look funny on your own,' she said caustically. 'I thought Marguerite had become a permanent attachment.'

'So did I.' He made a face. 'Who are you phoning?'

'Me daddy, to come and collect me, but it's broken. It doesn't matter. I'll walk.'

'It's snowing a bit outside.'

'A bit of snow won't stop me.'

He smiled and the laughter lines around his dark eyes deepened. 'You're pretty tough, aren't you, Marie Brennan?'

'Am I?' She hadn't thought of herself as tough before.

'Yes, as tough as ould boots, as me dear grannie would have said.'

'You say the nicest things,' she snapped. 'That's the first time I've ever been compared to a pair of ould boots. It's not exactly flattering.'

'It was meant to be. Come on,' he grasped her arm, 'I'll give you a lift home.'

'You've got a car?'

'Well, I wasn't intending to give you a lift on me back.'

His car was an old Anglia, in only slightly better condition than her father's van. The engine groaned in complaint when he switched it on and gave an anguished sigh when it was turned off outside the Brennans' cottage. They'd hardly spoken to each other in the time between.

'Thank you for the lift,' Marie said. 'Are you going back to the wedding now? Marguerite will be wondering where you are.'

'Then Marguerite can go on wondering. I managed to escape once, I'm not going back to be captured again.' He folded his arms, grinning. 'I was hoping you'd ask me in for a cup of tea.'

'Would you like to come in for a cup of tea, Mickey?'

He jumped out of the car with alacrity. 'I would indeed, Marie. By the way, what's happened to your freckles?'

Marie was rooting in her bag for her key. 'They're covered with make-up.'

Mickey put a finger under her chin and tipped her face towards his. 'I prefer you with them,' he said softly, kissing her cheek.

Marie didn't like Belfast from the start. There was too

much hatred there, too much prejudice. She didn't like Catholics having to stick to their own shops, their own roads, while the Protestants stuck to theirs. She had nothing against Protestants. Hadn't she gone dancing loads of times in Donegal with June Cummings, a Methodist, whose mam belonged to the same women's circle as her own? Didn't they worship the same God, after all?

But Mickey was a Northern Irishman with a good job at Harland & Wolff. Marie had known that if she married him it meant living in Belfast and she hadn't hesitated. She'd have married Mickey had he lived in the North Pole or at the foot of a volcano.

So, Belfast it had to be. The first house they rented was a mean little terrace, full of dry rot and old-fashioned furniture that she polished to death in the hope of making it look better. It did, but not all that much. On the first night there, half a dozen British soldiers came racing down the street, rifles at the ready, disappearing inside a house only a few doors away. Marie, a born worrier, was terrified Mickey would get shot merely for being a Catholic.

She got a job working full-time in a dry cleaners. With two wages coming in, they were soon able to afford to move to a better house in a Catholic area. The place was unfurnished and she was glad they could buy their own stuff, even if it was mostly second-hand.

Despite everything, she was happy, madly in love with Mickey and he with her. Enda Kelly had got married not long after them to a girl called Peggy, who quickly became a friend. Weekends, they went out in a foursome to places like Ballycastle for the day, for a meal in town, or just to the local pub for a sing-song – Marie was always worried a bomb would go off and kept a lookout for suspicious packages. They acquired loads of friends and were often invited to parties and threw a party themselves every few months. Best of all were the times she and Mickey went to Donegal and slept in the room in the loft, empty now, as there were only four Brennan girls left and they occupied the bedroom with the bunks and the double bed and the poster of Mick Jagger on the ceiling, where Marie had spent so many happy hours, wishing and dreaming that one day she would meet a man like Mickey Harrison and marry him.

They'd been married for two years when Marie discovered she was pregnant. Mickey was thrilled to pieces. 'It'll be a boy and he'll have red hair, a million freckles, and sea-green eyes,' he predicted. 'Let's give him a good old Irish name, Patrick, but no one on earth will be allowed to call him Paddy.'

'What will happen if he's a girl?'

'As long as she looks like you, me darling Marie, I won't care.'

Marie didn't care either. All she wished was that her child could be born in Donegal with all her family around her. Mickey's parents were dead and he was the youngest of five, the others scattered far and wide all over the world: two brothers in Australia, one in the United States, and his only sister, Patsy, of whom he was desperately fond, living in London and working in a posh hotel in Mayfair. Marie had only met her the once at their wedding.

Still, she had plenty of friends, not as good as family, but almost. It was a nice surprise when Peggy Kelly announced she was also expecting and they could go to the clinic together, although her baby wasn't due until three weeks after Marie's.

Patrick Russell Harrison was born without too much bother on 14 July 1983. As Mickey had predicted, he had red hair and freckles and was the image of Marie.

'He's a corker,' his father said admiringly when he nursed his son for the first time. 'Just like his mam, except for the blue eyes.'

'They'll turn green eventually,' Marie assured him.

'Well, if that's not a miracle, then what is?' Mickey marvelled.

Marie considered it a miracle that he'd fallen in love with her when he could have had the gorgeous Marguerite or any number of equally beautiful girls – girls who continued to make eyes at him, even though they knew he was a married man. But Mickey was the most faithful of husbands and Marie the happiest of wives.

Three years later, Marie gave birth to a second son, Daniel Gabriel, after ten hours of agonizing labour followed by a forceps delivery.

'That's it,' Mickey announced, mopping his brow when the whole painful business was over and Daniel lay screaming in his cot, his red hair on fire, his face screwed up into one big freckle. 'I can't go through that again. It hurt too much.'

Marie surprised herself by laughing – it was only hours since she'd thought she'd never laugh again. 'It hurt me far more than it did you,' she protested.

'I know, luv.' He tenderly stroked her brow. 'Seriously though, do we want a dozen kids like your mam, you spending half your life with your belly blown up like a balloon? Won't two be enough? It's a nice, neat number. They can both have their own room and we won't be stretched for cash.'

'Two will do us fine, Mickey.' She didn't say she wouldn't have minded another ten like Mam, but only if they could appear by magic. No way was she prepared to spend ninety months of the rest of her life in a state of pregnancy.

Mickey had always avoided anything political like the plague. Of course, if someone came round to the house collecting for a cause, he contributed, sometimes more than he could afford. Same at work. It was dangerous not to. It wasn't that you were expected to be *for* the cause, but it didn't do to be against it. It was easy to make deadly enemies on your own side.

Marie hated it when the boys started school and came home full of prejudices. She said nothing, not wanting them to stand out from their classmates by voicing contrary opinions they'd learned at home. Mickey said she was being over-cautious, but, since coming to Belfast, Marie had only felt safe inside their own four walls or with friends who were as indifferent to politics as she was herself. Only then could she talk freely.

The final decade of the twentieth century was only a few months old when her darling daddy died and the whole family went to Donegal for the funeral. It was the saddest occasion she'd ever known. Colette and Gerry were the only Brennans still at home and Gerry was courting and Colette was going steady, even though she was hardly fifteen. Pretty soon, Mam would be left in the cottage on her own.

'It was a day I thought about sometimes,' she said to Marie, 'but I couldn't for the life of me imagine what it would be like. Still, I'll know soon. But then, won't I still have eleven of me kids living no more than a few

324

miles away from their mammy and dropping in to see her every other day?'

'I wish *I* could, Mam,' Marie sobbed. 'I really wish I could. I miss you desperately. I miss everyone.'

'It can't be helped, me darlin'. You've got a fine feller in Mickey Harrison. A woman has to follow her husband wherever he goes. You're happy with him, aren't you?'

'More than happy, Mam.'

'Well then, that's all that matters.'

A ceasefire was called but, although the fighting lessened, it didn't go away altogether. The peace was accompanied by an influx of hard drugs: heroin and crack cocaine and the men of violence found something else to fight over. By then Patrick and Danny were in their teens and Marie breathed half a sigh of relief. All she'd ever wanted was to live with her husband and raise her family in an atmosphere free from danger, a very limited ambition to have, but one that had proved hard to achieve. She was working in a shop again, a jewellers, only part-time. The extra money paid for holidays and things for the boys that normally they couldn't have afforded, like a computer between them and a guitar for Patrick, who had decided he wanted to become a pop star.

A new priest had arrived at St Joseph's, the parish church. His name was Father O'Mara and he was even better looking than Father Murphy, who Marie had swooned over back in Donegal eighteen years ago. She was glad Mickey wasn't home when the father called at the house: she felt as tongue-tied as a teenager when the slightly built, brown-eyed priest, who had the aura of a film star with his thatch of thick dark hair and the faintest suggestion of a moustache, came to ask if Danny would play in the under-sixteen football team.

'Do you feel all right, Mam?' Danny asked after the priest had gone.

'I'm fine, son,' Marie replied. 'Why do you ask?'

'You looked awful sick while Father O'Mara was here and you hardly opened your mouth.'

'I'm fine,' Marie repeated, although her knees felt like jelly and she could hardly breathe, as if she'd just had Brad Pitt or Tom Cruise in her front room, shaking her hand and sitting on the Dralon velvet settee. She could understand why all the women, from the very young to the very old, were madly in love with the new priest.

It wasn't long after this that Mickey flew to London for his sister's fiftieth birthday. Patsy had never married and he thought it would be a nice surprise if her brother made an unexpected appearance on the day. Marie had met Patsy a few times over the years and grown to like her. She would have loved a trip to London where she'd never been, but wasn't prepared to leave the boys – that weekend, Patrick was playing the guitar with the group he belonged to and Danny had a football match.

'Give Patsy my love and insist she come and stay with us for a wee while,' she said to Mickey. 'And behave yourself,' she admonished. 'If any girls chase after you, tell them you're a happily married man.'

'And you tell Father O'Mara you're a happily married women if he comes calling while I'm away.' Mickey roared with laughter. All the men considered the way the women had a crush on the priest a huge joke.

Mickey was only gone two nights, but it felt like for ever. The bed seemed desperately strange without him: cold, although the weather was warm, and as big as a desert. He rang from London on the first night and she

326

rang him on the second: there was a party going on and someone was singing 'Danny Boy' in a beautiful tenor voice. Mickey was flying home the next afternoon. In the morning, Patsy was going to show him round the hotel in Mayfair where she worked.

'I can't wait to see you, darlin',' Marie breathed.

'I've missed you, Marie, me luv. I'll see you tomorrow.'

In the hours before he was due home, she made as much effort with her appearance as she'd done on the day of Brigid Kelly's wedding, washing her hair and winding it on to giant rollers, taking extra care making up her face, and putting on the green top and tiered skirt she'd bought in Marks & Spencer only the day before. Mickey liked her best in green. It went with her eyes.

It was a lovely June evening, a Sunday, when Patrick and Danny stood by the window to watch for their father. Patrick, being the tallest, spied him first. 'He's just turned the corner,' he shouted, so they spilled outside, Marie with them, to welcome home their daddy and the dearest husband a woman could ever have.

Micky grinned as he came nearer. 'Where's your mammy?' he shouted. 'Is that a new girlfriend you've got there, Patrick? She looks much too young to be the wife I left behind.'

He came inside. The boys fussed over him as if he'd been gone a year. Marie made tea. They sat in the front room while he told them about London. Patsy had pointed out a cheap hotel, very clean, where they could stay for a few days and she'd show them around the sights.

'Perhaps we could go in the summer holidays,' he suggested.

Marie, sitting on the arm of his chair, squeezed his

327

shoulder. She could never remember feeling quite so happy as she did at that moment: that peerless, sublime moment when the world seemed perfectly balanced and she couldn't imagine anything going wrong.

'How did the concert go, Patrick?' Mickey asked.

'Great, Dad. Someone took a photo, I've got a copy upstairs. It's going in the paper on Monday. Would you like to see it?'

'Of course, son. Is there another cup of tea, luv?' he said to Marie. 'I'm parched.'

'You've hardly been home a minute, Mickey Harrison,' she smiled, 'and you've already got me running round after you like a slave. Here, give us your cup. There's still half a pot out there.'

Patrick went to fetch the photo and Marie was in the kitchen, pouring the tea and, at first, couldn't quite make out the source of the terrific banging. It must be coming from next door. It sounded as if someone was trying to kick in the door. Then there was a crash in the hall and she realized it was her own door that was being attacked. When she looked, the door was swinging on its hinges and there were noises in the front room, a series of subdued bangs, and two men, dressed from head to toe in black, came rushing out and Marie went rushing in to find Danny staring, horrified and unbelieving, at the chair where his daddy had been sitting, now drenched in blood. There was a pool on the floor and splashes on the walls, and her darling Mickey's face was a mess of blood and brains because half of his face had been blown away.

People came: neighbours, friends, two members of the Royal Ulster Constabulary. Who did she think had done it, they wanted to know? What organizations had

Mickey belonged to? Why had he been to London? Who had he gone to see there?

Marie couldn't take the questions in. She was too traumatized, frozen in a state of shock, nursing Danny, who was crying like a baby in her arms, so Patrick took over, not quite seventeen, but already as fine a man as his father.

'Me dad didn't belong to any organizations,' he said bluntly while fighting back his own tears. 'He'd been to London for me Auntie Patsy's birthday. There's no reason on earth why anyone'd want to kill him.'

The police sergeant looked dubious. 'There's always a reason for this sort of thing, son. Was your daddy dealing drugs, do you know?'

'Indeed he was not. Whoever did this had the wrong name or the wrong address. It must be a mistake — they've been made before.'

A mistake! Mickey had been murdered by mistake! To lose him was tragedy enough, but for him to go so brutally, so incomprehensibly, was a tragedy with which Marie didn't think she would ever come to terms, never understand, and never forgive.

An old priest, Father McNarmara, presided over Mickey's Requiem Mass. The funeral was a day of quiet footsteps and subdued sobs as the hearse drove to the church followed by hundreds of mourners, Marie at the head holding Danny's hand and Patrick's arm around her shoulders, her family behind.

Mickey had lain in his coffin in the front room for five days, his face miraculously mended, a rosary threaded through the long fingers that had touched his wife so tenderly and passionately over the years. The front door had been repaired and put back on its hinges, the stains on the walls painted over, the carpet cleaned, and Mickey's chair was in Marie's bedroom, the red blood dried to black.

Enda Kelly came to the house late the same night. Enda had started at Harland & Wolff at the same time as Mickey and they'd been best mates ever since. He was shattered by his death and looked as if he'd aged twenty years since he'd come round to watch a football video the night before Mickey had gone away. Now he'd come to talk about old times, reminding Marie of the night he'd brought his friend up to their Rita's bedroom and he and Marie had clicked straight away.

'No we didn't, Enda. He clicked with Marguerite Kelly first, he didn't even notice me for a good half hour.'

'He liked you, though. He told me afterwards how much he liked you.' Enda sighed. 'Now I suppose you'll be going back to Donegal to live with your mam?'

'We will indeed. As soon as the lads finish school this summer.' She thought how much she'd always wanted to go back, but never under such heart-breaking circumstances.

'There're no Kellys left in Donegal any more. Most of them have moved to Birmingham.'

'I know, Enda. I still write to your Rita sometimes and she told me.'

'Of course you do. I'd forgotten for the moment. Me and Peggy and the kids might go there ourselves when all this is over.'

'When all what's over?' There was something about his face, usually so open, now threatening and dark, that worried her.

'Never you mind, Marie.' He looked at the carpet, refusing to meet her eyes.

'*When all what's over, Enda?*'

He shook his head. 'It's nothing to do with you, Marie. You go back to Donegal with your lads. You'll be nice and safe there. Forget about Belfast.'

Marie's heart began to thump and the pounding spread rapidly through her entire body. She hardly recognized her own voice when she said, 'You know who killed my Mickey, don't you?'

'Mickey rang from the airport on the way home from London and gave me the name of the boyo who must have given the orders, even if he didn't do the deed himself.'

She was losing her mind. Nothing was making sense any more. 'Tell me who it is,' she whispered. 'Tell me who it was, then give me a gun, and I'll put a bullet through his evil heart meself, so I will.'

'There's half a dozen fellers who can't wait to do that themselves, Marie, and I'm the first in the queue.' The pale eyes burned with hatred. 'Patrick and Danny have seen enough of murder to last a lifetime. Leave the bastard to me and Mickey's mates. As soon as you and the lads have gone, we'll see to him.'

Father O'Mara came even later, long after Enda had gone. He'd been twice before to say prayers over Mickey's body, but this was the first time Marie had spoken to him on her own.

'Where are the boys?' he asked.

'Asleep in their beds.'

'And your family?'

'All home by now. They came from Donegal in a hired coach.'

The priest nodded. His handsome face was set in an expression of the utmost gravity. 'Did Mickey say anything when he got back from London that might give a clue to who killed him?' he asked gently.

'No, Father. We only talked about holidays and things.' Patsy had told him about a cheap hotel in London where they could all stay for a few days.

The priest sighed. 'I suppose there's a chance we'll never know who did it.'

'Enda Kelly knows who's behind it, Father: him and a lot of other men. They're only waiting for us to leave before they sort him out.'

'I see.' The priest nodded and fell silent. 'I see,' he said again and there was another silence. 'The reason I came is that I have some bad news for you, Marie,' he said eventually.

She laughed bitterly. 'Things are already bad, they can't get any worse.'

'Yes, they can, girl.' He paused and looked at her pityingly. 'The men who murdered Mickey are out to get your Patrick too.'

'Don't talk daft, Father,' she said disparagingly. She didn't give a damn that he was a priest, although his words, said so flatly, sent a chill through her weary bones. 'Have you been drinking or something? Why should anyone want to kill our Patrick? He's only sixteen.'

'Age doesn't come into it, Marie. They think, these men, that Patrick was mixed up in whatever it was Mickey was involved in.'

'Mickey wasn't involved in anything, so how could our Patrick be? It was all a mistake. They killed the wrong man.'

'We both know that, child,' the priest said in a soft voice. She could tell he was trying to convey his terrible message in the gentlest possible way. 'But these are the sort of men who don't listen to reason. Now the funeral's over, everything will go quiet and they'll strike again.' He leaned forward and said urgently, 'They would have got Patrick at the same time as Mickey, except he was upstairs and when you appeared they panicked and ran.'

Marie shivered. 'How do you know all this, Father?'

'I'm a priest. People tell me things. I hear confessions.'

'Tell me what you've heard,' she commanded.

'You know I can't, Marie.' He jumped when a noise came from upstairs: one of the boys was using the bathroom. 'To tell the truth, I don't feel safe myself. I know too much.'

'We're going back to Donegal shortly to live with me mam,' she said resolutely. 'We'll be safe there.'

'I don't think you will, Marie. Everyone knows where you come from.'

'Enda Kelly said we'd be all right,' she protested.

Father O'Mara shook his head. 'Enda Kelly doesn't know the half of it. He might have got the odd name, but not the whole story. He can kill one man in revenge for Mickey, but that'll only start a war and Patrick will be in even greater danger.'

Marie's hands went to her head, as if she was trying to hold herself together. She had lost her husband and now, according to Father O'Mara, was about to lose a son. Life had become the worst of nightmares. 'Then what am I supposed to do?' she asked helplessly.

'Pack your bags,' the priest said urgently, 'be ready to leave first thing in the morning. I'll take you to Dun Laoghaire and you can catch the ferry to England. I'll arrange somewhere for you to stay in London. A big city's the best place to hide out.'

Hide out. 'Will it be for ever, Father?' Her voice trembled.

'I don't know how long it will be for, Marie.' He stood and she stood with him. 'You mustn't tell anyone about this: not your family, not Enda. The fewer people know, the safer you will be.'

He arrived at the crack of dawn wearing jeans, an open-neck checked shirt, and a tan anorak. The car was a big eight-seater thing that she'd often seen him use to take kids to football matches. She went outside to speak to him.

'Danny wants to know if he can bring the computer,' she said.

'Tell Danny he can bring anything he wants except the furniture.' He looked very tired, as if he'd been up all night: it turned out that he had. 'A gang broke into the Presbytery last night. They were looking for me, but I was out giving the Last Rites, thank the Lord.' He crossed himself. 'I hope you don't mind, but I'm coming with you, Marie. We'll be protection for each other. No one'll be looking for Mr and Mrs Liam Jordan and their two boys. I've a brother called Liam and me mother's maiden name was Jordan,' he explained in response to her look of bemusement. 'How did Patrick and Danny take the idea of going away?'

'They're very confused and frightened and just a tiny bit excited at the idea of going to London. I told them it would be dangerous to go back to Donegal and we had to leave for a while till all the fuss died down.' She hadn't mentioned it was Patrick who was specifically at risk. 'They're just packing the last of their things.' She shrugged, feeling incredibly sad. 'I'll just go and tell Danny it's all right about the computer.'

She sighed. Gulls were squawking angrily on the roofs and there was merely a suggestion of silvery light in the east where the sun would eventually rise. The curtains on the rest of the houses in the street were closed: there was no one awake to see them go and wish them goodbye.

No one spoke as the luggage was carried out. No one smiled. When everything was done and they climbed into the car – Patrick hugging his precious guitar as if he got some sort of comfort from it – Father O'Mara turned and said gravely, 'I'll be looking after you from now on. I owe it to Mickey. He was a fine man.'

'You've never spoken a truer word, Father,' Marie murmured.

'Liam,' the priest said. 'From now on, you must call me Liam.'

Thursday

12 JULY 2001

Chapter 11

It can't be raining!

When Marie woke, the room was flooded with sunlight, the sky a pale morning blue and the bit she could see was completely cloudless.

Yet she could hear rain. She got out of bed, padded across to the open window, and saw that Rachel Williams was watering the communal lawn with a hosepipe. The water made a sizzling sound when it hit the dry earth.

She stood for a moment looking at the houses. They looked perfect in their newness, like the Lego buildings the boys used to build when they were small. Some of the roofs were red-tiled, the others green. She hadn't noticed that before, although must have done and just not taken it in. All the curtains were closed, including those in the bungalow to her left that she could just about see and where, according to Rachel, a Mrs Moon was about to move in.

Rachel seemed to know everything. She was a terrible busybody, the sort of person Marie wouldn't normally like, but there was something desperately pathetic about her. Her eyes were full of sadness, as if, inside, she was hurting badly. Marie wondered if her own eyes gave the same impression to the world?

She pulled on jeans and a T-shirt, checked the boys were still asleep, didn't even glance at Liam's door when she passed it, and went outside. "Morning, Rachel,' she called as she walked towards the woman who looked a sight in an over-large man's shirt and grey leggings that were much too tight. Her flat, lifeless hair badly needed something doing to it – a perm, for instance, although a good brushing would have done for now.

'Good morning, you're up early. I thought I'd do this,' she indicated the hose, 'the poor grass looked awfully parched and I was worried the little tree might die without any water.'

'I'm not up as early as you.' Marie looked at her watch: five to seven.

'I can never sleep in daylight. I rise with the sun in summer.'

'That's a sensible thing to do. You can get so much more done in the early morning. My husband used to be amazed when he came down and saw the line full of washing.' She remembered Liam was supposed to be her husband now. It was Mickey who'd been impressed with the washing blowing on the line. 'You've been busy, luv,' he'd say sleepily. He was a night person, it took him ages to come to in the morning. 'I didn't even know you were up,' he'd say.

She caught her breath. He'd seemed so real just then when she'd thought about him. If only there was some way of telling him how sorry she was about what had happened with Liam. It was just that she'd been so mixed up and terrified: nothing was making sense any more. Her normal, very ordinary life had been turned upside down and she'd smothered her grief by thinking about Liam rather than the man who would always be the love of her life. It was a relief that she'd been strong enough not to sleep with him. She couldn't have lived with herself if she had. Her reverie was interrupted by a cry from Rachel.

'Gareth! You look as if you've spent a night out on the tiles.'

Gareth Moran had entered the square. He looked embarrassed. Marie suspected he would have turned round and waited until the coast was clear had he known she and Rachel would be there.

'Slept at a mates,' he mumbled.

'Leaving your wife on her own?' Rachel raised her eyebrows and Marie felt deeply for the young man. Rachel was awfully tactless.

'She's not there,' Gareth was forced to admit. 'She's at her mother's.'

Fortunately, Rachel didn't ask if they'd had a row, but said she hoped the little cat hadn't felt lonely by itself. 'If you ever want to go away, I'll look after her for you,' she offered.

'Thanks. She's a he, actually, although her – I mean his – name's Tabitha.' He looked anxious to get away. 'I'd better go. I've got things to do before I go to work.'

Gareth stumbled into Hamilton Lodge. He prayed the women hadn't noticed he'd come out of Victoria's house. It struck him what a dangerous thing he was doing, having an affair under the noses of the neighbours. If it got back to Debbie, she'd blow every single fuse in her perfect little body and their marriage would be over.

He stood in the hall, his back to the door, and wondered if that would be such an awful thing? She'd divorce him, take him for every penny he had, leaving him free to marry Victoria. On reflection, there weren't any pennies for her to take, only debts, which Debbie was welcome to – they were mainly hers, anyroad.

'Tabitha,' he yelled, 'come and get your brekkie.'

'I've already fed him,' said a small voice from the direction of the kitchen. Gareth went in. Debbie was sitting at the table wearing a frilly camisole top and bikini pants to match which he understood was the latest in sleeping gear. Her long black hair fell loosely over her sunburned shoulders and her face, bare of make-up, was dejected. She looked terribly appealing, but he didn't feel even faintly turned on. Until recently, he would have torn off her sexy outfit and made love to her on the table – had there been room amongst the dirty dishes that had been there since Sunday when his in-laws had paid them a visit. Now, he felt only irritation that she would distract him from thinking about the night he'd just spent with Victoria.

'I thought you were at your mum's,' he said stiffly.

'I came home, really late, because I wanted us to make up, but you weren't here. You weren't here the night before last either.' Her sniff was a mixture of pathos and indignation.

'There'd be no need to make up if you didn't keep running off to your mother's in a huff,' he pointed out, 'and you can't expect me to sit here by meself and mope every time you do.'

'You used to. You used to phone and plead with me to come back.'

'I've grown up, Debs. Those days are over. You make it sound like we were playing a game.' Tabitha came and rubbed himself against Gareth's ankle. He picked the kitten up. Poor little sod. Rachel was right, he *was* being neglected. Tonight, he'd take Tabitha with him to Victoria's – that's if he could get away. Could he really bring himself to have another row with Debbie so she'd go back to her mother's? It would be a really horrible thing to do, although it turned out that the row they were about to have was perfectly genuine . . .

'I love it when we make up,' Debbie said in a small voice.

'It still sounds like a game.'

'I don't think I understand you any more, Gareth.' There was a suspicion of tears in her big, brown eyes. 'What we need is a holiday, to get away and forget everything for a few weeks, just concentrate on each other.'

'I've already told you we can't afford a holiday. What's that you've got there?' he asked sharply. She was folding and unfolding a slip of paper on the table in front of her.

'It's a receipt. Yesterday, I paid in full for the holiday in Barbados with my credit card. Oh, Gareth!' she cried. 'It was silly to let the deposit go to waste: four hundred pounds and nothing to show for it. We'll have a wonderful time.'

'So, you paid another three thousand six hundred?' His voice had risen an octave. He felt himself go faint and hurriedly sat down. He'd meant to ring the travel agent and cancel the holiday, but there'd been so many other things to think about.

'I didn't think you'd mind,' she said sulkily, clearly alarmed by his tone.

'Mind! Mind! Mind is too mild a word to use. I'm totally horrified. How many times must I tell you, Debs, *we can't afford it*. Didn't we discuss this very same thing yesterday? Christ!' He banged his head on the table, but it didn't help. 'You didn't buy the Prairie Dog while you were at it, did you?'

'Of course I didn't, that's something we'd have to do together.'

Thank the Lord. 'What's the limit on your credit card?' he asked dully.

'I've never looked. I didn't know it had a limit.'

'Debbie, I think you should go back to your mother's.'

'What, now?'

'Yes, now, before I kill you, before the postman comes with more bills and I kill you again.'

Debbie stamped her foot. 'You're acting like a prima donna, Gareth. Mum always says you act like a prima donna.'

'Does she?' He didn't care what his gruesome mother-in-law thought. All he cared about were his monstrous debts and, of course, Victoria.

'What have you been up to?' Frank grunted when Rachel went indoors. He was dressed for work, but still had to put on a jacket and tie. The sun had never treated Frank kindly: the skin on his bald scalp was flaking and his face had turned an unflattering dark red.

'I've been watering the grass at the front,' she explained, knowing he was bound to tell her she was mad or something.

'It's not your job to do it. I thought it was communal?'

'It is, but I don't mind. It was terribly dry and I was worried that the willow tree would die.'

'What a pity you didn't show the same concern for Alice before *she* died,' he said, and the bitterness in his voice sliced through her like a knife. It hurt so much she could hardly breathe. Before she could think of a reply — *was* there a reply to such a stark, cruel statement? — he

344

had opened the fridge. 'Is there anything to eat in this house?' he asked sourly.

'There's always something to eat,' she replied, surprised at how steady her voice was when her insides were in turmoil. 'What would you like? There's bacon, sausage, eggs, tomatoes.'

'The lot with a slice of fried bread.' He slammed the fridge door shut, so hard it made her jump. Her hands were shaking. How he must hate her! You'd have to hate a person very much to say the things that Frank said to her.

'Do you think I have no feelings, Frank?' she asked in the same steady voice.

'Damn your feelings!' He pushed his angry, red face into hers. 'D'you think I give a shit about your feelings? Due to you, my little girl is dead.' His harsh voice became softer and his face seemed to melt. 'I dreamed about her last night. It was when she was in that nativity play at playgroup. She was an angel, all in white with silver wings and a halo – I think it was made of tissue paper. In the dream, she started to fly. I reached up to catch her, but she disappeared. It seemed so real when I woke up,' he whispered. 'I tried to go back to sleep, just so I could see her again, catch her this time, but I couldn't.' He gave her a look that made her feel sick to the stomach. 'If I were you, I wouldn't be able to live with myself,' he said.

'Oh, Frank,' she whispered, and wondered if he was actually suggesting she kill herself?

'You're always here, reminding me of the precious thing I've lost.' He paused and fixed his burning eyes on hers. 'I hate you, Rachel. I hate you with all my heart.'

Rachel sighed and bowed her head. 'I see,' she said

quietly. It was something she'd just have to live with, but she didn't know if she'd be able to do it for much longer.

'Victoria, are you there?'

'Come in whoever you are,' Victoria sang. The side door was wide open to let in the fresh air. 'I'm in the kitchen. Isn't it another glorious morning?' she remarked when Marie Jordan entered. 'Apparently, there's a heatwave in New York, it's even hotter than here.'

'This is the first time I've seen you when you haven't been cleaning or polishing or sorting things out to send to charity,' Marie said. 'You look quite lazy for a change.' Victoria, still in her nightie, was sitting in a little armchair, her feet on a stool, a mug in her hand. It was where Gran had sat during the day, never venturing into the parlour until evening.

'I *feel* quite lazy,' she announced. 'I'm flogging a dead horse washing wallpaper. The dirt's ingrained. I've decided to get the decorators in. When I can get up enough energy, I'll have a look through the Yellow Pages. No sensible person would want to rent this place the state it's in.'

'Oh, I dunno.' Marie gave the now bare kitchen an affectionate look. 'That dresser's probably worth a bit, it looks like pine. This reminds me of the house I grew up in. Mind you, me mam had a new kitchen put in last year. It's got a split-level cooker, just like mine, but she can't get used to the rings not being on top of the oven.'

'Me gran would have been the same,' Victoria assured her. 'This is all right to look at, but not to work in. The draining board's probably crawling with germs invisible to the human eye. Gran used to scrub it with bleach, but I've never bothered.' She nodded at the fat teapot on the table. 'There'll still be a cup in there if you want it.'

346

'Ta, but I'm on me way to the shops. I only came to say thank you for giving Danny and Patrick the computer. It's really nice of you. They're both as pleased as punch.'

Victoria smiled. 'It's nice to know it's going to a good home.'

'Well, I'll be off.' Marie edged towards the door. 'Enjoy your lazy day. I'll pop in on me way back, see if you've moved.'

'Only to have poured another cup of tea. Oh, I might be dressed by then, just in case I have any gentlemen callers.'

'Our Danny's wetting himself to come, but I told him not till after ten o'clock.'

'That means I've got half an hour.' Victoria yawned and stretched her arms. 'This is the life,' she muttered after Marie had gone. She remembered she must tell Sarah that she'd seen the ferocious Alex prowling around her house very early that morning.

'Victoria!' Another shout, a man this time. She would have recognized the voice anywhere.

'Gareth!' She ran into the hall. Gareth came in and kicked the door shut behind him.

'I had to see you before I left for work.' He took her in his arms and held her tightly.

'You're already late, for work that is,' she said into the collar of his shirt. 'Oh, but I'm glad you came. I was wondering if I could last out till tonight without seeing you.'

'I felt the same. The reason I'm late is, I've been thinking.' He pushed her away, put his hands on her shoulders, and looked at her intently. His glasses were crooked on his nose. 'Victoria, my darling, will you marry me?'

If only she could! If only! 'Gareth!' she said wildly. 'You seem to have forgotten something: you're already married.' She started to cry. 'I'd love to marry you. It's what I want more than anything in the world. But I can't. You know I can't.'

'Have you never heard of something called divorce?' He kissed away the tears that were streaming down her cheeks.

'Of course, but I don't want to break up your marriage,' she wept.

'It was a lousy marriage before I met you. Oh, *God*!' He pulled her back against him. 'I can't imagine life without you. Like I said last night, we were made for each other.'

'You probably thought you and Debbie were made for each other once,' she whispered. 'You're just going through a bad patch. After I've gone, everything will be all right again.'

'Without you, nothing will be right again. Let's go upstairs,' he said urgently. 'Let's remind ourselves how much we mean to each other.'

Victoria held out her hand and led the way up to her bedroom.

'I thought World War Three had started, all that noise.'

'I'm playing Battleships,' Ernest explained without looking up.

Anna said, 'I shall probably be the first woman to divorce her husband citing a computer as the third party.'

'I'm sorry, luv,' Ernest said abjectly. He sank another battleship and looked up. 'Did you want something?'

'I'd like my husband back for one thing, and I wouldn't mind my usual mid-morning cup of coffee. I tried to put the kettle on, but it's too heavy for me to lift.'

Ernest felt even sorrier. 'I'm neglecting you, aren't I?'

'You most certainly are. I thought the computer was bought for me?' She looked genuinely upset.

'It was.' He got to his feet and went into the kitchen. 'I'll show you how to use it later. We can play Battleships together.'

'That'll be nice,' she said in a neutral tone.

Five minutes later, he carried in a tray with two cups of coffee and a plate of assorted biscuits. 'There's some ginger creams there, luv, your favourite,' he announced.

'You're not going to get round me with a couple of ginger creams, Ernest Burrows,' she said in a severe voice. Then she laughed, 'Wouldn't it be awful if we broke up over a computer after all those perfect years together?'

'Don't talk daft, Anna.'

'I'm being serious.'

'You're being daft. Anyroad, aren't you forgetting something?'

'Such as?'

'The year we nearly got divorced. *That* wasn't exactly perfect.'

'Oh, Ernie.' She looked at him reproachfully. 'We didn't nearly get divorced. Oh, I know we discussed it, but we both decided we loved each other far too much to part.'

'You had an affair with that Italian count.' It still hurt, thinking about it more than thirty-five years later.

'So did you with that American woman.'

'I only did it to get me own back.'

'I know, darling.' She sniffed and studied her gold

sandals rather than look at him. 'I got the seven-year itch.'

'We'd been married for twenty-one years,' he pointed out.

'It came late. Oh, Ernie!' she cried, visibly upset. 'Do we really have to talk about it after such a long time?'

'It was you who brought up the subject of divorce, luv,' he said stiffly.

'I'm sorry! I'm really, really sorry. It was horrid of me to mention it.' She seemed to crumble in front of his eyes. 'I'm selfish. I expect you to be at my beck and call every minute of every day. I had no right to stop you playing on the computer, resent you enjoying yourself for once.'

He went and put his arms around her. 'Don't cry, luv. I'm sorry too.' He wasn't quite as sorry as she was. He still got angry when he thought about the Italian count.

After a few silent minutes, she lifted her head and surprised him with a grin. 'Have you been watching pornography, Ernie?' Her blue eyes sparkled with mischief.

'I've been doing no such thing,' he said appalled.

'I wouldn't mind seeing a bit of pornography. If we watched it together, we might get the urge.'

'To do what?'

She giggled coquettishly. 'The things we used to do when we were young.'

'The urge has never left me, Anna. We'll do them now if you like.'

'After I've eaten these biscuits, taken my tablets, limped into the bedroom and you've helped take off my clothes.'

He pretended to look disappointed. 'I didn't realize you were only joking.'

'What's that poem?' She closed her eyes and recited: "A man is not old when his teeth decay, a man is not old when his hair goes grey, but a man is nearing his last, long sleep, when his mind makes appointments his body can't keep." Change the man to woman and it describes me perfectly, Ernie.'

Ernest didn't answer and Anna went on. 'We've a visitor coming tonight: Charlie.'

'Charlie?' He looked at her, puzzled.

'Charlie Burtonshaw, your brother. Or, I should say, half-brother.'

'You've rung him!'

'Well, you asked me to sort it so that's what I've done. You'd have heard me on the phone if you hadn't been in the middle of a frightful sea battle.' She made a face at him. 'He sounds very nice. His Liverpool accent is much stronger than yours. He's coming tonight, but not bringing his wife, she's busy with something.'

'Did you ask about Gaynor?'

'Yes, she's married and lives in a place called Ormskirk. He said he'd get in touch with her.'

'So Gaynor might come too?'

'There's always the chance. Could you pour me another cup of coffee, darling? And hand us one of those ginger creams to dip in. They're much nicer when they're moist.'

Ernest did what she requested, noticing that his hands were shaking slightly. He was wishing now he'd never mentioned wanting to see Charlie or Gaynor. The gap had been too long. He should have contacted them – and Mam – sooner, like directly after the war was over in 1945, not waited until the next century was more than a year old.

★

Marie re-read the postcard she had written before leaving the house. The heading was, 'Computer For Sale,' and she wondered if a hundred pounds was too much to ask? Or it might not be enough. She hadn't liked asking the boys for their opinion as she felt slightly uneasy about selling theirs when Victoria was giving them a much better one and not expecting a penny for it.

'I'd have given it away, willingly,' she piously told herself, 'but there's no one to give it to. Sarah's children are too young, and Ernie and Anna would have been welcome to it if they hadn't bought a new one themselves only the day before. It's too good to give to charity.' Although Liam gave her plenty of money, another hundred pounds would always come in useful.

There'd been cards advertising things for sale in the shop in Allerton Road where Sarah had bought the chocolate the day before: O'Connor's it was called. Her lips curved in a smile when she thought about Sarah. Fancy having a nanny bring up your kids! Still, Sarah had been rather brutally thrust into the real world and was coping well.

I'm glad we left London and came to Liverpool, she thought. In London, they'd lived in what she could only describe as an old converted warehouse where everyone had been dead posh. Wish them 'good morning' or 'good afternoon' in the lift or going in and out, and they'd look at you as if you'd asked to borrow money or had pleaded to become their best friend. Their lips had difficulty forming a reply. Victoria Square was a very different kettle of fish, everyone knowing the neighbours, just like in Ireland, north as well as south. There were a few she hadn't met yet, like Gareth Moran's wife and Kathleen Cartwright's husband, but she'd see them at the barbecue on Saturday, which reminded her she must get a bottle of wine to take and ask Rachel if she wanted help with the food.

She arrived at O'Connor's and scanned the cards in the window in case there were other computers for sale and she could compare prices. There were plenty of three-piece suites, a garden shed going for free to someone willing to dismantle it, a couple of prams, loads of bikes, a few cars, and people offering their services as a window cleaner or plumber, but no computers. She looked the narrow shop up and down and went in. Inside was like an Aladdin's cave: the small counter spread with newspapers at one end and a rack of chocolate bars at the other. There wasn't a single inch of wall that wasn't covered with something or other: jars of loose sweets, cigarettes and tobacco, magazines, birthday cards, bubble-wrapped toys, cheap videos. A pleasant, grey-haired woman of about sixty with an Irish accent was serving a small boy with a quarter of Everton mints. She then attended to a man who wanted to pay his paper bill and put up a fierce argument when informed how much it was. He paid up eventually and left the shop, grumbling under his breath.

'They don't realize how quickly time passes,' the woman said to Marie. 'With papers the price they are now – some of the Sundays cost well over a pound – in no time at all, they can owe as much as twenty. What can I do for you, luv?'

'I'd like this card put in the window, please.'

'How long for? It's fifty pence a week, one-fifty for a month.'

'A week'll do.' If the computer hadn't gone by then, she'd leave it for another week, perhaps reduce it to seventy-five pounds.

As she was handing over the fifty pence the woman

said, 'Don't I know you from somewhere?' Her face broke into a smile of recognition. 'You're Marie Brennan, aren't you, our Rita's friend? You married me brother Enda's best mate at Harland & Wolff. What was his name now – Mickey Harrison. Oh!' The smile vanished. 'Mickey was killed, wasn't he? God rest his soul.' She made a quick Sign of the Cross. 'Enda said you'd gone back to Donegal to live with your mammy.'

Marie stood frozen to the spot and stammered something incomprehensible. Hadn't Enda said all the Kellys had gone to live in Birmingham? Perhaps he'd said most, not all.

'You don't remember me, do you?' the woman said kindly. 'I'm Brigid O'Connor, used to be Kelly. If I remember right, you came to me and Edward's wedding.'

'No, I didn't. I'm not Marie Brennan. Me name's Victoria. Victoria Jordan, and I've never been to Donegal in me life.' Marie fled from the shop. Her face felt as if it was burning and she was sweating cobs as she strode back to the square. She had almost reached home when she remembered she'd left the card on the counter and it had their telephone number on. Luckily, she hadn't included the address.

I'd better tell Liam, she thought when she entered the house, but there was no sign of him. He must have gone out – they'd hardly spoken since Patrick's outburst a few days ago. Danny would be well ensconced in Victoria's by now, and Patrick had gone to a summer day school with Rachel's daughter, Kirsty – script writing, or something.

Marie sank on to the settee and took several deep breaths. Was there any need to tell a single soul? None of the Kellys would wish her or her children any harm.

Weren't they all on the same side, after all? Anyroad, hadn't she denied she was Marie Brennan? Brigid Kelly, or O'Connor as she was now, would see no reason to disbelieve her.

Even so, if someone rang about the computer, she'd say it was sold rather than give their address to a stranger. 'None of this would have happened if you hadn't been so greedy,' she told herself, and tried not to think about all the nice things she could have bought with a hundred pounds.

'You mean he actually tried the door?' Sarah gasped. She was outraged and at the same time petrified by such unwelcome news. She and Victoria were sitting on the back step watching Jack paddle in the plastic pool, his blanket on his head. Alastair, wearing only a nappy, lay in the shade examining his toes and Tiffany was in Victoria's house, playing with Danny on the computer. Sarah had been feeling exceptionally contented with the world until her neighbour had arrived to describe what she had witnessed in the early hours of the morning.

'Well, he went up to the door,' Victoria said. 'I think he examined the lock. I couldn't see all that well.'

'And it was definitely Alex?'

'I couldn't swear to it — I only saw him for a minute the other day when he was being shoved into the police car, but there was a Rolls-Royce parked in the main road.'

'I didn't hear a thing. I would have phoned the police if I'd known he was prowling around outside.'

'I was wide-awake and the window was open. I could hear their voices, but not what they were saying, I'm afraid,' Victoria said regretfully. 'As to the police, I should've rung them meself. I didn't think fast enough.'

'My window was open too, but I was fast asleep and so was Alastair – his tooth's appeared. It's like a little white pimple on his gums.' She felt inordinately proud, as if she personally was responsible for the tooth coming through. But there were more important things than Alastair's teeth to think about at the moment. 'What on earth am I to do about Alex?' she cried. 'He'll probably come back tonight or another night, break down the door, snatch the children, and within an hour they'll be on a plane to who knows where.'

'Have they got passports?' Victoria asked.

'No, but that won't stop Alex,' Sarah said frantically. 'He's got his own plane, a little one with about six seats. I've never been in it, I was too scared. He only uses it to go to race meetings, sometimes in France.' Once the children were out of the country, she'd never get them back.

'Oh, Lord!' Victoria bit her lip. 'Tell you what, why don't you all stay at mine tonight? You'll have to bring your own bedding and Alastair's cot. You and Tiffany and Jack can sleep in Gran's old bed.'

'Thank you, Victoria, that's very kind of you and I'm very grateful. But we can't sleep in other people's houses for the rest of our lives.'

'Of course you can't,' Victoria soothed. 'Look, let's put our brains together and we might think of something constructive we can do.'

Sarah didn't think she was capable of thinking constructively. She wondered if Daddy would *still* have sold her to Alex Rees-James had he known the way things would turn out?

Kathleen and Steve had spent a blissful morning in bed. They hadn't exchanged a single cross word.

'This is how it ought to be,' Steve said with a complacent grin when, at midday, they decided it was time to get up. 'Perhaps we should stop talking to each other and just make love.'

'Perhaps.' Kathleen smiled, lazily stretched her arms, then reached for her cigarettes off the floor. 'Although, isn't that rather a bad thing, that we only get on when we're in bed?'

'I suppose we've got to learn to live together,' Steve said sensibly. 'We did all our courting in bed. We hardly knew one another when we left Huddersfield.'

'What if we don't like each other out of bed?'

'In that case, Kath, we're in trouble. As from Monday, I'll be working: a week nights, a week days, so half the time we'll hardly see each other, let alone sleep together.'

'And when *I* start working, we'll see each other even less, *and* I'll be on duty the occasional weekend.' Kathleen wrapped her scarlet dressing gown around her and silently contemplated this rather bleak future as she went into the kitchen to make breakfast. 'Do you want something fried?' she called.

'No, ta, just toast and cereal.'

It was time they turned the bungalow into a proper home, she thought. All they'd bought so far were essentials. They needed curtains or a pretty blind for the kitchen window, pictures, plants, a rug for the front room, little pieces of furniture like bedside cabinets and a coffee table – oh, and a microwave and some lamps.

Steve came strolling in wearing khaki shorts and a short-sleeved shirt. His legs and arms were thick, but shapely. She felt a surge of desire.

'Do you really *have* to take this security guard job?' she asked. 'Couldn't you wait until one comes up with regular hours? You just said we must learn to live together, but we're hardly likely to do that if we only see each other a few hours a day.'

'That's hardly my fault.'

Here we go again, she thought impatiently. 'I never said it was your fault, Steve,' she said in as reasonable a voice as she could muster. 'It's the fault of the job. I was just wondering if you couldn't get another where you worked nine to five, that's all.'

'Why do I have to change my job?' he said truculently. 'Why don't you change yours?'

'Because we only came to Liverpool because of my job.' Reason fled and she gave a sarcastic snort. 'I didn't realize you wanted to make a career as a security guard.'

'We're fighting again.' He sat down abruptly at the table.

'I know.' She caught the bread when it popped out of the toaster and began to butter it ferociously. 'What are we going to do about it?'

'I dunno. I think I must resent you.'

'For what?' she asked curiously.

'You have a better job than me, had a better education, you're better off than I am by a mile.' He shrugged. 'I suppose you make me feel inferior.'

'That's good,' she said encouragingly, pouring corn-flakes into a bowl, milk into a jug, and putting them on the table in front of him.

He raised his eyebrows questioningly. 'It's good that you make me feel inferior?'

'No, that you're putting your feelings into words. If we work through this together we might find what causes our fights and never have them again. Go on,' she urged.

'Me go on? What about you? Or am I the only patient in this psychiatric hospital, Doctor?'

She frowned. 'What do you mean by that?'

'Is it only *my* fault that we fight?' He regarded her thoughtfully. 'Believe me, Kathleen, you're very different now than you were in Huddersfield. You never used to be so sure of your bloody self. You seemed softer then, insecure, as if you needed me. Now, all you want to do is piss me around. I daren't open me mouth 'case you jump down it.'

'Who started this row, Steve? All I did was suggest you got a job with more convenient hours. Is that so awful?' She poured the tea then lit another cigarette. She was smoking herself silly.

'There was no need to rub in the fact that my job's shit and yours is so bloody worthwhile. I knew that already. It was only going to be temporary, anyroad, till I found something better. Don't you realize how important it is to me to bring some money into the house? I don't want you keeping me.' He picked up the tea and half drained the cup, returning it to the table with a thump. 'You belittle me, Kath. I think that's the word.'

'I'm sorry.' She realized his esteem was very low. She'd have to be careful in future. The rows were both their faults, hers as much as his. She picked up his hand and pressed her lips against the palm. 'I love you. Shall we go into town this very minute and have lunch, then buy some things for the house? There's no need to get changed, you look lovely as you are.'

He nodded, smiling, and told her he loved her too, so she poured the cornflakes back into the box, threw away the toast, and went to have a shower.

After she had dressed in her new black skirt patterned with roses and the top to match, she asked if he would mind if she just popped over to Rachel's for a minute. 'I won't be long, it's just to see how she is.'

'Be as long as you like.' He was by the kitchen window, looking out. 'It wants planting with something out there: bushes'd be best, and perhaps a little waterfall in the corner. While you're gone, I'll work out what's best to buy. Perhaps we could go to a nursery tomorrow and get 'em.'

'Could we have some climbing roses?' she said eagerly. 'I love roses.'

'What colour?'

'Yellow. I like yellow best.'

'Then yellow it'll be.'

As Kathleen walked across the grass, she could see Rachel sitting on the settee in the living room, apparently staring into space. She waved, but Rachel didn't respond. Perhaps she hadn't noticed. The back door was open and she called, 'It's me, Kathleen. Can I come in?'

There was no answer. She called again, but still no answer. Was it deliberate? Did Rachel not want visitors and this was her way of showing it? Somehow, Kathleen doubted it. She went inside and noticed the dirty breakfast dishes were still on the table in the kitchen, the white of an egg congealed to the plate. Two wasps crawled around the rim of an open jar of jam.

'Rachel – oh, what's the matter, love?' Kathleen never called anyone but her immediate family 'love', it seemed patronizing, but the word just slipped out. Perhaps love was what this poor woman needed.

Rachel's face was like death, her eyes were dark and haunted with pain. She turned her head towards the visitor and said in a thick, dull voice, 'Hello, Kathleen. How nice of you to come.'

'Would you like me to make you some tea, Rachel?'

'Yes, please. My throat's very dry.'

'I won't be a minute.'

Kathleen boiled the minimum amount of water, found the teabags and put one in a mug, took milk from the fridge. It was hardly a minute later that she took the tea into the living room where Rachel hadn't moved an inch since she'd left.

'Here you are.' She sat beside the woman and put her arm around her shoulders. Rachel's body felt unnaturally cold for such a hot day.

'Thank you.'

'What's wrong, love?'

Rachel was a long time answering and when she did, she spoke like a child, almost petulantly. 'I thought when we moved everything would be different, that we'd make a fresh start. But you can't escape the past, can you? Your troubles travel with you.'

'That's true. Drink your tea, Rachel. It will warm you up a bit.' Rachel obediently sipped the tea. 'What's brought this on? You seemed all right yesterday.'

'Frank said something this morning. Please don't ask what it was. It just made me realize that there's no way out. I'm trapped.'

'In what?'

'Trapped in this life, this awful life.' She stared at Kathleen, who wanted to shrink away from the haunted eyes, scared that she'd be contaminated by Rachel's hideous, all-consuming grief.

'Would you like me to help you up to bed? Perhaps you could take a tablet. You mightn't feel so bad after a good sleep.' Kathleen felt ashamed. She was trying to find an easy way out, not wanting to irritate Steve by staying too long, yet knowing she couldn't possibly leave Rachel in such a state.

'I'll never sleep. I'm all right here.' She leaned her head on Kathleen's shoulder. 'I'm glad you've come.'

'I can't stay long, love. Steve and I have to go out. Another ten minutes or so and I'll have to leave.'

Steve was in the garden when she got home, breathless from the short run from Rachel's house. 'I'm sorry I took so long,' she panted.

'That's all right,' he said easily. 'I've made a list of things to get from the nursery. Apart from plants, we'll need some garden tools and a hose. Are you ready to go now?'

'In just a minute.' She took the car keys out of her bag. 'Will you get the car out? I just want to have a quick word with Victoria.'

'Who's Victoria?'

'She lives in the old house on the corner. I met her yesterday and she's awfully nice. I want to ask if she'd call on Rachel. The state she's in, she shouldn't be left on her own.'

'Why don't you stay with her, luv? We can always go out tomorrow.'

'Would you mind? I was worried I'd upset you.'

'You must think I'm a monster.' He looked almost ashamed. 'I suppose I did feel a bit put out when you came back late the other day, but I was worried about you more than anything. If the woman's hurting, Kath, I'd feel a louse if you left her alone on my account. While you're gone, I'll find out where the nearest nursery is and get the stuff today.'

'Steve!' She threw her arms around his neck. 'Kiss me before I go. Shall we go out to dinner tonight? Unhappiness is catching. I'll need you to cheer me up as soon as I'm home.'

'I know the best way of doing that – we'll have dinner afterwards.' He kissed her soundly and Kathleen went back to Rachel.

They sat on the settee together talking about nothing much, until mid-afternoon when Rachel fell asleep. Kathleen eased her arm from behind her back and crept into the kitchen to tidy up. She had just finished washing the dishes and was looking for a tea towel when the phone on the wall beside the fridge rang. She took it off and said, 'Hello.'

'So, you're still managing to live with yourself I see,' a man's gruff voice said. 'Happy, are you?'

'Who is this speaking?'

There was a long pause then a clicking sound and the phone went dead. Kathleen stood holding the receiver for quite a long time. Was Rachel being terrorized? Was the man a stranger or someone she knew?

The phone must have woken Rachel. In a shaky voice, she called, 'Who was that? Are you still here, Kathleen?'

'I'm still here, yes. It was a wrong number.' Earlier, Rachel had told her that Frank had said something this morning, but she wasn't to ask what it was. So far, Kathleen hadn't even glimpsed Rachel's husband, let alone met him. Had that been him on the phone? If so, what the hell was he up to?

Charlie Burtonshaw arrived on the dot of six. He was shorter than Ernest by a good six inches and in remarkably good condition for a man not far off seventy. The skin on his face was pink and looked as soft and silky as a baby's and his white hair was tinged with yellow. He wore a white T-shirt tucked inside cream Terylene trousers held up with a frayed imitation crocodile belt.

'Long time no see,' he quipped in a hearty voice when he shook hands with his long-lost half brother.

'Yes, indeed.' Ernest, not a loquacious man under normal circumstances, was stuck for words. 'Come in,' he gulped. 'Come and meet me wife.'

'That'll be a pleasure.' Charlie stepped inside. 'Nice little place you've got here, Ernie. Nicely situated an' all.'

'It's the door on the right.'

Charlie disappeared into the living room to be greeted by a welcome cry from Anna. Ernest took a deep breath and followed. There was no need for introductions, Anna had already done it herself and was patting the chair beside her for Charlie to sit down.

'Would you like something to drink, Charlie?' she cooed. 'We've coffee, tea, whisky, and there's beer in the fridge, isn't there, Ernie?'

'Beer'll do me fine, ta. D'you mind if I smoke?'

'Go right ahead, Charlie. Ernie, is there an ashtray in the kitchen?'

'I'll have a look.' The smoke would get on Anna's chest. Ernest felt annoyed with Charlie for asking. He found an ashtray that hadn't been used in years, collected the beer and two glasses, and poured about half an inch of sherry for his wife.

'How's life treated you, Charlie?' he asked when he carried everything in, attempting joviality, but failing miserably.

'Well, Ernie, very well,' Charlie said in the same hearty voice. 'Served an apprenticeship as a turner and worked in the same place, Denver Tools on Kirkby Trading Estate, until I was sixty-five. Married Evelyn in nineteen fifty-eight, and we've got two kids, Ronnie and Tessa. Now we've got three grandkids,' he finished proudly.

'And Gaynor?'

'Gaynor's not been quite so lucky: married twice, widowed twice. Only son, Brian, works abroad most of the time: something to do with oil. Me and Ev go to see her as often as we can, but she's lonely on her own.'

'Poor dear,' Anna said sympathetically. 'We can go and see her now, can't we, Ernie?'

'Of course,' Ernest muttered, and then asked the question he'd been wanting to ask ever since Charlie had arrived. 'What happened to Mam?'

'Died two years after the war ended, I'm sorry to say.' Charlie blinked. His eyes were the palest blue Ernest had ever seen, surrounded by stubby, white lashes. 'She was only forty-four. Desmond Whitely looked after me and Gaynor, otherwise we'd have gone in an orphanage. Do you remember Des?'

'I remember him well. I always assumed Des was my father.'

'He moved in with Mam permanently as soon his own kids had grown up. We found out they'd had an affair years before and you were the result. Lived till nearly ninety, Des did, and was completely in possession of his senses until the day he popped his clogs.'

Anna raised her eyebrows questioningly at Ernest, but he ignored her. She must never have heard of the expression before.

Charlie took several mouthfuls of beer, wiped his mouth with the back of his hand, and said, 'What about you, Ernie? What have you and your lovely wife been up to for the last sixty years?'

'Not much,' Ernest grunted. 'We just travelled around a bit and ended up here.'

'Darling,' Anna trilled. 'You make our lives sound awfully dull.' She turned to Charlie. 'We've had some wonderful times, Charlie. We lived in Egypt for a while – that's where we met during the war. Then it was to and fro between Paris and Monte Carlo and all sorts of other exciting places.'

'You never had any kids, then?'

Anna's face changed, became sombre. 'We wanted children, but it just didn't seem to happen.'

'That's a shame.' Charlie slapped his knees and got to his feet. 'Well, I'd better be going. I told Ev I wouldn't be long. Tonight's Bingo night and she's always expecting us to win the jackpot.'

'You're not going already? You've hardly been here five minutes. We were going to offer you dinner, weren't we, Ernie?'

'I had me tea before I came. I couldn't eat another thing. Tara, Anna.' He shook hands. 'It's been nice meeting you. You too, Ernie.'

'I'll see you out.' Ernest went into the hall and opened the door. 'Perhaps you and Evelyn would like to come another night,' he said politely. 'Or Anna and I could take you both out for a meal.'

'I don't think so.' Charlie's smile didn't reach his eyes. 'I never want to see you again, Ernie. I only came this time out of curiosity. Do you know why Mam died when she did, eh? *Eh?*' he added belligerently when Ernest didn't answer. 'You broke her heart when you didn't come home after the war, that's why. She knew you weren't dead, Des wrote and checked. I don't think a day passed when she didn't cry her eyes out wondering where you were. After a while, she gave up hope, took to her bed and died. It would have been such a little thing to do, to send a letter and tell her you were safe. But you were too busy, flitting around the world, having a good time.' He started to back away and Ernest

366

couldn't help but notice that his trousers were too short and his T-shirt misshapen, as if it had been washed hundreds of times. 'I told our Gaynor where I was going and she said to tell you you're the last person on earth she wants to see. So, there you are, Ernie. Me and Gaynor want nothing to do with you.' His tone was triumphant, as if this was a speech he'd been practising for the best part of his life, but had never imagined it being delivered.

Ernest closed the door, shoulders bowed, hands trembling. He shuffled back into the living room where Anna was saying how nice Charlie had seemed. 'But he looked terribly poor. Did you notice all the snags in his trousers? Are you all right, Ernie? You're very pale.'

'I'm feeling a bit queasy,' Ernest admitted.

'Go and lie down for half an hour, darling, but pour me another sherry before you do – a proper one this time. There was barely two sips in the one you gave me.' She settled back in her chair and said contentedly. 'There's a good film on soon: *Notorious*, with Ingrid Bergman and Cary Grant. I've seen it loads of times before, but I love it.'

Ernie gave her the sherry and went to lie on his bed. He felt as if he had been kicked in the stomach. Mam had gone to an early grave and it was his fault. Charlie was right: all that had been needed was a letter just to show he cared, was still thinking about her. This morning, Anna had confessed to being selfish, but she was nothing compared to him. He called himself a socialist, yet he hadn't done a decent day's work since he'd left Cairo. He'd lived by his wits: a professional gambler. Ernest groaned and buried his head in the pillow. What an epitaph to put on someone's grave!

Sarah didn't seem to notice anything odd about Gareth's

presence that night when she came to Victoria's laden with bedding and accompanied by the two older children. She returned to fetch Alastair who was already asleep in his carrycot.

'Oliver's looking forward to sleeping in your house, Victoria,' Tiffany said. 'He told me so earlier.'

'Did he now?'

'Oliver seems to have lost an eye,' Gareth pointed out.

'I know. Mummy's going to make a patch and he'll look like Nelson McDella.'

'You mean Nelson Mandela?'

'I think Mummy meant Lord Horatio Nelson, Tiffany,' Victoria said. 'He lost an eye, just like Oliver?'

Gareth shook his head dazedly. 'This child always confuses me something rotten.'

'Victoria, Oliver wants to watch *EastEnders*.'

'Then take him into the parlour: you know how to switch the TV on, don't you?'

'Oliver does.'

Victoria grinned and Sarah came in with the carrycot. 'Jack's nearly dead on his feet. I'll take him and Alastair upstairs.'

Gareth offered to help and Victoria said she'd make a drink. 'Where's Tabitha?'

'Asleep on your bed,' Gareth said on his way upstairs.

A shriek came from the front room and Tiffany came galloping out, minus Oliver. 'Is Tabitha here? Can I nurse him?'

'I'll bring him down with me.'

'Won't Oliver be jealous?' Gareth enquired when he put the kitten in Tiffany's eager arms.

'Of course he won't, silly. He knows how much I love him. Come on, Tabitha, you can watch *EastEnders* with us.'

Gareth rolled his eyes. 'What time is she likely to go to bed?' he hissed.

Victoria shrugged and said she had no idea.

'Are you sure this Alex guy is going to come back tonight?'

'Pretty sure. I rang Speke airport earlier, said I had some important papers to deliver to Mr Rees-James and what time was his plane taking off. They said at half-past two in the morning.'

'Cor! That was clever of you, Vic.'

'Wasn't it?' Victoria looked pleased with herself. 'Sarah and I reckon he'll come – if he comes at all – at about half one. Once he's grabbed the children, he'll want to get out of the country as quickly as possible.'

'Have the cops been alerted?'

'They're on standby or something.'

Gareth grinned, though it wasn't the least bit funny. 'This is all very cloak and dagger.'

'You know what to do, don't you?'

Gareth saluted. 'Yes, ma'am. Do you think Tiffany will be asleep by then? More importantly, will Oliver? I don't trust that bloody little bear not to give the game away.'

The plan went like a dream. At twenty-five past one, Gareth, who was watching from the front window of Victoria's bedroom, hissed, 'They're here,' at Victoria and Sarah who were watching from the other. 'The Rolls has just stopped outside. Two men have got out and they're walking into the square at this very minute. I'm about to call the cops on the mobile and then I'll go out and let down the tyres.' This was merely a precautionary measure.

The women watched as the men walked quietly into

the square and approached the house where Sarah and her children would normally have been peacefully asleep.

'The tallest one is definitely Alex,' Sarah whispered. 'I recognize his walk. Thank goodness you were awake last night and saw him. Oh, look! He's going to kick down the door.'

Alex gave the door a single kick and it flew open. He beckoned to the other man and they entered the house. Within minutes, two police cars were at the scene, lights flashing. A struggling Alex and his partner were escorted from the house. 'I only wanted my kids,' Alex screamed. 'That's all I wanted, my children.'

'I almost feel sorry for him,' a shaken Sarah said when it was all over and the square was quiet again.

'Save your pity for someone more deserving,' Victoria advised.

Sarah yawned. 'I think I'll go to bed. Thank goodness the children didn't wake up. Goodnight, you two. I'll see you in the morning.'

'Is it all right if I stay, do you think?' Gareth asked when Sarah had gone.

'Yes, but you'd better leave early in the morning.'

'Is there a lock on your bedroom door?'

'There's a hook. Why?'

'Because I don't want Tiffany, Oliver and Tabitha barging in disturbing our slumber or whatever else we might be up to.'

Judy Moon let the bedroom curtain fall when the excitement appeared to be over and went into the kitchen to heat a cup of milk in the microwave. It didn't bode well for the future that, after only a few hours in her new home, there'd been a police raid. Donna said that Victoria Square appeared eminently respectable, the

370

people very nice, although when she'd come the other day to put up the curtains, the woman from next door, Rachel Williams, had been very pushy. She'd come again next morning and invited Donna for coffee.

'Pushy, but helpful,' Donna said in the crisp, no-nonsense tones that had scared the living daylights out of Judy when Joe had first brought her home and she could tell straight away it was serious. She had always expected that one day she would have two daughters-in-law and had vowed never to interfere, criticize or take sides, but to make friends with the girls so they had nice, easy-going relationships.

The microwave beeped and Judy carried the milk into the bedroom, switched on the bedside lamp, and hoisted a pillow behind her back. Making friends with Donna had proved easier said than done. For years, the girl had been positively *un*friendly.

But now that was all water under the bridge. In the course of time, Donna had turned out to be worth her weight in gold. It was all due to Sam. Judy smiled wryly. Because of Sam, she'd made a friend of her daughter-in-law and an enemy of her husband.

The milk finished, Judy didn't feel remotely like sleeping – she'd been tossing and turning when the police cars had arrived, blue lights flashing and casting an eerie glow over the room. She clasped her hands on top of the duvet. 'This is the first day of the rest of me life,' she told herself. It was a saying that applied to every day, but in her case was particularly apt: from this day onwards, she would be living alone for the first time, beholden to no one, able to go anywhere, do anything she wanted. It was a daunting prospect, vaguely frightening but, at the same time, exciting.

She'd never go to sleep at this rate. There was

something missing. After a few minutes, she remembered what it was and went over to her luggage, still unpacked, and rooted through a suitcase until she found a packet of incense sticks, a holder, and a box of matches. She chose Golden Orchid, lit the stick and put it on the chest that Josh had painted so beautifully, and got back into bed.

Almost immediately, the room was pervaded by a musky, pungent scent. She snuggled under the clothes, acutely aware that she was lying in Sam's bed, underneath his duvet, her head on his pillow and surrounded by his furniture. She was back again in the basement flat in Islington and, as she drifted into sleep, she could have sworn she could hear Isabella singing . . .

Judy Moon

Chapter 12

Judy Smith was a war baby. She was born in 1941 while her mum and dad, both avid film fans, were watching *The Wizard of Oz* in the Palais de Luxe in Lime Street. Mum experienced the first contraction just as Dorothy and her companions arrived at Oz and were waiting to see the wizard. She'd rather hoped to last the film out, but had another contraction almost immediately, more severe than the first. Time seemed to be at a premium. The manager had been asked to phone for an ambulance, but said it would be quicker if he took them to the maternity hospital in his car. After he'd delivered Mum – he meant to the hospital, not in his car – he'd take Dad back to Penny Lane where a neighbour was looking after the other children.

'If this one's a girl, you'll have to call her Dorothy,' he said on the way.

'Can't,' said Dad. 'We've already got a Dorothy, after Dorothy Gish. *Orphans of the Storm* was the first film I ever saw. I was only eleven and I've been hooked every since.'

'Judy then. Judy Garland's a real heart-stopper.'

'That's not a bad idea,' Dad mused. 'All our four kids are named after film stars. We were going to call this one Glenda, after Glenda Farrell who was in *I am a Fugitive From a Chain Gang*. It's my favourite film.'

'It's mine too,' the manager enthused. The siren went to signal an air raid had started, but both men ignored it.

'But Judy seems more appropriate. What do you think, luv?' he asked Mum, who was writhing in agony on the back seat and hoping they'd reach the hospital before any bombs fell.

'Judy's fine,' she gasped.

'What about if it's a boy?' the manager asked.

'Clark, after Clark Gable,' Dad replied.

'Have you seen *Gone with the Wind*?'

'Twice.'

'Magnificent picture, wasn't it?'

'Superb. You enjoyed it, didn't you, love?'

'It was marvellous,' Mum gulped.

Judy's two brothers and two sisters were called Dorothy, Paulette (after Paulette Goddard), Ronnie (Ronald Colman), and Fred (Fredric March). The Smiths were a happy family. They weren't exactly poor, but neither were they comfortably off. Dad didn't earn much in his exceedingly dull job in an insurance office. Fortunately, Mum could do wonders with a couple of pounds of mincemeat and the younger children didn't mind if they wore hand-me-down clothes.

Mum and Dad argued a lot, not over anything important, mainly the films with which they were obsessed: whether Ronald Colman was a better actor than Herbert Marshall; if Clark Gable was more handsome with a moustache or without; was it Jean Harlow or Rosalind Russell who had starred in *China Seas* – a few days later, Dad had gone round to the local picture house to ask the manager and it turned out to be both.

Judy did well at school. She had 'a quick brain', according to her father. All Sylvester Smith's children had quick brains, something of which he was inordinately proud, particularly when they all passed scholarships and went to grammar schools. They'd inherited their brains from their dad, he told them frequently, and their looks from their radiantly pretty, golden-haired, peachy-skinned mother, who could well have become a film star herself had she not fallen in love with you know who. 'Old monkey face,' he would add. It was his way of fishing for compliments, knowing that someone would insist he bore a striking resemblance to Spencer Tracy.

'Perhaps we should have gone to Hollywood when we first got married,' he would ruminate aloud, his brow furrowed, just like Spencer's. 'I could have become a director or a producer or something. We'd be living in a white mansion with a swimming pool by now, 'stead of Penny Lane.'

'But if Mum was busy being a film star, you wouldn't have had us,' Dorothy once pointed out.

'Oh, well, given the choice . . .' Dad said hastily, leaving the rest of the sentence hanging in the air so his children could only guess what the choice would have been had he been given it. Dorothy thought he'd sooner be in Hollywood and Fred thought Penny Lane. The others couldn't make up their minds.

Anyway, their house had a little touch of Hollywood about it. Dad collected the *Picturegoer* from the paper shop every Friday on his way home from work and, after he and Mum had read it from cover to cover, it would be passed on to the children who

377

devoured it just as keenly if they could read or, if they hadn't yet learned, just looked at the photos of the stars and scenes of the films they were in.

The magazines would then be put in a box in the cupboard under the stairs where they were easy to get at for reference purposes. If there was a photo of a star he or Mum particularly liked, Dad would buy another *Picturegoer* and the pictures would be cut out and pinned to the walls of their bedroom.

They grew up, the Smith children, thinking that the little, unpretentious house in Penny Lane had something extra-special about it. The stars were their friends. Sylvester referred to them by their first names: Clark, Franchot, Ingrid, Humphrey. 'I see Humph and Lauren are getting married,' he would say looking up from the *Picturegoer*, irritating Mum no end because she preferred to read it for herself.

At nine, Judy wrote to the studios for a photograph of Alan Ladd, the first man with whom she fell in love. When it arrived, she burst into tears because he was so handsome, yet unattainable.

It struck her then, although in a way she could never have put into words, that her family were brushing with the softest of wings against an alien world far away across the ocean to which they didn't belong and never would. Yet it seemed an innocent and charming thing to do, to escape from their own humdrum little world into a star-studded tinsel town in California, far better than being interested in nothing at all like most people.

From that day on, Judy regarded her family's fixation with Hollywood with an amused tolerance, although stayed in love with Alan Ladd until she was fourteen, keeping his photo underneath her pillow to look at before she went to sleep and first thing in the morning when she woke up.

It would seem all the children had come down to earth at some time during their young lives. Dorothy, the eldest, became a teacher, much to the disappointment of Sylvester who'd been hoping all his incredibly handsome children would go into show business. Then Ronnie chose a career in the Navy, Paulette went into nursing, and Fred took his A.M.I.Mech.E and became an engineering draughtsman. All her father's hopes were now centred on Judy, who was to disappoint him again by getting engaged during her final year at school and marrying the following Christmas after spending a few months in an office as dull as his own.

Judy met Harry Moon in the Cavern, a jazz club that had opened in Liverpool a few years before – her father was a keen aficionado. One wintry Sunday in February, she was with a friend from school listening to Cy Laurie's Jazz Band, when a young man appeared at the end of her row, his eyes searching for an empty seat.

'Who does he remind me of?' she asked herself and realized with a little thrill that it was Alan Ladd. He had the same blond hair and perfectly regular features. Someone moved up so the end seat became vacant and he nodded a 'thank you', and she saw he had the same smile and the same white teeth. He was smartly dressed in a grey tweed suit, woollen shirt, and check tie. The other men present were more casually attired.

During the interval, when people were milling around buying soft drinks from the bar and her friend had gone to stand in the queue for the Ladies, Judy managed to let her handkerchief fall at Alan Ladd's feet. She was looking her best that night, in a white angora jumper Paulette had given her because it itched, a maroon pleated skirt, a hand-me-down of Dorothy's, and high-heeled boots Mum and Dad had bought her for Christmas. She'd only recently begun to use lipstick and the pale rose on her lips was the same shade as her cheeks. Mum had set her wavy hair in a casual style very similar to Marilyn Monroe's.

'You've dropped something,' Alan Ladd said, picking the hankie up.

'Thanks very much, I hadn't noticed.'

'Do you come here often?' he asked conversationally. She identified a spark of interest in his blue eyes and wondered if it was reflected in her own that were a slightly darker shade of blue.

'About once a week, usually on Sunday. I'm not too keen on skiffle. I like New Orleans jazz best.' She felt slightly disappointed. Close up, he didn't look even faintly like Alan Ladd. His nose was a tiny bit bigger, or possibly smaller, his mouth wider, or it might have been narrower. He just wasn't the man she'd spent five years of her life madly in love with. She quickly got over her disappointment: despite the differences, he was just as handsome.

'What do you do for a living?' he enquired in a friendly tone.

'I'm still at school. In May, I'll be eighteen and I'll be leaving in July. What do you do? For a living that is.'

'I'm a photographer,' he said modestly, though she could tell he was rather proud of the fact. 'My dad's got his own shop in Menlove Avenue.'

'That's not far from us. We live in Penny Lane.'

'We might bump into each other sometime. Look, we'd better sit down.' People were returning to their seats. 'The Blue Genes Skiffle Group is on next.'

She wanted to spit, thinking that she'd lost him, but when the music ended and everyone was filing out, she felt a hand on her arm and turned to find Alan Ladd regarding her with slightly more interest than before.

'Will you be here next Sunday?'

'I expect so,' Judy said casually, although she wouldn't have missed next Sunday for the world.

'See you next week then. What's your name?'

'Judy Smith.'

'I'm Harry Moon.'

Within a month they were in love. They got engaged on her birthday and were married at Christmas. The youngest Smith, Judy was the first to marry. There was a flat over the photographer's shop, which the present tenants were about to vacate, where they could live at a nominal rent.

'Dad said we could have it for nothing, but that wouldn't be right. I insisted we pay something.'

Harry was twenty-two, a cautious, honourable man, easy-going to a fault. Judy loved him for it. Always careful to do what he considered was right, he gave back change if he'd been given too much and, if they were on a bus or tram and the conductor was on the top deck and he hadn't paid the fare when it was time to get off, he would run upstairs and pay, even if he sometimes nearly missed his stop – Judy and almost every other person she knew would have jumped off and considered themselves lucky. And kept any overpaid change.

She got married in her mother's carefully preserved wedding gown that she'd made herself: cream crêpe, full-length, with a boat-shaped neckline edged with pearls and otherwise completely plain apart from the leg-of-mutton sleeves.

'You look just as beautiful as your mum did on our wedding day,' Dad said emotionally in the car on the way to the church. 'Harry's a lucky chap. I'm glad you're marrying into an artistic family, Jude. Did you know his dad belongs to a film group? They actually make short films. He's invited me to join.'

The Moons and the Smiths got on extraordinarily well. The two sets of parents had already become good friends and it turned out that Harry's sister, Eve, was a teacher and already knew Judy's sister, Dorothy.

Life, it seemed, was perfect. The wedding was perfect. Living in the flat over the shop was perfect, particularly making love with Harry. They continued to go to the Cavern where rock 'n' roll had taken over from jazz and scruffy young men who would eventually become world famous played their wild, raucous music, sending the crowds into a delirium of excitement.

Judy gave up her office job to look after the shop while Mr Moon was in the studio taking photographs that flattered the sitters no end. Harry did all the outside jobs: the weddings, christenings, parties, and family portraits.

They'd been married six months when Judy discovered she was expecting a baby and Joe was born in the spring of 1961. By this time, they'd already moved into their own house: a large, comfortable semi-detached in Heathfield Road, no distance from the shop, Judy's mum and dad, and her in-laws. Harry was a partner in the business and could easily afford the mortgage. Their second son, Sam, arrived a year later, only missing his mother's twenty-first birthday by a day.

Judy felt as if she had been uniquely blessed, moving seamlessly from a supremely happy childhood to a blissfully happy marriage, now with the addition of two beautiful, healthy sons: Joe, with his delicate skin and golden curls took after her, whereas the more robust Sam had dark hair and navy-blue eyes and took after no one they could think of.

Her sisters hadn't been so lucky. Dorothy, who had married the year after her, was having trouble with a husband who drank too much and had already had one affair – 'That I know of,' Dorothy said darkly. Paulette, now twenty-five, longed to get married, but so far hadn't met a man with whom she felt inclined to spend the next fifty or sixty years.

Despite her state of utter contentment, Judy couldn't help but worry that it might not last. Life was so unexpected. No matter how good things were, you could never tell what was waiting around the next corner. Look at her father, for instance! He'd been seriously depressed when nearly all the cinemas in Liverpool had closed down and were converted into Bingo halls, used for storage, or just left to rot. It was the last thing he'd imagined happening. And who would have thought that the day would come when the *Picturegoer* would publish its final issue, as it did in April 1960? Dad felt as if his world was falling apart. His idols were either dead or retired and had been replaced by actors who hadn't the charisma of Clark or Humphrey, Rosalind or Rita, apart from Marilyn Monroe whom he worshipped. He was gradually sinking into a decline when his children clubbed together and bought him a television and he was able to watch old films in the comfort of his own home, although it didn't have the magic of a real picture house.

Judy and Harry suffered the usual traumas of parents, nursing the children through chickenpox, measles, coughs and colds that hinted of something far more deadly, but turned out to be nothing of the sort. When Joe was eleven, he broke his arm playing football, and Sam acquired a squint at the same age and had to have an operation to put it right – Harry sat with him in the hospital throughout his first night, much to the irritation of the staff.

The shared agony of these incidents brought them even closer. These two wonderful human beings were the results of their love for each other. Harry adored them and talked of little else, boasting to all and sundry of his sons' achievements at school or on the football or cricket pitch, boring his listeners silly and showing not even the slightest interest in *their* children.

'People will start avoiding you,' Judy warned.

He grinned. 'I don't care. If I run out of people, I'll talk to myself in the mirror.'

Then the day came that sixteen-year-old Joe brought home his first girlfriend, Shirley. Harry waited until they'd gone then, to Judy's utter astonishment, he said in a tone of voice she'd never heard him use before, a mixture of outrage and anger, 'She was nothing but a cheap little tart. All that eye make-up! And I suspect her hair was dyed.'

'She seemed quite nice to me.' Shirley had undoubtedly gone to town with the eyeliner, but Judy didn't see that it mattered. 'She's only fifteen. Her and Joe aren't likely to get married.'

'I didn't like her.'

'She probably didn't like you, either, the way you glowered at her. I just hope Joe didn't notice. Really, Harry,' she chided, 'you're going to have to be more tolerant. If Joe senses you don't like Shirley, it'll only make him want to go out with her more. Let him give her up in his own time – or she in hers.'

'Our Joe would never go out with a girl I disapproved of,' Harry said incredulously.

'Oh, yes, he would,' she assured him. 'Would you have given me up if your father had disapproved?'

'But you were perfect!'

'Joe might think Shirley's perfect – for the moment.'

Harry managed not to glower when Joe turned up with a succession of girlfriends, although always found something wrong with them. Judy began to wonder if there was a woman on earth good enough for his son.

'At least our Sam's got a sensible head on his shoulders,' he muttered. 'He's more interested in enjoying himself than bothering with women at his age.' Sam hung around with a crowd of young people of both sexes and appeared to be having a whale of a time.

'He will eventually.' For the first time, Harry was getting on her nerves. He was too possessive by a mile, too – she tried to think of a more appropriate word – too *involved* in his children's lives, not accepting that they had to be left to go their own way, choose their own wives.

Joe was twenty-one and obviously smitten when he came home with Donna Nelson, four years older than him, a severe looking woman with a permanent frown. Her jet-black hair was brushed smoothly back from a face that might have looked pretty had she ever smiled. Even Judy was faintly shocked when it emerged that Donna was divorced and had a two-year-old son.

'I trust you won't be going out with *her* again,' Harry exploded the minute he had his son on his own.

Joe looked taken aback. 'I'm sorry, Dad, but I don't think that's any of your business,' he stammered. 'I'll go out with whomever I like.'

'But she's been married before: she's actually got a *child*.' Harry could hardly contain his anger.

'Ashley's a really great kid. You'll like him.'

'Ashley!' Harry almost spat the word out. 'What sort of name is that?'

'Harry,' Judy said warningly. An old memory surfaced and she recalled Leslie Howard's character in *Gone with the Wind* had been called Ashley. She hadn't liked Donna much herself. The girl was too abrupt, too surly, almost rude when she'd tried to be friendly. But if she was Joe's choice . . .

It seemed that she was because not long afterwards, Joe announced that he and Donna were getting married.

Donna had a married sister with two children in their teens. Her parents were dead. At first, she rebuffed all Judy's offers to help with the register office wedding and pay for a hotel so they could have a proper reception with rather more guests than the handful Donna envisaged. With great reluctance, she conceded it would be unfair not to invite Joe's grandparents, his aunts, uncles, cousins, and a few of his friends, so Judy booked a room big enough for forty at a hotel in Woolton.

'I had a big wedding last time,' Donna said sullenly, 'and look at the way *that* turned out.'

Judy didn't ask the reason why she'd got divorced. As long as Joe knew and was satisfied, she didn't care.

It was a while since both families had gathered together for a big occasion. Judy's heart swelled with a mixture of love and pride when, in March 1983, she sat in the front row of the register office and watched Sam, the best man, hand the ring to his brother. Joe was the taller of the two, over six feet, lithe and graceful. He always looked a touch aristocratic with his long, thin nose and high cheekbones. At twenty, Sam was still very boyish, solidly built, with a lovely open face that always seemed to be set in a grin. She'd never had a favourite, but Sam had always seemed more vulnerable and easily hurt than his brother and she worried about him more. These two young, hand-some men were her sons and her love for them was absolute.

She would have enjoyed the wedding more if it hadn't been for Harry's scowling face, all because his son was marrying a woman he objected to. It was so unlike him. Usually so good-natured and free with his smiles, she realized that when it came to the boys, another side to her husband emerged, one that she hadn't known existed.

Fortunately, nobody else seemed to notice: even Donna, in a smart white suit, melted slightly at the reception when showered with so many kisses and good wishes for the future. She seemed particularly taken with Sylvester, who told her she reminded him of Louise Brooks, one of his all-time favourite stars of the thirties. Ashley, her little boy, was very sweet, dark like his mother and very well behaved – until he was noticed pouring champagne over the remainder of the wedding cake and eating it with a spoon. 'I've made a pudding,' he explained.

Judy was glad when Donna said, 'What a clever thing to do, sweetheart, but it might make you sick.' She'd dreaded that she might smack the child.

The day wore on. At six o'clock, the newly married couple left for their honeymoon in Brighton. Judy hadn't realized they were taking Ashley with them and thought it rather nice, but Harry's face darkened even more. 'It's not natural,' he mumbled. He'd had too much to drink, which was a first. 'Why couldn't Donna leave the boy with her sister?'

'I don't know,' Judy sighed. The room had been booked until ten. She was wondering how she would get through it with Harry in such a horrible mood and was glad when he went to talk to his father. She'd always imagined the boys' weddings being very different, her and Harry united in their delight that their sons had found wives they loved, but this wedding had been a bitter disappointment.

She noticed Sam was sitting by himself, a lonely figure. He'd miss Joe no longer living at home. They'd always been the best of friends.

'You look sad, love,' she said, sinking on to a chair beside him.

'I'm tired. Joe's stag party didn't finish until four this morning. I suppose I *am* a bit sad too,' he conceded. 'It's not every day you lose your brother.'

'Never mind, you'll be next.' Judy patted his knee.

There was a long pause before Sam said, 'I don't think so, Mum.'

Just five words, said in a quiet, steady voice, yet there was something about the words, or it might have been the voice – *too* steady, *too* quiet, too *positive* – that made the hairs tingle on Judy's neck.

'I'm sure you will, son.' *Please* say you will, another voice inside her shrieked. *Please* say you don't mean what I think you mean.

'No, Mum, I won't.' He looked at her compassionately, knowing that what he was saying would break his mother's heart. 'I like women, but I'll never marry one. I'm not attracted to them, not in the way our Joe is to Donna. I prefer . . .' He left the rest of the sentence unsaid.

Judy finished it for him. 'Men?' There was a quiver in her voice and waves of nausea were washing over her.

Sam nodded, his face crimson with embarrassment.

'Oh, Sam! Oh, my dear boy.' Her beloved son, was a . . . She refused to even *think* the word. 'What's to become of you?' she wailed.

'It's not the end of the world.' He took her hand and squeezed it hard. 'Please say you don't hate me, Mum.'

Suddenly, he was her little boy again needing the comfort of his mother's arms and soft words. 'Of course, I don't hate you, Sam,' she said fervently. 'I love you with all my heart and I'll never stop loving you until the day I die.'

'Ta, Mum.' He was still squeezing her hand, as if he needed her reassurance. 'I'd sooner have not told you in the middle of the wedding,' he said soberly, 'but a few people today have said, "you'll be next," just like you. It doesn't matter about them, but it does about you and Dad. I don't want you expecting me to bring a girl home one day and announce we're getting married.'

'Do you want me to tell your father?'

'If you wouldn't mind. I've been meaning to tell you for ages, but I didn't know how to begin. What do you think Dad will say?'

'He'll blow his top at first, but he'll soon get over it,' Judy said confidently.

She didn't pluck up the courage to tell Harry for another week, by which time he seemed to have recovered his good humour and was smiling again. They'd been to her in-laws for a meal. Mr Moon had talked about retiring from the shop in the near future. 'Your Sam's turning out to be a darned good photographer. Why don't you make him a partner when he's twenty-one, like I did you, and I'll disappear from the scene?' Sam had taken a photography course at the art college – Joe had shown no interest and had chosen hotel management as a career.

'Will you?' Judy asked when they got home. 'Make Sam a partner, that is?'

'If he wants. You don't think he's too young?'

'You managed OK at the same age.'

'I suppose I did.' He yawned and stretched his arms. 'Is Sam home?'

'He went to a disco. He'll be ages yet.'

'Oh, well. I think I'll turn in.'

Judy took a deep breath. 'Before you go, there's something I want to tell you. It's about Sam . . .'

She thought he took it very well, kept saying, 'I see,' from time to time, his face devoid of expression when she repeated what Sam had told her at his brother's wedding.

'I see,' he said again when she'd finished.

'Are you all right about it?' she asked anxiously.

'What do you think?' He went to bed without another word and she had no idea whether he was all right about it or not.

Harry was already up when she woke next morning: Sunday, she remembered, when she heard church bells ringing in the distance.

She went downstairs and found him and Sam seated at the table in the breakfast room. 'Good morning,' she said cheerily. 'Did you have a nice time at the disco, Sam?'

Before Sam could answer, Harry sneered, 'Yeah! He danced all night with his boyfriends.'

Judy's blood ran cold. 'What a terrible thing to say!'

'It's the truth.'

Sam said quietly, 'As it happens, it's not the truth.' He turned to his mother and she could have wept when she saw the grief in his dark blue eyes. 'Dad's just chucked me out, Mum. I'll pack my stuff in a minute and be on my way.'

'You'll do no such thing,' she snapped.

'This is *my* house,' Harry said in a grating voice, 'and I'm not having a bloody pansy living under *my* roof.'

Judy gasped. 'What on earth's got into you, Harry? You've changed out of all recognition. Sam is your son. How can you possibly throw out your own son?'

'Sam's no longer my son. I thought Joe was bad enough, marrying a divorced woman with a child when he knew that I, his father, was dead against it, but this!' To her surprise, he began to cry. His shoulders heaved. 'I don't know what the world's coming to. Everything's going wrong.'

Judy made no attempt to comfort him. It was his sheer pigheadedness that was making everything go wrong. They still could have continued, a perfectly normal family, accepting Joe's choice of a wife, accepting Sam for what he was, if only Harry could have understood he didn't *own* his sons. They weren't puppets and all he had to do was pull the strings and they would dance to his tune.

'I'll go, Mum.' Sam heaved himself wearily to his feet. 'It's for the best.'

'But where?' she cried.

He shrugged. 'I don't really know.' He seemed about to cry himself.

'Go to Gran and Granddad Smith's. They'd love to have you and there's plenty of room. I'll give them a ring, shall I?'

'Please, Mum.'

Harry must have been listening. 'You're not to tell them,' he said hoarsely. There was a look, almost of fear, in his eyes. 'You're not to tell *anyone* what you are. I'm too ashamed. I couldn't stand it. What Joe did was bad enough. But you, you're beyond the pale.'

Judy ignored him. 'After I've rung, I'll come upstairs with you, love, help you pack a bag.'

Half an hour later, she stood at the window, palms pressed against the glass, and watched her son walk away. Although the bag she'd helped him pack wasn't particularly heavy, he carried it as if it contained a ton of bricks; his shoulders curved like an old man's. She felt her heart contract and wanted to rush after him, fetch him back, but that just wasn't on, not with Harry the way he was.

'He'll be all right,' he said from the door.

'No, he won't. I'll go and see him later.'

'I'd sooner you didn't,' he said stiffly. 'I'd sooner you had nothing more to do with Sam. He's no longer a member of this family.'

She looked at him pityingly. 'He's my son, Harry. He'll always be my son. And I'll always be his mother. You can't argue with that, you can't change it.' When she glanced through the window again, Sam had disappeared. She said, 'I think I'll go to church.'

'I'll come with you.'

'I'd rather you didn't, Harry. I want to be by myself.' She wanted to pray for Sam, for Joe and Donna, for Harry and herself. Most of all, she wanted to pray that their marriage would survive the events of the last few weeks. She still loved Harry, but the love had been badly scarred and she had a feeling the scars would never completely heal.

Sam stayed with his grandparents for two months before moving to London. 'I'll fit in better down there.' He grinned. He seemed much more cheeful. 'There's more people like me around and they're quite open about it.'

'Are they really?' She'd never met a — she still refused to think the word — person of Sam's disposition in her life.

'There's an awful lot of us about, Mum. I'm not exactly one in a million.'

'Is it something *I* did that's made you like this, son?' she asked anxiously.

Sam laughed. 'I don't know what made me like this,

Mum, but it was nothing to do with you. You're still not used to it, are you?'

'I never will be, Sam. I'm afraid I don't understand any of it.'

'I don't think I do, either.' He shrugged.

'Write to me with your address as soon as you've got one.'

'To the house?'

'To the house. Your father will be cross, but that's his problem.'

'Wouldn't it be best if I sent the letters here?' he asked, meaning the house in Penny Lane where his mother had been born.

'No, it'll only worry your gran and granddad. They're already worried enough, wondering what's happened, why you left home in the first place.' Mum and Dad were in their seventies. Dad was as fit as a fiddle, but her mother was becoming very frail.

Everyone was getting older. In a few days, she would be forty-two and Sam twenty-one. She'd planned a big party, but that wouldn't happen now. She couldn't visualize ever going to a party again.

She did, of course, although it was a long time before she and Harry began to get along, and it was never the same as it had been before. She felt as if a curtain had fallen between them and they couldn't communicate with each other any more. If a letter came with a London postmark, Harry would ignore it. He wasn't interested in knowing how Sam was getting on. When he'd been away a few months, Judy paid him a visit and Harry went around, tight-lipped, hardly speaking, for days beforehand and for days after she came back.

Judy continued to visit and he accused her of being disloyal.

'You should be on *my* side, not Sam's,' he finished in a hurt voice.

'I'm not on anybody's side,' she replied. 'I'm not deserting Sam for you – or you for Sam. I'll see him whenever I like.'

Joe visited them often, sometimes bringing Ashley with him, but it was rare that Donna came and just as rare that they were invited to their house in Allerton. Judy didn't like to call unannounced, worried she mightn't be made welcome. She was resigned to the fact that she would never make a friend of her daughter-in-law.

She also got used to explaining to people why Sam never came home. 'He works for a newspaper and spends loads of time abroad. He keeps promising to come and stay, but never manages to make it.'

At least the newspaper bit was true and Sam did go abroad, but only occasionally. She felt annoyed at having to lie because of Harry's prejudices. 'Next time someone asks, I'll refer them to you,' she told him crossly, but people gradually stopped asking.

Nineteen eighty-five was a sad year. Mr Moon passed away in January, followed not long afterwards by Judy's mother. It was also the year when Joe discovered the truth about his brother. The two young men wrote to each other and frequently spoke on the phone but, in deference to his father, Sam had always kept his secret hidden.

Joe had been on a hotel management course in Kent. On the way home, he called on Sam in his basement flat in Islington. Back in Liverpool, the very next day, he came to see his mother. Harry wasn't there, having gone to work in the shop, as Joe had known he would.

'Sam's living with this black guy, Josh. They're a couple. Why didn't you tell me, Mum?' Joe said reproachfully. 'Did you think I'd mind or something? Sam said it's why Dad chucked him out and he's never come back, not even for a visit.'

'Your father didn't want anyone to know. He's too ashamed.'

'Ashamed of what?' Joe looked truculent. 'Sam said you've stuck by him all the way, but you could have told *me*. I'm his brother. I've a right to know. As for Dad, he's still living in the nineteenth century. Strange,' he said thoughtfully, 'I used to think he was the best father in the world, so laid back he was virtually horizontal, but it turned out he doesn't go along with divorce, let alone homosexuality.' Judy winced at the word and Joe went on, 'There are loads of openly gay men and women around nowadays: famous actors, pop groups, film stars. There's no need to make a big deal out of it. It isn't against the law.'

Judy sighed. 'Have you told Donna about Sam?'

'Of course I have. She's dead shocked – oh, not with Sam, but with Dad for making him leave. By the way, she's pregnant.' He smiled joyfully. 'We're dead pleased. We're having a little get-together on Saturday, just a few friends. Donna wants to know if you'll come. She's really impressed with the way you've stood by Sam. She thought you'd have gone along with Dad.'

Judy's heart leaped. It seemed as if she might make a friend of Donna, after all. 'I'd love to. I'll see what your dad's up to that night.'

'Dad's not invited. Anyroad, he wouldn't have come. He dislikes Donna as much as she does him.'

The curtain between them was getting thicker. Harry would get up and leave the room whenever Joe mentioned his brother. He wasn't even faintly thrilled when his first grandchild was born: a bonny little girl named Rosemary and wore the same scowl at the baby's christening as he'd done at her parent's wedding.

'Why don't you lighten up?' she asked when they got home. 'You're making yourself terribly unhappy just because your sons haven't conformed to the pattern you drew up for them. Joe and Sam haven't done anything evil.' He stared at her blankly, as if she'd spoken in a language he didn't understand. 'Harry,' she said gently, 'what's happened to us? Remember the night we met in the Cavern? For years afterwards, our lives were perfect. What's gone wrong, love?'

'I don't know.' The blank stare was replaced by a look of terror. 'I'm frightened, Jude,' he said piteously.

'I'm not surprised, love. You've made enemies of the people closest to you. Why not make a fresh start?' she urged. 'Make friends with Donna – and Joe: he's not exactly pleased about your attitude to his wife. Invite Sam home, even if it's only for a weekend.'

'Would he bring his boyfriend?'

From his glacial tone Judy could tell she was wasting her time. The family was now divided into two distinct camps: Harry in one camp, his sons in the other, herself somewhere in between, but slowly being drawn into the second camp and making an enemy of the husband she'd once loved so much.

★

Sylvester Smith refused to leave the house on New Year's Eve, 1989, to see in the new decade with his children. He reserved *Casablanca* in the video shop, a film that not only featured two much-loved stars, Ingrid Bergman and Humphrey Bogart, but had also been his wife's favourite of all time.

Dorothy, who lived nearest, bought him a couple of bottles of beer and a box of chocolates. 'Enjoy yourself, Dad. I'll give you a ring as soon as Big Ben chimes in nineteen ninety.'

But when Dorothy rang, there was no answer. Suspecting something might be wrong, she called Judy, Paulette and Fred – Ronnie had settled in New Zealand when he gave up the Navy – and they entered the house together to discover their father had passed peacefully away. *Casablanca* had finished and had rewound.

'I wonder if he saw it right through to the end or did it rewind itself?' Paulette moaned. 'We'll never know exactly when he died.'

'I reckon he saw it. The beer and the chocolates have all gone. He usually made them last out the whole film.' Fred closed his father's eyes for the last time. 'Didn't you, Dad?' he said fondly.

Dorothy made the cold body comfortable on the settee, Paulette went to ring for an ambulance, and Judy took the bottles and the empty chocolate box into the kitchen. The others followed and they sat around the old table where they'd eaten their mother's delicious casseroles. An ancient chrome alarm clock ticked loudly on the window sill. A poster advertising *The Godfather* was attached to the fridge.

'I bet Mum and Dad are in heaven watching *I am a Fugitive From a Chain Gang*.' Judy managed a smile.

'That was a ghastly film. Remember he asked us round the minute he got the video and we had to pretend to enjoy it so as not to hurt his feelings?'

It was a signal for the memories to come pouring out. They recalled how flattered their father had been to be compared to Spencer Tracy, how much he had adored their mother, the way he had eagerly devoured the contents of the *Picturegoer* every week.

'There's hundreds, if not thousands of them, under the stairs,' Paulette said. 'They'd probably sell for a small fortune, but I'd prefer we kept them. We could have a few boxes each.' She put her elbows on the table and cupped her chin in her hands. 'Are we as happy now that we're all in our fifties as we were then?' she asked.

'I'm not in my fifties,' Judy reminded her. 'I'm only forty-eight.'

'OK, I'll rephrase the question. Are we as happy now that three of us are in our fifties and our Judy's forty-eight?'

There was silence for a while. Then Fred said, 'Most of the time. Mavis and I have had our ups and downs, what marriage doesn't? But all in all I'd say I'm happier. What about you, Pauly?'

Paulette made a face. 'It wasn't as nice living here after you'd all gone. I was beginning to think I'd end up an old maid. I was thirty when I met John and we fell in love. We had four kids in four years and I couldn't be happier.' She turned to her sister. 'It's your turn, Dot.'

'Me?' Dorothy shuddered. 'I was dead *un*happy when I first got married. It was a good ten years before I became resigned to Kevin's affairs. I comfort myself with the thought that he always came back to me.

Now the kids are grown up and Kevin doesn't bother with other women. Perhaps he hasn't got the energy. We go on holiday together. We've become friends more than anything. I suppose,' she said thoughtfully, 'you could say that I'm happy.'

Everyone turned to Judy. 'I don't know what to say,' she stammered when faced with three pairs of curious eyes.

'Shall I repeat the question?' Paulette asked.

'No.' Everyone else had told the truth: this wasn't a time for lies. 'When I married Harry,' she began nervously, 'I was happier than I'd thought possible. It stayed that way for years and years, but then something awful happened and everything fell apart. It's never been the same since.'

'So you're the only one who's not as happy now as when we were kids?' Fred deduced.

'It would seem so.'

Dorothy's eyes narrowed. 'Is Sam being gay the awful thing that happened?'

Judy caught her breath. 'How did you know?'

'Dad guessed that time Sam stayed here years ago. Nobody said anything, we were waiting for you to mention it first.' Dorothy folded her arms and said, almost coldly, 'I wouldn't have described the thing with Sam as awful, Jude. Upsetting, maybe, but not awful. I can't believe you let Harry throw him out – your own *son*. For all his faults, Kevin would never have done a thing like that.'

'Neither would John,' Paulette chimed in.

'Harry was always a bit of a stuffed shirt,' Fred said with a critical sniff. 'He wanted his kids to grow up to be reflections of himself: nauseatingly moral and incredibly dull.'

Judy jumped to her feet. 'I think I'll go and sit with Dad until the ambulance comes.'

'I'm sorry, sis. That was a bit harsh.'

'No, Fred. It's the truth. I'd already come to the same conclusion myself, but you phrased it better than I ever could.'

Another decade passed. When Mrs Moon died, there were no grandparents left, but by then the children had become grandparents themselves. Time was marching relentlessly onwards, arriving at the twenty-first century with the tick of the clock, a burst of fireworks, and celebrations throughout the land.

Judy and Harry spent Millennium's Eve at Joe and Donna's with a few old friends and Harry's sister, Eve, and her family. Harry's opinion of Donna had softened with the years. She had proved a loyal and supportive wife to his son, but his judgement of his other son had never altered. It was eighteen years since Sam had left home, but his name was rarely spoken in the house in Heathfield Road.

Fireworks were being let off in the garden when Donna came and squeezed Judy's hand. 'While everyone's out here, I thought you might like to ring Sam from the extension in the bedroom.'

'Thank you, love.' Behind her rather grim exterior, Donna had a soft and tender heart and Judy had come to love her as a daughter.

'It sounds like pandemonium there,' she said when she got through to Sam and was met by thunderous music and a chorus of animated voices in the background. 'Happy Millennium to you and Josh, son. You sound as if you're having a good time.'

'The best, Mum. How about you?'

'We're at Joe's. Oh, but I wish you were here too!' Suddenly, she wanted to weep because the whole family weren't together on such a momentous night.

Sam chuckled. 'You never know, by the time the next Millennium comes, Dad might have accepted he has a gay son.'

Judy said she thought it would take more than another thousand years. 'He's thinking of retiring, your dad: selling the business and the house and moving to a smaller place in the countryside.'

'Do you fancy that, Mum?'

Judy shuddered. 'No!' There'd been a time when she would have looked forward to Harry retiring and wouldn't have cared where she lived as long as it was with him, but now she dreaded it. 'We haven't really got round to discussing it properly. I'll tell him how I feel when the time comes.'

Sam had met Josh, his long-term partner, not long after he'd arrived in London. Josh was a talented artist who made his living designing theatre sets and was rarely seen without a cigarette between his lips. He was also a brilliant guitarist. Small, as thin as a whip, with great dark eyes and a beautiful, soulful face, he and Sam loved each other very much.

When Judy went to visit her son in the summer, she was shocked at how ill Josh looked. His skin was taut over his already prominent cheekbones and his eyes had sunk deep into their sockets.

'Is Josh sick?' she asked Sam when they were alone.

Sam looked startled. 'Is it noticeable?'

'Very much so.'

'He looks just the same to me.' Tears began to trickle down her son's face.

'Oh, Sam! He hasn't got AIDS?'

'Gay men don't only die of AIDS, Mum,' Sam said a trifle impatiently. 'Josh has lung cancer – you've seen the way he smokes. It's inoperable. He's been having chemotherapy and it takes an awful lot out of him.'

'But he'll get better?' *Please* say he will, Judy prayed, but Sam's reply wasn't terribly satisfactory.

'I hope so, Mum. I don't know how I'll live without Josh.'

Judy took her son in her arms. She stayed silent, unable to think of anything to say.

The chemotherapy must have worked. By the time autumn came, Josh looked much better and seemed his own self again at Christmas.

'I didn't mention to Sam, but he might just be in remission,' Judy sighed next time she met Donna.

'Have you told Harry about Josh?' Donna enquired.

'He wasn't interested. Oh, I didn't mean it to sound like that,' she said quickly when Donna pulled a face. 'He wasn't interested because Josh is a man and he can't see how it can matter half as much as it would if Josh were a woman. He can't get his head around two men being in love. It's not just unnatural, it's impossible.'

'Poor Harry,' Donna said, smiling sadly.

Easter came and went and the house in Heathfield Road was put on the market. Judy was shocked when she returned from shopping and saw a For Sale board outside.

'You should have discussed it with me first,' she said crossly to Harry when she went in.

He looked surprised. 'We discussed it on Good Friday. I thought we'd agreed.'

'Did we?' She couldn't remember, too worried about Josh who was showing signs of having relapsed and was sicker now than he'd been before. 'Did we agree on where we were going to live?'

'Well, no,' Harry conceded. 'We went to look at that cottage over the water in Thornton Hough. I liked it, but you thought it was too far away from Liverpool.'

'It's much too far. Donna tells me there's a little estate being built right by the Mystery,' she said eagerly. 'It's called Victoria Square: just seven properties and three are bungalows. Perhaps we could take a look tomorrow?'

'No.' Harry shook his head. 'I'm tired, Judy.' He briefly closed his eyes as if to prove how tired he was. 'I want to get away from everything familiar and have some peace for a change. This house, this road, even the area, they're all full of too many horrible memories. I want to go where I won't be reminded of them any more.'

'The horrible memories are of your own making, Harry,' she told him sharply. '*Mine* are quite different. I love it around here. I don't want to leave.' She had a thought that made her head swim. 'Am *I* part of the horrible memories, Harry?' she asked, her voice kinder now. 'Just like the house and the road?' When he didn't answer, she went on, her heart in her mouth, knowing she was about to say something that she would have once thought inconceivable, 'Do you think it would be a good idea if we separated? You go your way, I go mine?' There would be enough money from the house and the business to buy the cottage in Thornton Hough and a bungalow by the Mystery.

Harry didn't answer immediately. Judy watched his blank face until it settled into an expression of relief, as if her suggestion was one he might eventually have made himself. 'You're right, Jude,' he said sadly, 'it *is* a good idea.' He closed his eyes again, as if to shut out the world in which everything had gone so horribly wrong.

'Don't worry,' Donna soothed. 'You can stay with us while you buy your furniture. Joe and I won't let you sleep on a cold, carpetless floor.'

'I won't need carpets, all the rooms will have wooden tiles.'

'Then what are you worried about?'

'I don't know,' Judy admitted. 'I would have liked to keep some of our old furniture, but I let Harry have first pick and the rest is far too big.'

She glanced around the half-empty room. It was three months later, the house had been sold, Harry had already moved into his cottage across the water and, as from yesterday, the bungalow in Victoria Square, as yet unfinished, was hers.

'You'll be able to buy new stuff, modern,' Donna said encouragingly. 'I'll come with you. It'll be quite exciting.'

'It's a bit much, having to furnish a house from scratch at my age.'

'What do you mean, at your age?' Donna pretended to look shocked. 'You're not yet sixty, still in your prime.'

'I'll be sixty in a few weeks and out of my prime,' Judy said fretfully.

'Would you like a lift to Lime Street Station?'

'No thanks, the traffic will be murder. I'll phone for a taxi. I'd catch a bus, but that suitcase weighs a ton. There's everything in there apart from the kitchen sink.'

'Well, you don't know how long you'll be in London, do you?'

They exchanged glances, both knowing she would stay until Josh died and, after that, for as long as Sam wanted her.

'Sam seems to think Josh is nearing the end.'

'It's going to be very sad for you, Judy.'

But the four weeks Judy spent in Sam's basement flat in Islington were anything but sad. She had never before known such a joyous and uplifting time.

The room was on two levels: half buried underground at the front with French windows opening on to a small garden at the rear. Even in the brightest sunshine, the room could be dark but, that evening when Judy entered, she gasped in surprise when she saw that almost every surface was covered with candles in vividly coloured glass containers so that the room shivered and glittered on all four sides. The smell of melting wax was mixed with the musky aroma of incense and the scent of flowers.

Josh was half sitting, half lying on the settee covered with a patchwork quilt. In front of him, on the floor, a small crowd were sitting, and he looked like a king among his admiring courtiers. To Judy's further surprise, two of the admirers were quite famous actresses. Sam whispered in her ear, 'All Josh's old friends are coming to say goodbye.'

'Hi, Jude.' Josh had noticed her arrival. He waved a

weak hand. 'Folks, this is Sam's mum, Judy. She's going to stay until yours truly has gone to meet his maker, aren't you, darling?'

Judy endeavoured a smile when everyone called, 'Hi, Judy.' In her experience, people didn't announce they were dying. Even when there was no possible chance of survival, the impression would be given by all concerned that there was always hope the patient would pull through.

But Josh appeared quite blasé about his imminent demise. He frequently began sentences with, 'When I'm gone . . .'

The days passed. When Judy got up from the camp bed in the tiny room that had once been a scullery, people would already have arrived bringing with them more candles, more incense, more flowers, and the boxes of Turkish Delight that Josh loved. The atmosphere in the flat was almost mystical, as if pilgrims had come to witness a supernatural event. Judy asked Sam how Josh could possibly remain in such good spirits, and he replied, 'Two reasons: firstly, he's a Catholic, so he believes he's going to a better place; secondly, he's as high as a kite on marijuana.'

'He doesn't smoke it, surely?' She thought of Josh's lungs, eaten away by cancer.

Sam grinned. 'No, Mum, he sprinkles it on the Turkish Delight. It works better than painkillers any day.'

That was the night Isabella came, a magnificent woman of about forty with pure white skin and bright red lips. She arrived very late because she was in a West End show and descended upon Josh, a bundle of black lace frills and wild black hair, arms outstretched, and gave him an enormous hug that made him wince and brought on a bout of coughing.

'I'm sorry, darling,' she cried. 'You are a delicate flower and I'm being too rough.' She planted a sloppy kiss on his thin cheek. 'Why didn't you tell me you were so ill? I only heard this afternoon. I came as soon as I could.'

'I'm not just ill,' Josh said, almost boastfully, 'I'm dying.'

Isabella screamed, 'You can't, darling. I won't let you.'

'Two weeks, maybe three, and I'll be dead.' Josh rolled his big brown eyes dramatically. 'I'm sinking rapidly.'

This was true. In the fortnight Judy had been there, he slept more, ate less, and was sometimes too tired to speak, just watched his friends and listened to their chatter, a beatific smile on his face that seemed to be growing more beautiful as he edged closer towards death.

'Sing to me, Isabella,' he said now, 'my favourite song.'

'Where is the guitar?'

Sam fetched the guitar from the bedroom. Isabella played a few notes, then began to sing 'Bridge Over Troubled Water' in a mellow contralto voice that spread like honey over the magical room with its flickering candles and heady scents.

Judy listened, entranced, letting the music and the spine-tingling ambience wash over, feeling as if her mind and her soul were being cleansed, made pure, that she would never have a bad thought again.

Isabella finished the song and began another, 'The

Streets of London.' This time, everybody joined in. Even Josh managed to croak a few words.

True to his word, two weeks later, Josh departed from this world. By then, the postman had popped his head around the door to say goodbye, and Mr Patel from the newsagent's had brought his last box of Turkish Delight. Judy hadn't counted, but reckoned about two hundred people had visited the flat since she'd arrived, most coming more than once.

Isabella always arrived late. It was after midnight, she was singing 'The Long and Winding Road', when Sam noticed that Josh, who appeared to be asleep, hadn't moved for a long time. Tenderly, he put his hand on his lover's throat to feel for a pulse, looked at his mother, and shook his head. Isabella stopped singing and began to weep. Everyone breathed a deep, concerted sigh. Perhaps it was just coincidence that a number of the candles went out, the flames flickering wildly before dying, just like Josh.

Friday

13 JULY 2001

Chapter 13

Donna came the next morning. Judy was in the kitchen examining the new units, making sure the drawers ran smoothly and the cupboards closed properly. The room was very clinical: white units, white tiles, white walls. Donna had left the ornaments and the smaller odds and ends from Sam's flat for Judy to find places for herself. Later, she'd search for bright, colourful things for the window sill out here. She was just thinking how hard her daughter-in-law must have worked to have arranged everything so nicely, when the front door opened and Donna shouted, 'It's only me.'

'I'm in the kitchen,' Judy shouted back. 'Oh, aren't they lovely,' she gasped when Donna came in and presented her with a bunch of dark red roses. 'Thank you, love.' She kissed her daughter-in-law fondly. 'I'll find a vase in a minute. You've worked wonders with the house. Everything is exactly where I would have put it myself.'

'I've stored what was over in the second bedroom. It's beautifully painted, the furniture,' Donna said admiringly. She leaned against a worktop and folded her arms. On the other side of the room, Judy did the same. 'You say Josh did it?'

'When he first became ill, before he was bedridden. It was Sam's idea, just to keep him occupied. You know Josh was a set designer, don't you? Well, he painted a

413

different backdrop on every piece of furniture: a jungle, a garden, the night sky, a desert and so on.' Judy sighed with pleasure. 'The place feels just like home – not Heathfield Road, but where I've been living for the last month or so. By the way, there were two police cars here last night. I hope it doesn't happen often.'

'It was probably just a one off,' Donna said comfortingly. 'Maybe someone ran into the square and the police chased them.'

'Let's hope so.' Judy crossed her fingers. 'Would you like some tea? I'll have to get a little table for out here, it's one of the things Sam and Josh didn't have.' Judy bustled around, putting the kettle on, looking for mugs. 'Oh, and thanks for the tea bags and the milk and the other things. I really appreciated them last night. I got here awful late. I went to Heathrow with Sam to see him off to India, then back to Islington for my luggage. It was all hours by the time I got to Euston and caught the Liverpool train.'

'How is Sam?' Donna asked.

'Rather subdued, but quite serene.' Judy smiled tenderly. 'He had a long time to get used to the fact that Josh was dying. But he couldn't stay in the flat. He never wants to live there again and was dead pleased when I said I'd like the furniture. He's going to wander the earth, taking photographs and making videos, until he feels like coming home. I'll sort out the other bedroom in case he wants to live with his mum for a while. He's never been able to do it before.' Judy couldn't hide her delight at the idea of having her son to stay.

'Joe said Josh's funeral was lovely and there were loads of people there.'

'Sam was so pleased that Joe came. It was the only time he nearly broke down, when he saw his brother.

Shall we take the tea into the living room? There's nowhere to sit out here.'

They sat on the squashy blue linen settee on which Josh had died, although it seemed too morbid a thing to tell Donna – not that there'd been anything remotely morbid about Josh's dignified and moving death. Judy had brought a ghost with her to her brand-new house and was conscious of its friendly presence.

Donna regarded her mother-in-law critically. 'You look different. I'd expected you to come back all washed out, but you're quite radiant. And those clothes! They're not the sort you usually wear.'

Judy flushed and smoothed her hands over her tiered, filmy cotton skirt, the colour of red wine. 'Isabella gave it me for my sixtieth birthday,' she said shyly. 'She said my clothes were too mature for such a young-looking woman. Sam bought the embroidered top. There's more stuff like this in the suitcase.' It wasn't that she was changing her image, but she could no longer see why age should dictate the way a person dressed or what they did or how they led their lives. She intended learning to play Josh's guitar, doing all sorts of things she wouldn't have dreamed of doing before.

Donna left, promising to come back that night with Joe and the children. 'We'll bring a take away. What would you prefer, Chinese or Indian?'

'Either, I like both, but nothing with meat in. While I was away I became a vegetarian like Sam and Josh. That reminds me, I must ring our Dorothy, Paulette, and Fred and tell them I'm home. I'll invite everyone to tea on Sunday. I'll have sorted myself out by then. Bye, love.'

Judy wandered into the kitchen, stood at the open back door and frowned at the area of dry grass that badly needed watering – it was almost as hot here as it had been in London. She'd get rid of the rotating clothes line, it would take up too much room when extended – one of those pull-out lines that were attached to the wall would be sufficient – and do something really exciting with the garden: get some exotic plants, statues, hanging baskets, and fast-growing ivy to cover the bare wooden fence. The Mystery was on the other side, she remembered, where the Smith children had played when they were young: rounders was the favourite, although the boys had been keen on football that the girls were hopeless at. Dad used to come with them on Sundays. Ever since he'd taken Ronnie and Fred to see *The Babe Ruth Story* with William Bendix, he'd called rounders 'baseball', she recalled with a smile. She could hear children playing a ball game of some sort right now and it brought the memory of her own time there even closer.

That afternoon she'd get a book on Japanese bonsai from the library. She jumped, startled, when there was a knock on the door. Another thing to get was a doorbell and she'd ask Joe if he'd fit it tonight – no, she wouldn't, she'd do it herself. Now she was living alone, she'd have to learn to do things like fitting doorbells. In the past, Harry had always done those sorts of jobs, but Harry was no longer around.

She opened the door. A woman was standing outside, her face red and dripping with perspiration. She wore baggy, knee-length khaki shorts and a T-shirt that was much too tight. Her feet were bare.

'Oh, hello,' the woman said brightly, a bit *too* brightly: her voice was tinged with hysteria. 'I'm Rachel Williams from next door. I've come to welcome you to Victoria Square . . .'

★

'I wonder why she does it?' Kathleen mused aloud. She was standing by the window watching Rachel at the door of the bungalow that she'd thought was empty. The woman must have moved in overnight.

Steve raised his head from the *Daily Mirror*. 'Why who does what?'

'Why Rachel calls on the new arrivals, why she organizes things like barbecues and coffee mornings when she's clearly not up to it. It's just piling on the agony. Any minute now she'll tip over the edge.' She noticed Rachel wasn't wearing shoes. Was it deliberate, or had she forgotten to put them on?

'You should be able to read Rachel's mind. You've got a degree in psychiatry – or is it psychology? Or is it both?'

'Neither. I have a degree in medicine, that's all.'

'I thought you had degrees in just about everything.'

Kathleen turned and was relieved to see he was grinning. She grinned back. 'I was worried then you were gearing up for a fight, but I assume that was a pathetic attempt at being funny.'

'I thought it was quite a good attempt meself.' He threw the paper on to the floor and patted his knee. She went over and sat on it, murmuring that they must get some net curtains so people couldn't see inside.

'You've never asked what qualifications *I* have,' Steve said in an injured tone.

'I didn't know you had any.'

'Well, I have, so there! I have a cycling certificate, a swimming diploma, a runner-up cup for snooker, two B grade O levels, one for English, the other for Geography, and a very official looking piece of paper informing me I'd failed the rest. Oh, and a photo of me in the fifth-form football team. I played right half. Does that count?'

Kathleen kissed his nose. She had forgotten about Rachel. 'You were quite clearly a brilliant student. Would you like a certificate from me?'

'What for?'

'To certify that you have passed a very rigid test with flying colours and are, without a shred of doubt, one hell of a lover and the sexiest man alive.'

Steve looked at her gravely. 'I think I need testing on that again.'

'Shall we do it now?'

'This very minute. I'll carry you into the classroom. You needn't bother with your gown and mortarboard. I'll do the test better if you've got nothing on.'

He stood, Kathleen in his arms, lifting her effortlessly. His strength always turned her on. She was looking forward to the next hour, when Steve groaned and nearly dropped her. 'Sod it!'

'What's the matter?'

'Anna's tottering in our direction and she looks awful, poor old soul.' He put Kathleen down. 'Next time I have an affair it'll be with a lap dancer or a model, definitely not a doctor. They're too much in demand.'

He went into the garden to get on with preparing the soil for the plants he'd bought the day before and Kathleen let Anna in.

Steve was right. She looked awful, nothing like her normal glamorous and chirpy self: no make-up on or jewellery, her silver hair a wild halo around her deeply wrinkled face. She wore a white blouse, buttoned crookedly, a dirndl skirt and fluffy mules. Kathleen helped her inside and into a comfortable chair.

'I hope you weren't in the middle of anything important,' she said in a cracked whisper.

'Not at all,' Kathleen lied. 'Don't you feel well, dear?'

'I'm all right. It's Ernie. There's something wrong with Ernie.' Her eyes, usually so brightly blue, were watery and faded. 'He helped me to get up and dressed and made my breakfast, then went back to bed. Now he won't talk to me. I'm sorry about my hair.' She made an attempt to pat it, but her hand wouldn't reach that far. 'Sometimes I can comb it, sometimes I can't, and then Ernie does it for me. This morning, he didn't even ask, nor what shoes I wanted. And he buttoned my blouse all wrong. It's not like him at all.'

'Would you like me to go and see him?'

'I'm not sure. I really came because I wanted to talk to someone. I'm frightened, Kathleen.' Her bottom lip trembled. 'I couldn't live without Ernie. It would be the end of everything and there'd be no point. He'd feel the same if I died first. We need each other and it keeps us both alive.'

'There, there!' Kathleen patted her hand, although it seemed very inadequate. 'Has anything happened recently that might have upset him?'

'His brother came last night, Charlie. Ernie hadn't seen him since the war. They seemed to get on all right, although it was me who did most of the talking.' Anna sniffed. 'Ernie tells me I could talk the hind leg off a donkey. When he came back from showing Charlie out, he was very pale and said he felt nauseous. I had expected him to go and play on that damned computer, but he went to lie down instead.'

'I think the best thing to do is make you some coffee and then I'll go and have a word with Ernie, see if I can discover what's wrong.'

Ernest lay on the bed, hands clasped behind his head, and stared at the ceiling. He was responsible for Mam's death.

The words had hammered through his brain all night long as he'd lain in the same position and sleep had refused to come. *He* was the reason why she'd cried herself to sleep, night after night, year after year. 'You broke her heart,' Charlie had said. Not normally given to melodrama, Ernest was forced to concede that, to all intents, he was a murderer who'd led a frivolous, useless life, contributing nothing to society. Not even the numerous casinos he had frequented had profited from his custom, as he'd always won far more than he'd lost.

It wouldn't have mattered quite so much if he hadn't been so close to Mam. Until she'd married Cuthbert Burtonshaw there'd only been the two of them, not counting Desmond Whitely whose occasional visits hadn't been much help. He remembered how happy they'd been in the dingy little room in Chaucer Street, Mam knitting like a maniac, him lying in bed, watching the patterns the fire made on the ceiling or reading a book. Mam and him had been best mates. How could he have treated her so cruelly?

The phone started to ring, but he didn't move. It was on the little table beside Anna's chair, easy for her to answer. Ernest began to feel uneasy when the ringing went on and on.

'Anna,' he called. When there was no reply, he swung his feet off the bed and stood up so quickly his head swam. Feeling dizzy, he stumbled towards the door. The telephone was still ringing, but there was no sign of Anna in the lounge. Neither was she in the kitchen or the bathroom. He threw open the door to the second bedroom that was going to be a study: the door slammed against the wall, swinging back and almost hitting him. He'd forgotten to turn off the computer the night before and a multi-coloured blob floated across the screen, changing shape as it moved.

'*Anna!*' Ernest shouted, his voice hoarse now. He'd forgotten about Anna! He'd actually *forgotten* about her. The past didn't matter, he told himself. It was over and done with and there was no going back. 'It's no good crying over spilt milk,' Mam used to say. What mattered was *now*, the present, and his beloved Anna.

The back door opened and he turned expectantly, but it was the woman from next door, he couldn't remember her name although they'd gone to lunch together only the other day.

'Anna said it was unlocked.' She smiled at him. 'Are you all right? She's very worried about you.'

'Is she with you?' He recalled the woman's name: Kathleen.

'Yes. I've left her with some coffee. She's fine, just worried, that's all.'

'I'll come and fetch her.'

'Hadn't you better put some shoes on first?'

'Oh!' Ernest looked down at his feet, encased in navy-blue socks. 'Oh, yes.'

'I'll go back and tell Anna you're all right, shall I?' She looked at him searchingly. 'You *are* all right, aren't you, Ernie?'

'As all right as I'll ever be.' He looked at his feet again and mumbled, 'Have you ever done something in the past that you're deeply ashamed of?'

'Of course,' Kathleen said kindly. 'Haven't we all? But it's no good crying over spilt milk, is it? We can't go back and put right whatever the something was. See you in a minute, Ernie.'

'You're as soft as a brush, Ernie Burrows,' Anna said

421

gently, stroking his hair after he'd told her the whole story from beginning to end.

'Daft, luv, daft as a brush. I know,' he sighed. 'I don't know what got into me. Charlie made me feel like a murderer.' They were home again, together, Anna in her chair, he crouched on a stool at her feet.

'Charlie's not a very nice man. I didn't like the look of him from the start. He seemed rather sly.' Ernest recalled last night she'd liked him, but didn't bother to point it out. 'What a thing to say to someone you haven't seen for sixty years! I'll have something to say to Charlie if I ever see him again,' she finished indignantly.

'I doubt if you will, luv.' He certainly hoped not. 'Anyroad, what he said was true. Mam died of a broken heart and it was all my fault.'

Anna shook her head dismissively. 'I don't believe it. She had two other children, didn't she? Her lover, your father, had come to live with her. She was probably upset at not hearing from you, but not upset enough to let it break her heart, not when she had everything to live for. Charlie's having you on, darling, he was just being spiteful, Lord knows why.'

'I never looked at it that way.' He hoped and prayed she was right, but would never know.

She continued with her ruthless mission to demolish every single one of his worries. 'As to that other thing, that you've led a completely useless life, what nonsense! Remember when you took the Montands all the way to Palestine? That was incredibly brave. And that job you had in Cairo was terribly important: you would never have left if they hadn't treated you so unfairly. You may never have had a proper job since, but just think of some of the jobs you *could* have had: a door-to-door salesman, for instance – everybody loathes them.' She began to tick them off on her fingers. 'A politician – they're loathed even more. You could have made weapons of mass destruction, poison gas, guns; worked for one of those dreadful firms that lend money at extortionate rates; become a bailiff, which is probably one of the worst jobs in the world.' She'd run out of fingers on one hand.

'All right, luv, all right, you've made your point,' Ernest said hastily when she looked about to start on the other hand. He found her logic somewhat confusing, yet comforting.

'I could go on and on. We've led a fine life, Ernie. We never hurt anybody so you must stop thinking like that. We can't all be Mother Teresa.' She patted his head. 'Have you finished, darling?' she cried gaily. 'Have you told me everything that's been worrying you? If so, let's go out and have the most expensive lunch that money can buy. The weather's beautiful again and it's not going to last for ever. But comb my hair first and button my blouse properly. And fetch my gold sandals and those gypsy earrings I got in Woolworths the other day. Oh, and a lipstick: the raspberry pink. And some blue eye shadow. What's the matter, Ernie?' she said apprehensively when he didn't move. 'Is something else bothering you, darling?'

Ernest decided to get everything off his chest in one go. Normally, he was the stronger of the two, but today he was letting Anna take a turn. 'I'm losing me memory, luv.' He sniffed pathetically. 'I keep forgetting words, quite simple words. I think I'm getting Alzheimer's. What'll become of us then?'

'You're nothing but a damn fool, Ernie.' Her voice was so cutting that he winced. 'You've always been a hypochondriac. Remember that time in Monte Carlo when you were bitten by that dear little poodle and were terrified you'd caught rabies? There's been loads of other instances, too many to list. Cut your finger, and you've got blood poisoning; the suggestion of a rash, and it's skin cancer; forget a few words and you've got dementia.' She paused for breath. 'Stop being such a ninny and comb my hair. I feel like a tramp – what is it they call female tramps in America?'

'Bag ladies,' Ernest said promptly.

'See!' she said triumphantly. 'You remembered that.'

He fetched the comb, suitably humbled. She'd always had the knack of turning his troubles into little ones or making them vanish into thin air. He wasn't entirely convinced by everything she'd said, but it had been enough to set his mind at rest.

By now, Victoria could say she was leaving for New York the day after tomorrow. It was *that* close. She could actually count down the hours: forty-eight, forty-seven, forty-six, and so on until it was time to leave the house and her new friends. Every time she and Gareth made love she tried not to think it could be for the last time: tonight, Debbie might be there and he'd find it impossible to get away; tomorrow was the barbecue and he would have to go because he'd invited his mother. Anyroad, they couldn't let Rachel down.

That morning, after Sarah and her family had gone home – the police were coming to interview Sarah at ten o'clock about Alex's abortive attempt to kidnap the children – Victoria and Gareth sat down to breakfast, grinning at each other stupidly across the table because they were high on love, having spent a truly fantastic night together.

'If we got married, we could do this every morning

for the rest of our lives,' Gareth reminded her as he bit into a piece of toast.

'You're already married,' she reminded him.

'Have you never heard of divorce?'

'You've asked me that before.'

'And what was your answer?'

'I can't remember,' she admitted. She changed the subject. 'Why aren't you at work?'

'You asked me *that* before. I told you, I don't care about work. Anyroad, I hardly ever take days off. I called earlier and told them I had the flu.'

'Nobody gets the flu in a heatwave.'

'I somehow managed to. It's your fault. Every time I look at you my temperature soars. It's like that Peggy Lee song, "You give me fever."' He sang a few lines and Victoria clapped.

'I *love* that. It's ages since I heard it.'

'I've got a Peggy Lee CD at home. I'll bring it next time I come.'

'I haven't got a CD player,' Victoria told him.

'Then I'll bring my portable CD player with me.'

Victoria sighed. 'You've got an answer for everything.'

He reached across the table and took her hand. 'I haven't had the answer I want from you. I've had *an* answer, but not the right one.'

'I can't marry you, Gareth,' she said piteously. 'I *can't*.'

'They why don't we just live together?' he said urgently. 'I could come and join you in New York. Not straight away, obviously, but in about a month's time, after I've given in my notice, sorted things out here. I'll tell Debbie I'm leaving her, not say I'm in love with someone else so she won't feel quite so hurt.'

'She'll feel hurt enough.' Victoria closed her eyes and

imagined living with Gareth in New York. It would be so totally wonderful that it almost took her breath away. She opened her eyes and murmured, 'It would be heaven.'

'Wouldn't it! Will you at least *think* about it, darling?'

'I'll think about it,' she promised.

Tabitha strolled in yawning, yawned again, and collapsed into a heap on the floor. After Victoria and Gareth had gone upstairs, he jumped on to the table, ate the remainder of the toast, knocked over a mug and drank the spilled coffee.

'You are a very naughty kitten,' Gareth told him, hours later, on the way back to Hamilton Lodge. 'Your manners are appalling. You have no idea how to behave in other people's houses. Or in your own, come to that,' he muttered, unlocking the door and stepping over half a dozen letters that had arrived that morning. He shouted, 'Debbie!' just in case she was home, although it was most unlikely at one o'clock in the afternoon.

He'd come back to have a shower, change his clothes, and give the cat some genuine cat food. The poor little bugger hadn't had anything proper to eat since yesterday morning. He went into the kitchen, opened a tin of rabbit, spooned half into Tabitha's plastic bowl, and filled a saucer with milk.

'After you've stuffed yourself, we're going back to Victoria's,' he promised. 'I'd better look through the post first.' He'd only open those on which the address had been written by hand; typed, and they meant trouble. None of the letters was handwritten, so he threw them on to the hall table to look at another time, ran upstairs, had the speediest shower he'd ever had in his life, put on clean jeans and a T-shirt, and returned to the kitchen.

'Haven't you finished yet?' he said impatiently. Tabitha was vigorously licking the bowl and, so far, hadn't touched the milk. The kitten gave him a filthy look and continued to lick.

Gareth sat down to wait. 'She's thinking about it, Tab,' he chortled. 'How about that, eh? When you become a fully grown cat, don't get married until you're a hundred per cent sure you've found the right female. Me, I just drifted into it like a sleepwalker. Oh, look! Madam's left me a note. I hadn't noticed.'

A large piece of paper covered in Debbie's barely decipherable scrawl was attached to the fridge with a magnet disguised as a gnome, GARETH, in big block letters at the top, heavily underlined:

(1) Do you still live in this house? I came home last night and you weren't here (again) so went back to Mum's.
(2) Out of interest, will you be at the barbecue tomorrow, or shall I stay with Mum for the weekend?
(3) I'm pregnant.
    Debbie, your wife. (Just in case you've forgotten.)

Gareth stared at the third item for a very long time. The only sounds audible were of Tabitha noisily lapping the milk and the collapsing of his world around his ears: a thunderous crashing and rolling.

Debbie was having a baby! *His* baby. The enormity of it was taking some time to register in his brain, until the searing recognition came that he couldn't possibly leave her now: it was out of the question. He couldn't let his child grow up without a father. He dropped his head in his hands and began to weep.

Alex Rees-James was in prison and, according to the police sergeant who'd been to see Sarah that morning, had been charged with breaking and entering and attempted kidnapping. 'He's unlikely to be allowed bail since there's always a chance he'll try again.'

'That's good to know,' Sarah breathed. As soon as the man had gone, she put Alastair in his pram in the garden and began to put fresh water in the paddling pool – she must buy a hose, it took ages to fill with a bucket and Tiffany and Jack insisted on helping and the kitchen got flooded. It was another fantastic day and her shoulders felt light with relief, although she wasn't entirely confident she would ever be completely free from Alex. Even in jail, he posed a threat.

Marie Jordan came into the next-door garden with a basket of washing and began to peg it on the line. 'Have the police been?' she called.

'Yes.' Sarah repeated what the policeman had said. 'Would you like a coffee?' she asked when she'd finished.

'I'd love one, except I'm waiting for an important phone call. I don't like to leave the house. When the children get tired of the pool, perhaps you could come round here? By the way, do you think they'd like a computer? Victoria's letting us have her much better one, so ours will be going spare.'

Tiffany had been listening, as always. She leaped out of the pool. 'We'd love a computer, wouldn't we, Mummy? I can already play loads of games: Danny taught me. Where *is* Danny?' she demanded. 'I thought he'd be in Victoria's, but when I knocked on the door she didn't answer.'

'Danny knocked too,' Marie said. 'She must have

gone out. He's gone into town with Patrick and Kirsty, Rachel's daughter.'

'He didn't ask me,' Tiffany said sulkily.

Sarah told her not to be silly and that she wouldn't have let her go anyway, she was far too young.

'I don't *feel* young,' Tiffany said with an angry toss of her head and stamped indoors.

'I'm glad she's gone.' Sarah put her elbows on the fence and said in a hushed voice. 'That chap, Gareth, from Hamilton Lodge, was at Victoria's last night. I thought he'd leave after the police had gone, but he was still there this morning.'

'Perhaps he stayed in the spare bedroom,' Marie suggested.

'There's only two and we slept in one of them.'

'Or he slept downstairs?'

'Perhaps,' Sarah said doubtfully. 'He and Victoria seem awfully close. I wonder if he's still there and that's why Victoria isn't answering the door?'

'Isn't he married?'

'Yes. I've never spoken to his wife. I've seen her leaving for work a few times. She's very pretty and always wears the latest fashions.'

'Oh, well.' Marie shrugged. 'Victoria's off to America the day after tomorrow. If anything's going on, it'll have to end.'

'Don't repeat what I've told you, will you? I wouldn't want to spread gossip,' Sarah added a trifle sanctimoniously.

'Me lips are sealed,' Marie assured her.

'Mummy!' Tiffany said stridently from the door. 'We've got a visitor.'

'Who is it, darling?'

Tiffany made a grotesque face. 'Midge.'

'*Midge!*' Sarah groaned.

'Who's Midge?' Marie asked.

'Alex's first wife. I wonder what the hell *she* wants.'

'All I want,' Midge said meekly, 'is to know if I can see the children every now and then.' Her accent, like Alex's, was upper class with a hint of cockney. They were standing in the kitchen so Sarah could keep an eye on Jack who was playing in the pool. There seemed something odd about him and she realized he had parted from his blanket and thrown it on to the grass. Alastair had woken and two tiny naked feet could be seen waving in the air. Tiffany was by the door, listening avidly: Sarah couldn't be bothered telling her to go away.

'No.' She shook her head emphatically at Midge and wondered how anyone could be so thin and stay alive. The woman's hips were scarcely wider than Sarah's thigh and her bones, including every single rib, were visible under her silky, clinging frock. Her narrow face and pale green eyes were drawn, as if she'd been up all night – probably waiting for Alex to return with the children so they could all fly off to God knows where.

'I know Alex and I have acted very badly. By rights, I should be in prison with him, but I've grown to love those children, Sarah.' Her voice broke. 'I can't stand the thought of never seeing them again.'

'You didn't seem to care if I, their mother, never saw them again,' Sarah said accusingly.

'I'm sorry.' Midge bent her head in shame. 'You turned out to have far more character than we'd expected. We didn't think you cared two hoots for the children. Once you and Alex were divorced, he presumed you'd be quite happy for him to keep them.'

'*I* wouldn't have been happy,' Tiffany interjected.

'Shush, darling.'

'But Mummy, I wouldn't. I would have been terribly, *terribly* unhappy. And so would Oliver. And so would Jack and Alastair. And I wouldn't have met Danny or Victoria or Tabitha. I love Danny very much,' she said gravely to Midge. 'We're going to get married when I grow up.'

'Are you really, darling?' Midge was staring at the little girl, real hunger in her eyes. 'Have you got a kiss for your Auntie Midge?'

'No.' Tiffany backed away, a look of distaste on her haughty little face. 'I don't like kissing you. Neither does Jack. I hope you don't come again. This is *our* house, not yours.'

'I think that answers your question,' Sarah said quietly, not wanting to gloat when Midge appeared to be devastated by Tiffany's blunt message.

'I'd better go,' she muttered, her skeletal frame looking as if the bones had turned to spaghetti and she was about to land in a curled heap on the floor. Sarah squeezed Tiffany's shoulder, hoping to stop her daughter from issuing any more home truths.

Sarah followed her unexpected visitor to the door. The silver Rolls was parked outside, a driver behind the wheel: someone must have pumped up the tyres that Gareth had let down last night. Midge turned, 'I don't suppose it's much use suggesting Tiffany and Jack come back to the house from time to time to ride Boots?'

'No use at all,' Sarah said emphatically.

'A photograph then,' she pleaded. 'Could you at least let me have a photograph of them, just once a year? It's not much to ask.'

'I'll have one taken at Christmas,' Sarah promised.

Midge was right, it wasn't much to ask, but still far more than she deserved.

Marie finished hanging out the washing and went indoors. To her surprise, Danny had arrived home. 'I didn't hear you come in, son. Tiffany's been looking for you.'

Danny wrinkled his nose. 'Tiffany's OK, but she gets on me nerves. Why are you selling our old computer, Ma?' he asked. 'It seems a bit mean when we're getting a new one for nothing.'

'I'm not selling it, it's going next door.' An awful suspicion entered her head. 'What made you think I was?'

'The phone just went. It was some man about the computer. He said he'd seen a card in a window somewhere.'

Marie felt herself go very hot. 'What did you tell him?'

'He asked for our address, so I gave it him. Is there anything to eat, Ma? I'm starving.'

'I'll make you a sandwich in a minute. What did the man sound like? Did he say when he was coming round to look at the computer?'

Danny shrugged. 'Like a man and he just asked for the address. What sort of sandwich?'

'Corned beef. Did he have an Irish accent?'

'Yeah, I think he did.' His eyes widened. 'I haven't done anything wrong, have I?'

'No, Danny, it's just that I've changed my mind about the computer. I'm letting Sarah have it. You're right, I shouldn't have thought of selling it when we're getting one for free.' She cursed herself for being so greedy.

'You'd better go to the shop and ask for the card back.'

'I'll go later.' Except she couldn't, not when Brigid O'Connor née Kelly, sister of Enda, Mickey's friend, would be behind the counter, insisting Marie had been at her wedding – which Marie had. She hadn't mentioned the card to Liam when he'd come home last night, very late. He'd gone out again this morning without saying when he'd be back, and would think her very foolish: they were supposed to be keeping their heads down, not advertising things for sale. If he heard about the telephone call, he might decide they should move when Marie liked living in Victoria Square and surely Patrick was in no danger after all this time from the men who'd murdered her dear Mickey in cold blood?

'You've been hours,' Victoria cried when she threw open the door to Gareth's special knock – he had to use a special knock so she would know it was him and not Danny or Tiffany who'd be very much in the way. 'I thought you were only going to be five minutes. Where's Tabitha?'

'I forgot to bring him.' His face was very grave.

'What's the matter? You look as if you've lost a pound and found a sixpence. Gran always used to say that,' she explained.

'My mum ses it too.' Gareth came in and closed the door.

Victoria said, 'You know I promised to think about you coming to New York, well I've decided . . .' To her astonishment, Gareth pressed his hand hard against her lips, 'Don't say it,' he whispered urgently. 'Please don't say what you've decided, I'd sooner not know.'

'But Gareth,' she managed to splutter through the fingers that smelled of orange-flavoured soap.

'Debbie's expecting a baby.' He removed his hand and

they stood looking at each other for a very long time, neither speaking.

Eventually, she asked, 'How did you find out? Is she home?'

'She left a note on the fridge. There hasn't been the opportunity to tell me face to face. We've hardly seen each other all week and whenever we did we had a fight.'

'You can't possibly leave now,' she said dully.

Gareth sighed. 'I know.'

During the time he'd been away, Victoria had come to a decision. 'All's fair in love and war,' was another thing that Gran used to say. She would never love another man the way she loved Gareth and took it for granted he felt the same about her: God had made him for her and she for him. It was selfish, yet seemed only right that they should spend the rest of their lives together. Debbie would suffer in the process, but she couldn't love Gareth all that much or she wouldn't make him so unhappy. One day, she felt sure that Debbie would find someone else.

But now Debbie was having a baby and it was all over.

'I'll always love you,' Gareth murmured.

'And me you.' Victoria stood there, arms hanging limply by her side, feeling as if her heart was breaking to pieces in her breast.

'Can we go upstairs?' he asked in quivery voice.

'I'd sooner not.' Victoria numbly shook her head. 'It's one thing, *thinking* it might be the last time, but *knowing* would be too sad for words. I couldn't stand it.' She'd probably cry the whole way through. 'I'll make us some coffee.'

After she'd made it, they sat staring into the cups, not at each other, until the drink went cold and Victoria had to heat it up in the microwave. They began to talk then, about last night's adventure, the square, her house . . .

'Have you been in touch with a decorator yet about having the place done up?'

'I keep forgetting,' Victoria confessed.

'That's good, because I was thinking . . . I was thinking . . .' Gareth slammed the mug on the table. 'Oh, Victoria! *Please* can we go upstairs?'

So they did, and they made love, but as Victoria had expected, she couldn't stop crying the whole way through.

Judy had bought two bottles of wine: one red, one white. She put the white in the fridge for when Joe, Donna, and the children came and began to set the table. It was a good thing that Sam's table folded into such a narrow strip because anything larger wouldn't have fitted into the room. Extended, it took up almost half the floor space and she had to push the settee out of the way. It was a bit like putting a jigsaw together: it would take a while getting used to such a small house after Heathfield Road.

She fetched five chairs from the second bedroom and went to get the place mats and cutlery from the drawers in the kitchen where she'd put them earlier. On her way back, she opened the front door an inch to save her visitors from knocking – Donna had insisted on returning the key.

Sam's cutlery was just a pile of odds and ends: some knives with highly decorative handles, although none were the same and the rest were wooden. The occasional knife matched the occasional fork and the spoons didn't match anything, not even each other. Still, she wouldn't have changed them for the world. She was laying them on the table when she heard the door open and a voice called, 'Are you there?'

'Come in, Joe. I'm in the living room.'

A spoon dropped with a clatter on the table when, instead of her son and his family, her husband entered the room. 'Harry!' she gasped. 'You're the last person I expected. What on earth are you doing here?'

'Just came to see how you were settling in, Jude,' he said in a friendly voice.

She'd never known him dress so casually: jeans, a grey sweatshirt, trainers, and had forgotten how handsome he was: an older version of the man she'd met in the Cavern over forty years ago. She responded gladly to his friendly tone, having expected when they met again for the atmosphere to be strained. 'I've hardly had time to settle in. It's lovely to see you. Are you happy living in Thornton Hough?'

'Extremely. It's very quiet, no distractions. I read a lot, watch TV, think. I've started writing a book on photography.' He seemed very content, clearly enjoying life on his own. 'That's a pretty frock,' he said approvingly, 'it suits you.'

Judy had discarded her skirt and top for a flowery chiffon dress with a cape collar and fluted hem. 'It makes me feel young,' she declared. In the past, during the bad years, he'd sometimes criticized her choice of clothes.

He glanced at the table. 'Are you expecting company?'

'Just Joe and Donna and the kids. They're bringing a take away.'

'I'd better not keep you.'

'Why don't you stay?' she offered impulsively, hoping Joe and Donna wouldn't mind. 'There's bound to be too much food. Would you like some wine while we wait?'

'Yes, please.' He smiled, and it was the smile of old,

his Alan Ladd smile. Perhaps they should have separated a long time ago.

She showed him around the house. Inevitably, he remarked on the furniture and she told him Josh had painted it. He was silent for a while, then said, 'How is Sam taking things?' It was the first time he'd spoken Sam's name in a normal tone since his son had left home.

'Pretty well. He's gone abroad.'

'I'll never accept it you know, Jude.' He shoved his hands in the pockets of his jeans. 'Sam really let me down. I won't forgive him for that.'

It was his attitude to Sam that had driven them apart. There'd been a time when his words would have driven her cold with rage, but now they meant nothing. She said, 'Let's not talk about it. You have your views and I have mine. Now that we're not living together, it doesn't matter what the other thinks.'

'True, but we can still be friends, can't we? See each other occasionally, have dinner?' He looked at her keenly. 'You've been the most important person in my life for over forty years, Judy. I'd hate it if we never saw each other again.'

She didn't remind him that Sam had also been part of his life, but he'd managed to shut him out completely. There'd be no more scoring points.

They sat on the back step in the late afternoon sun, sipping wine and discussing what best to do with the garden, completely at ease. Judy felt as if she'd climbed a mountain and come safely down the other side.

Rachel lay flat on her back in the garden listening to the muted voices on the other side of the fence. She could just about make sense of what was being said. Judy Moon and her visitor sounded as if they were good friends. Were they lovers? she wondered.

A bee buzzed angrily close to her ear and the parched grass prickled her arms and the back of her neck and wasn't terribly comfortable, but she couldn't be bothered going all the way to the garage for a garden chair – they'd have to find somewhere more convenient to keep them. Frank had started complaining about the lack of space to store things. 'We shouldn't have bought this bloody place,' he'd grumbled that morning.

'I love it here,' Kirsty had argued. 'Could we have a conservatory built, Mum? We could keep stuff there.'

Frank had thrown his daughter a thunderous look. He hated being reminded that it was his wife who had the money for things like conservatories.

'I'll look into it,' Rachel had promised, although she hadn't. It meant searching through the Yellow Pages for a builder, picking up the phone, tapping in the number, speaking to a stranger, and she no longer had the confidence, or the willpower, even the strength, to carry out such a daunting task. Instead, after going next door to introduce herself to Judy Moon, seeing the wary look in the woman's eyes – she quite obviously considered her mad and hadn't invited her in, muttering something about having to meet someone in town in a short while – Rachel had returned home to lie on the grass where she'd been all day thinking about Alice: her first steps, her first words, her first day at playgroup, at school, the clothes she had been bought, the presents, the pictures she had drawn, the stories she had loved, her attempt to knit a scarf for her favourite doll. She remembered every single little thing that Alice had done before her life had been so cruelly cut short.

Kathleen had come round a few times, banging on the

door, calling her name, but hadn't thought to look in the garden. Rachel had ignored her, not because she didn't want to see Kathleen, but couldn't be bothered shouting back or rising from her bed of prickly grass.

It was well past the time she should have started on the tea, but felt too scared to go into the kitchen. 'I don't know how you can live with yourself,' Frank had said again that morning. Was he going to say that to her every day for the rest of her life until she decided she *couldn't* live with herself and ended it? Was it just her imagination that he'd looked from her to the cooker, than back again, as if suggesting a way out? By then, James had left for work and Kirsty had gone over to the Jordans to call for Patrick. Shortly afterwards, Frank had gone himself without saying goodbye. The dream he'd had about Alice seemed to have brought back the horror of their loss and his grief was as raw as it had ever been. As usual, he was taking it out on his wife.

Rachel's mother had had an electric cooker when they'd lived in the countryside and had never ceased to complain about it. Rachel had preferred gas ever since. They'd been asked for their preference before moving into the square. 'Gas,' Rachel had said emphatically.

She'd read somewhere that gas was the least unpleasant way of killing yourself. All you had to do was turn it on, put your head in the oven, and fall peacefully asleep. It was quite painless and much more efficient than lying on a railway line, swallowing tablets, or hanging – she'd only make a mess of the knot.

Tiffany had come to play outside. 'Here we go round the mulberry bush,' she sang in a clear, childish voice, 'the mulberry bush, the mulberry bush. Here we go round the mulberry bush on a cold and frosty morning.'

She was probably dancing around the willow tree with Oliver.

Alice had used to sing the same song as she'd danced around the little apple tree in the garden in Lydiate holding James and Kirsty's hands. Rachel had used to watch from the kitchen window, smiling, thinking what a beautiful sight it made. Sometimes, she'd join in.

'Here we go round the mulberry bush . . .'

Rachel got to her feet with enormous difficulty. Her arms and legs felt as if they'd turned to concrete during her hours on the grass. The house was calling to her, inviting her inside, telling her it would be painless and afterwards her mind would be at peace. She walked stiffly, like a robot into the kitchen, turned the gas full on and opened the oven door. She removed the two top shelves, forced her concrete legs to bend so she was sitting on the floor and, with a deep sigh, rested her head on the remaining shelf. It was the only way out, the only thing left to do.

Ernest was watering the clematis in the pots by the front door. 'I think they've grown at least an inch,' he called to Anna.

'Are there any signs of flowers?'

He examined the plants carefully and was forced to admit there wasn't the faintest sign. 'We've only had them a fortnight, luv.' She got too impatient with plants, expecting them to become full-grown overnight. One of these days, he'd fix a strip of lattice each side of the front door for the flowers to climb up and wondered if he'd still be alive by the time they met at the top.

The little girl from across the square, Tiffany, was dancing around the willow tree with the teddy bear she was so fond of and singing a nursery rhyme. All of a sudden, she made for Three Farthings and danced through the back door. A few minutes later, she danced back. 'Excuse me,' she said politely to Ernest, 'but can you spare a glass of milk? Jack emptied ours into the paddling pool and Mummy's gone to buy more. She's very cross. Rachel wouldn't answer when I asked her.'

'Why, is Rachel cross too?' Ernest had had no experience of talking to children and always felt very awkward with them.

'No. She's baking her head or something. She left the back door wide open.'

'That's a funny thing to do,' he said in an attempt at joviality.

'It smells really horrid.' Tiffany pretended to be sick.

'What did you just say?' A white-faced Anna had come into the hall, holding on to the walls for support. 'What was it you just said, darling?'

'Rachel's kitchen smells really horrid.'

'Before that. Did Rachel have her head in the oven?'

Faced with Anna's breathless urgency and stricken expression, the little girl had lost some of her composure. She stammered, 'Yes,' turned on her heel and ran away, clearly frightened. Ernest had cottoned on and was already hurrying towards Three Farthings. For the second time that day, Anna made her laborious way to Kathleen's.

Ernest had turned off the oven and dragged Rachel into the fresh air by the time Kathleen arrived, closely followed by Steve. Kathleen dropped to her knees beside Rachel's prone body.

'Shall I phone for an ambulance?' Ernest made to return to the house, but Steve told him curtly not to. 'Don't touch anything in there, it's dangerous.' He turned to Kathleen. 'Do we need an ambulance, luv?'

'No, she's breathing quite steadily. I think she might have fainted. She'll come to in a minute and, hopefully, vomit.'

At that very moment, Rachel groaned, raised herself to a sitting position, and was sick. Steve supported her with his arm. She opened her eyes and a dark flush spread over her already red face when she remembered what had happened. 'I'm sorry,' she said hoarsely. 'So sorry. I didn't want to inconvenience anybody.'

'Shush, love,' Kathleen said gently. 'Can you walk? Let's go to our house and I'll make some tea. You need to rest awhile.'

'Don't tell Frank, will you? Please don't tell Frank.' She looked at them pleadingly, her eyes resting first on Ernest, Steve, then Kathleen. 'Don't tell anyone.'

Ernest opened his mouth as if to argue, but Kathleen frowned at him and shook her head. He closed his mouth without a word and Steve hoisted Rachel to her feet.

'Ernie,' Kathleen said briskly, 'will you please keep an eye open in case Frank or the children arrive home shortly? Tell them there's been a gas leak but it's already been seen to. In a little while, you can go inside and open the windows. The smell might have gone by the time anyone comes and they won't know a thing about it. Just say Rachel's feeling a little bit off colour and she's with me.'

'You saved her life, Ernie,' Anna said when Ernest came home. She'd been watching the proceedings from the front door.

'No, luv, it was you. Me, I'm as thick as two short planks. When Tiffany said Rachel was baking her head,

442

it never crossed me mind what she really meant. You're the clever one.'

'I suppose it's Tiffany who should be taking the honours. I bet she doesn't tell her mother. She probably thinks she's done something wrong. Can I have a glass of wine, darling? I don't know about you, but I'm shaking like a leaf.'

Ernest's own hands weren't exactly steady. He fetched the wine and a whisky for himself, after telling Anna not to move from the window in case Rachel's husband or children appeared. But it was almost seven by the time they arrived: first Frank, then James, followed shortly afterwards by Kirsty. By then, the smell of gas had completely gone and Rachel had insisted on going home.

'But do you feel well enough?' Kathleen asked anxiously.

'Yes,' Rachel said steadily. 'I want to be there when Frank and the children come. I'd sooner they think it's been a perfectly normal day. I'm sorry for causing such a fuss, Kathleen.'

'Stop being sorry. You apologize far too much.' Kathleen put her hands on Rachel's shoulders and looked into her eyes. 'Rachel, love, I don't know what goes on inside your head, but please, please, don't do anything like that again. Imagine if your son or daughter had come in and found you!'

'I think I reached my lowest point and now I'm about to climb up again.'

'That's good, really good. Look, I can't possibly let you go back by yourself. I'll wait downstairs while you have a shower and get changed – your clothes smell a bit of gas.'

Rachel gave a slight smile. 'I'd sooner you didn't,

Kathleen. You've been kindness itself, but I can manage on my own. I promise I won't drown myself in the shower.'

Kathleen had no alternative but to let her go. Tomorrow was the barbecue and she hoped Rachel would be able to cope.

'It's all over, Gran,' Victoria whispered. 'All over,' she sighed. 'He's the love of me life, but after Sunday I'll never see him again. I don't suppose you'd have approved, him being married like, but people can't stop themselves from falling in love.' She caught her breath when a light came on upstairs in Hamilton Lodge. 'I wonder if that's him! Have he and Debbie talked about the baby? Will he make love to her tonight?' It would be best if she didn't think about it because it hurt too much. Tomorrow, at the barbecue, they'd have to pretend they hardly knew each other.

'I'm glad, now, that I'm leaving on Sunday, Gran. Until now, I was in two minds about it, what with everyone coming to live in the square and being so friendly. But now I can't wait. Oh, Gran!' Victoria wept. '*Do* something: make me strong, because I don't think I can live without Gareth.'

Outside, in Victoria Square, the leaves on the tiny willow tree trembled in the slight breeze. In number one, everyone was asleep except for baby Alastair who was thinking about food and wondering if he should send a signal that he was hungry to the person who fed him. But the person had stopped offering the nice, squashy things that tasted so good. These days, food came on something hard and cold and wasn't nearly so nice. If he couldn't have the nice squashy things, he'd sooner not bother. Alastair uttered a little regretful sigh and fell asleep.

In the house next door, Marie Jordan lay in bed, rosary beads threaded through her fingers, unable to sleep. That afternoon, she'd gone shopping in Allerton Road and had peeked in the window of O'Connor's shop, but the card advertising the computer hadn't been in. So, who was it who had rung and asked for their address?

Judy Moon was dreaming about her new garden that, because this was a dream, was at least ten times as big as the real one. The grass was emerald green and spotted with pink and white blossom that had fallen from trees that were at least a hundred feet high and the fence was covered with vines bearing bunches of luscious purple grapes. She plucked one and wasn't at all surprised when it tasted of chocolate.

In Three Farthings, Rachel was poised on the edge of sleep, relaxed, her mind at peace. Things couldn't go on as they were or she'd go completely insane. Tomorrow, the next day, as soon as she had the opportunity, she'd tell Frank the truth.

Gareth Moran pounded madly on the keyboard. He didn't bother to look at the screen, knowing he was making no sense at all, that he'd have to do the work again. It helped get rid of his frustration, his . . . his . . . he clicked on to the computer's Thesaurus . . . aggravation, irritation, annoyance, disappointment, dissatisfaction . . . every single one of those damn bloody things. He looked at his watch and groaned: almost two o'clock and he'd never felt less like sleep in his life. Tonight, he and Debbie had had the mother of all rows and he'd kept thinking, 'I could be with Victoria. I don't have to listen to this,' except he *did*, because Debbie was his wife and she was expecting their baby and somehow, in some way, he had to make things work.

In Clematis Cottage, Anna and Ernest were watching a video: *Top Hat* with Fred Astaire and Ginger Rogers. They'd seen it so many times that every scene was indelibly printed in their minds. Anna's eyes sparkled with anticipation just before Fred and Ginger burst into a favourite song followed by a brilliant display of dancing. 'Here it comes,' she murmured, when the fabulous couple were sheltering from the rain in a bandstand in Hyde Park. 'Isn't it a lovely day to be caught in the rain,' Ginger began to sing . . .

Kathleen and Steve were fast asleep in each other's arms when the telephone rang. 'I'll get it,' Kathleen murmured, but Steve stumbled out of bed and into the front room, saying, 'It's all right, I'll do it,' and Kathleen woke up properly. Was he expecting someone to ring? Or did he think that a phone call in the middle of the night could only be for him?

He was back within a few minutes, his face grim. 'That was Brenda. I have to go to Huddersfield first thing in the morning. Jean's been taken to hospital. She's had a heart attack.'

'What sort of heart attack?' Kathleen's voice was cold.

'I dunno,' he replied irritably. 'I didn't know you could have different sorts.'

'You can have a mild heart attack, a severe one, and all shades in between.'

'I didn't ask.'

'It might be nothing.'

'Or it might be something.' His mouth set in a hard line. 'I'm going to see her, Kath, so there's no point in trying to talk me out of it.'

'Take the car, go now,' she said shortly.

446

He looked at her uncertainly. 'Are you sure?'

'Oh, for Christ's sake, Steve, go and see Jean. I'm sure she's far more important to you than I am.'

'You know that's not true.'

She ignored him, went to look for her bag, found the keys and threw them at him.

He caught them and left without another word.

'Anyroad, I suppose I should try and get some sleep. I'll speak to you again tomorrow night, tell you how the barbecue went. Goodnight, Gran.'

And goodnight, Gareth.

Victoria closed her eyes.

Saturday

14 JULY 2001

The Barbecue

Chapter 14

The sun was a stark sliver of gold on the horizon and the sky a pearly grey when a milk cart glided into Victoria Square for the first time, the only sound the faint rattle of bottles in their metal crates. The elderly driver stopped the vehicle in front of Clematis Cottage and placed two pints of milk and a small toast loaf outside the door – Anna liked the milk fresh, not bought in bulk and left in the fridge for days. Ernie had only placed the order the day before.

The driver glanced speculatively at the other houses: was there any chance of more business here? When he came to collect the money, he'd deliver a leaflet to each house saying he could provide free-range eggs, yoghurt, and fresh fruit juice as well as milk and bread. Since supermarkets had started selling milk in cartons, he'd found it hard to make a living. He sighed: it was going to be another blisteringly hot day. It wasn't that he longed for rain, but this sort of weather was unnatural and it would be a relief to see some clouds back in the sky. The milkman got in the cart and glided away, having not disturbed a soul.

Two hours later, the sun by now a pale shimmering ball, a postman strode briskly into the mews: new, young, and enthusiastic, determined to get his round done in record time. He wore a short-sleeved shirt, navy-blue shorts, and three-quarter-length white socks – people could laugh all they liked: it was the way postmen dressed in *Neighbours*.

There was nothing for numbers one and two, one letter for number three – it felt as if there was a card inside. Number four had decided to call itself Three Farthings and most of the letters had been re-directed from their previous address in Lydiate. The next house was Hamilton Lodge – how bloody pretentious, the young man thought as he pushed a pile of official looking envelopes through the letterbox. Clematis Cottage had joined a book club and sent for a mail order catalogue. He stood the catalogue outside the door – it didn't look the sort of place where it would be pinched. Number seven had a letter from Liverpool General Hospital – he hoped it wasn't bad news.

The post alerted Gareth who was wide awake, but still in bed. He cringed when he heard the thud of letters on the floor. They were bills, he could tell from the sound: ominous and threatening. He groaned. He had a grinding headache and what felt very much like a hangover, although he hadn't had a drop to drink last night. Downstairs, Debbie was throwing dishes at the wall. He groaned again, turned over, turned back again and rolled out of bed. She would be leaving for work soon and he wanted to clear the air before she went.

Debbie wasn't throwing dishes, but stacking them in the dishwasher. It was new and he'd forgotten they had it. There was no sign of Tabitha, who'd probably gone to hide in a place of safety.

'Did you sleep well?' he asked politely. He'd slept in the guest room: they had three and he was the first guest.

'What do you think?' Debbie snarled. 'What were you

doing to the computer last night – attacking it with a hammer?'

'I was typing,' he said truthfully. 'About last night . . .'

Debbie turned on him, eyes ablaze. 'I am *not*,' she repeated the word, putting even more stress on it, 'NOT going to live in that crappy little house and rent my lovely one to strangers. NOT, Gareth, *not, not, not*.'

'In that case,' he said mildly, 'would you kindly explain how we can pay the mortgage, keep up with the hire purchase payments, give the credit card companies their monthly pounds of flesh, buy food, pay the council tax, the gas, electric, and water bills, the house and contents and various other insurances, run the car, entertain your large and avaricious family?' He paused. 'Have I missed anything? Of course: your regular supply of very expensive clothes and the holiday in Barbados that I'm really looking forward to. How can we do all that, Debbie, when you're no longer working because you'll have a baby to look after?'

It was last night's row all over again. Debbie said, 'I told you, Gareth, I have no intention of leaving work. I'll take maternity leave and then Mum will look after the baby.'

And *he* said, 'And I told *you*, Debbie, that you'll leave my baby with your mother in that filthy house over my dead body.'

'*Your* baby!' Debbie snorted.

'Isn't it?' He raised his eyebrows.

'Of course it bloody well is. How dare you suggest it isn't?'

'You said, "*your* baby" in the tone of voice that made me think otherwise.'

'Anyroad, what's wrong with my mother?' she

453

demanded aggressively. 'She's already had five children of her own.'

'Yes, and they're all slobs, apart from you. You're the only one who turned out a decent human being.'

'Am I?' She looked slightly flattered for a second then returned to the attack. 'Why don't *you* give up work to look after the baby?'

'Oh, yeah! Your wages wouldn't meet a fraction of the bills. We're not managing now, I don't know how many times I have to tell you.' He looked at her thoughtfully. 'Strange how such a tiny head can be so thick.'

She threw a plate at him. Fortunately, he caught it, a relief, as he had a feeling the dinner service had cost about a million pounds. 'It wouldn't be for ever,' he continued, 'living in the corner house. It's furnished and we could rent this place out for two, even three, times the cost of the mortgage. It'd be what's called, "an executive let". Victoria doesn't want much in rent. A couple of years and we'd be straight. Then we could come back, free of debt. It's a great idea, Debs.'

'It's a daft idea. We'd probably find all the furniture's been chopped up for fire wood.'

'Not all families are like yours.' It was probably the wrong thing to say, but he couldn't resist it.

Debbie looked at him, eyes like daggers, and he realized he was wasting his time. She positively refused to listen to reason: she behaved as if he was trying to convince her that black was white.

Victoria was making the bed when she saw Debbie Moran march out of the square. It was obvious from her scowling face that there'd been a row. Debbie worked in a beauty parlour. Even from here, Victoria could see

454

how perfectly made-up she was. She wore bright red matador pants, a white off-the-shoulder top, white hoop earrings that touched her shoulders, and strappy sandals with enormously high heels as thin as pencils.

Debbie disappeared and Victoria sat on the bed and hugged a pillow to her chest. If Gareth persuaded Debbie to come and live in her house, he'd probably bring her to look at it. If so, Victoria would make herself scarce, go for a walk or something. She couldn't stand the thought of showing them around, knowing that one day they would sleep together in this very bed, face each other across the kitchen table.

She wondered if Gareth had gone to work, or was he home, still pretending to have the flu, and feeling as miserable as she did? But it wasn't just misery, more an all-consuming ache and sense of despair that she would never see him again after tomorrow. She buried her head in the pillow and began to cry. There was a saying, ''Tis better to have loved and lost than never to have loved at all,' but Victoria didn't believe it.

'Your catalogue's come, luv,' Ernest shouted, 'and details of that book club I sent for. We'd better get one of those cooler things to put outside for the milk,' he said when he took the catalogue into Anna. 'It might go off in this weather.'

'Shall we go shopping this afternoon, just locally? We could have lunch in that nice pub again where everyone was so friendly.'

'Of course, luv,' he said contentedly. He liked having a programme arranged for the day ahead.

'I was wondering what to wear for the barbecue.'

'Jeans, boots, check shirt, leather belt, handkerchief around the neck, and a Stetson hat.'

Anna looked at him doubtfully. 'Isn't that square dancing?'

Ernest conceded it might be. He'd never square-danced or been to a barbecue in his life and could have got confused.

'Hi, Julie. It's me, Sarah. Did you have a nice holiday in the Lake District? Good, but I'm not surprised you're tired after living in a tent for yonks. Julie, you'll never guess what's happened. I've left Alex. Yes, *left* him. I bought a house, awfully tiny, but terribly sweet. Alex came round and tried to drag the children away, then he tried to kidnap them and now he's in jail and Midge came wanting to know if she could see them, but Tiffany told her to go away. Didn't you, darling?'

Tiffany nodded proudly as she leaned against her mother and listened to the amazed squawks coming from Aunt Julie at the other end of the phone.

'Oh, and Julie, I've been doing simply loads and loads of washing. Yes, all on my own, although Marie from next door explained how the machine worked and showed me how to iron things. I've got a vacuum cleaner, too. It's enormous fun. And I can fry sausages and fish fingers and eggs. Did you know you could make chips in the oven? Alastair has stopped teething, and Jack actually paddles in the pool without his blanket, and Tiffany's made friends with the boy next door, and we're getting a computer and tonight we're going to a barbecue. Oh, and I'm reading a book. Yes, a book. It has loads of pages and is about a dear little boy called Harry. It's frightfully interesting. Of course you can come round, Jules. Tomorrow? Tomorrow's fine. Come to tea. Well, I won't keep you, I'm just about to ring Mummy's and see if she's back from Monte Carlo.'

'I'm off now, Marie,' Liam said stiffly when he came into the kitchen where Marie was making jam tarts for tonight. Rachel hadn't asked, but she thought it would nice to take some refreshments to the barbecue as well as wine. 'I don't know what time I'll be home.'

'Don't forget the barbecue,' she reminded him, wishing she hadn't the second the words were out of her mouth.

To her relief, he pulled a face. 'I'm not sure if I'll be back by then.'

'That's a shame,' she lied. She wanted him to be late. Not only was he out most of the time and they hardly saw each other, but she felt awkward when they did. Since the shameful night she'd let him kiss her and only a superhuman effort on her part had stopped them making love, everything had changed. He'd changed, she'd changed, and so had the boys. Before, they'd managed to pass off as a reasonably normal family. Liam had made friends of Patrick and Danny, but now they were enemies. It couldn't go on like this. Something would have to give.

There'd been no more calls about the computer, which wasn't surprising, seeing as the card hadn't gone in the window of O'Connor's shop. It was very mysterious and a little bit frightening. She tried not to think about computers, or Liam, and concentrated all her attention on the jam tarts.

Rachel had been baking all morning: fairy cakes, sausage rolls, biscuits, two giant fruitcakes. Kirsty had given her a hand. 'How many people are you expecting, Mum? There's enough here to feed the five thousand.'

'I don't know how many will come, but I'd sooner

have too much food than too little. It can always be kept for another day.'

'Did you remember to get the burgers?'

'There are fifty in the freezer and fifty rolls, and beer in the garage. I'll get the rolls out in a minute so they'll be nice and soft for tonight. Is everything done, apart from the cakes I've still to take out the oven?'

'That's the lot.'

'In that case, you go and do your own thing, love. I'll see to the cakes. After that I'm going into town. There's something I want to buy. Thanks for your help, Kirsty.'

Kirsty gave her an odd look and went upstairs. She was probably wondering why her mother wasn't dropping things all over the place and being her usual wretched, useless self. Rachel opened the oven, removed the cake from the top shelf, and put the cake underneath in its place. She closed the door with her foot and stared at it for a good minute. Say if Tiffany hadn't come in and found her? If Ernest hadn't been outside watering his clematis? If Anna hadn't been astute enough to understand the significance of what Tiffany had said?

Rachel put the cake on the draining board, removed her oven gloves, and stared unseeingly out of the window. She'd come a hair's breadth close to killing herself. And it was such a cowardly way out. She still had her health and strength. She still had two lovely children. Alice was dead and she would never cease to mourn her, but she wasn't the only woman in the world to lose a child. Life went on and she'd just have to learn to live with it.

Kathleen had moped about the house all day, smoking cigarette after cigarette until she'd had to open the back door and all the windows when the place began to smell.

Steve should have rung hours ago. Perhaps he was furious with her for being so furious with him for rushing off to Huddersfield just because Jean had had a heart attack that could well be merely a bout of indigestion. She'd known it happen loads of times before.

She lit another cigarette, put the kettle on for more coffee and made it strong. Fine doctor she was: lungs full of smoke, stomach full of caffeine. She'd go out if it didn't mean she might miss Steve's call, although he could always try again.

Back in the living room, she stood by the window, half expecting the Mercedes to drive in and for a cross Steve to get out and say it had all been a waste of time: there'd been nothing wrong and he'd told Jean and the girls to stop bothering him.

Victoria walked past, a big brown envelope in her hand. She waved and came over to the window. 'Would you mind doing me a favour?' she asked. Close up, Kathleen saw the girl's eyes were red, as if she'd been crying.

She wasn't in the mood for doing favours, but it seemed churlish to refuse. 'Of course, what is it?'

'I've just drawn up a Will on the computer. I was going to ask Anna and Ernie if they'd witness it for me, but they're out and so is Rachel. Sarah and Marie are busy with the children, and I wondered if you'd do it and I can ask my friend, Carrie, when she comes to see me off in the morning. I need two signatures, you see.'

'You'd better come in.' You're a bit young to be making a Will, aren't you?' she said when Victoria was inside.

'I know, but I've suddenly acquired loads of money and the house is worth a bit. If I had a fatal accident,

459

everything would go to the State – unless my father could be traced, but he walked out when my mother died. It doesn't seem fair that he should get everything.'

'That seems very sensible.' It also seemed very sad that someone so young should be thinking about Wills and death. 'Of course I'll sign it for you. I'll get a pen and you can show me where.'

'I've brought a pen. You sign here, on the second page. You don't want to read the first page, do you?' Victoria looked anxiously at the other woman.

'As long as you can assure me it really is a Will I'm signing and not anything compromising,' Kathleen laughed. Victoria obviously wanted to keep the identity of her beneficiary a secret.

'Oh! Oh, no!' The girl blushed. 'Look, it says "Last Will & Testament" on the top of the first page.' She held up the document so Kathleen could see.

'I was only joking, Victoria. You're the last person in the world I would expect to deceive anyone.' The girl was completely without guile. She signed the document 'Kathleen Quinn', although, as Steve's 'wife' her name was supposedly Cartwright. Hopefully Victoria wouldn't notice and query it. She gave the Will back and Victoria put it in the envelope without even glancing at the signature.

'Thank you very much,' she said politely. 'I hope I didn't disturb you.'

'I'm glad you came,' Kathleen said sincerely. 'I was worrying myself to death over something and you took my mind off it for a good ten minutes.'

'Would you like to talk about it?' Victoria offered. 'People say I'm a good listener and I promise I won't repeat it if it's personal.'

Kathleen shrugged and made a face. It wouldn't hurt

to get things off her chest. 'It's nothing much. I'm probably getting upset over nothing, but Steve's wife – his *first* wife – has been taken ill and he's gone to Huddersfield to see her. I've been expecting to hear from him all day, but I was so cross with him for going, he's probably taken umbrage and hasn't phoned.'

Victoria looked surprised. 'Why were you cross?'

'Wouldn't *you* be? I'm his wife now. His first loyalty should be to me.'

'Only if you were ill too,' Victoria said practically. 'Then there'd be no question he should put you first. But as you're not, it's only right he should go to his first wife. She hasn't re-married, has she?'

'No,' Kathleen said sulkily, at the same time praying that one day Jean would.

'Would you still like him if he knew his first wife was ill and didn't care?'

'*Like* him?' Kathleen was puzzled.

'Well, it wouldn't be very honourable, would it, not to give a damn about someone you'd been married to for years?' It seemed an old-fashioned word for someone so young to use: 'honourable'. 'There's this girl I know,' Victoria continued gravely, 'who's been having an affair with a married man. They love each other very much and were going to go away together, but the man learned that his wife was expecting a baby, their first, and he and the girl decided he couldn't possibly leave. It would have been dishonourable and terribly selfish.'

'How is the girl now?' Kathleen asked gently.

'Broken-hearted.'

'I'm so sorry, Victoria.'

Tears, like tiny, shimmering diamonds, trickled down Victoria's smooth, creamy cheeks. 'So am I,' she said in a cracked voice.

'If everyone's going to sit looking out of their windows waiting for someone else to go first, then none of us will go to the barbecue,' Anna argued.

'I'd sooner not be the first.' The Williamses had opened their windows and music issued forth, very loud – Anna claimed it was rap, Ernest insisted it was hip-hop. A table and four garden chairs had been placed on the communal lawn and a pasting table was covered with a gingham cloth on which stood half a dozen bottles of wine and plates of food covered with cloth napkins.

'You're eighty-one-years-old, Ernie,' Anna hooted. 'At your age, I wouldn't have thought you'd care if we were first or last. Poor Rachel will think no one's coming. If you're going to be such a coward, I'll go by myself.' Anna got to her feet. 'Where's that wine we bought?'

'In the fridge. I'll get it.' Ernest loathed being the first to arrive at a party, but the barbecue was supposed to start at seven and it was now ten past. He returned with the wine and Anna ordered him to go back and fetch the plastic chairs from the garden. 'Or else there won't be enough.'

Anna was proved right, as always. They had hardly set foot outside when, as if this had been taken as a signal, other doors opened: Marie Jordan appeared with her boys, the older one carrying a guitar, and Tiffany came whooping out of the house followed by Sarah, the baby in her arms, and a cautious Jack who'd been persuaded to leave his blanket behind.

When she heard the music, Kathleen cursed for not having left earlier. She'd intended giving Rachel a hand to get things ready, but had forgotten all about the barbecue. She quickly got changed into jeans and a loose blouse and brushed her hair. Steve still hadn't called, but it would be silly to stay just in case he did. After her talk with Victoria, she realized how selfish it was expecting him to cut off all contact with his family. What Victoria didn't know and Kathleen didn't explain, was that the selfishness was caused by fear that Steve might not come back.

Victoria was about to leave when there was a knock on the door and she found her friend, Carrie, outside. They hugged warmly. 'I thought you were going to dinner with some chap,' she cried.

'I was, but I decided to come to the barbecue with you instead. The chap's bound to turn out to be a louse, like all men.' Carrie grinned. 'Anyroad, I like you much better than him.'

'Let's go then, I can hear music. It must have started.' Victoria linked her friend's arm. 'I'm so pleased you came, Carrie.'

Judy Moon was also conscious of the music and the chatter of voices on the lawn outside. She remembered the strange woman next door was holding a barbecue – Donna had propped up the invitation on the mantelpiece. It wouldn't hurt to go, meet her new neighbours in one fell swoop as it were. She'd just stay an hour because she felt dead on her feet and had been looking forward to a long soak in the bath and an early night.

Her morning had been spent traipsing around the familiar shops in the area where she'd shopped her entire life. It would have been horrid to move away. She'd walked as far as the Moons' old photography shop in Menlove Avenue – Mr Moon had always referred to it as 'the studio'. The interior had been gutted and there was a notice outside to say it would shortly become an estate agency.

During the afternoon, she'd finished the unpacking and every one of Sam and Josh's lovely ornaments now had its own special place and every picture hung on a wall.

I'll have a shower instead of a bath, she told herself. Fortunately, she'd bought wine for tomorrow's lunch with her brother and sisters and their respective partners. She'd take a bottle with her and could always get more in the morning.

After showering, she put on the maroon skirt and embroidered top she'd been given for her birthday, examined her reflection in the wardrobe mirror – Josh had painted roses in each corner – and thought she didn't look too bad for a woman of sixty. She gave a sigh of happiness, it was a long time since life had been so good, and set forth.

'Are we going to this bloody barbecue or not?' Debbie snapped.

'Mum's come straight from work and she has to get washed and changed,' Gareth explained for the second time. His mother worked afternoons in the pay booth of a garage in Birkenhead and didn't finish until six. 'Do you have to be so rude? She might hear.'

'You usually do a bunk when *my* family come. You can't get any ruder than that!'

'I only do a bunk after they've been here so long I worry they've moved in for good. Mum's only been here fifteen minutes.' He felt a sudden flare of anger. 'I warn you, Debbie, you're not to be nasty to my mother. We don't see her often. If you upset her, well . . .' He left the threat unsaid, mainly because he couldn't think of one.

'Well, what?' She looked at him tauntingly. 'What exactly will you do if I upset your bloody mother?'

Gareth heard his mother go into the bathroom. He thought of how selflessly she'd worked to help him through university, despite her poor health. He said levelly, 'My mum's worth ten of you, Debbie. If you upset her, I'll leave you. You can have the house and everything in it. I don't think I want to live here any more.' He'd never spoken a truer word. Baby or no baby, he'd had enough. He wasn't prepared to live like this for the rest of his days, engaged in a continual war with his wife.

'*Gareth*! You can't mean that?' Her face had turned ashen. She grabbed the wrought-iron balustrade for support.

'I do.' He went into the kitchen and splashed his face with cold water. Christ, it was hotter today than ever!

Debbie came to the door. 'That was a terrible thing to say.'

'Go away, Debbie. I'm not in the mood for another argument.'

'You can't just say stuff like that and get away with it.' He didn't answer and she pressed on. 'You can't, Gareth.' Still he didn't answer. She asked sharply, 'Have you lost your voice or something?'

'Have *you* gone deaf? Didn't you hear me tell you to go away?'

His mother came downstairs, slightly breathless, in the blue brocade outfit she'd bought for his and Debbie's wedding. 'Sorry to have kept you both. I was as quick as I could.'

'Mum,' he said gently, 'you don't wear a hat to a barbecue.'

'Don't you, son? I've never been to one before.' She removed the hat, swathed in blue net, and laid it carefully on the hall table.

'Shall we go?' Gareth ushered her outside and completely ignored his wife. She could come if she wanted. It was up to her.

It was a beautiful evening: still hot, but slightly cooler than the day. The sun was a brilliant orange as it dipped towards the houses on the far side of the square, casting shadows on to the grass. For a moment, Gareth felt as if he and the people at the barbecue were the only ones left on earth, excluded as they were from the world outside.

The music had been turned off and Patrick Jordan was seated on the grass playing the guitar surrounded by a small crowd of admirers: his brother, Danny; Marie their mum; the gorgeous Sarah and her baby; Tiffany and Jack; Rachel's daughter Kirsty, to whom Gareth had never spoken; a strange, formally dressed young man who turned out to be Rachel's son James; a pretty, pert young woman who reminded him a bit of Debbie; and, of course, Victoria, the woman he loved and would love for ever. His heart turned over as his eyes met hers and he saw how melancholy they were, reflecting the expression that was bound to be in his own.

'There you are, Gareth!' Rachel approached. 'I thought you weren't coming. Hello, Debbie.' A subdued Debbie lagged behind.

'This is my mother, Ellen.' Was it his imagination, but did Rachel look different tonight? She'd had something done to her hair so it wasn't so limp and lifeless, and she wore a smart green dress. He hadn't thought it possible that Rachel could look so nice.

'It's lovely to meet you, Ellen. There's drink and refreshments on the table, so please help yourselves. But first come into the garden where my husband's attending to the barbecue. His name's Frank, by the way.'

Frank Williams wore a tall chef's hat and his red face glistened with perspiration, not surprising, as he was poised over a rack containing half a dozen spitting burgers.

'Hiya, neighbours.' He gave them a leery look and a burger each and they returned to the front. Gareth hadn't liked Frank the first time they met and now liked him even less.

Tiffany came running up and grabbed Gareth's leg. 'Why haven't you brought Tabitha? He'll be lonely on his own. I've brought Oliver: he's listening to the music.'

'Gareth,' Anna called, 'if that's your mother, bring her over here so I can tell her what a wonderful son she has.'

Gareth duly complied and sat his mother in the chair next to Anna. Ernie looked very morose, as if he heartily wished he were somewhere else. 'Did I hear you say your name was Ellen?' Anna gushed. 'I'm Anna, and this handsome gentleman is my husband, Ernie. The lady next to him is Kathleen. She's married to Sean Connery or someone remarkably similar who's away at the moment. Next to Kathleen is Judy Moon – isn't that a pretty name? Judy only moved in yesterday. Now,' Anna paused for breath, 'about Gareth, he kindly helped us install our computer . . .'

How come all these people knew Gareth? Debbie wondered. Virtually every person there had shouted a greeting of some sort: not just the adults, but the kids as well. When exactly had he managed to install the ancient couple's computer? How come the little girl knew about Tabitha? How did he know the stunning blonde's baby was called Alastair? And, come to that, how did he find out that this Victoria, whoever she was, was going to live in America and renting out her dingy little house? It was all very mysterious.

Debbie was sitting on the grass, munching her burger, and feeling a bit out of things. She was glad when the little girl came, sat beside her, and held out her teddy bear. 'My name's Tiffany and this is Oliver. You can shake his hand if you like.'

'How do you do, Oliver?' Debbie loved children and was looking forward to having one of her own. She shook the bear's paw. It had a hankie wrapped around its head covering one of its eyes.

'Mummy said you're Gareth's wife,' Tiffany said gravely. 'I thought Victoria was his wife.'

'What on earth makes you think that?'

'Well, she makes him meals and sleeps with him like wives do. Do you make his meals and sleep with him too?' For a few seconds, the child's brow furrowed then cleared. 'I know, Gareth has *two* wives!' she exclaimed.

'No, he hasn't. There's just one: me.' Powerful alarm bells were clanging at full volume inside Debbie's head. 'Is Victoria here?' she asked in a voice that sounded strange, even to herself.

'She's over there, talking to Gareth. She's awfully nice. She lets me and Danny play on her computer all the time. But she's going to America tomorrow. I'm awfully sad.' Tiffany sniffed. 'Tomorrow, I think I might cry.'

Debbie wasn't listening. She was watching Gareth in deep conversation with a girl who looked as if she belonged in a different era. Her black curly hair wasn't cut in any sort of style and she hadn't a scrap of make-up on, although her skin was flawless and the lashes on her large brown eyes were extremely long. She wore a plain blouse, a denim skirt, and flat sandals. Her head was almost touching Gareth's, but they were staring at the grass rather than at each other. If it hadn't been for Tiffany, Debbie would have thought the scene quite innocent, but now she could tell that whatever they were saying was private, important only to them, and of no concern to *her*, who happened to be Gareth's wife.

I'll kill him.

I'll never speak to him again.

I'll leave him.

The jumbled thoughts, the threats, the promises, raced like wildfire through Debbie's hot brain. She threw the burger on to the grass and ran into the house.

'Are you all right?' Rachel shouted as she ran past.

'I'm just going to fetch Tabitha for Tiffany.'

Tabitha was curled up in a ball on the white leather settee. Debbie knelt and laid her cheek against his warm, furry body. 'He's been having an affair, Tabs. What am I to do? It's no use killing him, because I love him, and it's no good saying I'll never speak to him again because he's already not speaking to me. Oh, and he threatened to leave me.' She began to cry. She'd thought the threat an empty one, never for a minute thinking that there was someone else, another woman that he'd leave her for. It was her own fault. She'd driven him to it, being so horrible about his mother. She quite liked her mother-in-law, although she was a bit long-suffering and inclined to speak in a whiny sort of voice.

'What's happened to us?' she asked Tabitha, but he merely curled himself into a tighter ball. They'd used to get on so well, but since moving to Hamilton Lodge, all

469

Gareth did was go on and on about money, about tightening belts and reining things in a bit. But Debbie hadn't wanted to listen. She was so proud of the house and wanted everything in it to be perfect. She didn't know anyone who had a nicer house, not even the woman who owned the beauty parlour where she worked.

Mum's place was a slum – Gareth was right – it was filthy. Growing up, she'd been ashamed to invite her mates inside. She'd used to dream about one day having a house of her own where all the furniture would match and it would be kept sparklingly clean although never, in the wildest of these dreams, had the house been half as big or half as smart as Hamilton Lodge – nor had it been *detached!* She loved inviting her family, knowing how proud they'd be for her – and how envious.

Perhaps Gareth was right about something else too. Perhaps she had been spending too much money – it had been like a drug, the money, and the supply had seemed endless. And now they were almost broke. Why else would he want them to move into Victoria's? If it was anything like Victoria herself, the house would be dead old-fashioned.

'But I'll have to, Tabs. I'll have to, or I'll lose him.' She wouldn't mention what Tiffany had told her. It would be awfully hard, but she'd pretend she didn't know. From now on, she'd be as nice as she could be. Her relationship with Gareth was hanging by a thread that a wrong word from her could very easily break and she loved him far too much to let him go.

'You're Ernie, I recognized you straight away.' The woman gave a throaty laugh. 'Anyroad, you're the only one here old enough.'

Ernest looked up. He was bored out of his mind and longed to go home, but Anna would call him all the names under the sun if he did. The woman wore an elegant yellow linen frock and her smooth blonde hair was knotted in a bun at the back of her head. At first, he thought she looked about fifty, but noticed her heavily wrinkled neck and added on a good ten or fifteen years.

'You don't recognize me, do you?' The woman giggled merrily.

Ernest felt obliged to confess he'd never seen her before in his life and she giggled again. 'I'm Gaynor, your little sister. Our Charlie told me you'd been in touch. The old sourpuss, I had to threaten to cut off his wretched balls before he'd give me your address. I didn't realize there'd be a function.' She glanced around the crowded lawn. 'I hope I'm not interrupting anything.'

'Gaynor!' Ernest struggled to his feet. '*Gaynor!*' he repeated, overcome with emotion.

Gaynor flung her arms around him. 'My big brother, home at last.' She patted his back. 'It's lovely to see you, Ernie.' She gave another of her throaty laughs. 'You haven't changed a bit.'

'I was only nineteen when I left, luv.'

'You still haven't changed.'

'Excuse me.' Anna coughed loudly, 'Are you intent on starting an affair right under my nose, Ernie, or are you going to introduce me to this lovely lady and claim it's all quite innocent?'

'This is Gaynor, luv, Gaynor, me sister. She's come to see us.' Ernest could hardly speak, he felt so choked. 'This is me wife, Anna.'

'How do you do, Anna?' The two women shook hands.

'Pardon me for not getting up, Gaynor, but I've had

471

two glasses of wine and feel quite tipsy. I'm not supposed to drink, you see, so I'm not used to it.'

'Take no notice,' Ernest growled. 'She drinks all the time. Can I get *you* a drink, luv? There's white and red wine and beer. Come on over, there's food there an' all and you can take your pick. Charlie said you didn't want to see me,' he remarked when they reached the table and he handed his sister a paper plate.

'Our Charlie's a prick,' Gaynor said bluntly, picking up two sausage rolls. 'His wife, Evelyn, has led him a miserable life, and their Ronnie's done time for burglary. Tessa, his daughter, is a nice girl, but she's in throes of getting divorced for the second time. Poor Charlie, eh?' Gaynor shrugged. 'He's more to be pitied than loathed. He's jealous of me – I've had a great life, Ernie, two wonderful husbands and a marvellous son – and now he's jealous of you. He told me he gave you a good ticking off.' She looked at him keenly. 'I hope he didn't upset you.'

'A bit,' Ernest acknowledged, although it had been rather more than that. 'It was about Mam, mainly. He said she died of a broken heart and it was me that broke it.'

'What nonsense!' Gaynor gave her attractive laugh. 'Mam died in her sleep at eighty. Oh, she worried about you at first, wondered where you were, why you hadn't come home, but she got over it in time. Why didn't you come home, Ernie?' she asked curiously.

'I was too taken up with Anna,' he confessed. 'We met during the war and I couldn't wait to get back to Cairo where she lived. Bootle, me family, didn't seem important any more. I know I should've written, luv, and I can't really explain why not.'

'Never mind, Ernie, it's all in the past. As Mam used

to say, "It's no good crying over spilt milk." Look, d'you think we should get back to Anna? She'll be feeling lonely on her own.'

'Anna will never feel lonely while there's another human being left on the planet. No, I want to introduce you to everyone, show me little sister off to the neighbours. See that lady over there,' he pointed to Rachel, 'she's the one who organized the barbecue. 'Rachel,' he called. 'I'd like you to meet me sister, Gaynor. This is the first time we've seen each other in sixty years . . .'

The sun had sunk lower and the grass looked greener where the shadows had spread. No one noticed the black cloud that was creeping into the sky from behind Victoria's house. The wine had almost gone, the food eaten. The charcoal in the barbecue was cold now, and Frank Williams, his labour no longer required, was sprawled on the grass beside Sarah Rees-James, carrying on a trite conversation while he stared at her breasts and drank his tenth can of beer − not that he'd counted.

Patrick, ignoring the advice given by Liam a whole week ago that he not play anything Irish, was doing just that. 'There was a wild colonial boy,' he crooned in a pleasant baritone voice, spurred on by the copious amount of wine he'd drunk of which his mother was totally unaware. Tiffany was dancing around the willow tree with Tabitha, the kitten held tenderly in her arms. Jack and Alastair were asleep. Judy Moon, who'd only meant to come for an hour, was still there, talking animatedly to Anna, who was in the course of telling her about the film she'd made. Judy had just explained where her Christian name had come from: 'Mum and Dad were at the pictures watching *The Wizard of Oz*, when Mum had her first contraction . . .'

'Have you enjoyed yourself, Gareth?' Debbie asked in a subdued voice.

'Yes,' Gareth said shortly. 'Yes, it's been great,' he added in a friendlier tone.

'I'm sorry I was so impatient with your mum. And we'll move to Victoria's house if that's what you want.'

'Will you?' This was a turn-up for the books. He wondered what on earth had happened to make her change her mind? Earlier, he'd meant it when he'd threatened to move out but, on reflection, it just wasn't on. Somehow, he and Debbie would have to learn to live together without fighting all the time. 'Before we move, I'll decorate the place from top to bottom,' he promised. 'We could get the paint and stuff tomorrow. Would you like to have a look around now? Victoria won't mind.' He looked at Victoria, who was looking at him while she spoke to his mother.

'No, I'd sooner wait till she's gone. I don't care what it's like as long as I'm with you. And I'll cancel the holiday in Barbados, tell them I'm pregnant and not allowed to fly.'

'Leave it,' he said impulsively. It would be the last extravagance for a long while. Their marriage needed mending and perhaps the repair could be done in Barbados.

Patrick finished 'The Wild Colonial Boy', and Rachel tapped a bottle with a spoon in order to grab everyone's attention.

'Two things,' she said in a strangely authoritative voice. 'Firstly, I'd like everyone to join with me in congratulating Patrick on reaching his eighteenth birth-day. Happy birthday, Patrick.'

'Happy birthday to you,' the crowd sang, 'happy birthday to you. Happy birthday, dear Patrick. Happy birthday to you.'

Patrick blushed, but looked pleased, not as pleased though as Marie, his mother, who was thrilled that such an important birthday had been celebrated in public. She and Danny had sent cards and so had Victoria and Kirsty – there'd been nothing from Liam who must have forgotten – but had circumstances been different, Patrick would have received dozens and dozens of cards from his aunts, uncles, and cousins back in Donegal, and from his friends in Belfast where there'd have been a party that would have gone on all night and half the next day.

'Secondly,' Rachel continued when the singing stop-ped, 'this is the last time we'll have Victoria with us. Tomorrow, she'll be flying off to a new life in New York. Let's drink to Victoria and wish her all the luck in the world.' She raised a cardboard cup. 'Victoria!'

'Victoria!' people echoed.

'Thank you,' Victoria said in a small voice, and Tiffany burst into tears.

Kathleen slipped home, unnoticed. She'd been too worried about Steve to enjoy herself. Anna was delight-ful, but she never shut up and had been getting on her nerves.

The first thing she did was pick up the phone to see if there was a message on voicemail, but the even tone indicated there was none. All of a sudden, she remem-bered that, if Jean had genuinely had a heart attack, then she had the phone number of the hospital where she would be in her address book – she'd had several friends there. She found the book and, after some hesitation, picked up the phone, dialled the number, and asked for the Cardiology ward.

'You have a patient, a Mrs Jean Cartwright,' she said when she'd been put through. 'I'd like to know her condition, please.' She prayed the nurse who answered would deny having a patient of that name or say it had been a false alarm and she'd been sent home.

'Are you a relative?'

'I'm her sister-in-law.'

'I'm sorry to say that Mrs Cartwright's condition is critical.'

'I see.' Kathleen drew in a deep breath. 'Is her husband with her?'

'Yes, he's been here all day, and her daughters.'

'Thank you.' She put the phone down, feeling shocked and horribly ashamed. Critical! There was actually a chance that Jean might die. And if she did, Kathleen knew for certain that Steve would be with her until the end and that he'd blame himself for the heart attack. Then there'd be a funeral and he might feel obliged to stay with his girls, at least for a while – or perhaps for ever!

And if Jean recovered? Kathleen dropped her head into her hands. If Jean recovered, she had no idea what would happen then. There were too many ifs and buts for her to cope with.

She should be feeling sorry for Jean, not herself. Perhaps Steve hadn't rung because he expected she'd fly off the handle if he said he wasn't coming home, didn't even *know* when he'd be home.

'God, I'm such a bitch,' she groaned aloud. She lit a cigarette, but stubbed it out almost immediately. Right now, she wasn't very keen on her own company. She'd go back to the barbecue, listen yet again to the story of how Anna had once starred in a film. It would be a sort of penance.

'When Irish eyes are smiling,' Patrick sang and everyone joined in. 'All the world is bright and gay . . .'

Some people had become aware of the black cloud that was getting fatter and fatter as it climbed towards the heavens.

'I hope it doesn't rain.'

'So do I, but we could do with a good shower.'

'As long as it's just a shower . . .'

Tomorrow was St Swithin's Day, Rachel remembered as she eyed the cloud. If it rained, then it would rain for another forty days and nights. She was glad she'd had the barbecue today. Everything had gone so well, much better than expected. It was almost nine o'clock, but no one showed any sign of wanting to go home. Kathleen had disappeared, but only for a while. Frank couldn't very well complain it had been a failure as he'd predicted. He was sitting on the grass, eyeing up Victoria's friend, Sarah having managed to escape his attentions. He might be trying to think up spiteful things to say to his wife when everyone had gone.

That afternoon, Rachel had gone into town and bought gold sandals and the green silky dress that she'd tried on the other day. The hairdressers were very busy, but said they could just manage a wet cut. She'd come out, her hair transformed. It would never be thick like Kathleen's or curly like Victoria's, but it looked respectable for a change. She'd felt quite proud of her appearance tonight and no one had looked sorry for her, as they usually did.

Gareth's mother approached. 'I just wanted to say I've

had a lovely time, Rachel. Thank you, very much. I've really enjoyed myself.'

'Do you have far to go?'

'Wallasey. It's quite a way, but Debbie has asked me to stay the night with her and Gareth.' She looked very pleased about it.

'In that case, we'll probably see each other in the morning.'

'Tiffany,' Sarah called, 'time to go home, darling. I want to put Jack to bed and give Alastair his bottle.'

'Don't want to go home, Mummy.' Tiffany was playing football with Danny Jordan. The child was tireless. Judy Moon was nursing Tabitha and talking about getting a cat of her own.

'I'll bring Tiffany over later if you like, Sarah,' Rachel offered. Patrick started to sing, 'I've been a wild rover for many a year . . .'

'Thank you, Rachel,' Sarah said, and Frank rose to his feet and said in a loud voice, 'I wouldn't trust *her* with your little girl, Sarah. You're not likely to see her again.'

Patrick stopped singing and guitar gave an angry twang when his fingers pressed the wrong strings. The buzz of conversation ceased and everyone looked uneasily at Frank, swaying slightly, his face as red and angry as Rachel had ever seen it. Saliva dripped from his mouth on to his shirt, as he continued, '*We* had a little girl, but she died and it was all *her* fault.' He nodded at Rachel. 'She all but killed her with her own bare hands.' His face collapsed and he began to weep, the tears streaming like rivers down his puffy cheeks.

'Shush, Dad, you're drunk.'

Kirsty took a step towards her father, but Rachel held up her hand and shouted, 'Stay!' She felt tall and powerful, very strong. Nothing on earth was going to prevent her from saying what she was about to say.

Her daughter stopped in her tracks and everyone jumped. Rachel turned to her husband and said in a voice even louder than his, 'If anyone killed our Alice, Frank, it was you. The day she died, I phoned the showroom because I was too sick to collect her from school. You'd said you were coming home early and I asked Margot, the receptionist, to make sure you left in time to pick up Alice.' Rachel cocked her head on one side, remembering. 'You'd just come back from lunch and I heard Margot call to you, "Rachel's on the phone and she said will you please collect Alice," and you replied, "OK".'

'That's not true!' Frank blustered, but his eyes were bright with fear. 'I would have remembered if it were.'

'Perhaps you would have remembered if you'd been sober, Frank: but you were drunk. That's the only mistake I made, not realizing you were drunk. You'd been out having a Christmas drink with your mates.'

Thunder rumbled in the distance, but no one stirred. Tiffany and Danny had stopped kicking the ball, aware something of tremendous significance was happening between the grown-ups. Anna opened her mouth to speak, but Rachel saw Kathleen lay her hand on her arm and whisper something in her ear.

'Margot rang the next day when she heard what had happened, that Alice had drowned, and I told her not to say anything about the phone call. I was willing to take the blame, you see.' She threw back her shoulders and could feel even more power coursing through her veins. 'I'm stronger than you, Frank,' she said proudly. 'You could never have stood up to knowing you were responsible for our little girl's death.' She looked at her husband pityingly. 'But *I* could, at least, I could have if I'd had your support. But you behaved as if I'd taken Alice to the canal myself and held her head under the water.' There was a chorus of horrified gasps from the rapt crowd. Rachel looked at them and said conversationally, 'He turned my children against me. He tells me over and over how much he hates me, that if he were me he wouldn't be able to live with himself.'

'Mum!' Kirsty ran and threw her arms around her mother. 'Oh, Mum.'

James, her son, who'd been so cold with her, groaned, 'I didn't know, Mum. I didn't know.'

Rain had begun to fall, only lightly at first, quickly turning into a downpour. A bolt of lightning split the sky, but still no one moved until they realized that Rachel had finished. Only then did they collect their belongings and make a dash for home. Frank Williams collapsed, weeping, on to the grass. No one went near him.

'Leave the chairs, Ernie. It doesn't matter if they get wet,' Anna commanded.

'Well, that's the most dramatic barbecue I've ever been to,' Gaynor remarked, as she and Ernie between them helped Anna home. 'Poor woman, what an awful time she's had. I'm glad she got everything off her chest. Yes, I'd love some cocoa, Ernie. Thanks for asking.'

Kathleen remained, not caring that she was getting soaked, watching Rachel being embraced by her children. Then Kirsty removed the sodden cloth from the table, James began to fold it, and Kathleen said, 'You were magnificent, Rachel. I can't believe you've been holding that in for so long. Me, I'd never had stood up to it.'

'I loved him, that's why,' Rachel explained. She

looked weary all of a sudden, all her power gone. 'I used to love Frank very much.'

'What's going to happen now?'

'I don't know. We'll sort it out tomorrow.'

'Good luck then, Rachel.' Kathleen went indoors and picked up the phone, but Steve still hadn't rung.

Marie had noticed the car parked outside the row of garages and assumed it belonged to Ernie's sister or Victoria's friend. She was having difficulty unlocking the front door. Her hands were wet and the key felt slippery. Patrick was urging her to hurry. 'Will you stop your nagging?' she barked. 'I'm doing the best I can.'

'But me guitar's getting soaked, Ma.'

'I'm sure a drop of rain won't harm it.'

'It's more than a drop.'

The key worked at last and they fell inside. Marie turned to close the door and saw a man coming towards her. 'I've been waiting for you in the car,' a familiar voice said. 'I didn't like to intrude on the party.'

'Enda!' Marie took a step backwards and bumped into the guitar. It made an echoey, booming sound and Patrick tut-tutted irritably. 'Enda Kelly. Come in, come in, before you get drenched.'

'You're a sight for sore eyes, Marie.' He gave her a warm hug, aimed a pretend punch at each of the lads, and grinned, still the same old Enda: tall, big-boned, white-blond hair as flat as a pancake. Marie was transported back to the night she'd gone to his sister's house and he'd come into the bedroom accompanied by her future husband.

'How did you know where we lived?' she demanded, a mere second before realizing it was a stupid question. He knew because his sister, Brigid, had given him the telephone number off the card advertising the computer and he'd rung and asked Danny for the address. 'It doesn't matter. I already know. Let's go into the kitchen and I'll make a cup of tea. Liam will be back in a minute,' she said when Enda and the boys had seated themselves around the table. This was all wrong, Enda shouldn't be there, but Marie no longer cared.

'Right now,' Enda said flatly, 'Liam Jordan's in the police station being questioned about his drug dealings.'

It took a long time for the meaning of the words to sink in. 'But he's a priest!' Marie protested when they had. She was shocked to the core, so much so, that the water she was pouring into the kettle missed its target and splashed all over her skirt.

'I know he's a priest, Marie. He's also a murderer. It was Liam who arranged to have your Mickey killed.'

There was another long silence, during which they were conscious of the rain pounding against the windows and thunder rolling in the sky.

Patrick was the first to speak. 'Liam killed our da?' His fists were clenched, the knuckles white. 'If I ever get near him, I'll kill him with me own bare hands, so I will.'

'And so will I,' Danny cried.

'No, you won't, boys. Me and a few other lads have been searching for him every-bloody-where over the last twelve months so we could do that very thing ourselves. We never dreamed he was with you, Marie.' Enda's blue eyes narrowed. 'Did you not realize you were protecting your husband's killer?'

'Indeed I knew no such thing.' Marie's face turned as red as her hair. Just as if! 'I was protecting our Patrick, or so I thought. He said – Liam said – that the men that killed Mickey were after Patrick too.'

482

'But why would anyone want to kill me?' Patrick spread his hands in a helpless gesture.

Marie angrily banged her fist on the draining board. 'Enda Kelly, will you kindly explain what's been going on? Oh, will someone make this tea? I've lost the hang of it.' She couldn't remember how to switch on the kettle. The wind had risen and sheets of rain were being blown against the windows – the bedroom windows were open and everything would be getting wet, but she didn't care if they had to swim upstairs.

Danny got up to attend to the tea making. Marie sat and wondered if she was going mad or had she already lost her brain when Mickey died?

'You know the weekend Mickey went to London to stay with his sister for her birthday?' Enda began. 'Before he left, he took her back to the hotel where she worked – what was her name, Marie?'

'Patsy. Still is, unless she's died herself while we've been away.'

'The hotel's one of those grand places that cost the earth to stay in and a small fortune to buy a drink. Patsy took Mickey into the bar and got him a lager: she probably got it buckshee, her being on the staff like.'

'What's this nonsense in aid of?' Marie asked impatiently. 'What's it got to do with my Mickey being murdered?'

'I'm coming to it, girl,' Enda replied, just as impatiently. 'Who did Mickey see in the bar, but Father O'Mara, now known as Liam Jordan, not dressed as a priest, but all done up in a posh suit and sitting with two other guys. Mickey recognized one: a Unionist racketeer, well known in the drugs trade. He would've run a mile, but it was too late. The priest had already seen him.

And that, my darling Marie, is why your Mickey had to be killed.'

'I remember,' Marie said slowly, 'it saying in the papers that kids were being offered drugs in schools, in parks, discos: all over the place. And Father O'Mara – Liam – was behind it and he had to kill Mickey before the truth came out.' It was *that* simple. Her darling husband had been in the wrong place at the wrong time and had had to die to save Liam's miserable life and protect the drugs business. Marie didn't think she would ever set foot inside a church again, ever say another rosary. It was so unfair. What sort of God would let such a heinous thing happen? They all grimaced when thunder shook the house and the windows rattled in their frames. She asked, 'How do you know this, Enda?'

'Because Mickey rang me from the airport and told me what he'd seen.'

Patrick said, 'I was offered cocaine at school, Ma. It happened more than once.'

'Jaysus, Mary, and Joseph, what is the world coming to!' Marie fell silent. She didn't possess the words to describe how she felt about Liam Jordan. Eventually, she said, 'But why did he want our family out the way? He insisted we leave, said it was dangerous to stay.'

'It wasn't Liam's hand that held the gun that saw Mickey off, Marie. There are men even more ruthless than him. Perhaps he genuinely thought you were in danger, that Mickey had said something the minute he got home. Or maybe he thought you'd be good protection while he hid himself away. We weren't searching for a family man when we searched for Father O'Mara.'

'That's probably it, Enda,' Marie cried. 'Like a fool, I went and told him that you knew who'd done for

Mickey and that you weren't the only one. It was only afterwards he started going on about Patrick and us having to hide out. Jaysus!' She felt like killing herself. 'Me sisters use to tell me I had the biggest mouth in Donegal.'

'There's been no harm done, Ma,' Patrick said philosophically, patting her hand. 'We just spent a lot of time away when we didn't have to.'

'Even so, son.' She sighed and said to Enda. 'What made you ring this number and ask for the address?'

'Because our Brigid thought it just a wee bit peculiar that you denied being Marie Brennan when she knew full well you were. There'd been a rumour the priest had made his way to Liverpool – this city is a hot spot for drugs. Did you know that, Marie?'

She shook her head. 'No, I did not. The people I've met here have been charming through and through.'

'Anyway,' Enda went on, 'I didn't exactly put two and two together, but we got someone to watch this house and they saw his holiness leave.' He smiled grimly. 'They followed him and he met up with a couple of unsavoury looking boyos in a pub on the Dock Road, spent a lot of time on his mobile, people came in and out to see him and went away with some very suspicious looking packages.' He sat back in the chair and folded his arms. 'The peelers were onto him like a shot when we fingered him – anonymously mind.'

'So,' Marie said slowly, 'it's all over. Now we can all go back to Donegal and live with me mam.' She couldn't wait. Tomorrow morning, first thing, she'd start to pack, although it would be desperately sad to say goodbye to Sarah and the other friends she'd made.

'Ah, no, Ma,' Danny wailed. 'I'd sooner stay.'

'Me too,' echoed Patrick.

'We can't, lads,' Marie told them. 'I've no idea who this house belongs to and I've no intention of sitting here waiting to be thrown out.'

'But will we still be getting Victoria's computer?' Danny persisted.

'In the morning, before she goes. She said so at the barbecue tonight. Now, Enda,' she said briskly in an attempt to take charge, be herself again, 'would you like a sandwich of some sort and I'll make more tea, not that I made the first lot? And there's a bed upstairs free if you want it, although I'll change the bedding first. I'm sure you won't be wanting to sleep between Liam's old sheets.'

'I'll have the tea, Marie, but say no to the sandwich and the bed. There's supper and a bed waiting for me at our Brigid's just along the road.' He stretched. 'I'll sleep better tonight, knowing that the priest's had his come-uppance, although I'd rather have shot the bastard and sat and watched him die.'

'And so say all of us,' Patrick murmured.

Marie didn't say anything, just made an involuntary Sign of the Cross and thought about her darling Mickey.

'This is my last night, Gran. My last night in our house.' Victoria sighed as she sat on the bed and changed the pillowslips for dry ones – the window had been open and they'd got wet. 'What am I supposed to do with the bedding in the morning,' she asked her grandmother fretfully, 'roll it up in a ball and throw it away? Or shall I put it in a plastic bag and ask Gareth to give it to charity? Debbie won't want our old sheets and stuff, that's for sure . . .'

'They're coming to live here, Gran.' Victoria stroked the bed on the side where Gareth had slept the few nights they'd been together. 'I suppose I'll learn to live without him. After all, I've hardly known him a week, but you can find out an awful lot about a person in just seven days, almost everything there is to know in fact, enough to realize you want to spend the rest of your life with them.'

She looked out of the window. Victoria Square looked different tonight: the wet bricks looked darker and the roofs shone like they were covered in silk. The lamps seemed to be drooping, as if the weight of the water was too much for them, and the light they emitted was weak, casting a pale, feeble circle underneath.

'I suppose I'd better get to bed. I'll have a busy day tomorrow.' Her suitcases were already packed, but there were bound to be last-minute things she'd forgotten. 'Anyroad, Gran, goodnight. Next time I talk to you, it'll be from America.'

Sunday

15 JULY 2001

St Swithin's Day

Chapter 15

Victoria had been up for two hours when the telephone rang. The taxi was coming at ten to take her to Manchester airport and she was already dressed for the journey in a cream linen suit with a blue T-shirt underneath. Her passport and airline tickets were in her bag, along with a book to read, a packet of paper handkerchiefs and two packets of mints. The rest of the bag contained all the rubbish she usually carried around: she hadn't thought to clear it out.

She picked up the phone. It was Carrie, calling to wish her good luck and have a safe journey. 'As soon as I get to a computer, I'll send an email,' Victoria promised.

The receiver had hardly been replaced a minute, when the phone rang again. This time it was Gareth. Her heart melted at the sound of his voice.

'Hi,' he said huskily.

'Hi, yourself.' She nursed the phone against her face, as if it was Gareth himself.

'I'll be coming over to say goodbye, but I thought I'd ring and say my own, personal goodbye first.'

'Goodbye, Gareth,' she whispered.

'Goodbye, my darling Victoria. If I say adieu does that mean we'll meet again?'

'No, its au revoir.' She could hardly speak her voice was so thick with sadness and longing.

'Then au revoir, my one and only love. Be happy, won't you?'

'You too, Gareth. Au revoir.'

'Just in case I won't be able to stop meself from leaping on a plane one day very soon, where will you be working in New York? I forgot to ask.'

She knew, and she knew that he knew, that he would never be free to leap on a plane and fly to New York. Nevertheless, she told him where she would be. 'My office is in the World Trade Center. I'll be on the ninety-somethingth floor.'

'Wow! That'll be some view. You never know, I might turn up one of these days.'

Someone was knocking on the back door. 'I have to go, Gareth.'

'I know, I heard the knock. It's the Jordan boys. I'm in my office and I saw them go in.'

'Bye, Gareth.' She put down the phone and opened the door to the Jordans. Their red hair was wet after the short walk from their house. It had rained steadily all night and now it danced in the pools that had formed in the concrete path around the emerald green lawn. She hadn't been able to sleep for the monotonous drumming on the roof.

'We're going back to Ireland, to Donegal,' Danny announced. 'Me Uncle Gerry's coming over in a van tomorrow to take us and our stuff back.'

'And we bought you this.' Patrick handed her a tiny cardboard box. 'It's a little St Christopher medal to attach to your watch.'

She thanked them both profusely and said she'd attach it before she boarded the plane. 'Then I'm bound to arrive safely, aren't I? Now you'd better go upstairs for the computer.'

At precisely ten o'clock, a horn sounded signalling the taxi had arrived. She picked up the suitcases, strung her bag over her shoulder, and went outside, leaving the key on the kitchen table for Gareth – she'd given him the spare the night before. She wondered how long she would be gone before he would come to show Debbie around?

She felt tears come to her eyes when she saw that nearly everyone in the square had come to see her off. They stood in line, smiling beneath their colourful umbrellas: like a row of flowers of all different sizes.

'Goodbye, Victoria, love.' Anna was in her wheelchair. She reached for Victoria's hand and held it as hard as she could, as if she never wanted to let her go. 'You'll always have a special place in my heart.'

'Bye, luv,' Ernie said gruffly. 'Here, let me put them suitcases in the taxi for you.'

'I hope you have a marvellous time in New York,' Sarah said warmly. 'Wave bye-bye, Alastair, and you too, Jack.'

'Bye, Victoria,' Tiffany sniffed wretchedly and threw her arms around Victoria's waist. 'Thank you for the hat and things. Can I come and see you in America and bring Oliver?'

'If Mummy will let you, darling.'

'Enjoy yourself, Victoria. I hope the job turns out all right.' Marie Jordan kissed her on both cheeks. 'Did the boys tell you we're moving too?'

'Yes. Donegal sounds lovely. I hope you'll be happy there. Good luck, Danny.' She kissed Danny on the cheek and shook hands with Patrick. 'Good luck.'

'You'll probably think me an idiot when we only met last night, but I didn't want to be left out.' Judy Moon smiled and gave her a kiss. 'Look after yourself, dear.'

'I've brought you a little present,' Rachel said, 'a gold St Christopher medal to wear around your neck. Shall I put it on for you?'

'Please.' Two St Christopher medals! Now she would be doubly safe. 'Thank you, Rachel. It was a wonderful barbecue last night. I couldn't have had a nicer send-off.' She lowered her voice. 'How are things in your house?'

'Grim,' Rachel said grimly.

Victoria was beginning to feel like a general inspecting her troops, sheltering briefly underneath each umbrella. The next person in line was Kathleen. 'Has Steve rung?' she asked in a whisper.

'No.' Kathleen made a valiant attempt to smile. 'But I'm sure he will eventually. Have a great time, love. Write to us, won't you? We'd like to know how you're getting on over there.'

'Farewell, sweet maiden,' Gareth said in a deep, Shakespearean voice. 'May flights of angels sing thee to thy bed of rest – in the city of New York.' Everyone clapped and he grinned. 'Did I ever tell you I was once in amateur dramatics?'

Victoria laughed and shook her head. It was just one of the things there hadn't been time to get to know about him.

'I've brought Tabitha to say goodbye.' He reached inside his jacket for the sleepy-eyed kitten and Victoria kissed the soft tortoiseshell head.

'You're going to miss your flight if you don't get a move on, missus,' the taxi driver shouted.

'Coming.' She formally shook Gareth's hand. 'Goodbye.'

'Au revoir, Victoria.'

'Goodbye, everyone.' She ran to the taxi, paused, and threw kisses to them all. 'You never know, I might be back one day soon.' It was strange, but when she looked at the house, she had the strongest feeling she would never see it again.

Ernest closed the taxi door, returned to Anna, and began to push the wheelchair towards their house.

'Let's put a video on as soon as we get in,' Anna said, sniffing loudly. 'Something cheerful that'll make us laugh. I feel terribly sad at seeing Victoria go.'

'Anything you like, luv,' Ernest said easily. Perhaps a sherry and a whisky wouldn't come amiss at the same time. He'd put water in the sherry and hope Anna wouldn't notice.

The Jordan boys rushed indoors to play with the new computer, already plugged in and ready to go, despite Ma insisting they should get on with the packing and take the old machine next door where Tiffany was probably on edge waiting for it to arrive. 'In a minute, Ma . . .'

When Kathleen entered the house, the phone was ringing. 'Steve!' she breathed when she picked it up and heard his dear, familiar voice. Jean had been on the critical list, he said, but was feeling much better this morning. He might come back later that day because he desperately wanted to see her. 'But it'll only be for a few hours, Kath,' he said warily.

'That's all right, darling. I desperately want to see you too.'

'You must come round at tea time and meet my sister,' Sarah said to Marie. 'Oh, we must write to each other. I could bring the children to Donegal some time. Tiffany's broken-hearted, what with losing Victoria one day and Danny the next.'

Rachel marched stiffly towards Three Farthings. Frank was pleading with her to forgive him, but she wasn't sure if she could. There were some things that were beyond forgiveness – Frank had obviously thought so because he'd never forgiven her.

When Victoria looked out of the rear window of the taxi, only Gareth was left. They waved and waved until the taxi turned the corner and they couldn't see each other any more.

Gareth walked disconsolately back to his showpiece house, Tabitha tucked inside his jacket. 'She's gone, Tabs. What am I going to do without her, eh?'

When he went inside, Debbie looked at him strangely. She'd been unusually quiet that morning. His mum had stayed the night and had gone to Mass at the cathedral. 'Would you like some tea?' Debbie asked.

'No, thanks.' He was on his way upstairs when he changed his mind. Debbie was trying to mend fences: hadn't she agreed to live in Victoria's house? Perhaps he should do the same. He returned to the kitchen. 'On reflection, I wouldn't mind a cup of tea,' he said gruffly.

Now every door in Victoria Square was closed tight against the rain that continued to pour relentlessly down.

Judy Moon looked out of the window and shivered. The place looked like a graveyard, no sign of life anywhere. It was a relief when a lamp went on in Clematis Cottage where the old couple lived – Anna and Ernie. She'd soon get the hang of everyone's names. She went round the house, switching on lights in every room: an extravagance, but it was that sort of day.

Boxing Day 2001

Epilogue

It had been dull and deathly miserable all day and the sky was already growing darker as it prepared for night. The roofs of the houses in Victoria Square glistened with frost and the frozen grass was a blanket of white that crunched agreeably when walked on. Christmas trees twinkled cheerily in every window and more lights adorned the little willow tree in the centre of the grass, the sort that changed colour: white, pink, red, blue, purple, green, then white again. Quite a few hours had been wasted by people staring through their windows at this hypnotic sight when they should have been doing something more important. Tiffany had christened it 'Victoria's tree', no one knew why, but the name had stuck and the willow would remain Victoria's tree forevermore. Despite the dreariness of the day, the square was a welcoming place.

The only sounds were coming from Clematis Cottage where the Burrows were having a party: three till six. Anna said she would have preferred one in the evening and wouldn't have minded had it gone on all night, but Ernest told her not to be so foolish.

'You're an old woman,' he reminded her, knowing how exhausted she would be after just three hours, let alone a party that went on into the early morning. Trouble was she liked to pretend she was eighteen, not eighty-two.

'There's no need to remind me that I'm old,' she said tartly. 'It doesn't mean I can't enjoy myself.'

'You'll just have to enjoy yourself in the afternoon,' he told her firmly.

'We'll play some of our old records to put people in the mood – and let's buy loads more decorations, darling. I *love* buying Christmas decorations.'

They already had enough to decorate Buckingham Palace but, if it made her happy, they'd get more – it was him who'd have to put them up and he didn't mind a bit.

'I wish Victoria were coming to our party, Ernie.'

'So do I, luv, but it's not to be.'

Everyone had said they'd come apart from the middle-aged couple in number two, the Jordans' old house. No one could decide whether the Forresters were anti-social, stuck up, or just plain shy, but they'd hardly spoken to a soul since they'd moved into the square in August, despite all attempts by the present residents to be friendly. Now, the only guests still to come were Sarah Rees-James and her children . . .

Really, Sarah thought impatiently, getting three small children ready to go out took longer than preparing an expedition to the top of Everest.

'Mummy,' Tiffany said in an outraged voice when they were at last ready to leave, 'you haven't put the television on for Eric and Jason.'

'Darling, cats and dogs don't watch television,' Sarah protested for the umpteenth time, nevertheless turning the set on – anything to shut Tiffany up.

'Eric *loves* football. He sits on top and tries to hit the ball with his paw. Not *EastEnders*, Mummy,' Tiffany snorted. 'You know the music makes Jason howl.' Jason was an incredibly curly puppy of unknown origin and Eric a smooth, white-haired kitten. They were both eight months old. It had proved terribly embarrassing, months ago, when the real Jason had turned up out of the blue and discovered a dog had been named after him. It had been even more embarrassing to have to tell him, with the utmost tact, that Sarah was no longer interested. She'd hardly thought about him since she'd left Alex. One of these days she might start thinking about boyfriends again. Right now, her children occupied every minute of her time.

She obediently changed the channel. 'All right, darling. Have you got the handbag that Anna bought you for Christmas? She'll be so pleased if she sees you using it.'

Tiffany picked up the blue leather bag and gave it a look of disdain. 'It's only a little girl's handbag.'

'You're only a little girl, Tiff. Put it over your shoulder this minute. Jack, let me zip up your anorak, it's below freezing out there.' She fastened Jack's anorak and picked up Alastair, who let out a roar of protest. 'You're not walking, darling, absolutely not. I know you like showing off, but you'll only slip on the ice and break your little legs or something. Is everyone ready?' Three young faces looked at her blankly. Sarah took this for agreement and said, 'Come on then, let's go.'

A beaming Ernest opened the door of Clematis Cottage. 'Sorry we're late.' Sarah pushed Tiffany and Jack inside out of the cold and set Alastair on the floor. He immediately staggered into the parlour to be met by a scream of welcome from Anna. 'I've brought some mince pies. I made them myself,' she said proudly. 'I've discovered I'm frightfully good at making pastry and it's such fun rolling it out.' She didn't wish him Merry

Christmas as she'd brought the children round the morning before to show him and Anna their presents.

'Take yourself into the parlour, luv, that's where most people are. What would you and the kids like to drink? Here, let me take your coats.'

'White wine for me: orange juice or something for the children. Oh, but do let me see to things, Ernie. I'm sure you must have loads to do. Is someone helping in the kitchen?'

'Rachel and Judy are out there. Me, I'm taking it easy while trying to keep an eye on Anna. She's already had too much wine and the party's hardly started.'

'I'll keep an eye on her too.' Anna's predilection for wine was well known throughout the square and sternly discouraged.

Kathleen was standing in the corner of the heavily garlanded, over-decorated room half listening to Fred Astaire singing 'They Can't Take That Away From Me' and, yet again, Anna tell about the film she'd once made. She wondered how many times poor Ernie had heard it. Today, she was telling the story to the young American couple who'd taken over Hamilton Lodge for a year.

'Y'don't say,' Pete Scheider drawled when Anna finished with a great deal of rolling of eyes and waving of hands. 'You've certainly led an adventurous life, ma'am.' He was terribly polite and called all the women 'ma'am', apart from his wife, Hetty, whom he addressed as 'honey'.

Hetty said, 'People in Liverpool are so-*oh* interesting!'

'Aren't we?' Anna preened herself, although she'd been born in Hungary and had only lived in Liverpool a small fraction of her long life.

Kathleen sighed and wished Victoria was there – she

wasn't the only one. Sarah and Rachel had just wished the same. Only Victoria had known how upset she'd been when Steve had gone rushing off to Huddersfield because his wife had had a heart attack. She would have loved to tell Victoria how well everything had turned out. Jean had recovered, for one thing. Having come so near to death, she'd left the hospital with a far more philosophical attitude to life than when she'd gone in, apparently resigned to the fact that Steve had found someone else. So resigned that she'd actually agreed to a divorce and had sent them a card at Christmas!

A few weeks before, Annie, Steve's youngest daughter, had telephoned and she and Kathleen had had quite a pleasant chat.

'I thought you couldn't possibly be quite as bad as our Brenda made out when you let Dad come all the way to see Mam in hospital,' Annie had said. Kathleen wondered if she would still have rung had she known how deeply she'd resented it. 'There's some women who wouldn't have stood for it. Mam *can* be a pain. It's not all that surprising that our dad did a bunk.'

Then Maggie had written a nice, friendly letter, and Sheila had sent a Christmas card. There were suggestions from both sides that they all meet up at some time in the future. So far, there'd been no word from Brenda, but she might come round one day. All Kathleen could do was wait and see.

She sighed again, blissfully this time. Steve had got a job as a porter at the hospital where she worked so their hours were more compatible. They still had the occasional flaming row – she was beginning to wonder if they enjoyed them.

Steve came up. 'You look like the cat that ate the cream.'

'I feel as if I've just eaten an entire pint. I was just thinking how happy I am.'

'You can't be happier than me.'

'I can.'

'You can't.' He grinned. 'Shall we go home and have a fight about it?'

'Would either of you like a fill-up?' Frank Williams paused beside them, a bottle of white wine in one hand and red in the other.

'Red, please.' Kathleen held out her glass.

'Mine's whisky and soda. Don't worry, Frank. I'll go in the kitchen and help meself in a minute.'

'It's all right, Steve,' Frank said heartily. 'I'll do it for you.'

'He's trying awfully hard,' Steve whispered when Frank left with his glass.

'He needs to.' Kathleen's voice was steely. 'He nearly drove Rachel to kill herself. I wish you'd been at that barbecue: the things she said! The man's a monster.'

I really shouldn't have let all that stuff spill out at the barbecue, let everyone hear, Rachel thought when Frank came into the kitchen with Steve's glass. He was trying his utmost to rehabilitate himself. The fact was, although it sounded childish, it was *him* who'd started it by saying to Sarah that it wasn't safe to leave Tiffany with her. Rachel couldn't help herself. It was as if a dam had burst its banks and the words – the truth – had come pouring forth.

From that night on, everything had changed and would never be the same again. Rachel didn't *want* things to be the same. She hadn't been prepared to continue with Frank's notion of what an ideal marriage should be: the man at the head of the family, a submissive wife who never did anything that might show her to be smarter than her husband. These days, she was her own woman. James and Kirsty were astounded when they discovered their mother could do *The Times* crossword.

'I never realized you were so clever, Mum,' Kirsty said admiringly.

'She's been hiding her light under a bushel all these years,' commented James.

Both seemed to comprehend that she'd been living a lie in order to please their father – and it hadn't been just since Alice had died, but throughout their entire married life. Next October, she was starting at Liverpool University as a mature student and studying for a degree in Women's Literature. She didn't need Frank any more. Oh, she felt sorry enough for him, spoke to him civilly, made his meals and washed his clothes, listened sympathetically while he flailed himself for not collecting Alice from school but, to all intents and purposes, their marriage was over.

'What's that song?' she asked Judy Moon who was in the kitchen with her. They'd finished sorting out the food – everyone had brought a contribution – and had remained gossiping about this and that. Judy and Rachel had become good friends.

' "The Way You Look Tonight," ' Judy said promptly. 'It's from a film called *Swing Time* starring Fred Astaire and Ginger Rogers and directed by George Stevens. That's Fred singing. Jerome Kern wrote the music. It came out in nineteen thirty-six.'

'Wow!' Rachel looked at her, impressed.

'My mum and dad were obsessed with films. I think I've told you before. Us kids are walking encyclopaedias.'

'Perhaps we could start a quiz team, call ourselves The

505

Victoria Squares, get Ernie to join. He seems to know a lot about politics and the war.'

'That's not a bad idea.' Judy cocked her head. 'Gosh, that music's romantic. I find it a bit disturbing.' Now Fred Astaire was singing 'Night and Day.'

'Disturbing? In what way?'

Judy shrugged and wrinkled her nose. 'I'm not sure. Something happened last night: my son and his wife had a party and Harry turned up with a woman young enough to be his daughter.' She laughed. 'Actually, it's rather funny. Sue's divorced and has two teenaged sons, both tearaways by the sound of it. Harry was so hard on our two and was totally opposed to divorce. It will be interesting to see how things turn out if it gets serious.'

'Are you jealous?' Rachel asked curiously.

'Not at all!' Judy cried. 'Harry and Sue are welcome to each other.' She clasped her hands together and pressed them against her breast. For a moment, she looked quite lost. 'I'm not sure what it is I feel.'

'Look, we'd better go in the other room or people will think us very rude. They can get their own food from now on and Frank's seeing to the drinks.'

It was standing room only in the parlour. Judy positioned herself behind Anna's chair where an animated discussion about films was taking place. Anna claimed that nowadays there was too much blood and gore and the American chap, Pete, said it merely reflected the world today. He called them 'movies' as her father sometimes had.

It was the sort of conversation that she would have normally enjoyed, but she had other things on her mind. It had come as quite a shock when Harry had arrived at

506

last night's party with Sue. Although they were separated, there'd been no suggestion of divorce and she had assumed that they would always remain man and wife. It had been extremely disconcerting to see him with someone else.

Since moving to Victoria Square, she'd made quite a nice life for herself, working mornings for the estate agent who had taken over the Moons' photographers – answering the phone, mainly, and doing the filing. She was learning to play the guitar, had taken up oil painting, met up regularly with her family and had got into the habit of going to the cinema with Rachel on Saturday afternoons. Until last night, everything had been going swimmingly, but now she felt that something was missing: a man. It hadn't crossed her mind before, but all of a sudden it chilled her to think that she might never again be kissed on the lips or held in a pair of strong arms, that candlelit dinners were a thing of the past, and anything else faintly romantic . . .

Well, she wasn't going to go looking for a man: she wasn't that sort of woman. She'd leave it to fate, but she cursed Harry for disturbing the smooth rhythm of her happy and contented existence.

'Darling,' Anna said in a low voice to Tiffany, 'see that bottle on the window sill, would you mind fetching it over and filling up my glass? Ernie's busy and we don't want to bother him, do we?' The film discussion was over and a few people had drifted into the kitchen for more food.

Tiffany looked at Anna doubtfully. 'Ernie said you'd already had enough wine. I'd better ask him first.' She trotted away.

Anna swore. 'Damn!'

'What's the matter?' Kathleen asked.

'Ernie's got his spies everywhere: he's even employing children. I was just trying to sneak another glass of wine, but Tiffany's gone to ask his permission.'

'You know it interferes with your medication,' Kathleen said severely. 'He's only looking after your best interests.'

Anna sniffed indignantly. 'I think I'm the one to do that, not my tyrant of a husband.'

'He does it because he loves you, Anna.'

'I know.' Anna smiled a touch sadly. 'How awful if I drank myself to death and no one cared.'

'We all need someone to care, Anna.' She glanced at Steve who was deep in conversation with Frank Williams – he felt sorry for the chap. Anna's eyes sought out Ernie who had just entered the room and the look of love on her old, wrinkled face made Kathleen want to weep.

'I won't drink any more today,' Anna said, 'not if it upsets Ernie.'

'When is the baby due?' Sarah asked an enormously pregnant Debbie Moran.

'In less than a month: the twentieth of January. I'm dreading it,' Debbie confessed. 'I'll scream my head off, I know I will.'

'It doesn't hurt much,' Sarah said comfortingly, although she'd gone through excruciating agony with Alastair who'd weighed over ten pounds.

'My mum had a terrible time with all five of us, loads of stitches. I wish she wouldn't keep on about it.' Debbie shuddered. 'She thinks I'm mad, wanting a water birth.'

'I've often thought I wouldn't have minded water births with my three. They say they're very relaxing.'

'I hope so.' Debbie looked doubtful.

'I'm going to be there, holding her hand.' Gareth joined them. He put his arm affectionately around his wife.

Sarah remembered how close he'd seemed to Victoria and wondered if they'd really had an affair? If so, he'd got over it very quickly as he obviously loved Debbie very much.

Hetty and Pete Scheider were the first to leave. 'We've got another party later,' Pete said. He shook hands with Ernest and kissed Anna on the cheek. 'Don't forget, all of you are invited to dinner a week from today.' He smiled at the assembled guests. 'I'd just like to say, folks, that Hetty and I consider ourselves very lucky to be living in Victoria Square. We were warned the Brits were very cold, but we couldn't have met a warmer, friendlier crowd of people. You've all made us very welcome and it's like belonging to one big happy family. We're not looking forward to going back to the States in six months.'

Hetty smiled. 'I go along with that.'

'Steve and I had better be going. We're meeting friends for a drink in town,' Kathleen announced not much later, and Judy Moon said she should leave too. She was going to tea at her sister's, she said a trifle gloomily.

'It's about time we made a move.' Rachel returned from washing the dishes, leaving Ernest without a single thing to do. 'We've got Kirsty and James's party tonight. I've told them not to make too much noise.'

'Marie's ringing from Donegal at around seven. I'd like to get Alastair and Jack asleep before then.' Sarah clapped her hands. 'Come along, darlings, time to go.'

'Can I speak to Danny?' Tiffany asked eagerly.

'Of course you can, Tiff.'

Gareth said Debbie urgently needed to lie down. 'She usually has a bit of a sleep in the afternoons, but she missed today.'

Clematis Cottage felt strangely empty and unnaturally quiet when everyone had gone. Anna looked quite desolate. 'What shall we do tonight, Ernie?' she asked. She seemed terribly downcast.

'Watch telly, luv. Is there a video you'd like to see?'

'No. I feel like doing something incredibly exciting: going to a grand ball, for instance, or strolling along the Champs-Elysées and eating in that restaurant we loved – you know, the one with the aquarium.'

'I remember, luv.' If only, if only, Ernest thought sadly. 'I expected you'd be too tired to do anything but watch telly.'

'Darling, I feel very much alive and full of beans.'

She didn't look it. Her mind and spirit might be very much alive, but her body was letting her down. Despite her words, her eyes were blinking with tiredness. 'Why don't you have a little nap?' he suggested. 'If you still feel like it when you wake up, I'll ring around a few restaurants and see if there's a table just for two.'

'Oh, Ernie, what a marvellous idea.' She closed her eyes and was asleep within minutes. These days she was sleeping more and more and eating less and less. He'd be surprised if she woke up in time for dinner.

He went into the kitchen, helped himself to a glass of whisky and some of the leftover party food and took them into the spare bedroom that Anna insisted on calling the study. He switched on the computer and began to play Battleships, but quickly got bored, so transferred to the parlour to be with Anna and remember times gone by – something *he* seemed to be doing more and more these days.

Gareth was seated before his computer reading for the hundredth time the last email that Victoria had sent him. It was dated 10 September. She was loving New York, but missed him. 'Perhaps I shouldn't say things like that,' she had written, 'but it's the truth. I doubt if the day will ever come when I won't think of you – and miss you badly.'

His desk was in the bedroom where they'd slept together: Debbie had preferred the front bedroom that had belonged to Victoria's Gran. She was fast asleep in there right now, a white cot beside the bed ready for when their baby came. The baby would sleep with them until they moved back to Hamilton Lodge in six months when it would have a room to itself and Gareth could have his office back. They were moving much sooner than expected.

Debbie had been a brick. She'd settled without complaint in the old house on the corner, had enjoyed picking the old-fashioned patterned wallpaper that suited the old-fashioned rooms, the frilly duvets and curtains, and colourful glass lamps. The other day, she'd actually confessed she'd miss it when they went home. 'It's so cosy and snug here. It's got personality, not like Hamilton Lodge.'

'We'll give it personality,' Gareth promised. 'Turn it into a home instead of a show house.'

He got up from the desk, stretched, and went over to the window from where Victoria had looked out on to the square. It was like a scene from a fairy-tale: the ice-covered roofs, the white grass, the sparkling Christmas trees and, in the middle of all this magic, Victoria's tree, brightly lit, the colours chasing each other around and around, but never quite catching up. He turned away. He couldn't bear to look another minute.

Victoria was dead. The day after she'd sent her last email, the World Trade Center where she worked had been attacked by terrorists and had collapsed in a great heap of rubble. Victoria was just one of the thousands of innocent people who had died. Gareth had watched the scene on television over and over again, horrified, trying not to imagine how she had felt when the terrible tragedy happened. He'd always nursed the faint hope that one day they would be together or, at the very least, that they would meet again. Although he was doing his best to commit himself wholeheartedly to Debbie, still the hope had remained.

A few days after the catastrophe in New York, Victoria's friend, Carrie, had telephoned him at work. 'I need to see you,' she'd said, and he'd told her she could come to the house any time.

'I need to see you alone,' Carrie had insisted.

They'd met later that day in a pub close to where he worked. He assumed she wanted to talk about Victoria, but it wasn't just that.

'Victoria told me about you and her the night of the barbecue when we went back to her house,' Carrie said. Her eyes were red with weeping and her voice was lacklustre. 'She asked me to sign something for her. I've got a copy of it here.' She produced a folded sheet of paper from her bag. 'I deposited the original with a solicitor.'

Somewhat bemused, Gareth had taken the paper and could never have described how he'd felt when he read it: stunned, moved, griefstricken all over again because

Victoria had made a Will and the house and the money she had received for the piece of land that was now Victoria Square had been left to him.

It was weeks before he could bring himself to visit the solicitor, more weeks before he felt able to tell Debbie, expecting the third degree: 'Why you, of all people? Why, Gareth, why?'

But Debbie had just nodded and kissed him dispassionately and he wondered if she'd known about the affair all along.

He read Victoria's email again, although he knew it word for word. 'I doubt if the day will ever come when I won't think of you . . .' Well, the day *had* come, he thought, breaking so many hearts.

'Gareth!' Debbie called fearfully from the bedroom. 'I've just had this awful pain.'

Gareth hesitated for the briefest of seconds, pressed 'delete' and the email vanished from the screen. He would never read it again. It was time to dwell on the future, not the past. Move on.

'Coming, Debs,' he shouted.

Outside, in the empty square, nothing moved except the lights on Victoria's tree that continued to chase each other around and around and around . . .

All Orion/Phoenix titles are available at your local bookshop or from the following address:

Mail Order Department
Littlehampton Book Services
FREEPOST BR535
Worthing, West Sussex, BN13 3BR
telephone 01903 828503, *facsimile* 01903 828802
e-mail MailOrders@lbsltd.co.uk
(Please ensure that you include full postal address details)

Payment can be made either by credit/debit card (Visa, Mastercard, Access and Switch accepted) or by sending a £ Sterling cheque or postal order made payable to *Littlehampton Book Services*.
DO NOT SEND CASH OR CURRENCY.

Please add the following to cover postage and packing

UK and BFPO:
£1.50 for the first book, and 50p for each additional book to a maximum of £3.50

Overseas and Eire:
£2.50 for the first book plus £1.00 for the second book and 50p for each additional book ordered

---

BLOCK CAPITALS PLEASE

name of cardholder ....

address of cardholder ....

....

....

....

postcode ....

delivery address
(if different from cardholder)

....

....

....

....

postcode ....

☐ I enclose my remittance for £.................................

☐ please debit my Mastercard/Visa/Access/Switch (delete as appropriate)

card number ☐☐☐☐☐☐☐☐☐☐☐☐☐☐☐☐☐☐

expiry date ☐☐☐☐   Switch issue no. ☐☐

signature ....

prices and availability are subject to change without notice